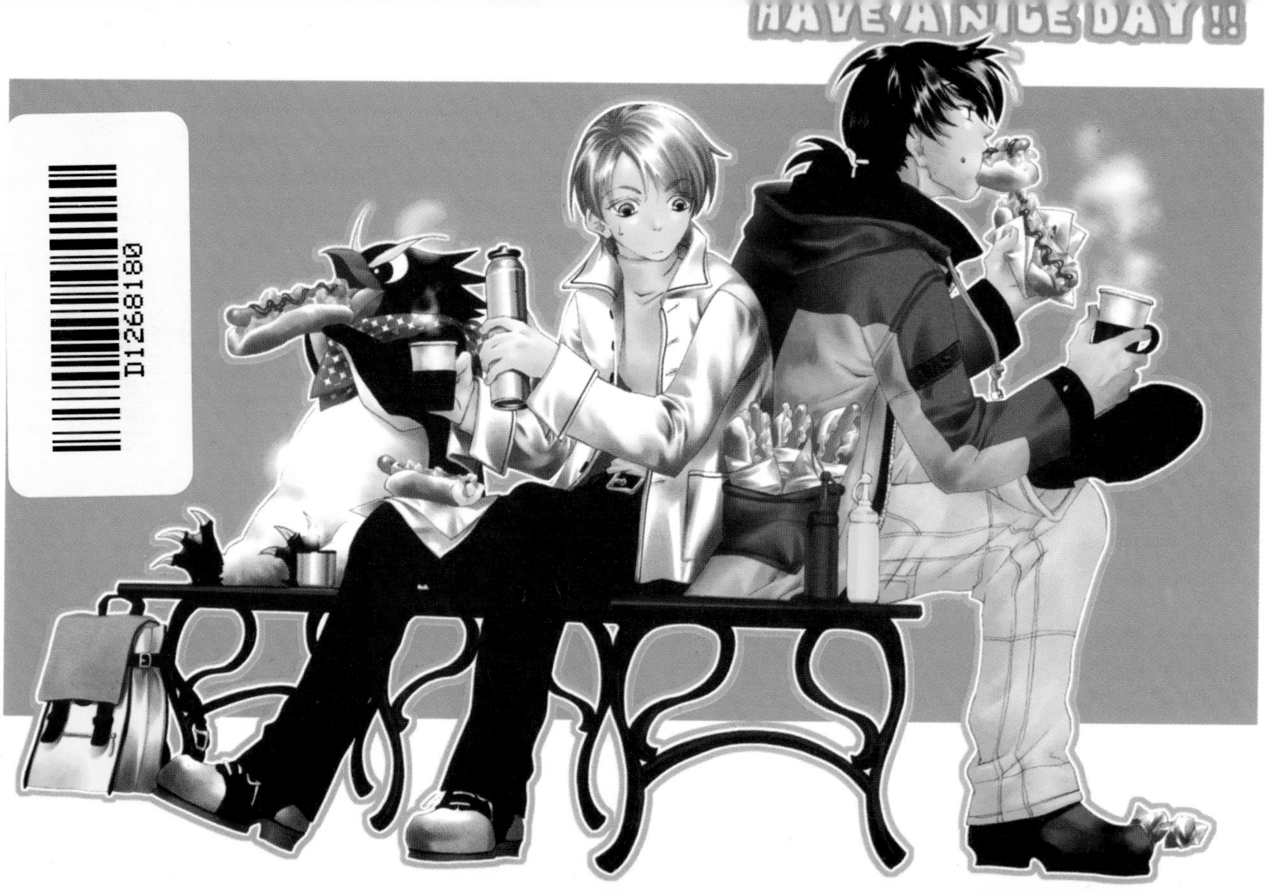
HAVE A NICE DAY !!

TRASH
SANAMI MATOH

CONTENTS

"TRASH"
Presented by SANAMI MATOH

By

Sanami Matoh

HAMBURG // LONDON // LOS ANGELES // TOKYO

Trash
Created by Sanami Matoh

Translation - Amy Forsyth
Copy Editor - Hope Donovan
Retouch and Lettering - Fawn Lau
Graphic Designer - Kyle Plummer

Editor - Lillian Diaz-Przybyl
Digital Imaging Manager - Chris Buford
Production Managers - Elizabeth Brizzi
Managing Editor - Lindsey Johnston
Editor-in-Chief - Rob Tokar
VP of Production - Ron Klamert
Publisher - Mike Kiley
President and C.O.O. - John Parker
C.E.O. and Chief Creative Officer - Stuart Levy

A  Manga

TOKYOPOP Inc.
5900 Wilshire Blvd. Suite 2000
Los Angeles, CA 90036

E-mail: info@TOKYOPOP.com
Come visit us online at www.TOKYOPOP.com

ISBN: 1-59816-516-X

First TOKYOPOP printing: July 2006
10 9 8 7 6 5 4 3 2 1
Printed in the USA

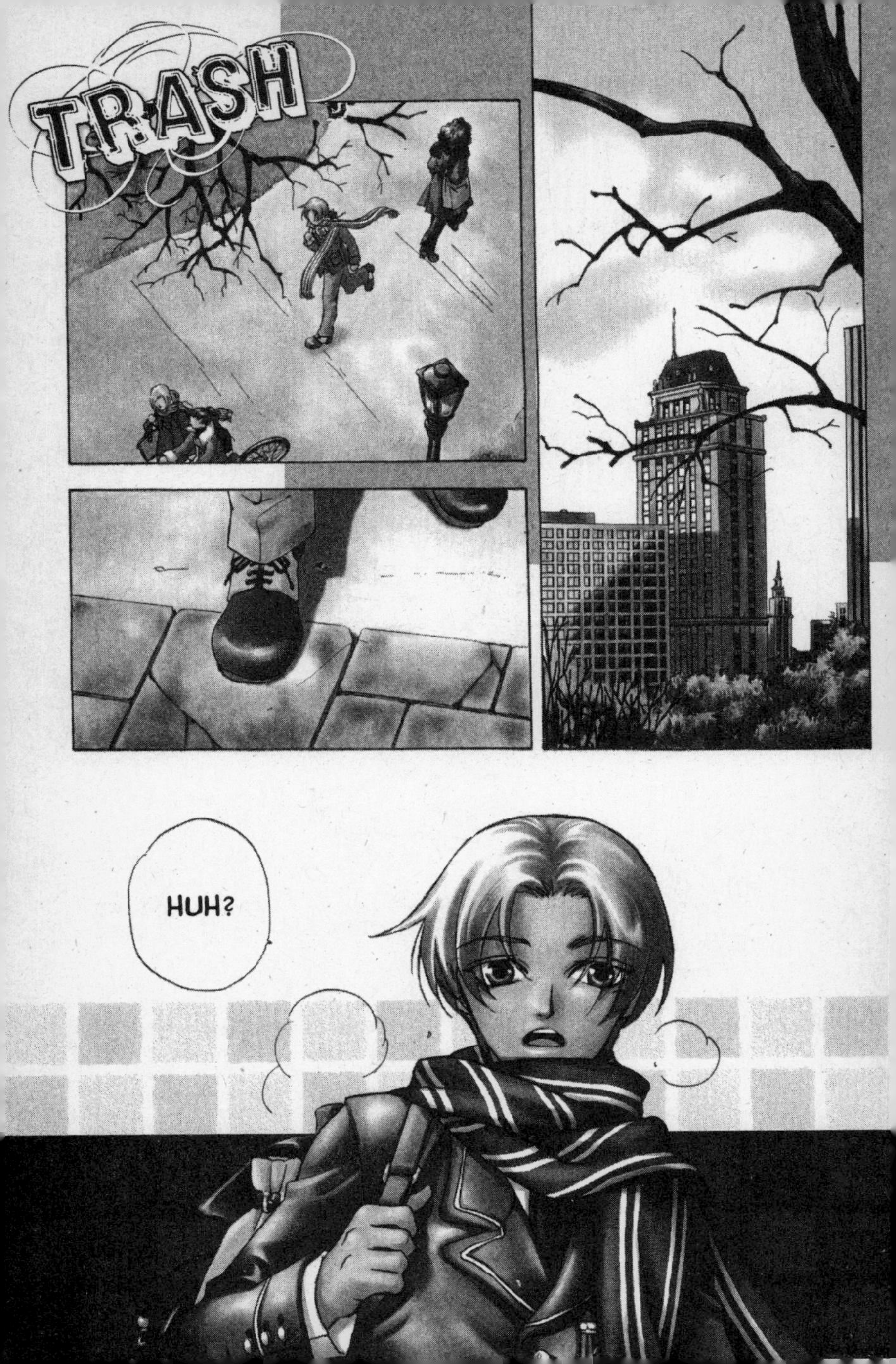
TRASH
HUH?

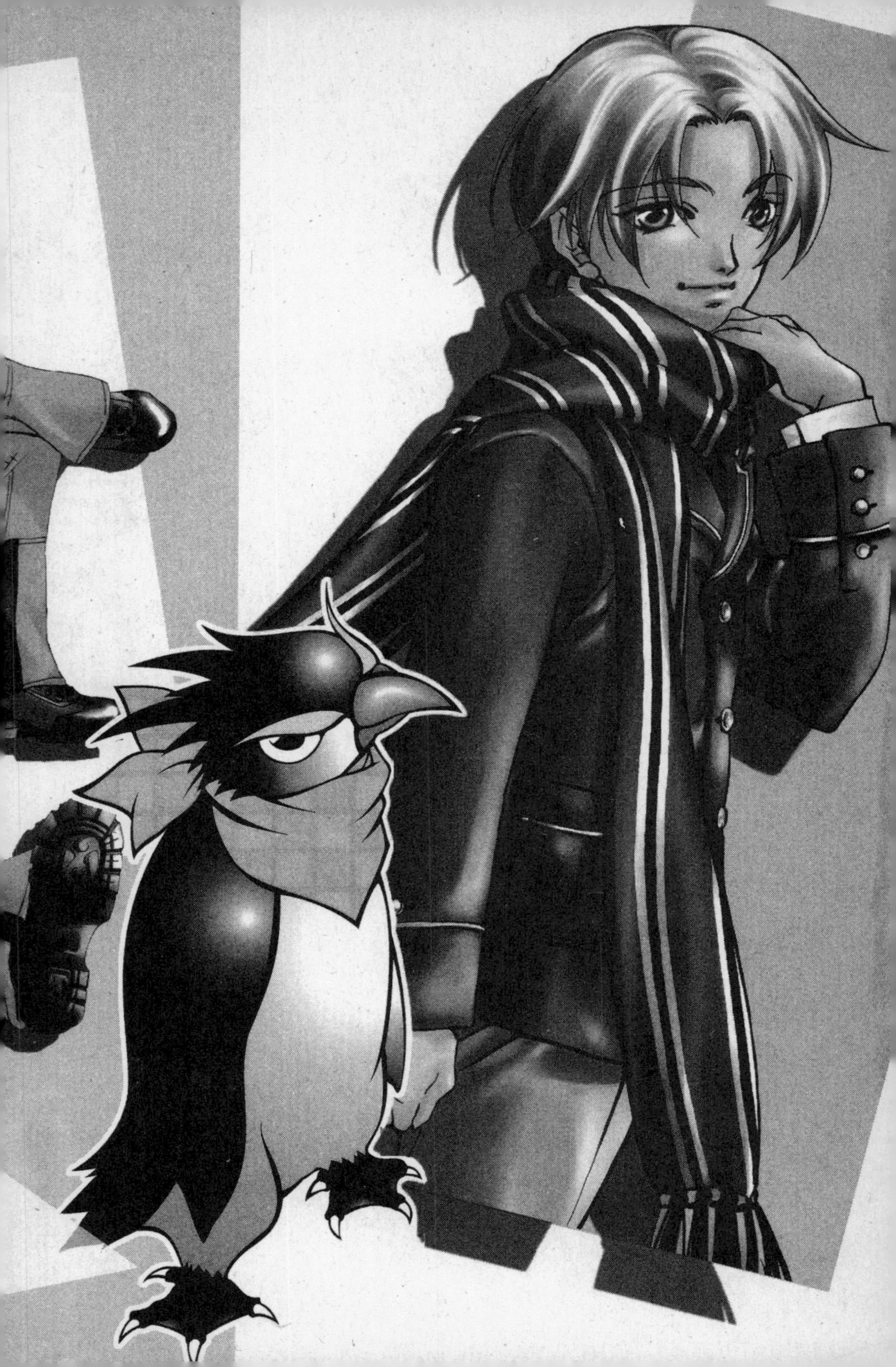

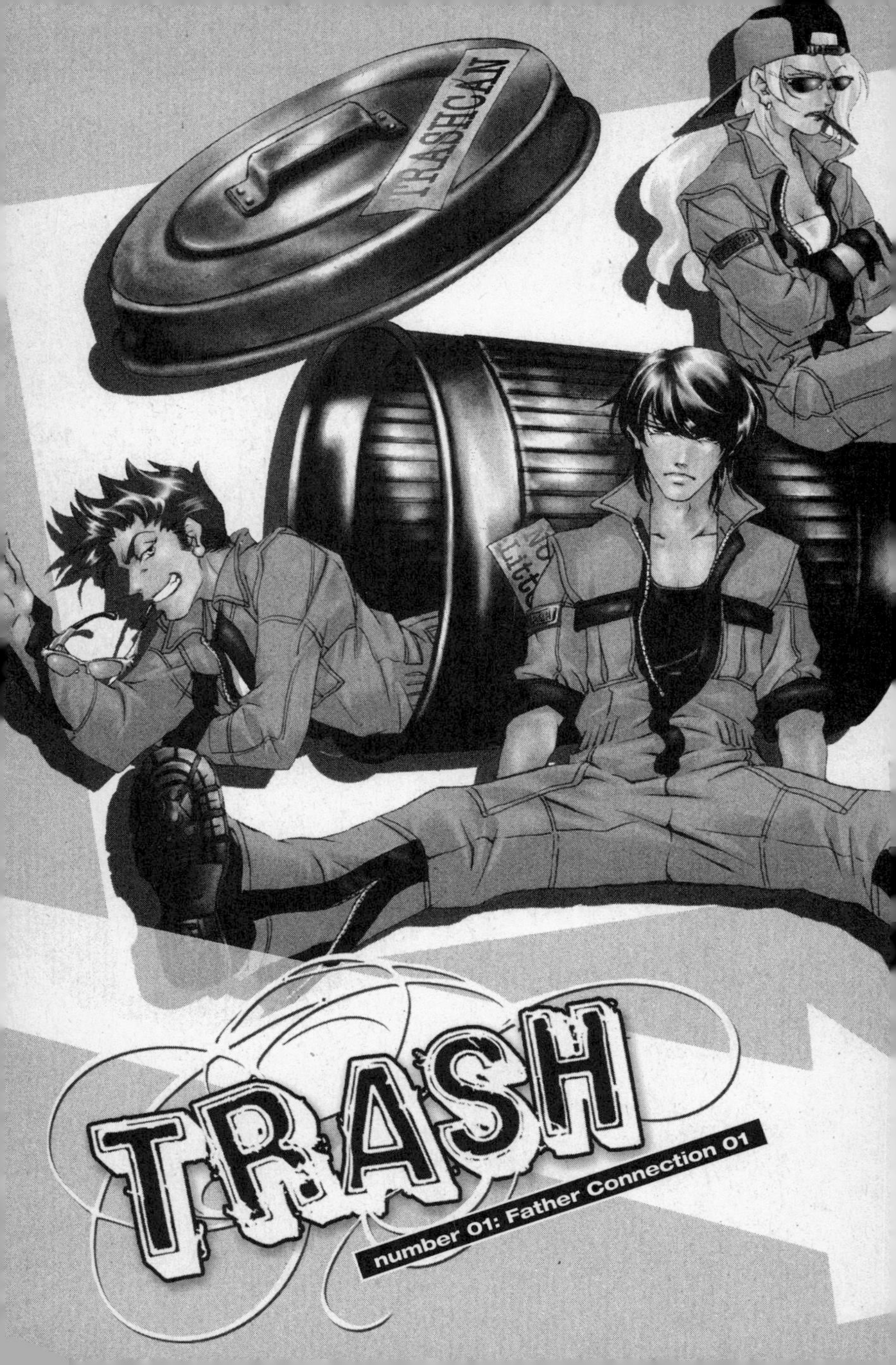
TRASHCAN
No Litter
TRASH
number 01: Father Connection 01

Father Connection
&
First Contact

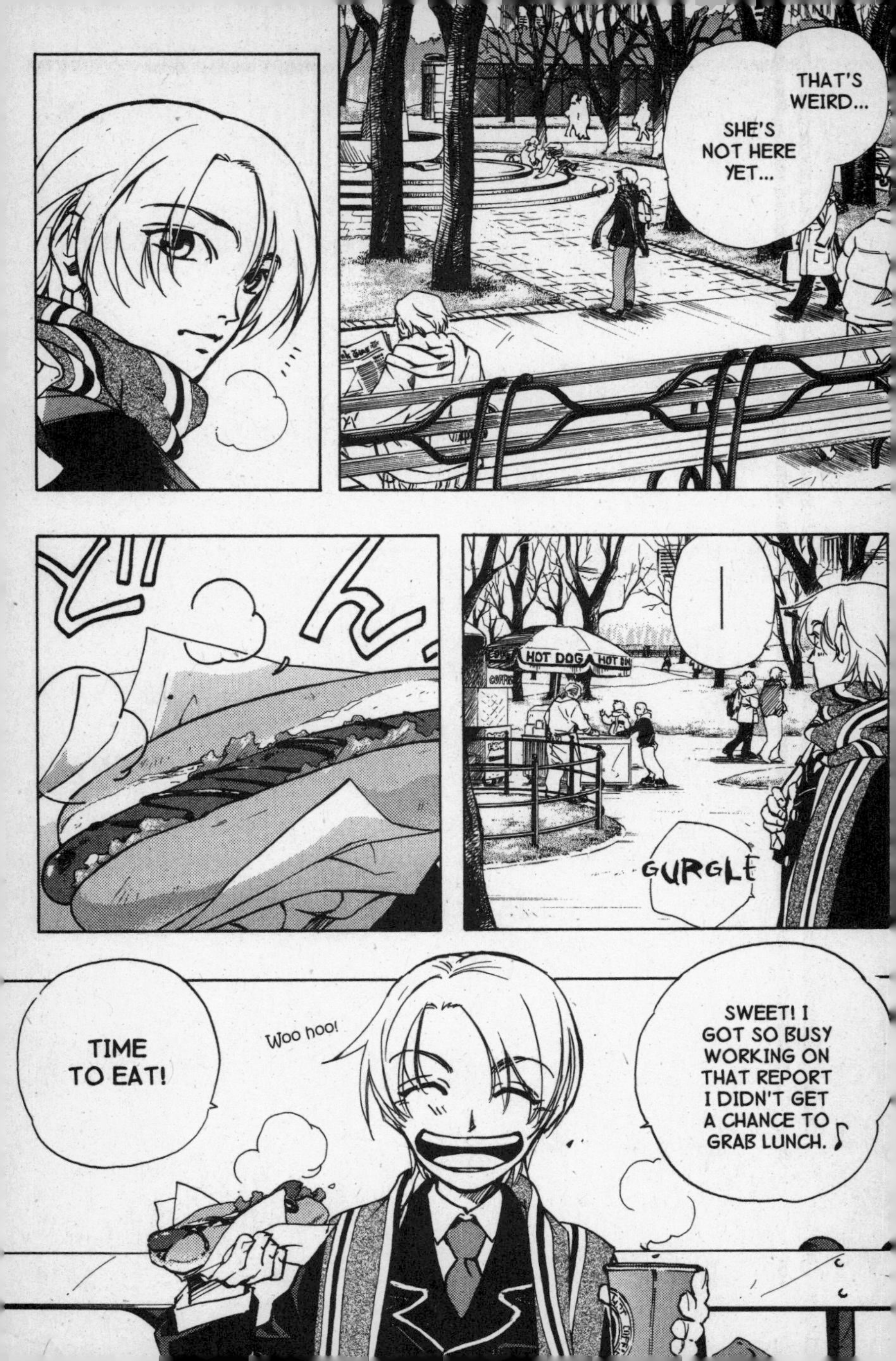
THAT'S WEIRD...
SHE'S NOT HERE YET...
GURGLE
SWEET! I GOT SO BUSY WORKING ON THAT REPORT I DIDN'T GET A CHANCE TO GRAB LUNCH. ♪
Woo hoo!
TIME TO EAT!

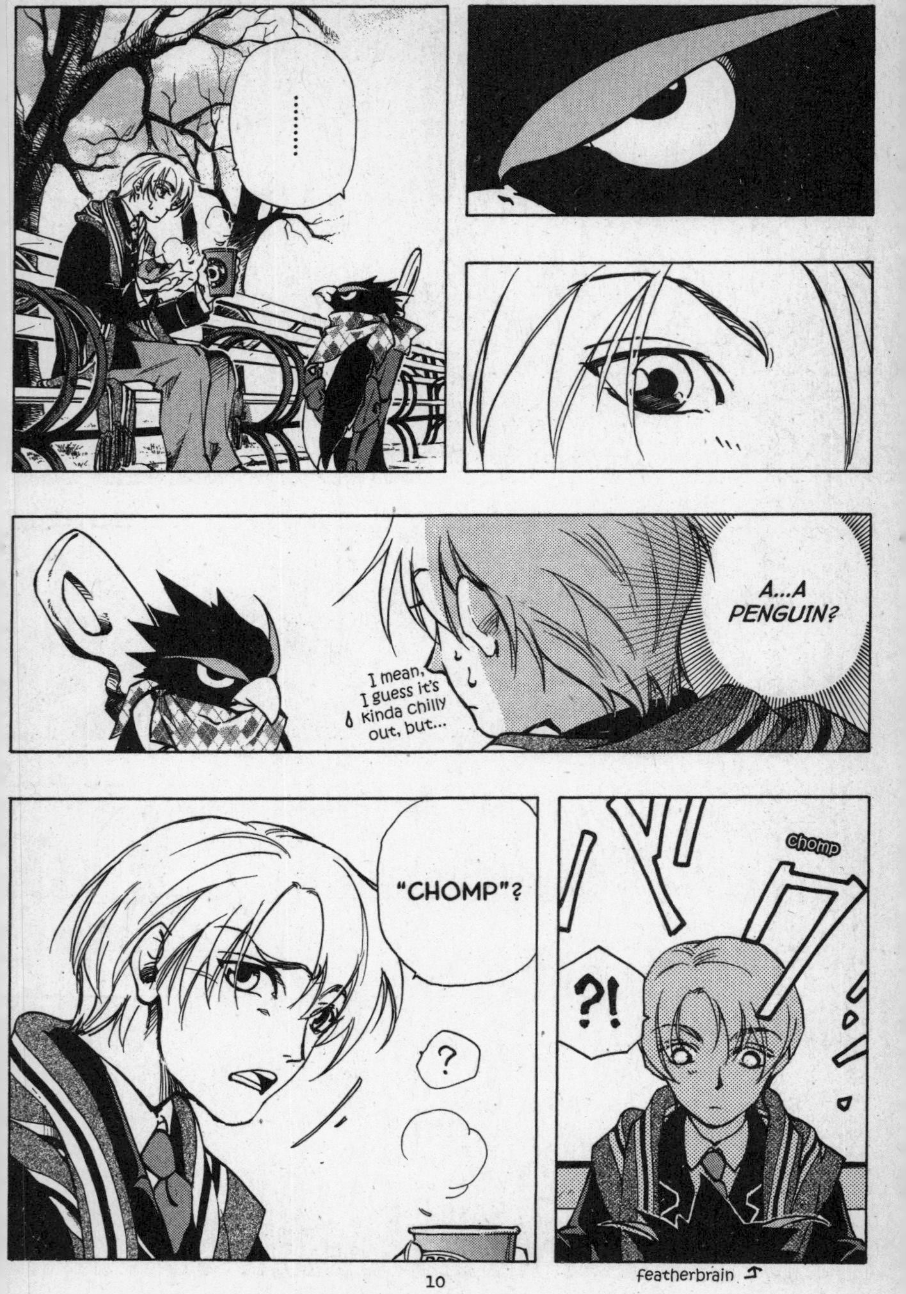
......
A...A PENGUIN?
I mean, I guess it's kinda chilly out, but...
chomp
?!
"CHOMP"?
?

featherbrain

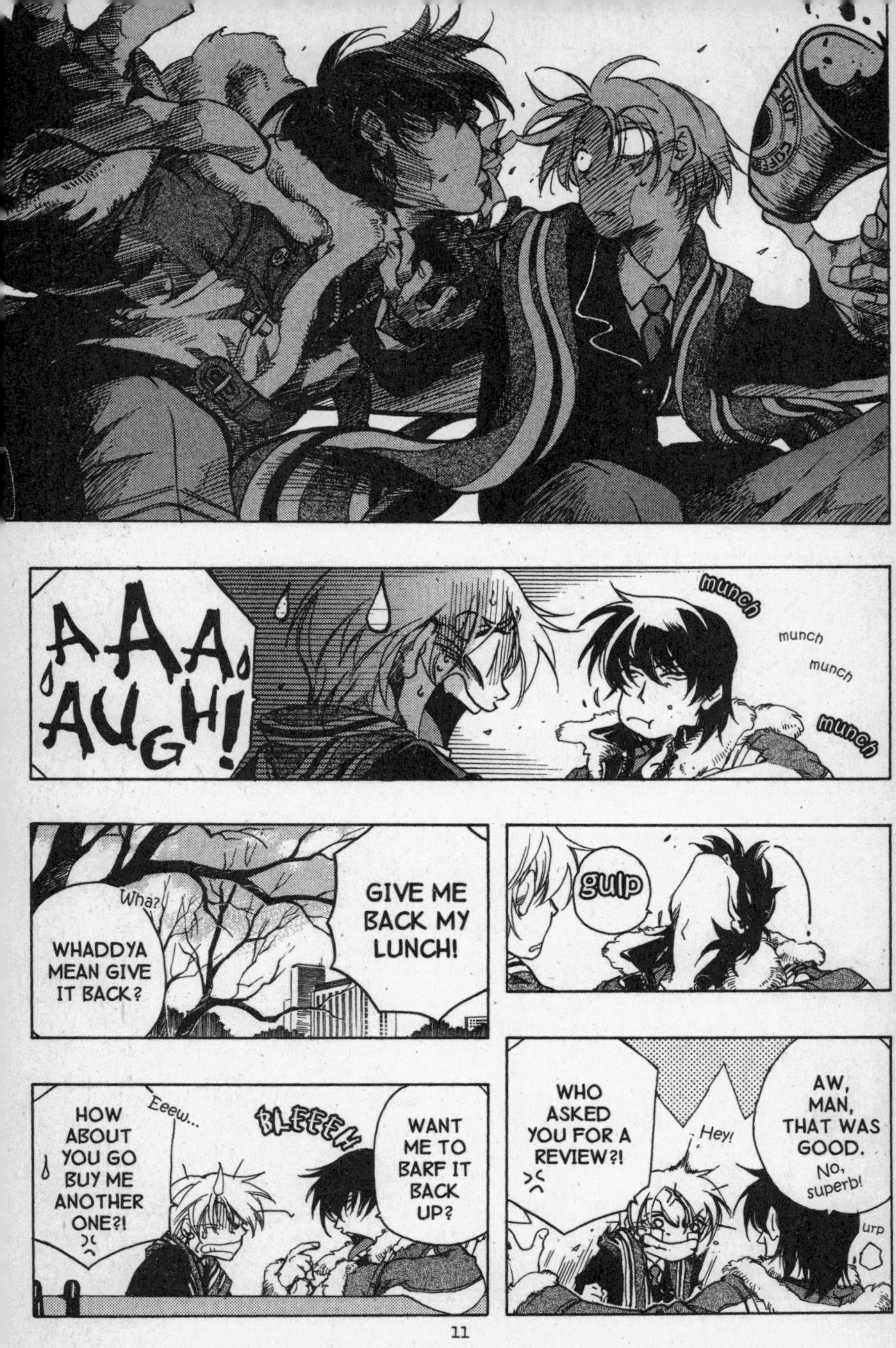
munch
munch
munch
munch
AAAAUGH!
gulp
GIVE ME BACK MY LUNCH!
Wha?
WHADDYA MEAN GIVE IT BACK?
AW, MAN, THAT WAS GOOD.
No, superb!
Hey!
WHO ASKED YOU FOR A REVIEW?!
urp
WANT ME TO BARF IT BACK UP?
BLEEEEH
Eeew...
HOW ABOUT YOU GO BUY ME ANOTHER ONE?!

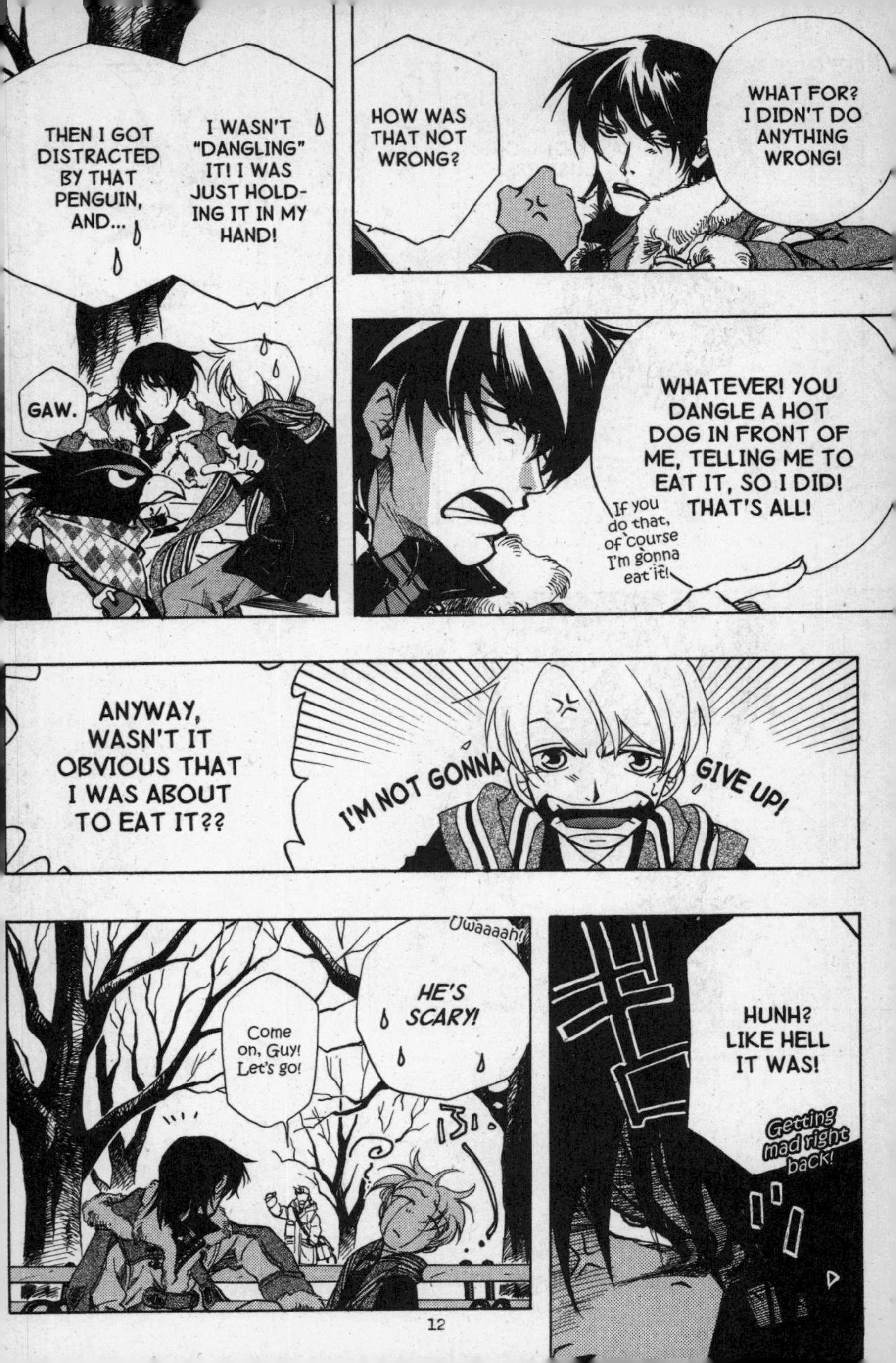
WHAT FOR? I DIDN'T DO ANYTHING WRONG!
HOW WAS THAT NOT WRONG?
WHATEVER! YOU DANGLE A HOT DOG IN FRONT OF ME, TELLING ME TO EAT IT, SO I DID! THAT'S ALL!
If you do that, of course I'm gonna eat it!
I WASN'T "DANGLING" IT! I WAS JUST HOLDING IT IN MY HAND!
THEN I GOT DISTRACTED BY THAT PENGUIN, AND...
GAW.
I'M NOT GONNA GIVE UP!
ANYWAY, WASN'T IT OBVIOUS THAT I WAS ABOUT TO EAT IT??
HUNH? LIKE HELL IT WAS!
Getting mad right back!
Uwaaaah!
HE'S SCARY!
Come on, Guy! Let's go!

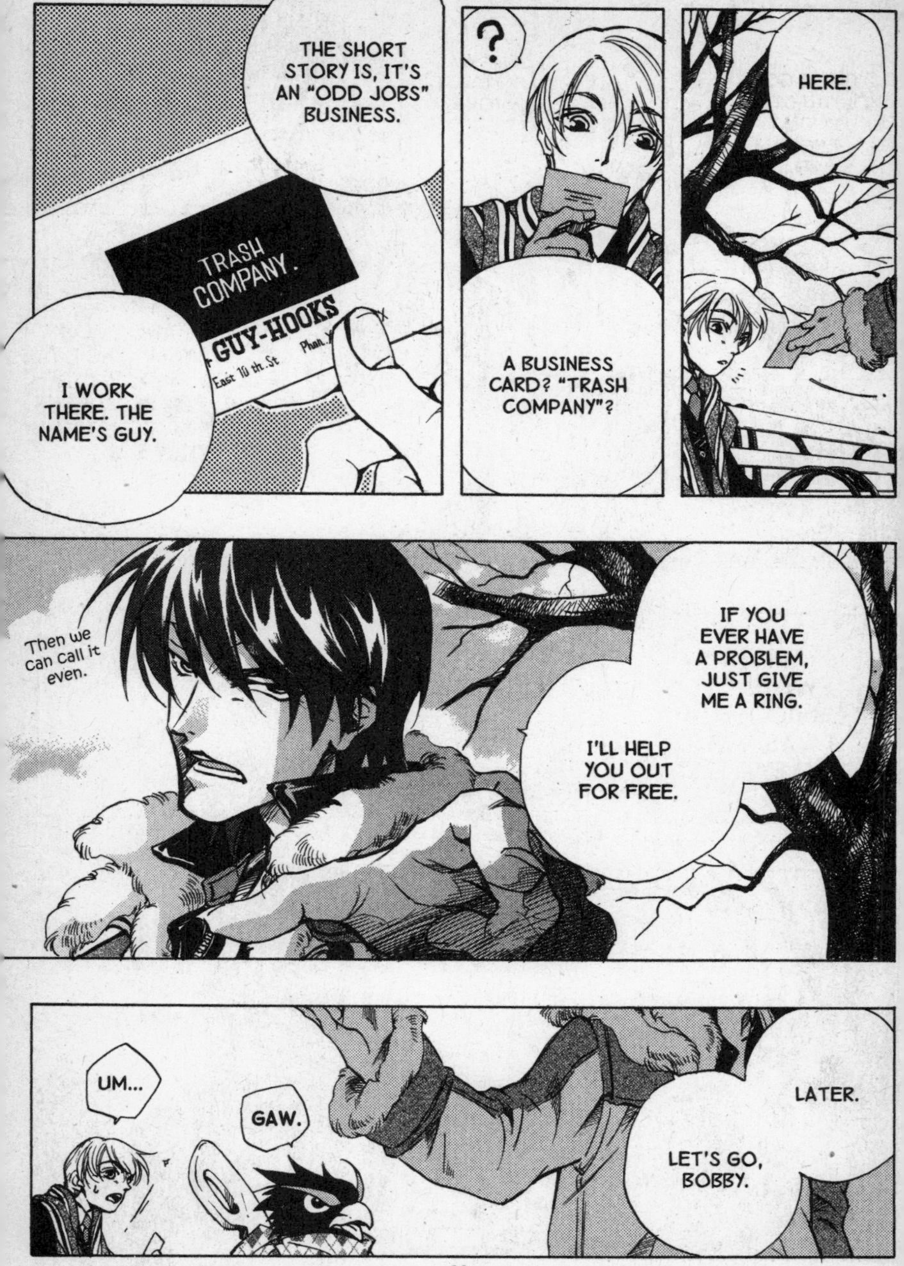
HERE.
?
A BUSINESS CARD? "TRASH COMPANY"?
THE SHORT STORY IS, IT'S AN "ODD JOBS" BUSINESS.
TRASH COMPANY.
GUY-HOOKS
East 10 th. St
I WORK THERE. THE NAME'S GUY.
IF YOU EVER HAVE A PROBLEM, JUST GIVE ME A RING.
I'LL HELP YOU OUT FOR FREE.
Then we can call it even.
LATER.
LET'S GO, BOBBY.
GAW.
UM...

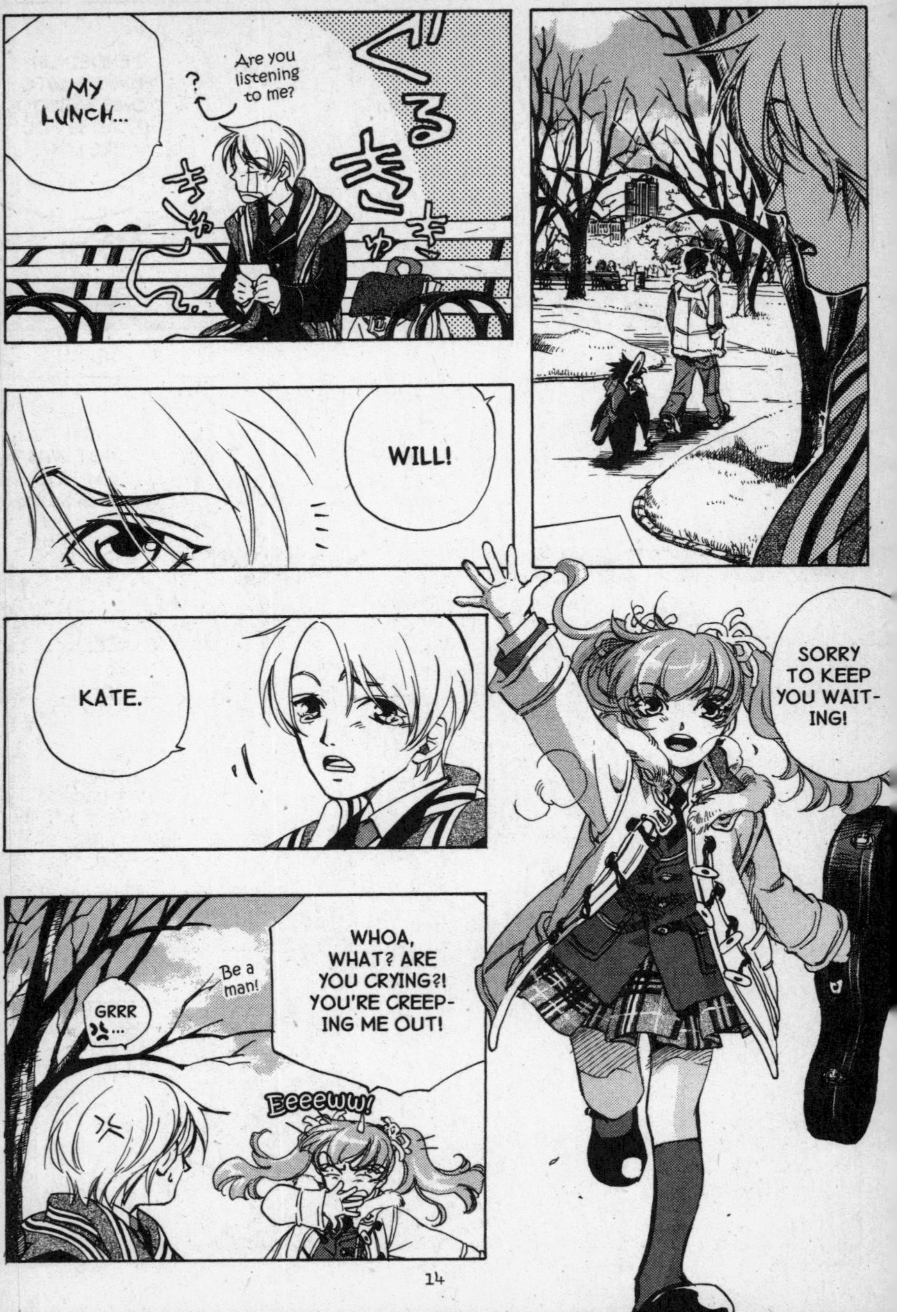
MY LUNCH...
Are you listening to me?
WILL!
SORRY TO KEEP YOU WAIT-ING!
KATE.
Be a man!
WHOA, WHAT? ARE YOU CRYING?! YOU'RE CREEP-ING ME OUT!
GRRR...
Eeeeww!

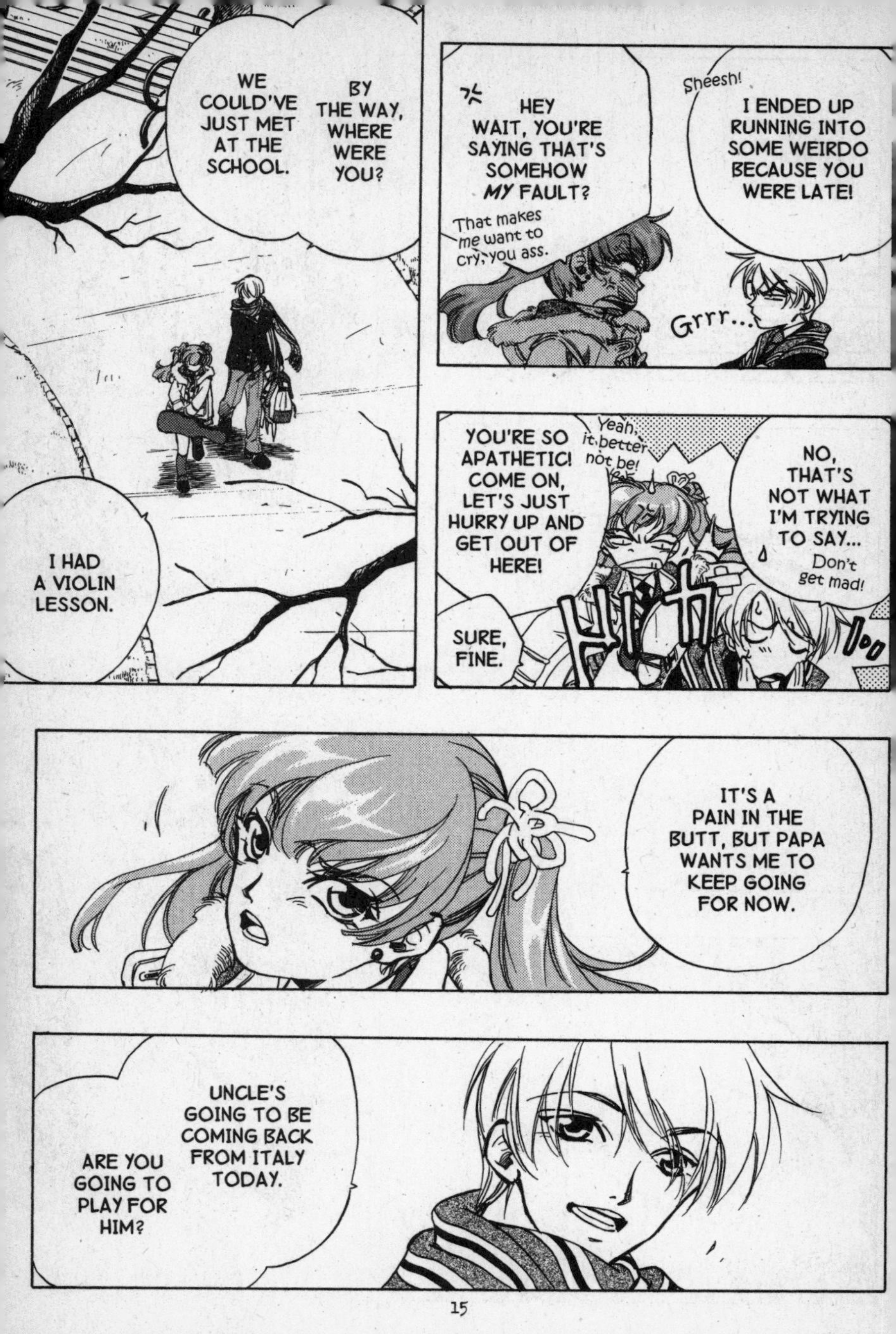
Sheesh! I ENDED UP RUNNING INTO SOME WEIRDO BECAUSE YOU WERE LATE!
HEY WAIT, YOU'RE SAYING THAT'S SOMEHOW *MY* FAULT?
That makes me want to cry, you ass.
Grrr...
NO, THAT'S NOT WHAT I'M TRYING TO SAY... Don't get mad!
Yeah, it better not be!
YOU'RE SO APATHETIC! COME ON, LET'S JUST HURRY UP AND GET OUT OF HERE!
SURE, FINE.
BY THE WAY, WHERE WERE YOU?
WE COULD'VE JUST MET AT THE SCHOOL.
I HAD A VIOLIN LESSON.
IT'S A PAIN IN THE BUTT, BUT PAPA WANTS ME TO KEEP GOING FOR NOW.
UNCLE'S GOING TO BE COMING BACK FROM ITALY TODAY.
ARE YOU GOING TO PLAY FOR HIM?

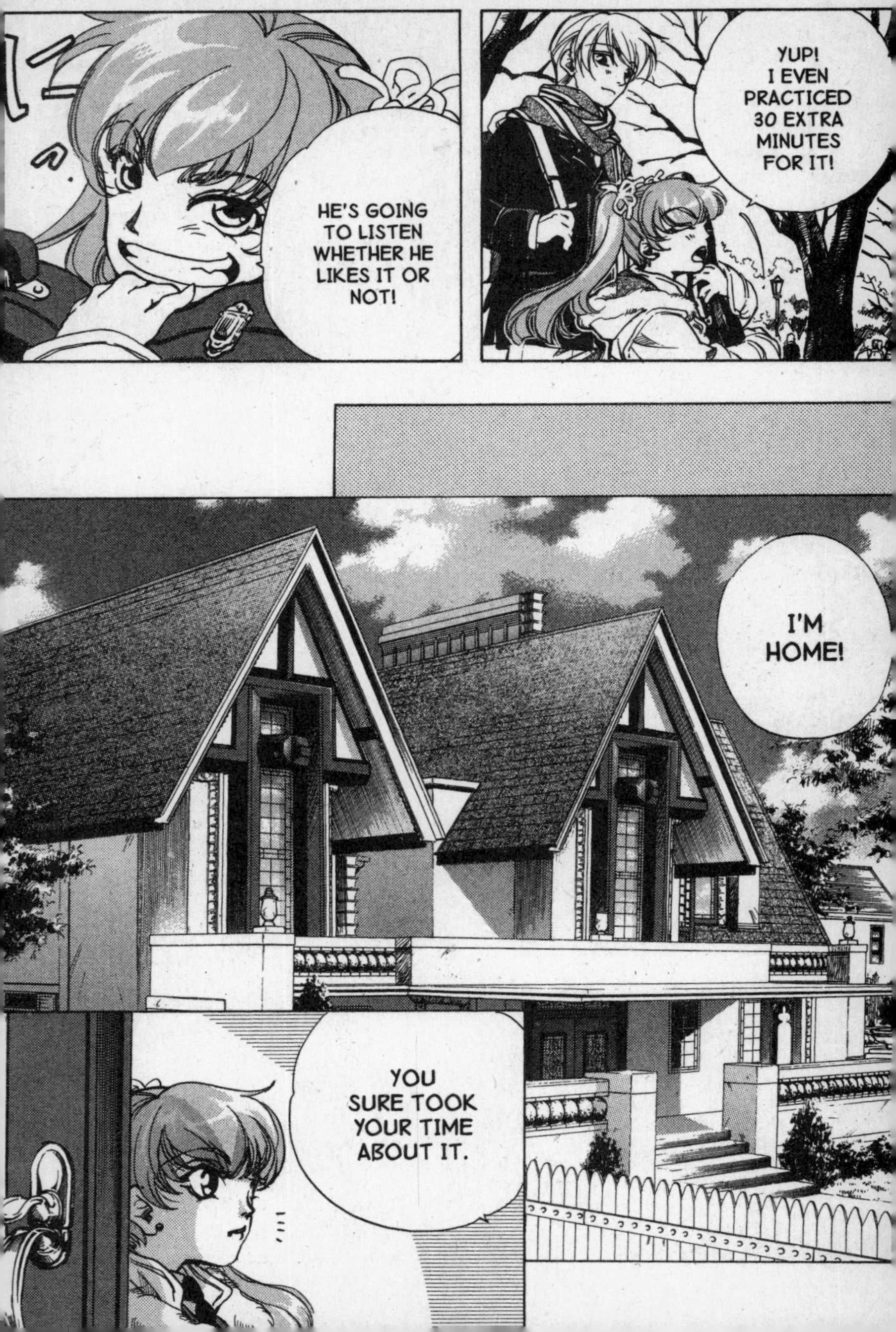
YUP! I EVEN PRACTICED 30 EXTRA MINUTES FOR IT!
HE'S GOING TO LISTEN WHETHER HE LIKES IT OR NOT!
I'M HOME!
YOU SURE TOOK YOUR TIME ABOUT IT.

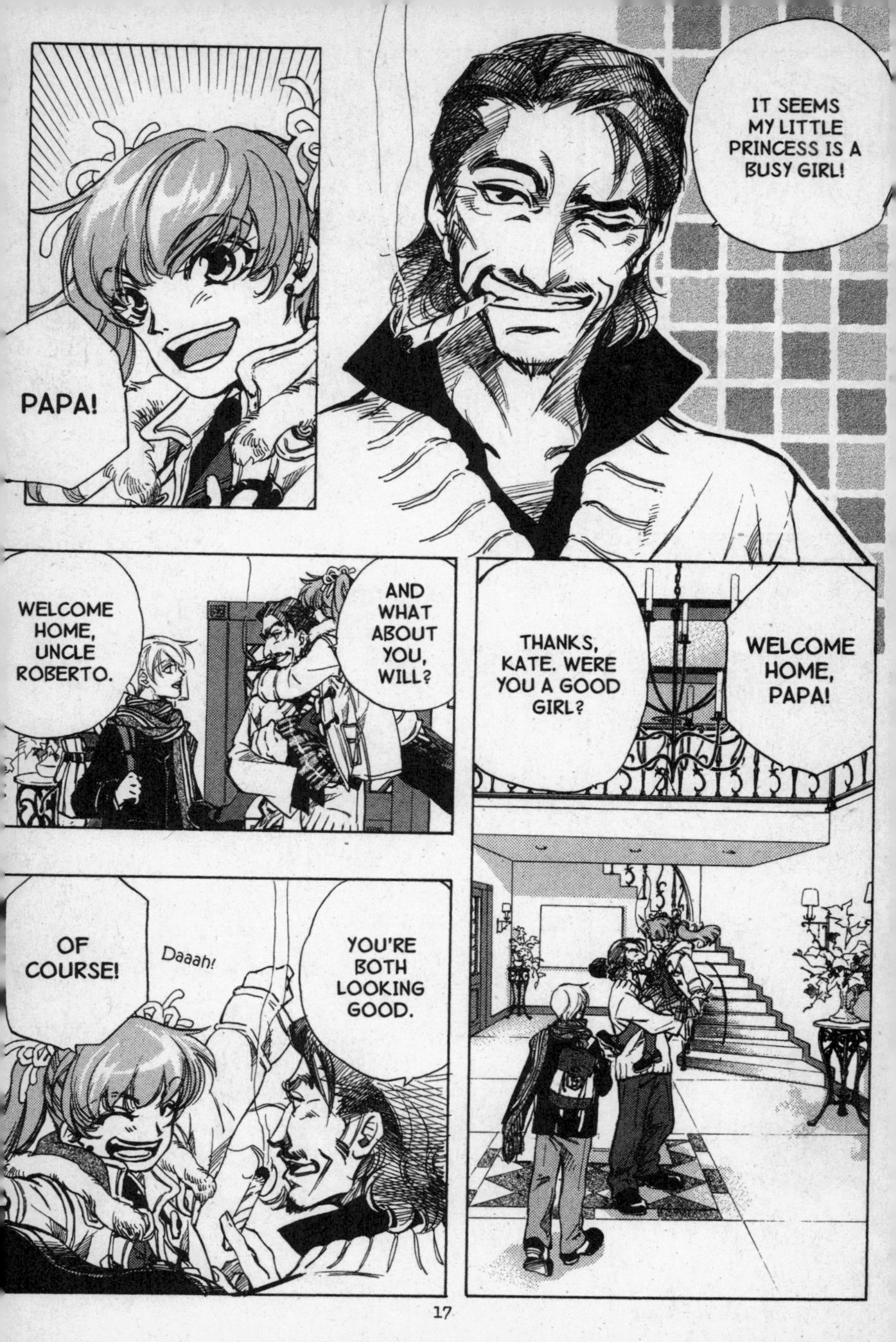
IT SEEMS MY LITTLE PRINCESS IS A BUSY GIRL!
PAPA!
WELCOME HOME, PAPA!
THANKS, KATE. WERE YOU A GOOD GIRL?
AND WHAT ABOUT YOU, WILL?
WELCOME HOME, UNCLE ROBERTO.
YOU'RE BOTH LOOKING GOOD.
Daaah!
OF COURSE!

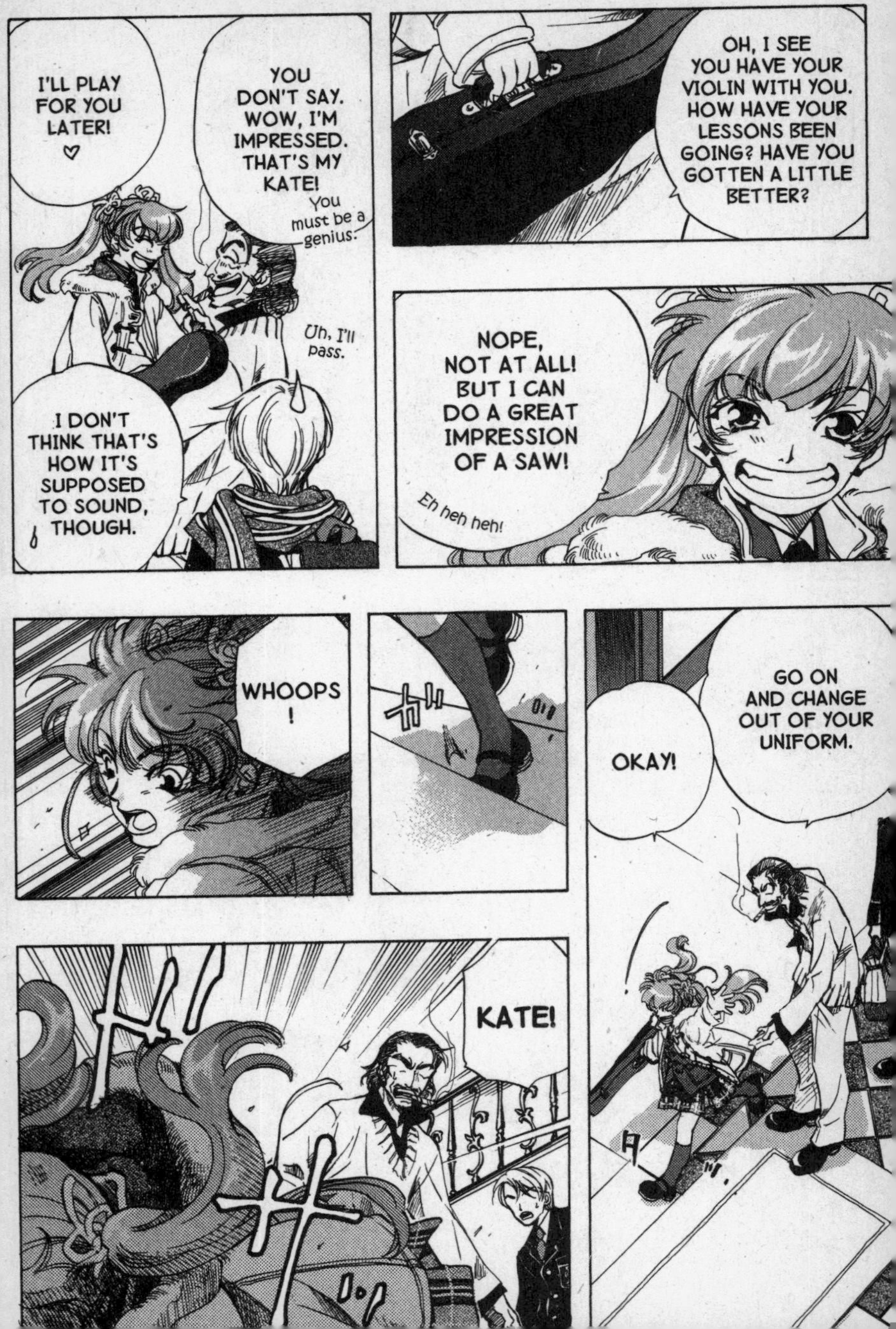
OH, I SEE YOU HAVE YOUR VIOLIN WITH YOU. HOW HAVE YOUR LESSONS BEEN GOING? HAVE YOU GOTTEN A LITTLE BETTER?
NOPE, NOT AT ALL! BUT I CAN DO A GREAT IMPRESSION OF A SAW!
Eh heh heh!
YOU DON'T SAY. WOW, I'M IMPRESSED. THAT'S MY KATE!
I'LL PLAY FOR YOU LATER! ♡
You must be a genius.
Uh, I'll pass.
I DON'T THINK THAT'S HOW IT'S SUPPOSED TO SOUND, THOUGH.
GO ON AND CHANGE OUT OF YOUR UNIFORM.
OKAY!
WHOOPS!
KATE!

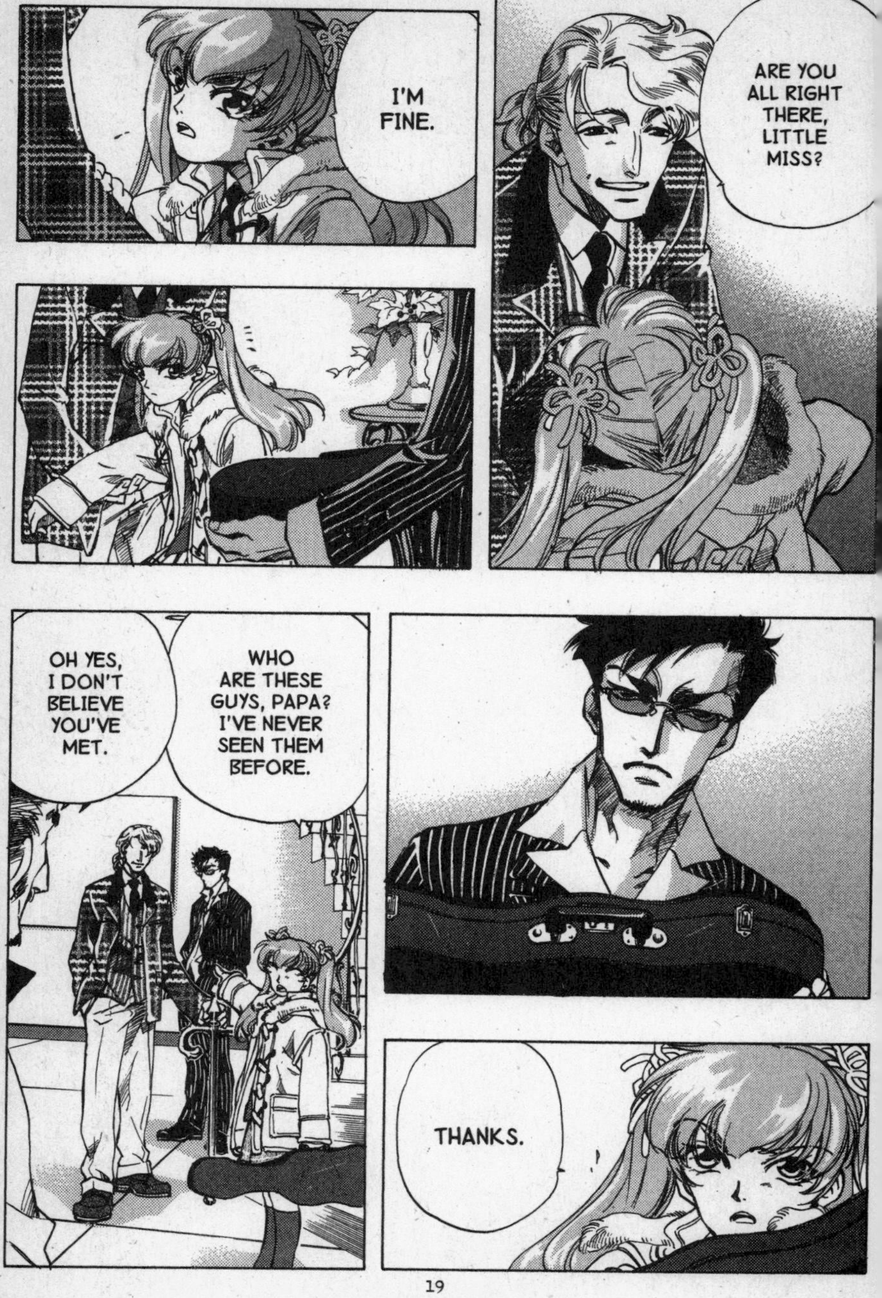
ARE YOU ALL RIGHT THERE, LITTLE MISS?
I'M FINE.
THANKS.
WHO ARE THESE GUYS, PAPA? I'VE NEVER SEEN THEM BEFORE.
OH YES, I DON'T BELIEVE YOU'VE MET.

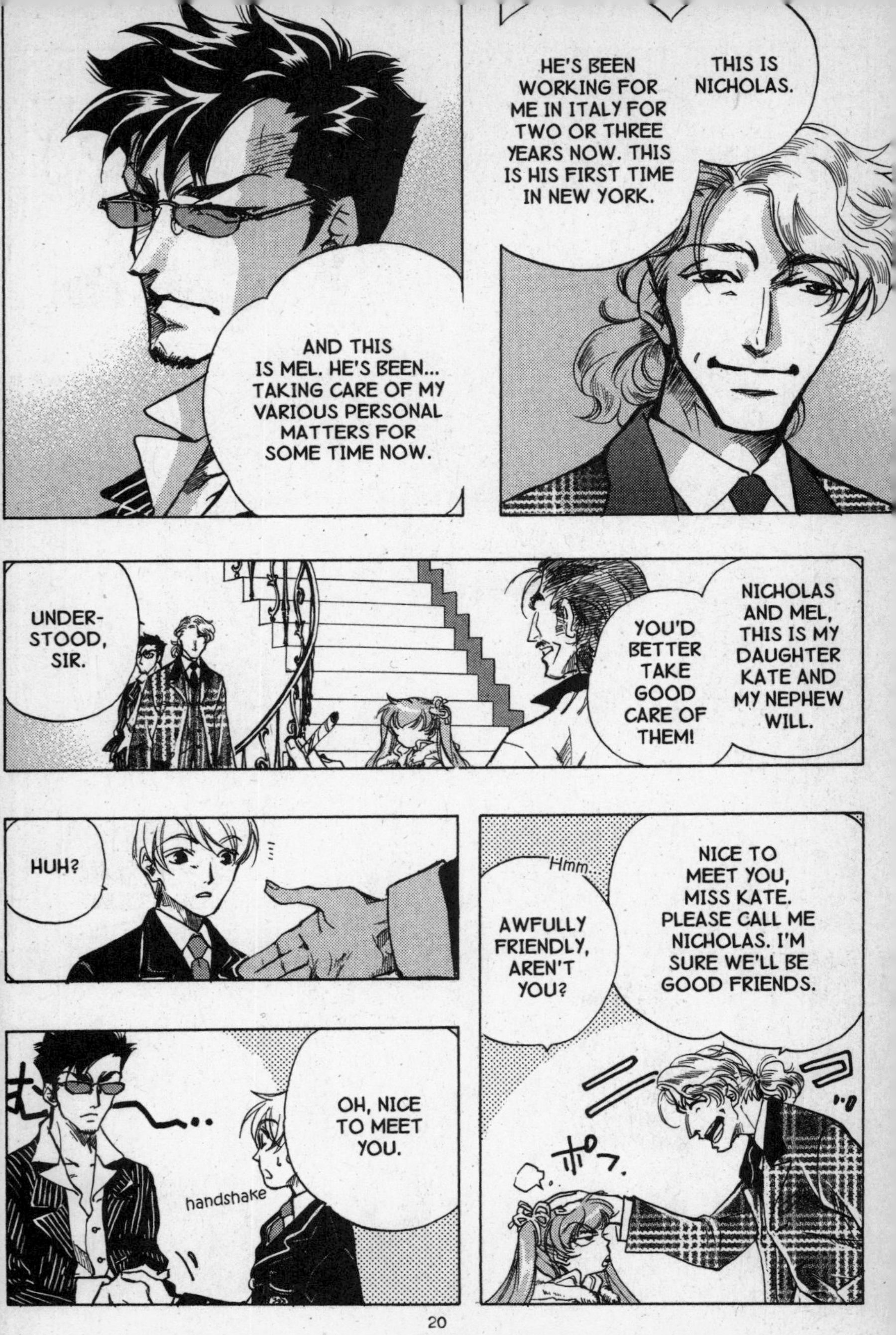
THIS IS NICHOLAS.
HE'S BEEN WORKING FOR ME IN ITALY FOR TWO OR THREE YEARS NOW. THIS IS HIS FIRST TIME IN NEW YORK.
AND THIS IS MEL. HE'S BEEN... TAKING CARE OF MY VARIOUS PERSONAL MATTERS FOR SOME TIME NOW.
NICHOLAS AND MEL, THIS IS MY DAUGHTER KATE AND MY NEPHEW WILL.
YOU'D BETTER TAKE GOOD CARE OF THEM!
UNDER-STOOD, SIR.
NICE TO MEET YOU, MISS KATE. PLEASE CALL ME NICHOLAS. I'M SURE WE'LL BE GOOD FRIENDS.
Hmm..
AWFULLY FRIENDLY, AREN'T YOU?
ポフ
HUH?
OH, NICE TO MEET YOU.
handshake

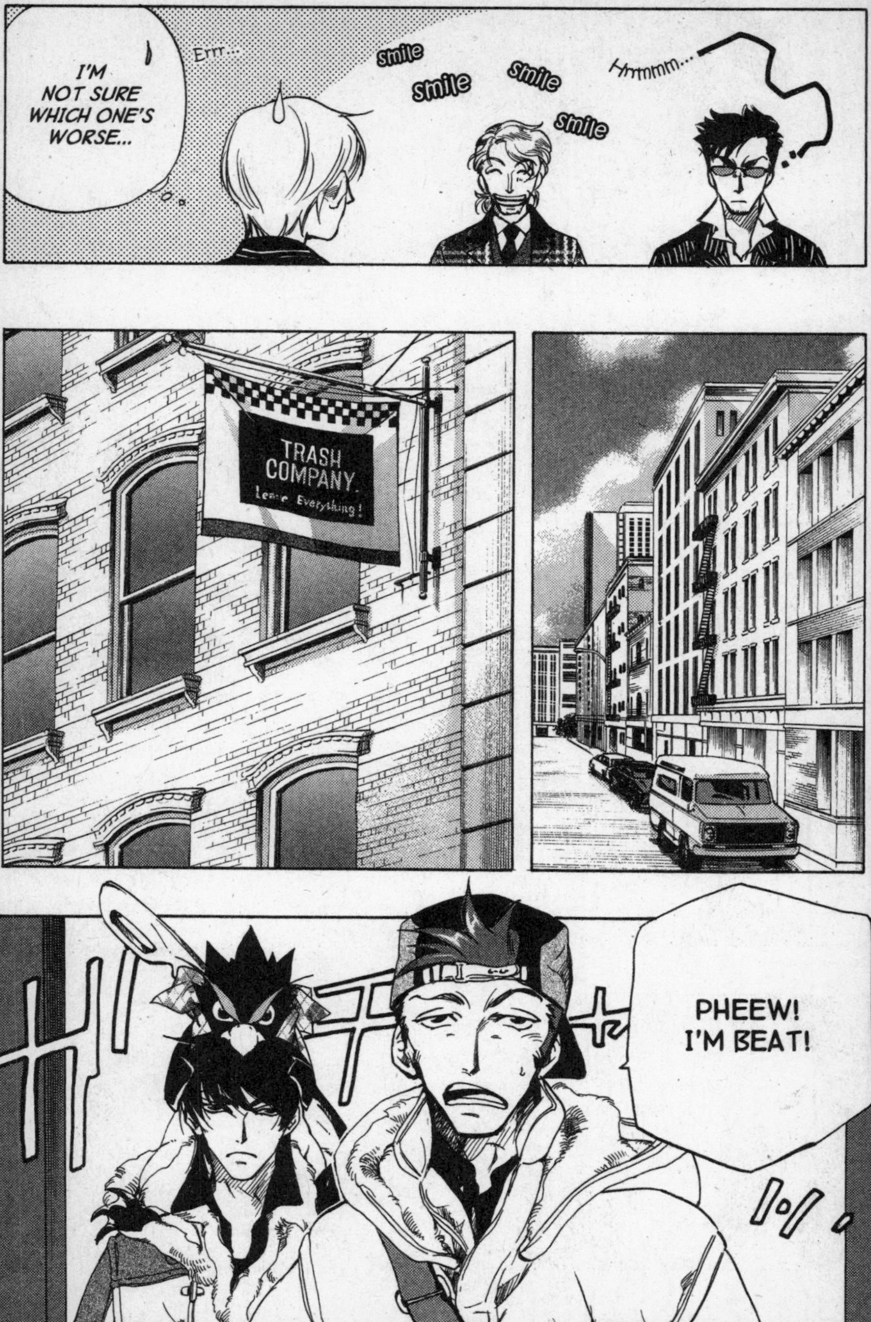
Hrmmm...
smile
smile
smile
smile
Errr...
I'M NOT SURE WHICH ONE'S WORSE...
TRASH COMPANY
Leave Everything!
PHEEW! I'M BEAT!

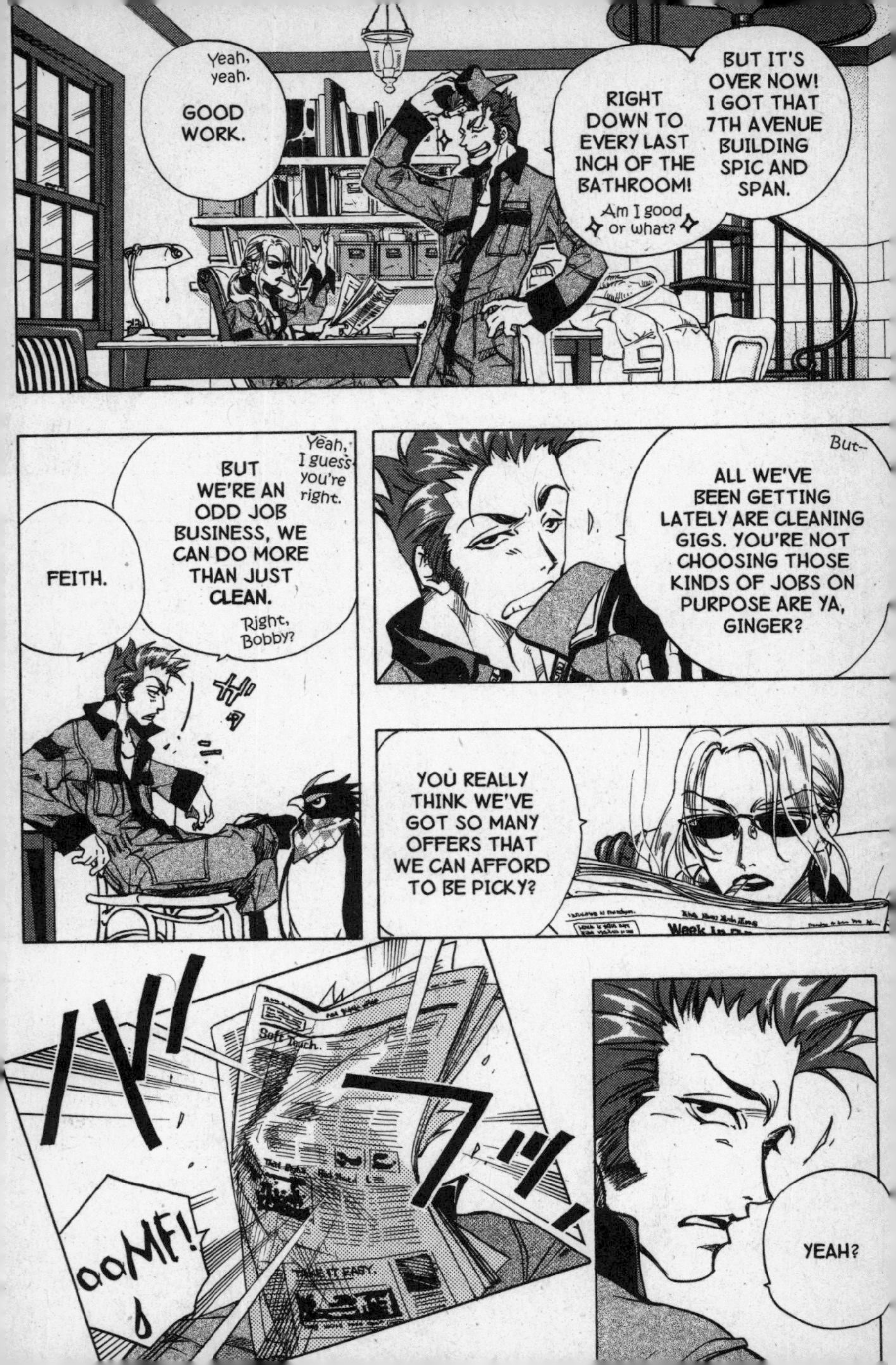
BUT IT'S OVER NOW! I GOT THAT 7TH AVENUE BUILDING SPIC AND SPAN.
RIGHT DOWN TO EVERY LAST INCH OF THE BATHROOM!
Am I good or what?
Yeah, yeah.
GOOD WORK.
But--
ALL WE'VE BEEN GETTING LATELY ARE CLEANING GIGS. YOU'RE NOT CHOOSING THOSE KINDS OF JOBS ON PURPOSE ARE YA, GINGER?
YOU REALLY THINK WE'VE GOT SO MANY OFFERS THAT WE CAN AFFORD TO BE PICKY?
Yeah, I guess you're right.
BUT WE'RE AN ODD JOB BUSINESS, WE CAN DO MORE THAN JUST CLEAN.
Right, Bobby?
FEITH.
YEAH?
OOMF!

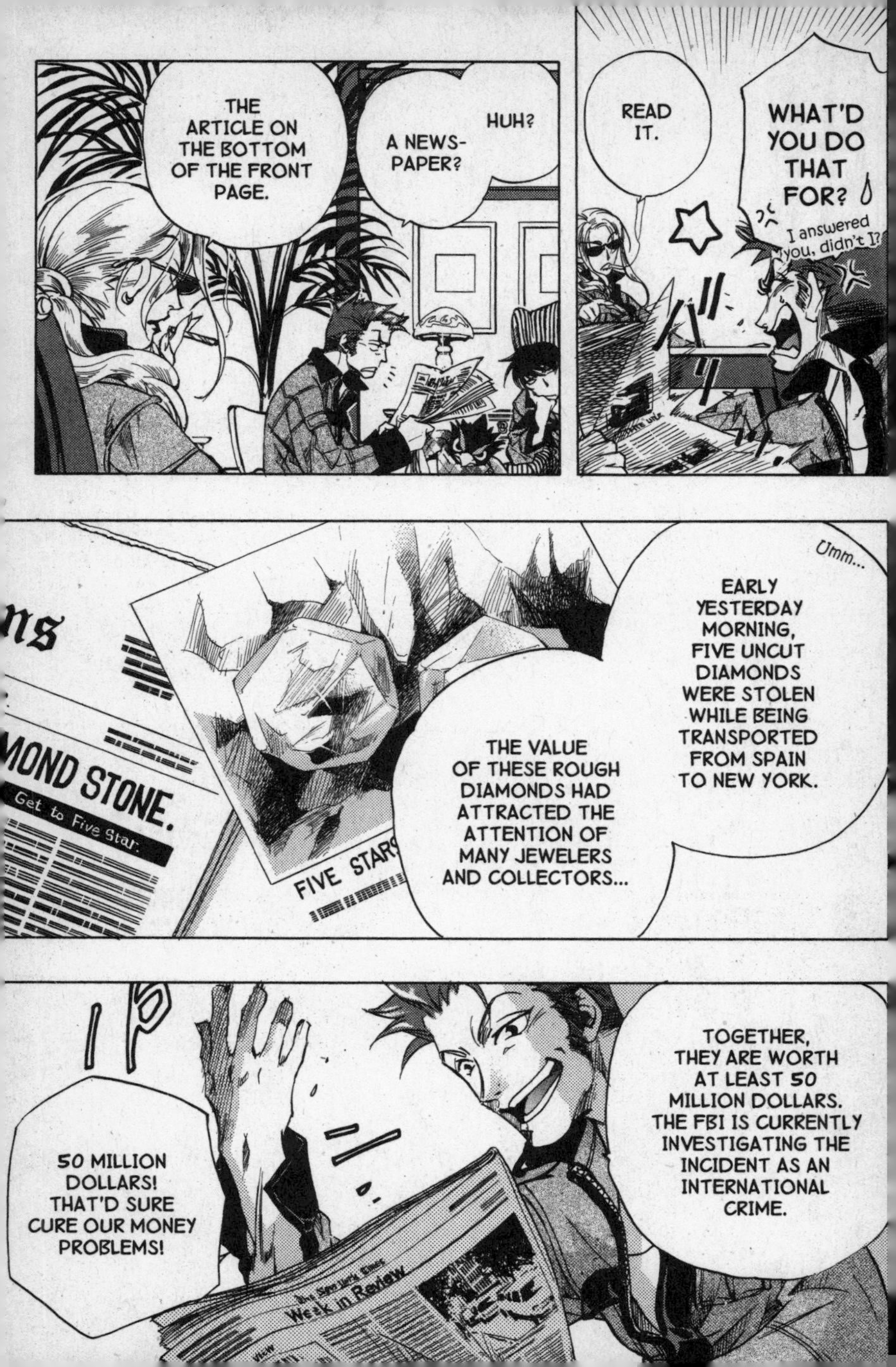
WHAT'D YOU DO THAT FOR?
I answered you, didn't I?
READ IT.
HUH?
A NEWS-PAPER?
THE ARTICLE ON THE BOTTOM OF THE FRONT PAGE.
Umm...
EARLY YESTERDAY MORNING, FIVE UNCUT DIAMONDS WERE STOLEN WHILE BEING TRANSPORTED FROM SPAIN TO NEW YORK.
THE VALUE OF THESE ROUGH DIAMONDS HAD ATTRACTED THE ATTENTION OF MANY JEWELERS AND COLLECTORS...
MOND STONE.
Get to Five Star.
FIVE STARS
TOGETHER, THEY ARE WORTH AT LEAST 50 MILLION DOLLARS. THE FBI IS CURRENTLY INVESTIGATING THE INCIDENT AS AN INTERNATIONAL CRIME.
50 MILLION DOLLARS! THAT'D SURE CURE OUR MONEY PROBLEMS!
Week in Review

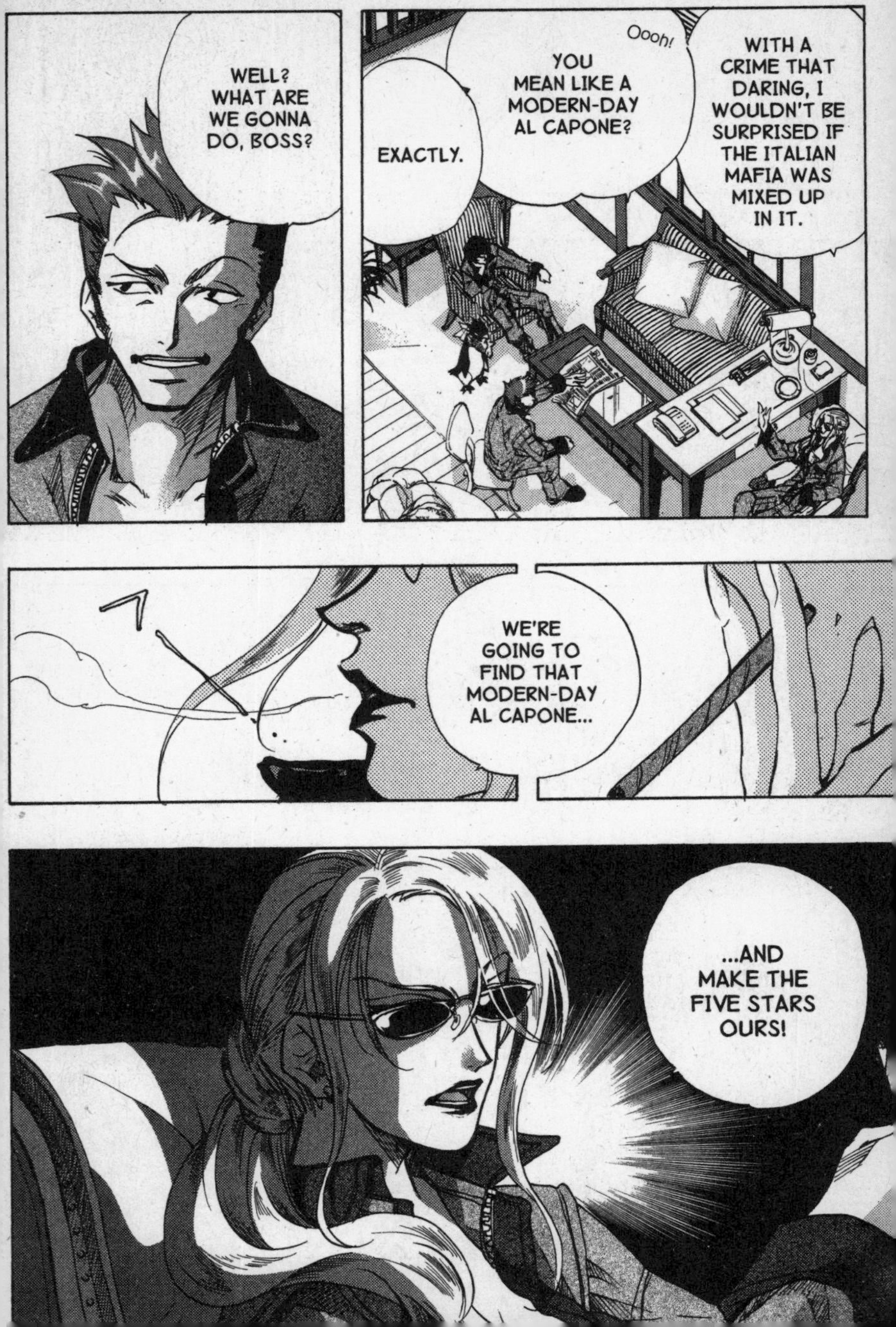
WITH A CRIME THAT DARING, I WOULDN'T BE SURPRISED IF THE ITALIAN MAFIA WAS MIXED UP IN IT.
Oooh!
YOU MEAN LIKE A MODERN-DAY AL CAPONE?
EXACTLY.
WELL? WHAT ARE WE GONNA DO, BOSS?
WE'RE GOING TO FIND THAT MODERN-DAY AL CAPONE...
...AND MAKE THE FIVE STARS OURS!

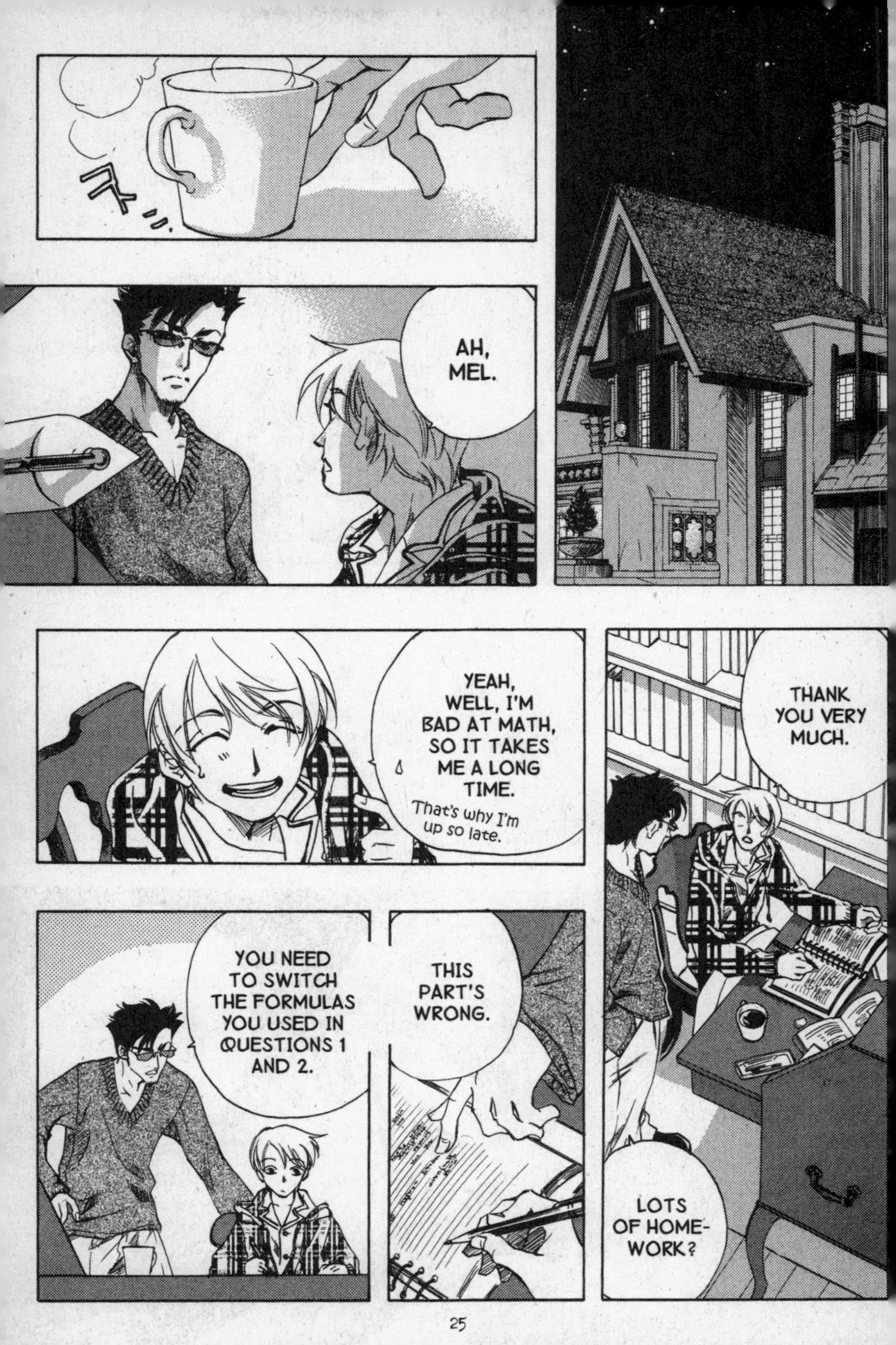
AH, MEL.
THANK YOU VERY MUCH.
LOTS OF HOME-WORK?
YEAH, WELL, I'M BAD AT MATH, SO IT TAKES ME A LONG TIME.
That's why I'm up so late.
THIS PART'S WRONG.
YOU NEED TO SWITCH THE FORMULAS YOU USED IN QUESTIONS 1 AND 2.

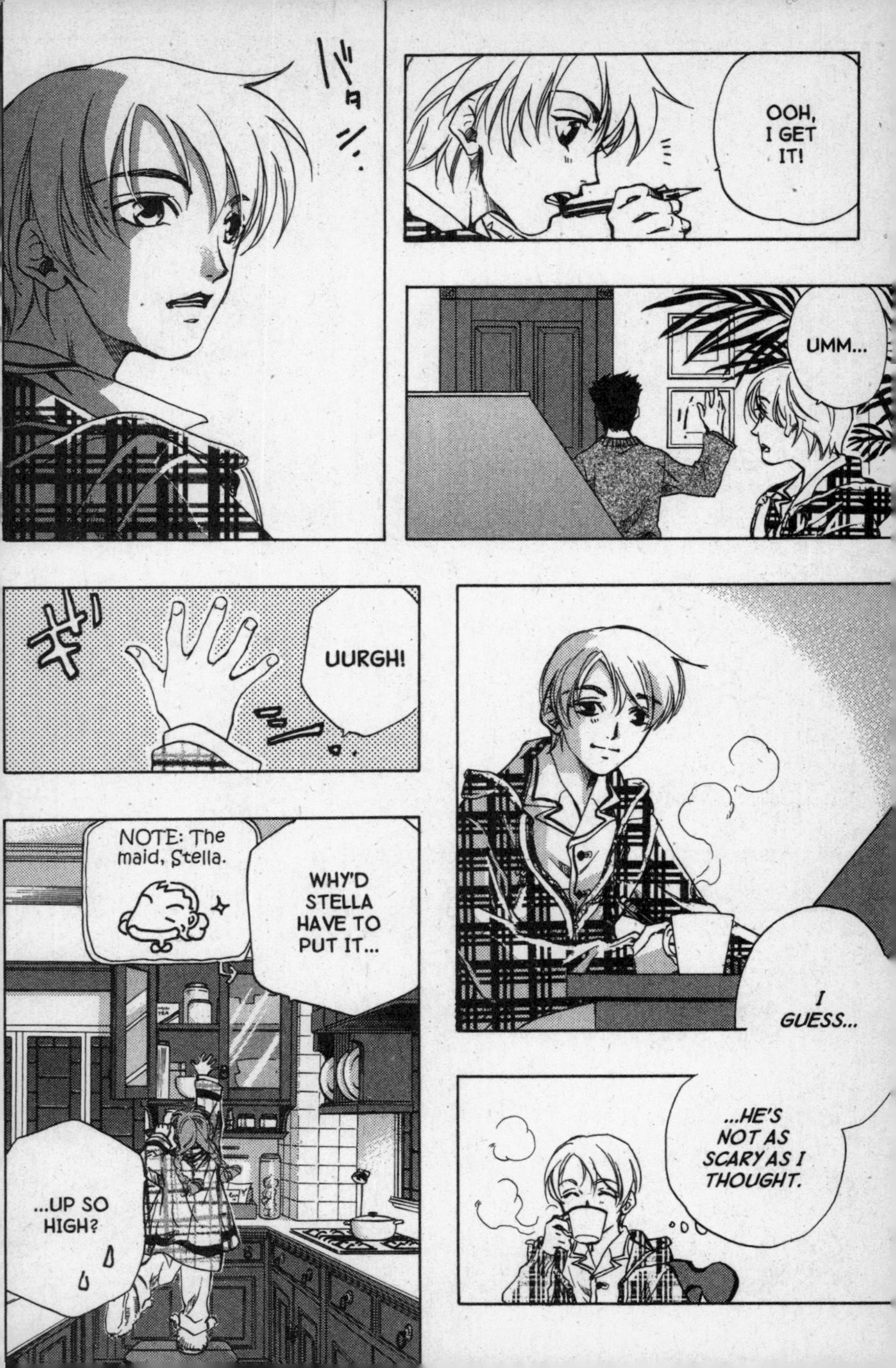
OOH, I GET IT!
UMM...
I GUESS...
...HE'S NOT AS SCARY AS I THOUGHT.
UURGH!
NOTE: The maid, Stella.
WHY'D STELLA HAVE TO PUT IT...
...UP SO HIGH?

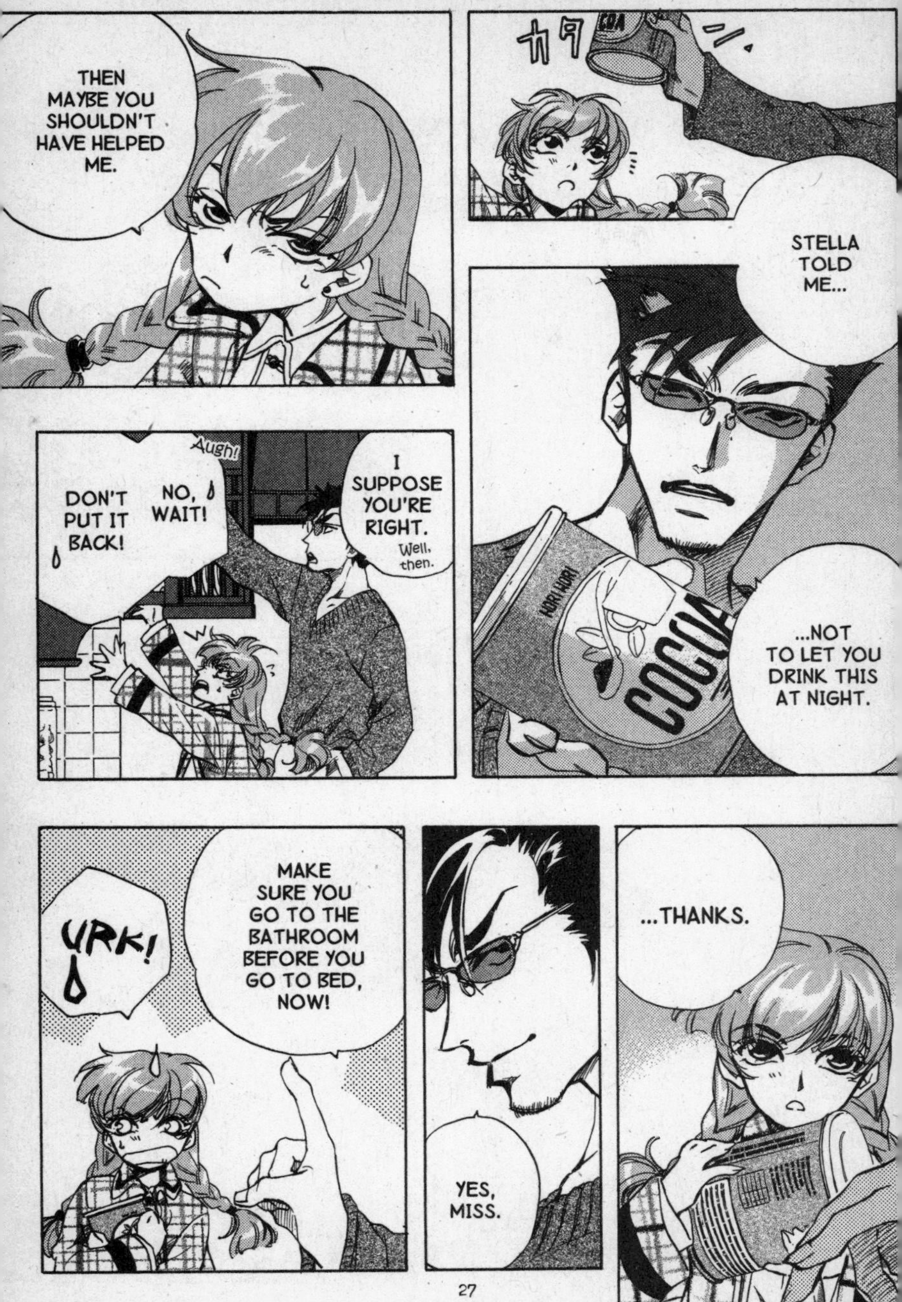
カタ
STELLA TOLD ME...
...NOT TO LET YOU DRINK THIS AT NIGHT.
THEN MAYBE YOU SHOULDN'T HAVE HELPED ME.
I SUPPOSE YOU'RE RIGHT.
Well, then.
Augh!
NO, WAIT!
DON'T PUT IT BACK!
...THANKS.
YES, MISS.
MAKE SURE YOU GO TO THE BATHROOM BEFORE YOU GO TO BED, NOW!
URK!

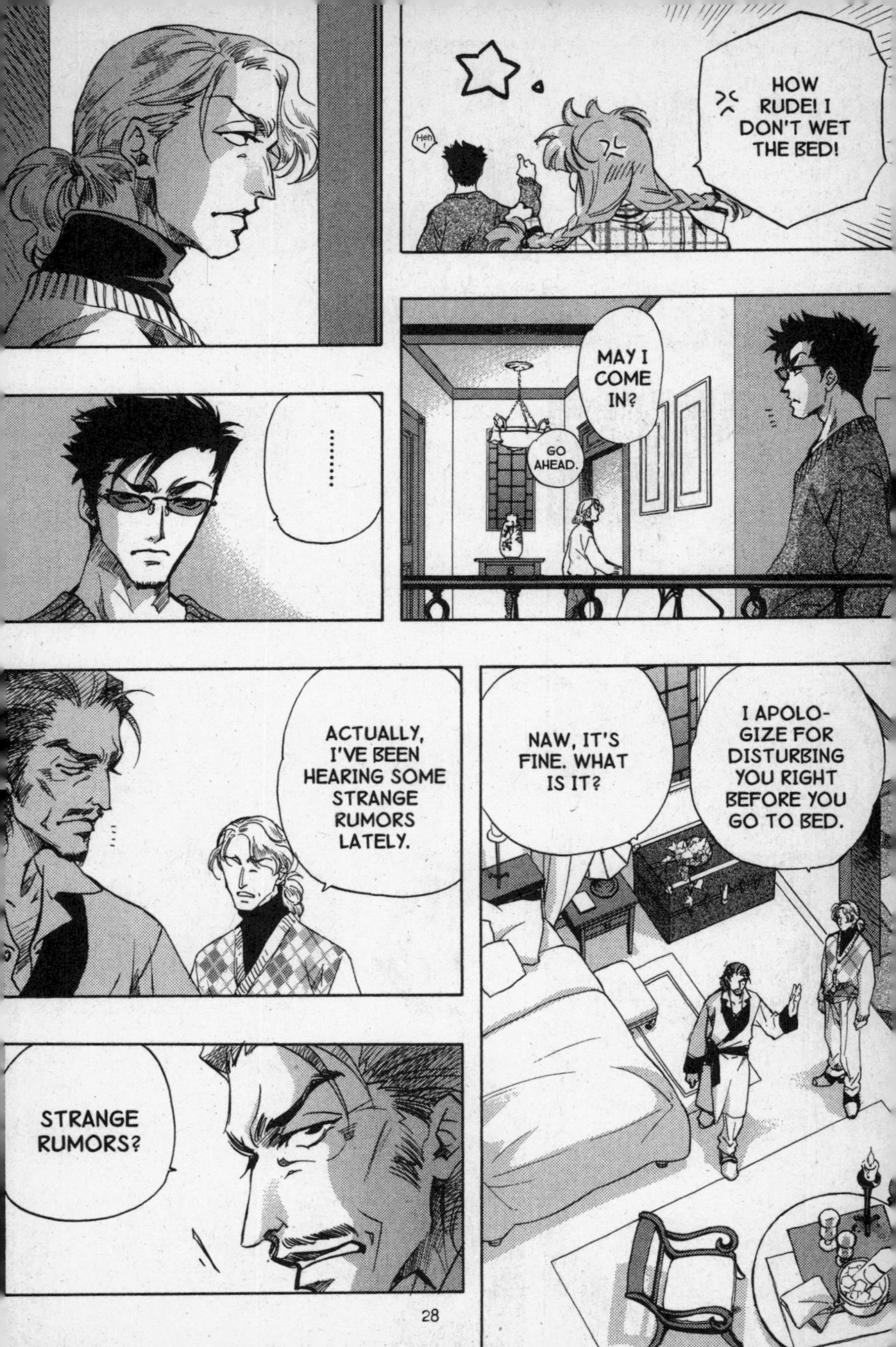
HOW RUDE! I DON'T WET THE BED!
Heh!
MAY I COME IN?
GO AHEAD.
....
I APOLOGIZE FOR DISTURBING YOU RIGHT BEFORE YOU GO TO BED.
NAW, IT'S FINE. WHAT IS IT?
ACTUALLY, I'VE BEEN HEARING SOME STRANGE RUMORS LATELY.
STRANGE RUMORS?

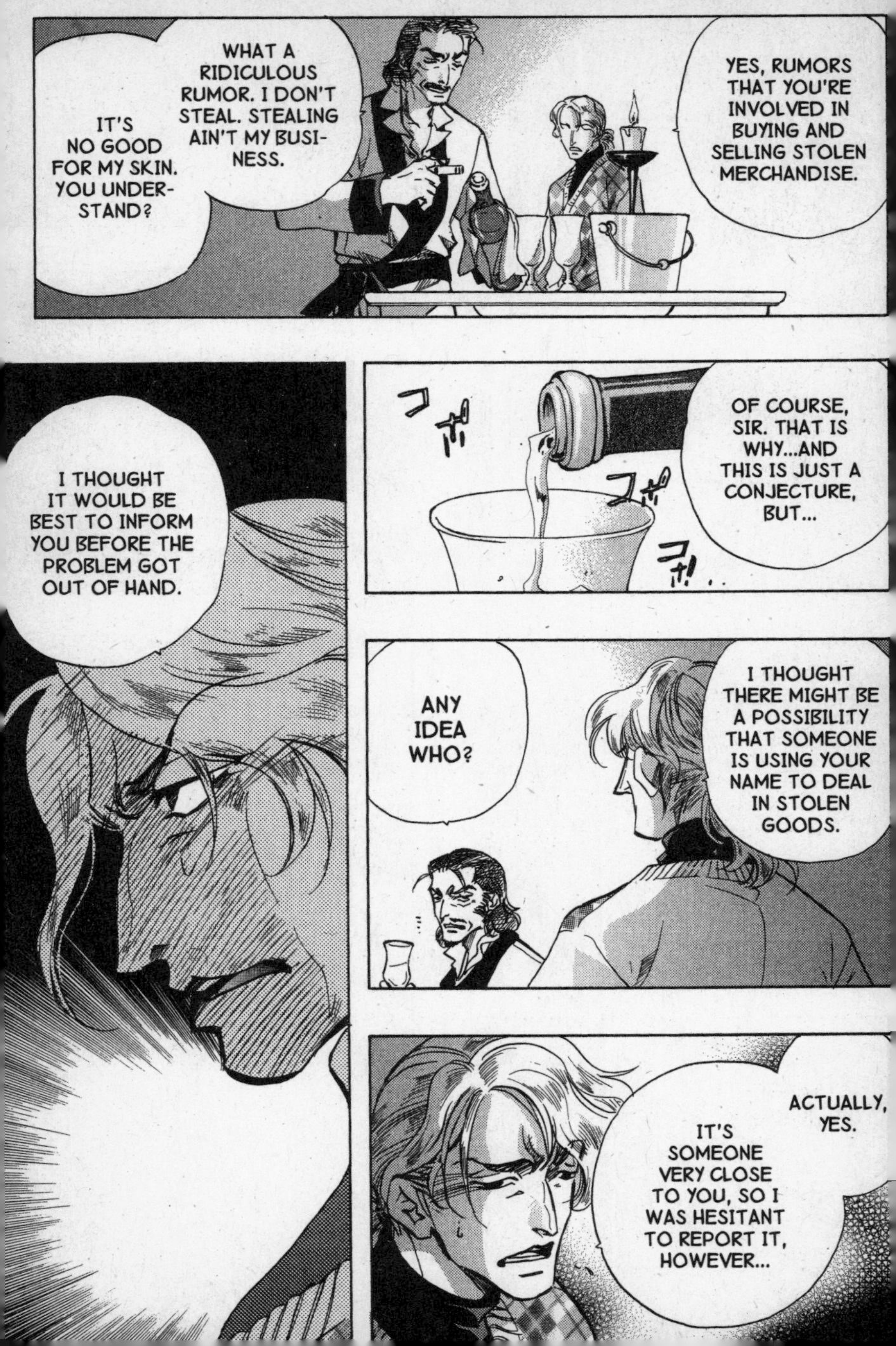
YES, RUMORS THAT YOU'RE INVOLVED IN BUYING AND SELLING STOLEN MERCHANDISE.
WHAT A RIDICULOUS RUMOR. I DON'T STEAL. STEALING AIN'T MY BUSI-NESS.
IT'S NO GOOD FOR MY SKIN. YOU UNDER-STAND?
OF COURSE, SIR. THAT IS WHY...AND THIS IS JUST A CONJECTURE, BUT...
コポ
コポ
コポ!
I THOUGHT THERE MIGHT BE A POSSIBILITY THAT SOMEONE IS USING YOUR NAME TO DEAL IN STOLEN GOODS.
ANY IDEA WHO?
ACTUALLY, YES.
IT'S SOMEONE VERY CLOSE TO YOU, SO I WAS HESITANT TO REPORT IT, HOWEVER...
I THOUGHT IT WOULD BE BEST TO INFORM YOU BEFORE THE PROBLEM GOT OUT OF HAND.

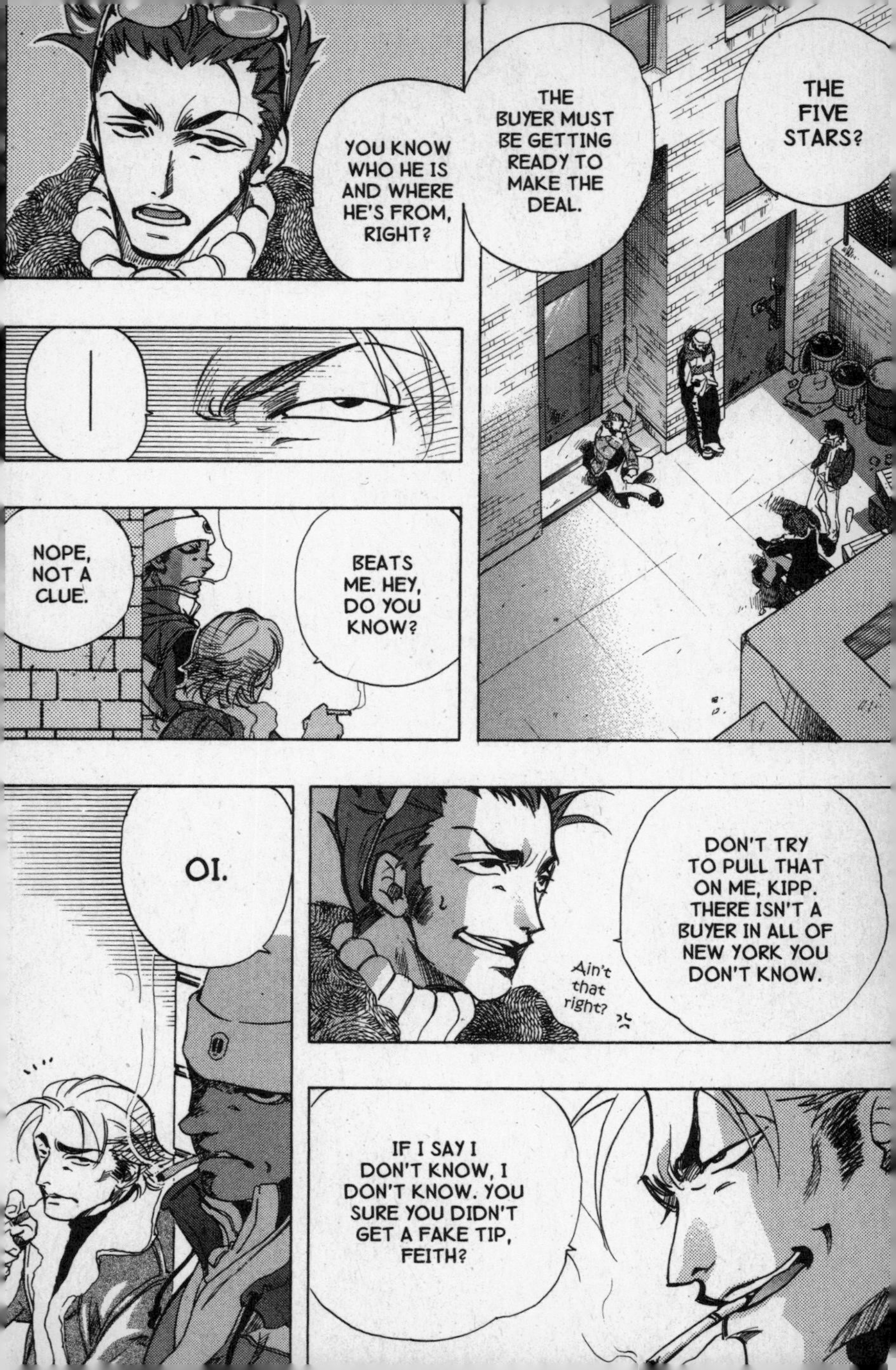
THE FIVE STARS?
THE BUYER MUST BE GETTING READY TO MAKE THE DEAL.
YOU KNOW WHO HE IS AND WHERE HE'S FROM, RIGHT?
—
BEATS ME. HEY, DO YOU KNOW?
NOPE, NOT A CLUE.
DON'T TRY TO PULL THAT ON ME, KIPP. THERE ISN'T A BUYER IN ALL OF NEW YORK YOU DON'T KNOW.
Ain't that right?
IF I SAY I DON'T KNOW, I DON'T KNOW. YOU SURE YOU DIDN'T GET A FAKE TIP, FEITH?
OI.
...

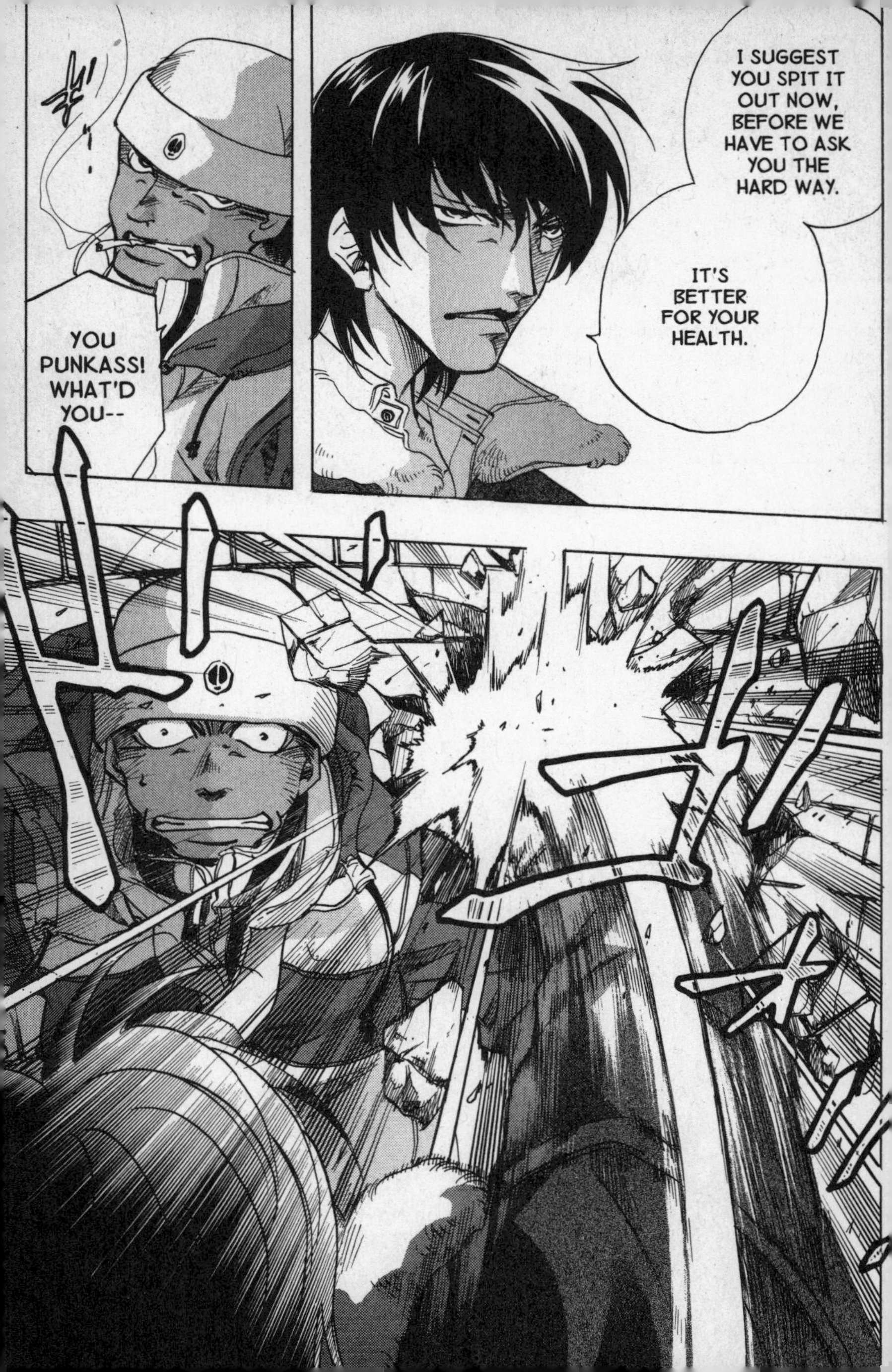
I SUGGEST YOU SPIT IT OUT NOW, BEFORE WE HAVE TO ASK YOU THE HARD WAY.
IT'S BETTER FOR YOUR HEALTH.
YOU PUNKASS! WHAT'D YOU--

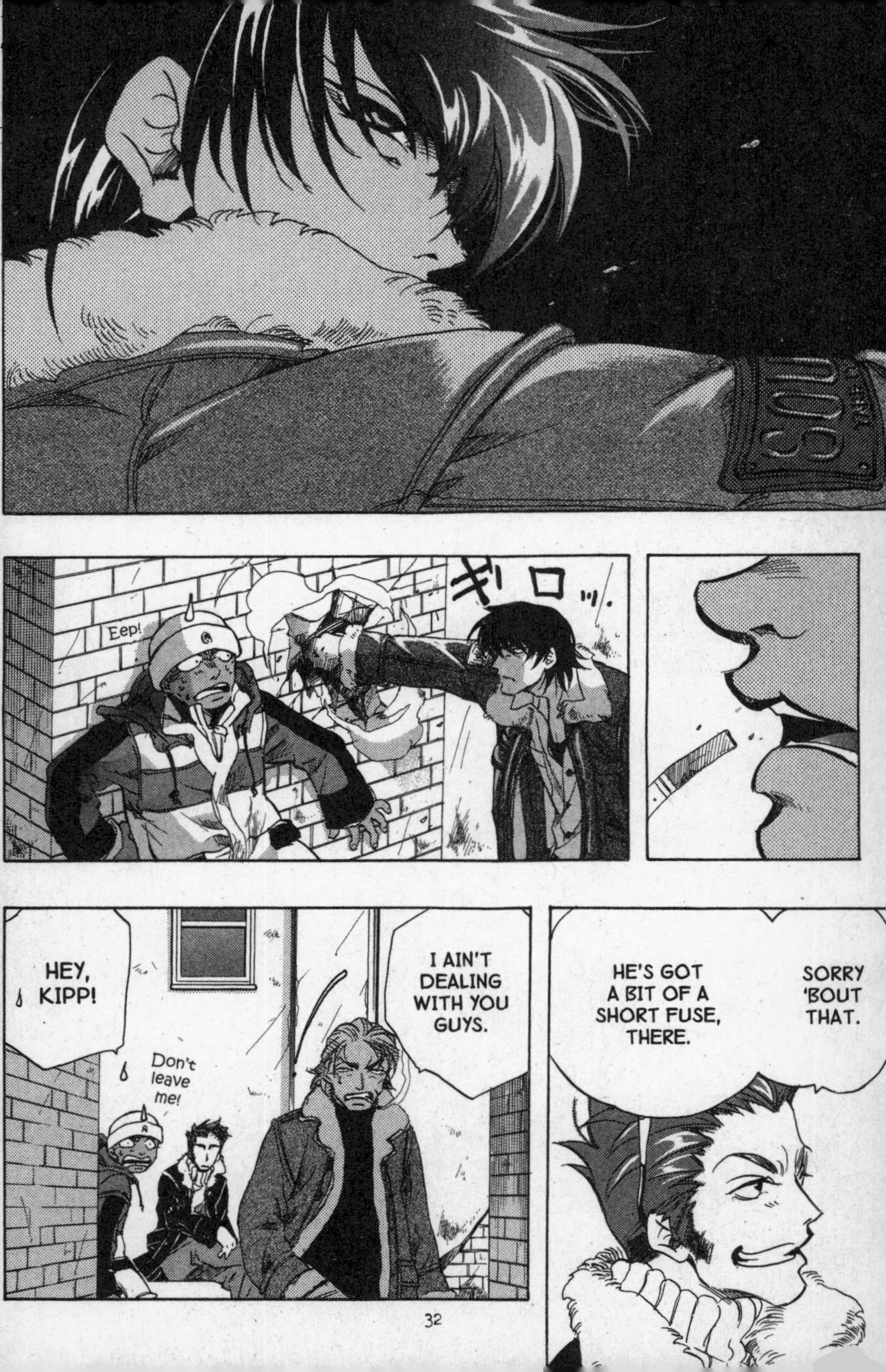
ギロッ
Eep!
SORRY 'BOUT THAT.
HE'S GOT A BIT OF A SHORT FUSE, THERE.
I AIN'T DEALING WITH YOU GUYS.
HEY, KIPP!
Don't leave me!

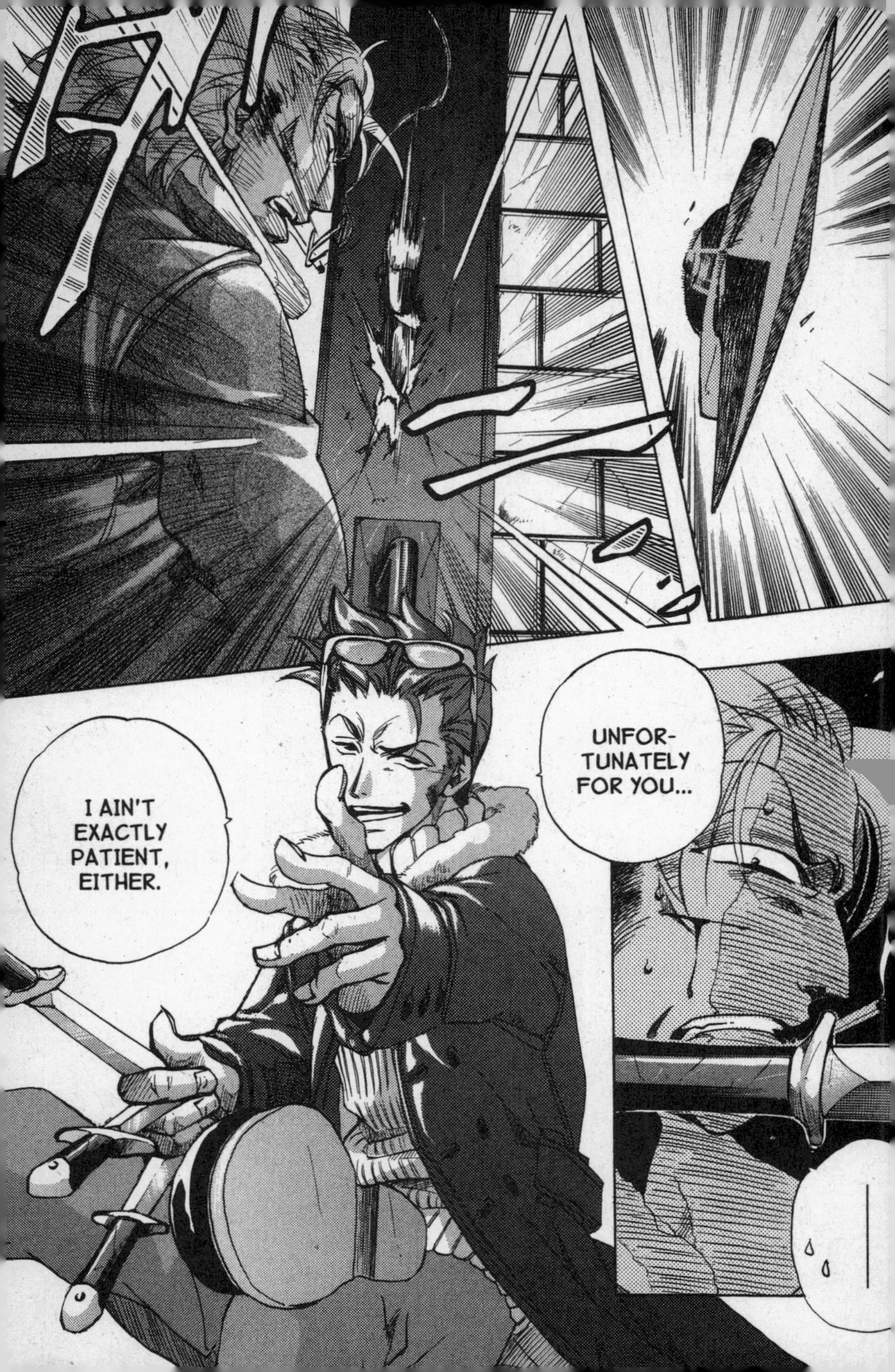
UNFOR-TUNATELY FOR YOU...
I AIN'T EXACTLY PATIENT, EITHER.

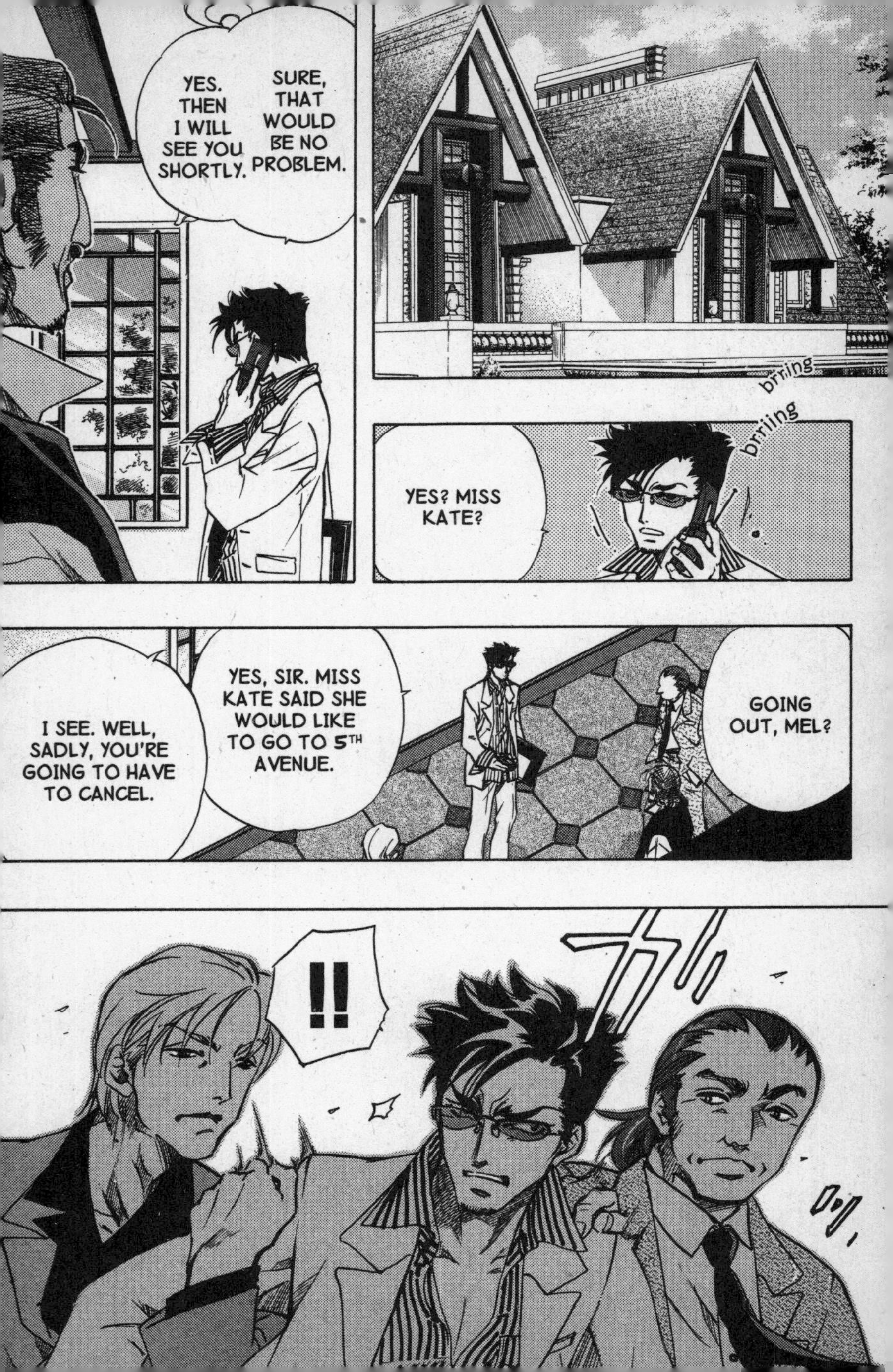
brring
brriing
YES? MISS KATE?
SURE, THAT WOULD BE NO PROBLEM.
YES. THEN I WILL SEE YOU SHORTLY.
GOING OUT, MEL?
YES, SIR. MISS KATE SAID SHE WOULD LIKE TO GO TO 5TH AVENUE.
I SEE. WELL, SADLY, YOU'RE GOING TO HAVE TO CANCEL.
!!

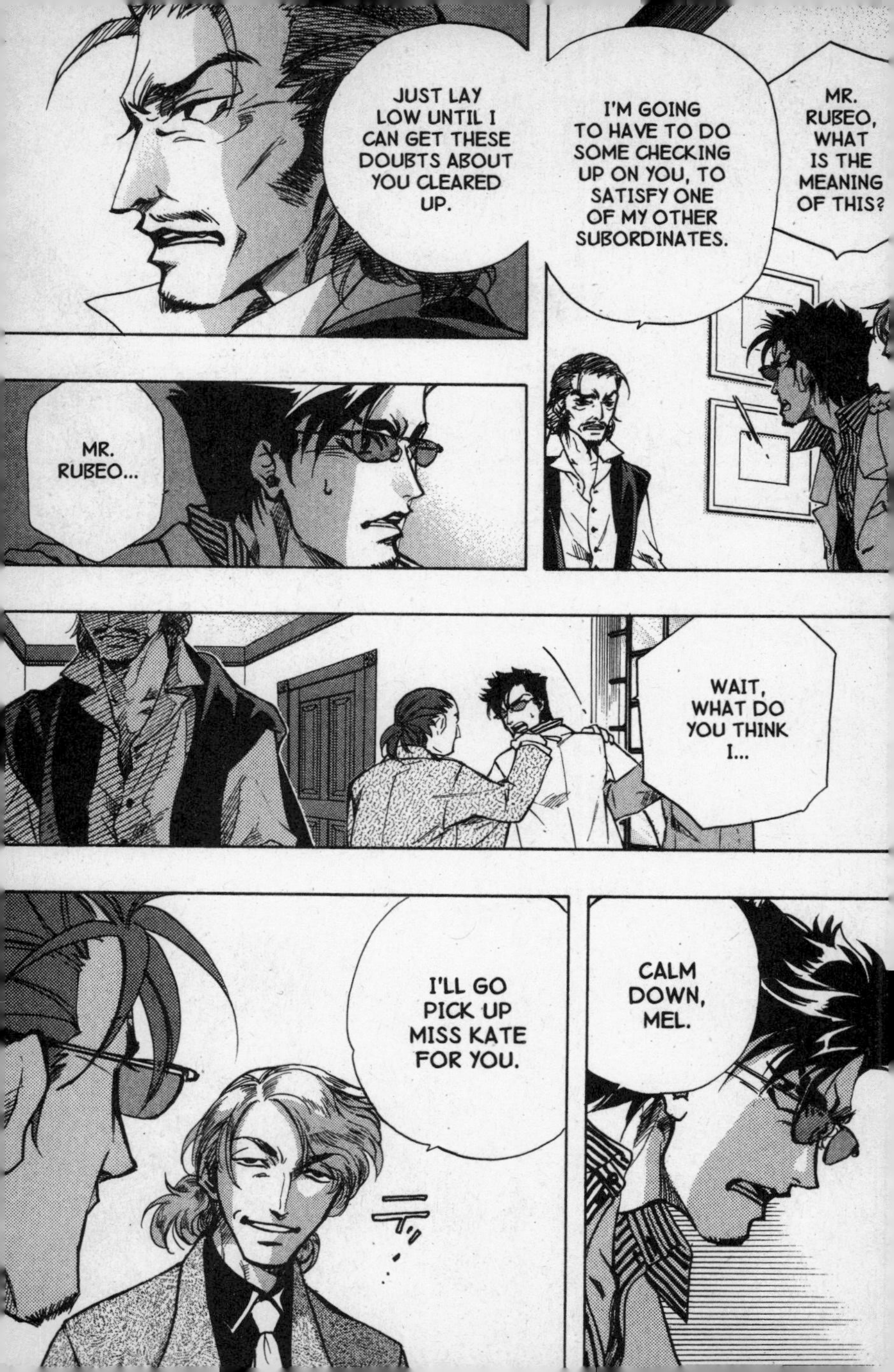
MR. RUBEO, WHAT IS THE MEANING OF THIS?
I'M GOING TO HAVE TO DO SOME CHECKING UP ON YOU, TO SATISFY ONE OF MY OTHER SUBORDINATES.
JUST LAY LOW UNTIL I CAN GET THESE DOUBTS ABOUT YOU CLEARED UP.
MR. RUBEO...
WAIT, WHAT DO YOU THINK I...
CALM DOWN, MEL.
I'LL GO PICK UP MISS KATE FOR YOU.

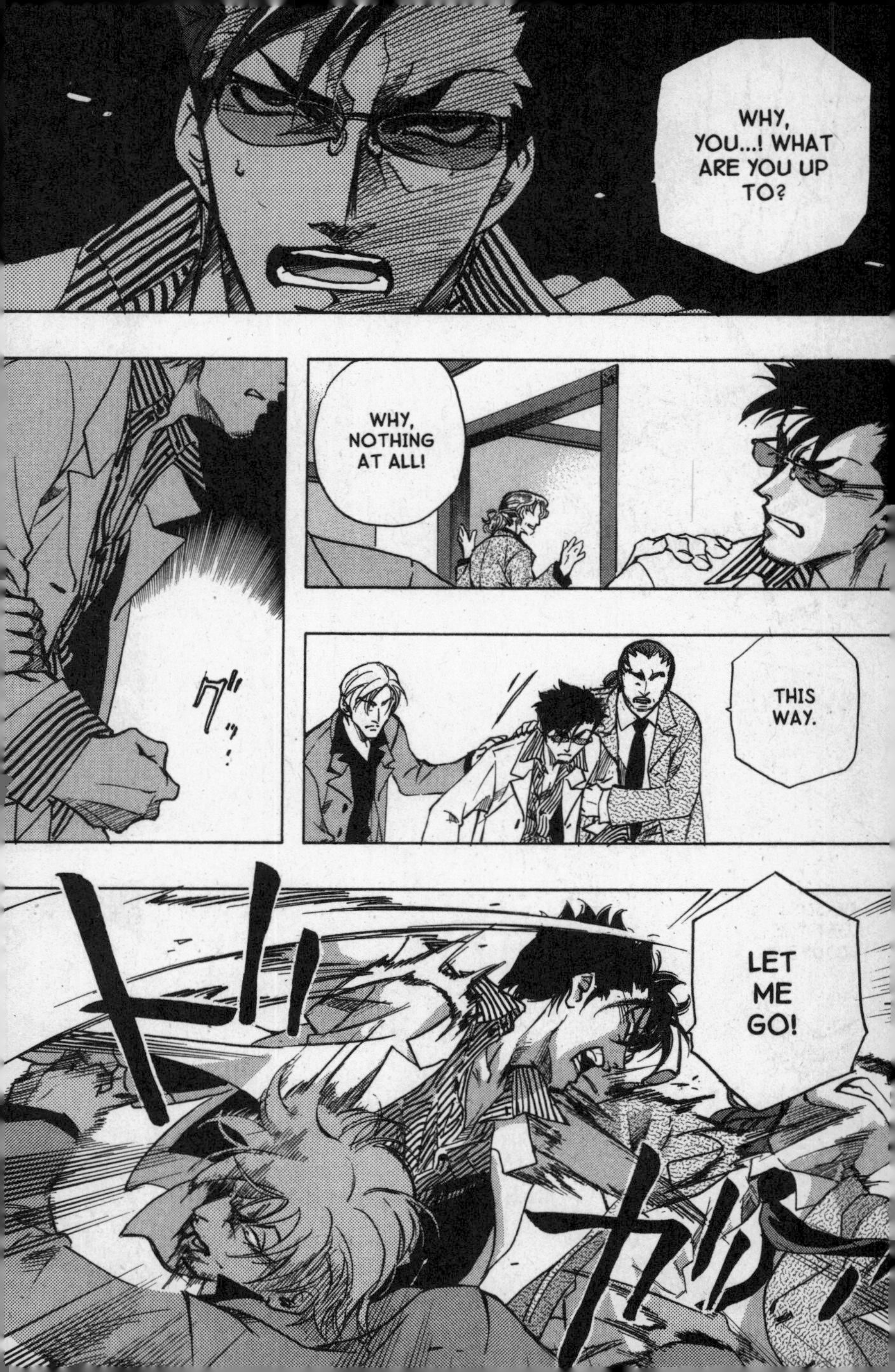
WHY, YOU...! WHAT ARE YOU UP TO?
WHY, NOTHING AT ALL!
THIS WAY.
グッ
LET ME GO!

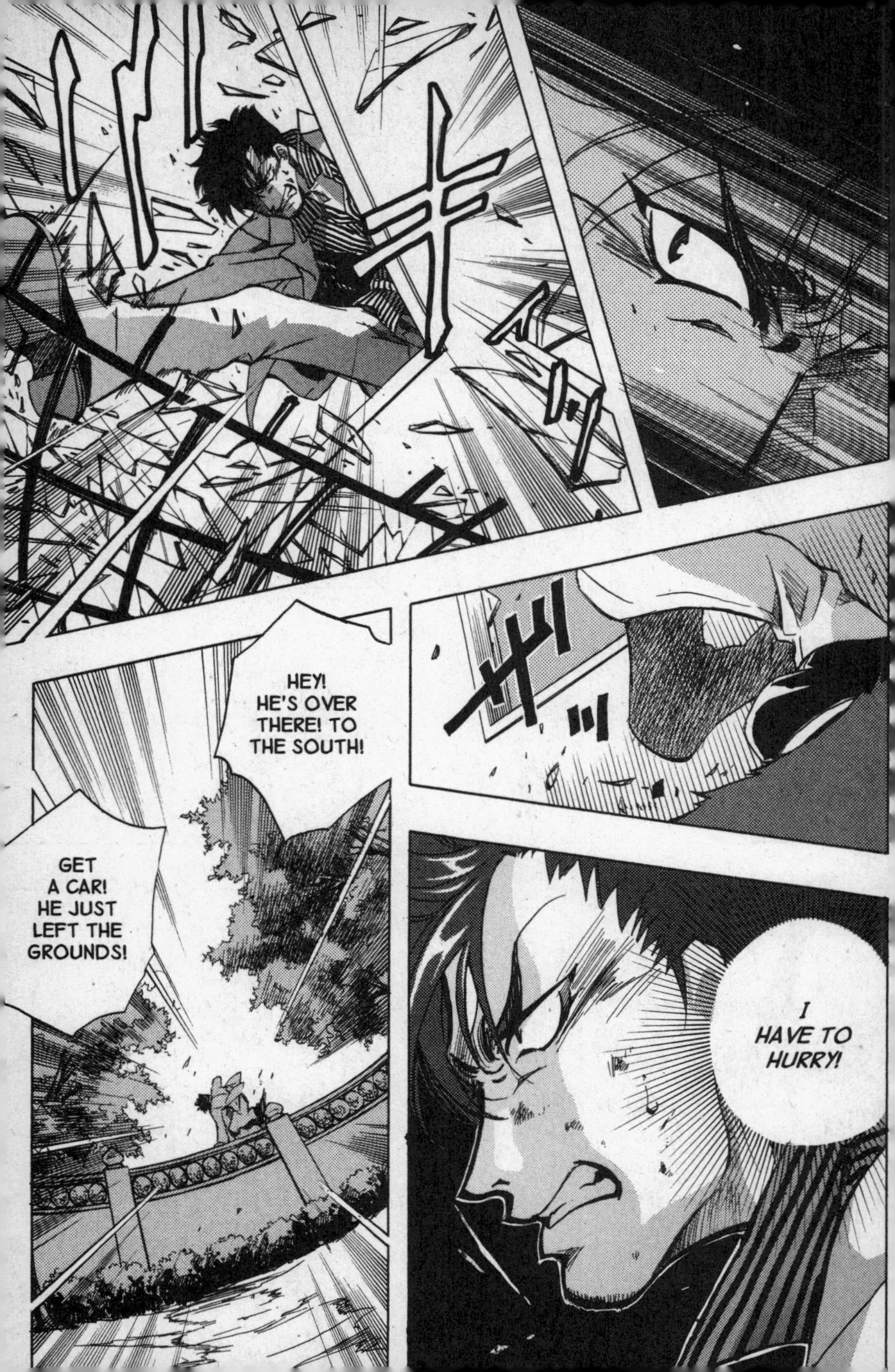
I HAVE TO HURRY!
HEY! HE'S OVER THERE! TO THE SOUTH!
GET A CAR! HE JUST LEFT THE GROUNDS!

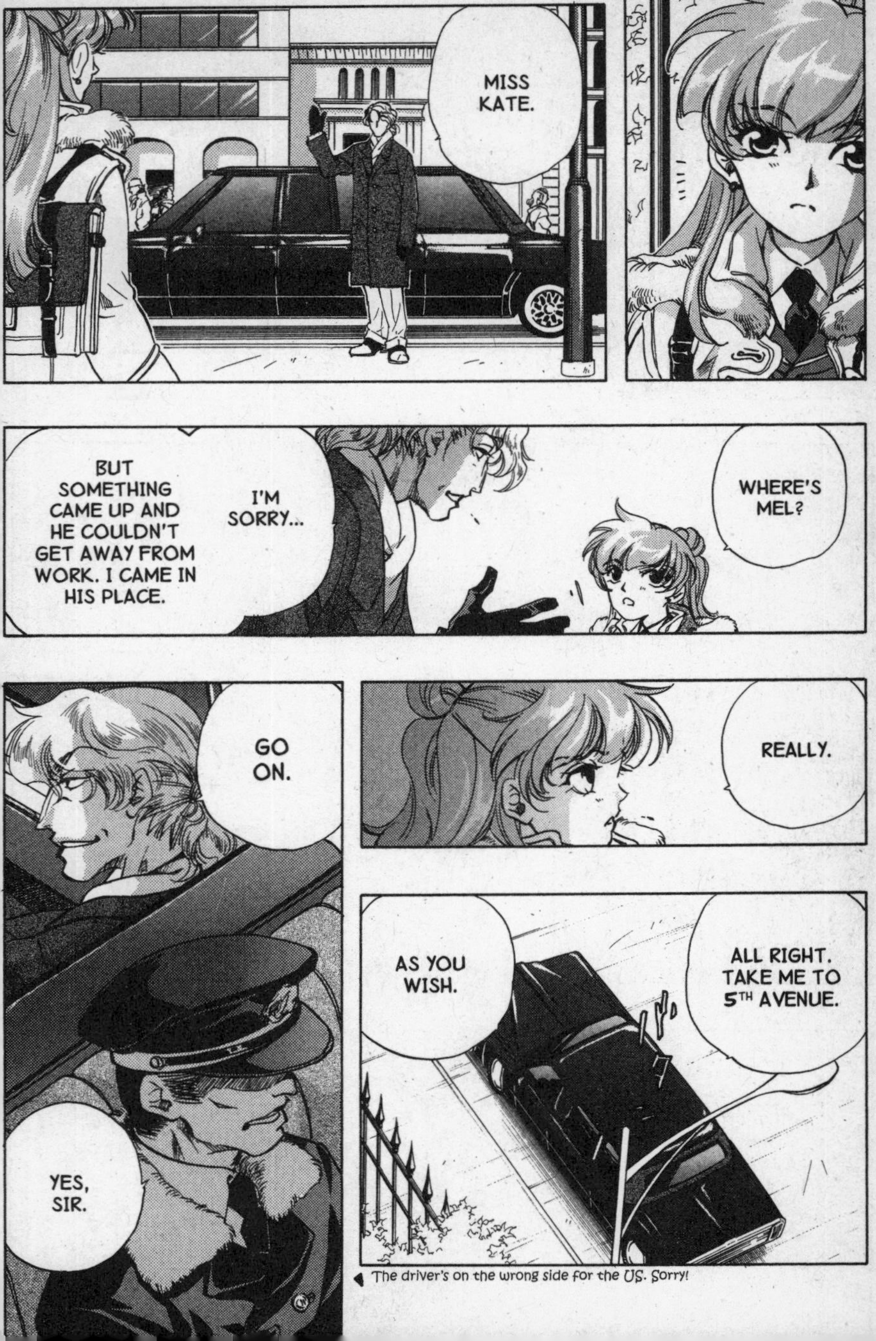
MISS KATE.
WHERE'S MEL?
I'M SORRY...
BUT SOMETHING CAME UP AND HE COULDN'T GET AWAY FROM WORK. I CAME IN HIS PLACE.
REALLY.
ALL RIGHT. TAKE ME TO 5TH AVENUE.
AS YOU WISH.
GO ON.
YES, SIR.
The driver's on the wrong side for the US. Sorry!

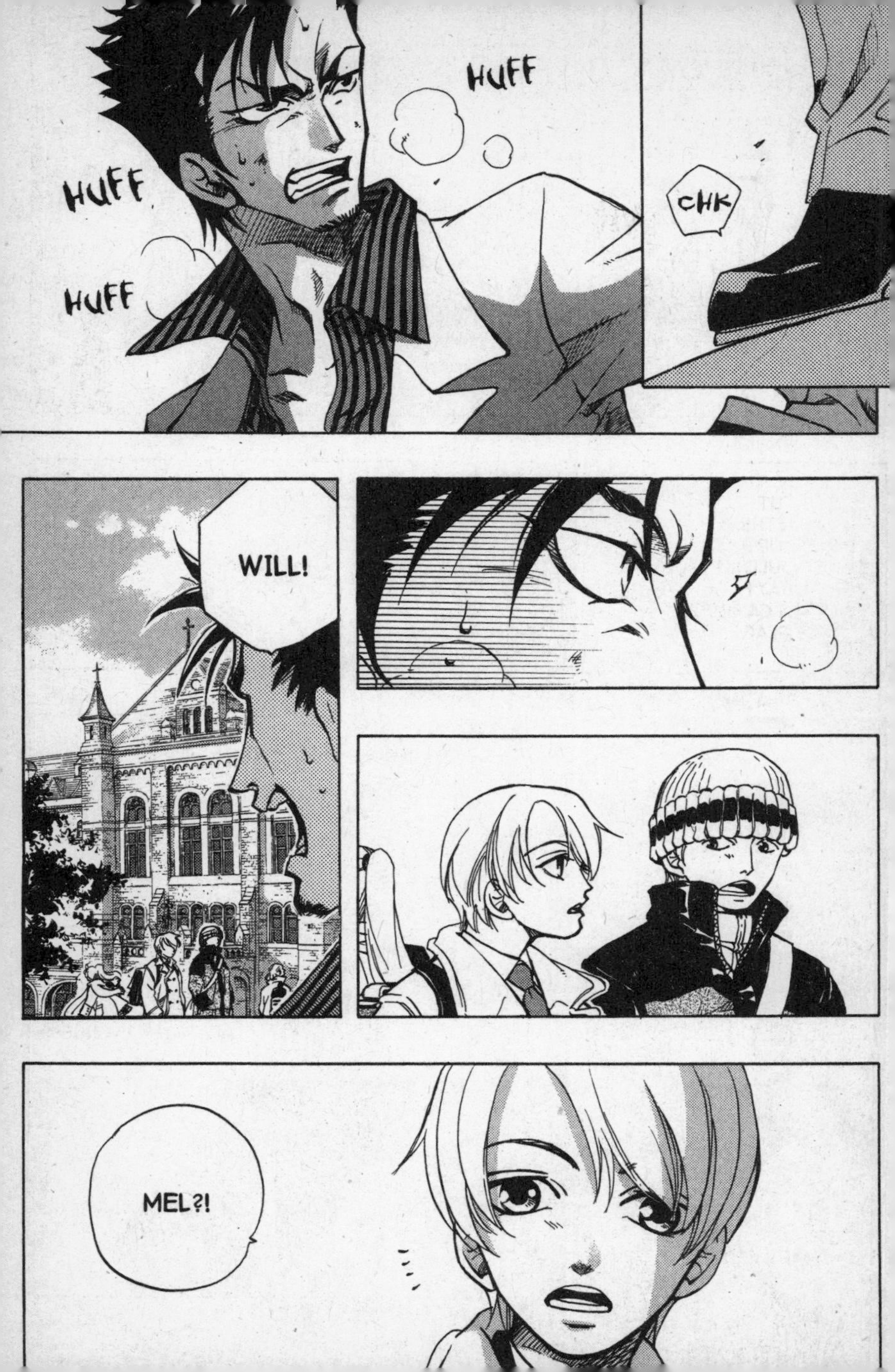
CHK
HUFF
HUFF
HUFF
WILL!
MEL?!

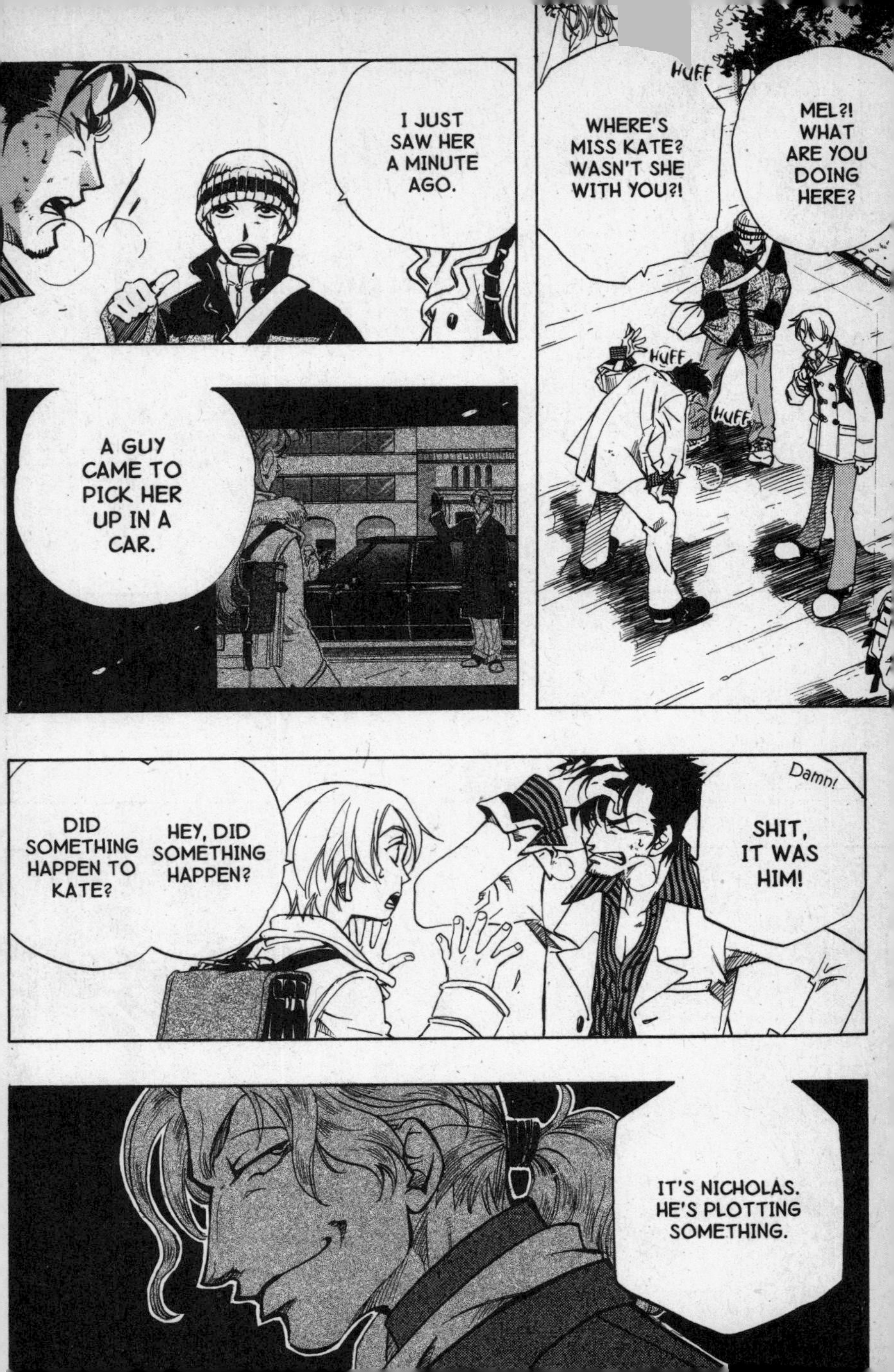
MEL?! WHAT ARE YOU DOING HERE?
HUFF
WHERE'S MISS KATE? WASN'T SHE WITH YOU?!
HUFF
HUFF
I JUST SAW HER A MINUTE AGO.
A GUY CAME TO PICK HER UP IN A CAR.
Damn!
SHIT, IT WAS HIM!
HEY, DID SOMETHING HAPPEN?
DID SOMETHING HAPPEN TO KATE?
IT'S NICHOLAS. HE'S PLOTTING SOMETHING.

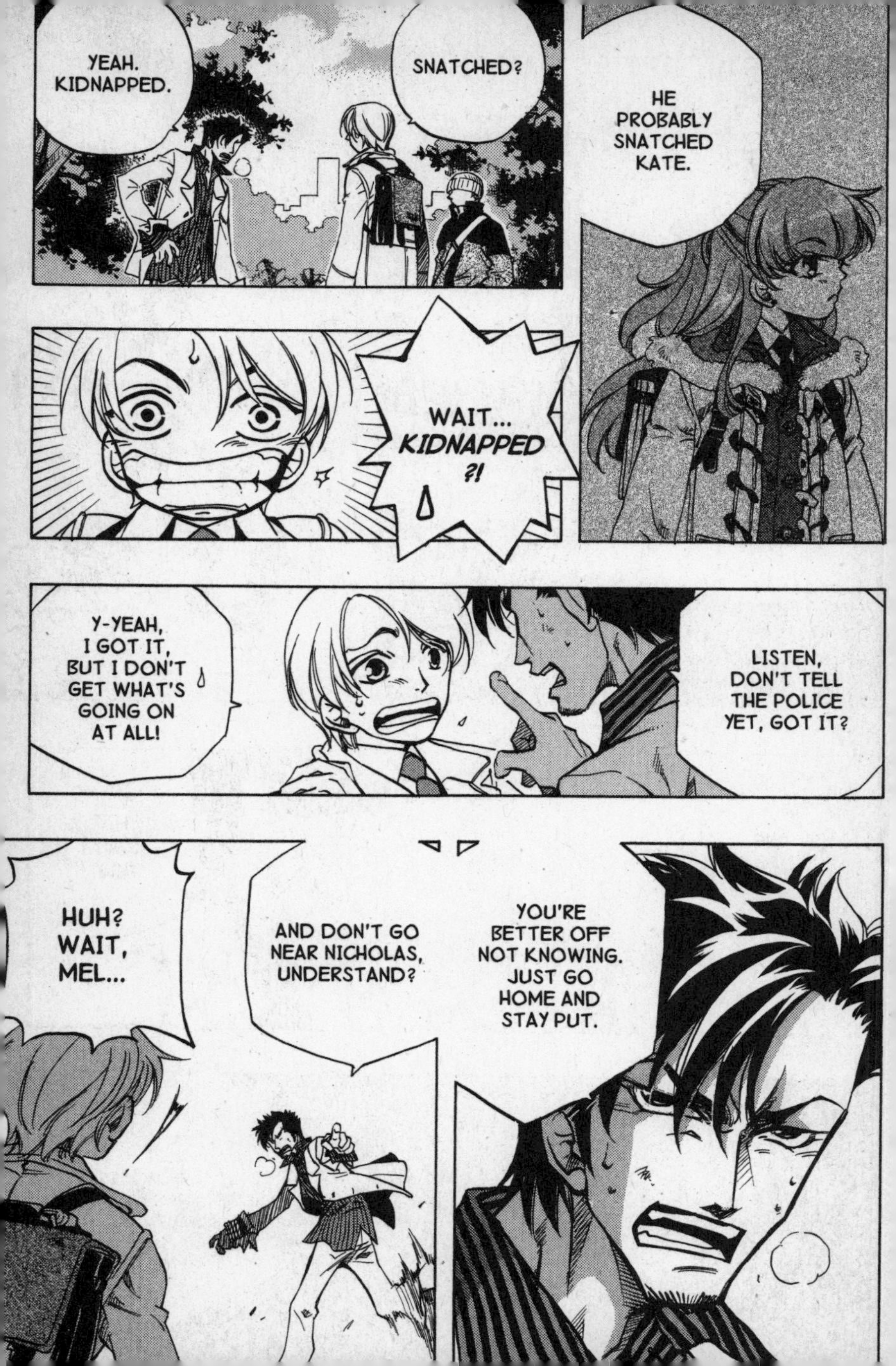
HE PROBABLY SNATCHED KATE.
SNATCHED?
YEAH. KIDNAPPED.
WAIT... KIDNAPPED?!
LISTEN, DON'T TELL THE POLICE YET, GOT IT?
Y-YEAH, I GOT IT, BUT I DON'T GET WHAT'S GOING ON AT ALL!
YOU'RE BETTER OFF NOT KNOWING. JUST GO HOME AND STAY PUT.
AND DON'T GO NEAR NICHOLAS, UNDERSTAND?
HUH? WAIT, MEL...

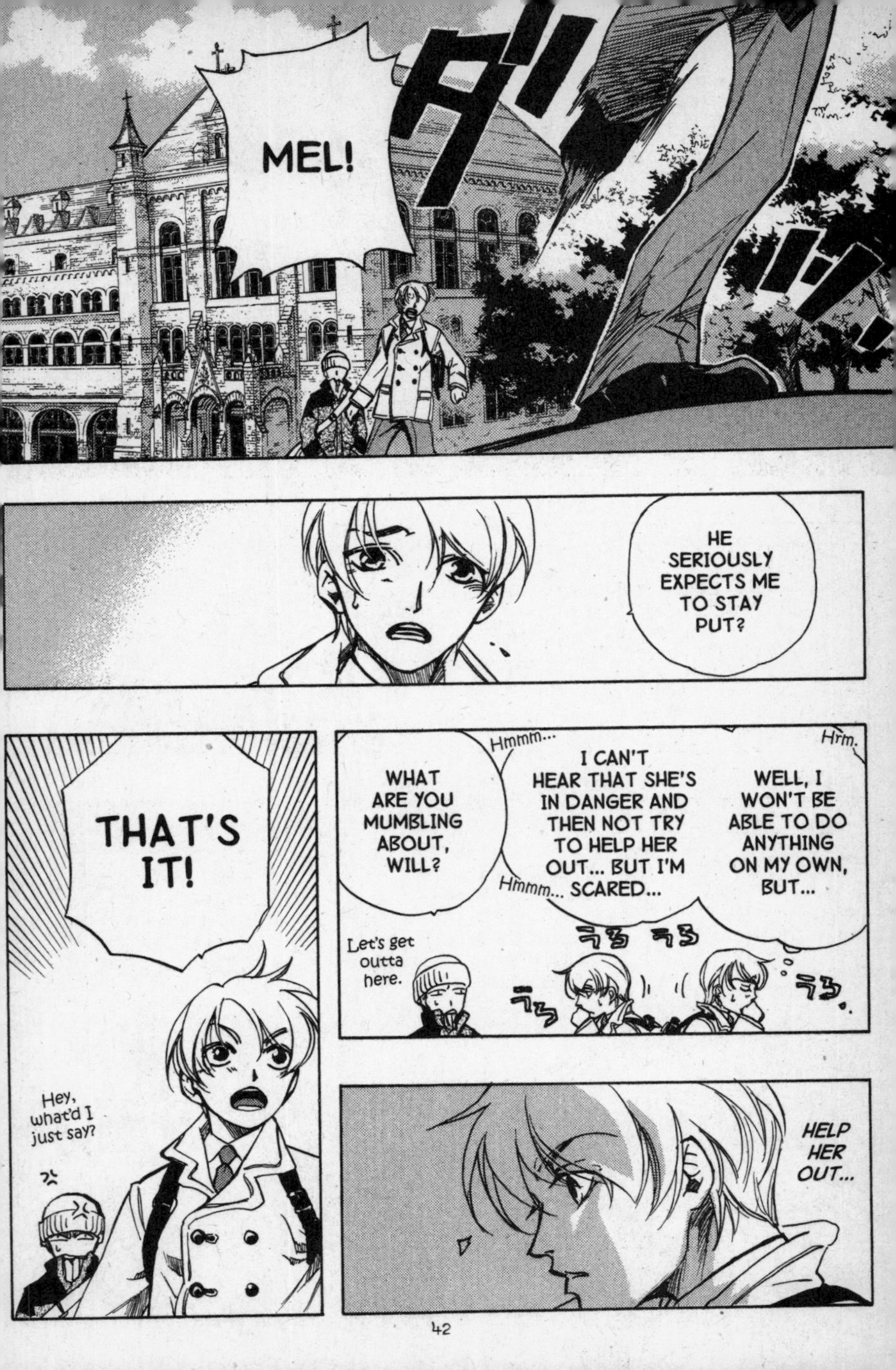
MEL!
HE SERIOUSLY EXPECTS ME TO STAY PUT?
Hrm.
WELL, I WON'T BE ABLE TO DO ANYTHING ON MY OWN, BUT...
I CAN'T HEAR THAT SHE'S IN DANGER AND THEN NOT TRY TO HELP HER OUT... BUT I'M SCARED...
Hmmm...
Hmmm...
WHAT ARE YOU MUMBLING ABOUT, WILL?
Let's get outta here.
HELP HER OUT...
THAT'S IT!
Hey, what'd I just say?

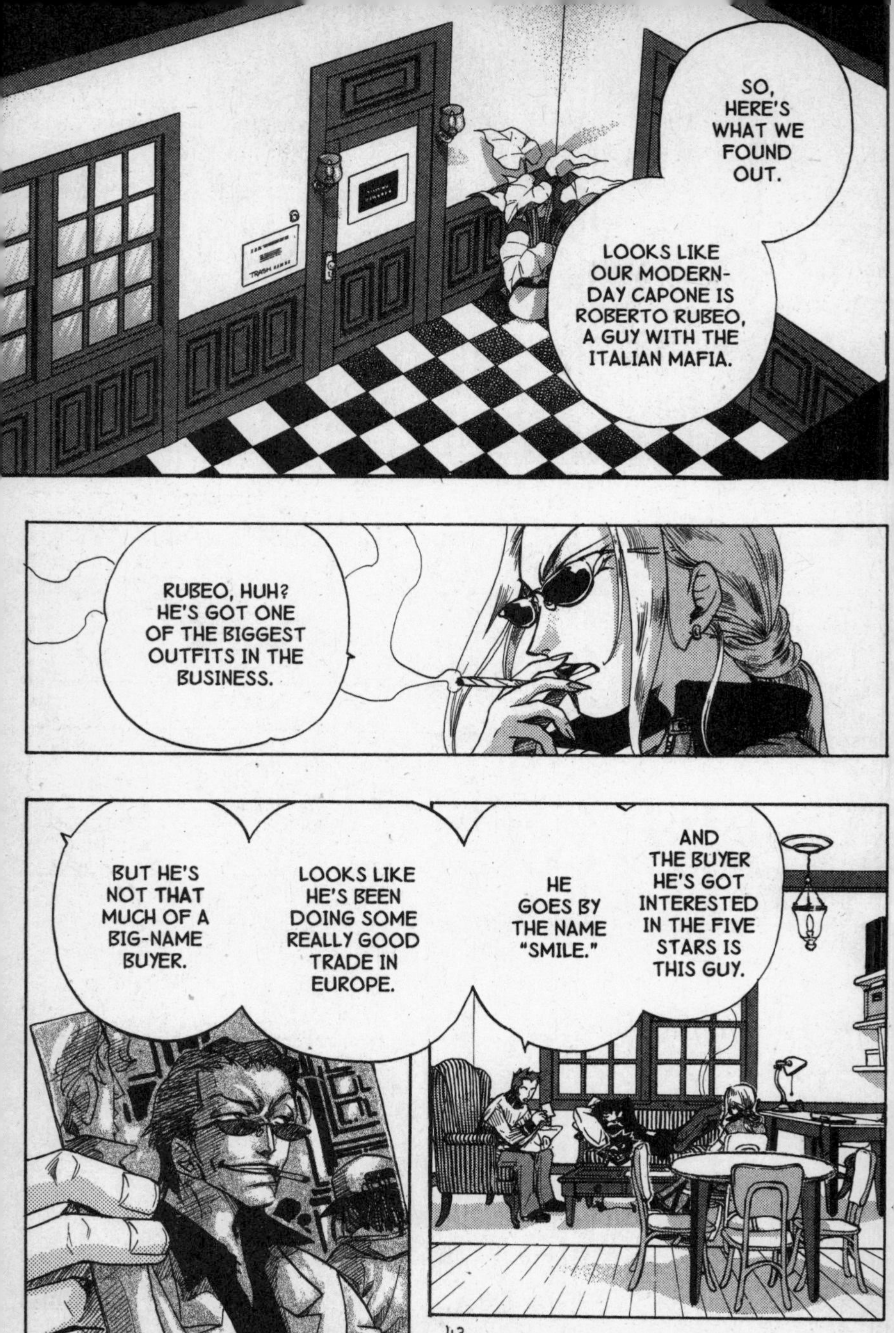
SO, HERE'S WHAT WE FOUND OUT.
LOOKS LIKE OUR MODERN-DAY CAPONE IS ROBERTO RUBEO, A GUY WITH THE ITALIAN MAFIA.
RUBEO, HUH? HE'S GOT ONE OF THE BIGGEST OUTFITS IN THE BUSINESS.
AND THE BUYER HE'S GOT INTERESTED IN THE FIVE STARS IS THIS GUY.
HE GOES BY THE NAME "SMILE."
LOOKS LIKE HE'S BEEN DOING SOME REALLY GOOD TRADE IN EUROPE.
BUT HE'S NOT THAT MUCH OF A BIG-NAME BUYER.

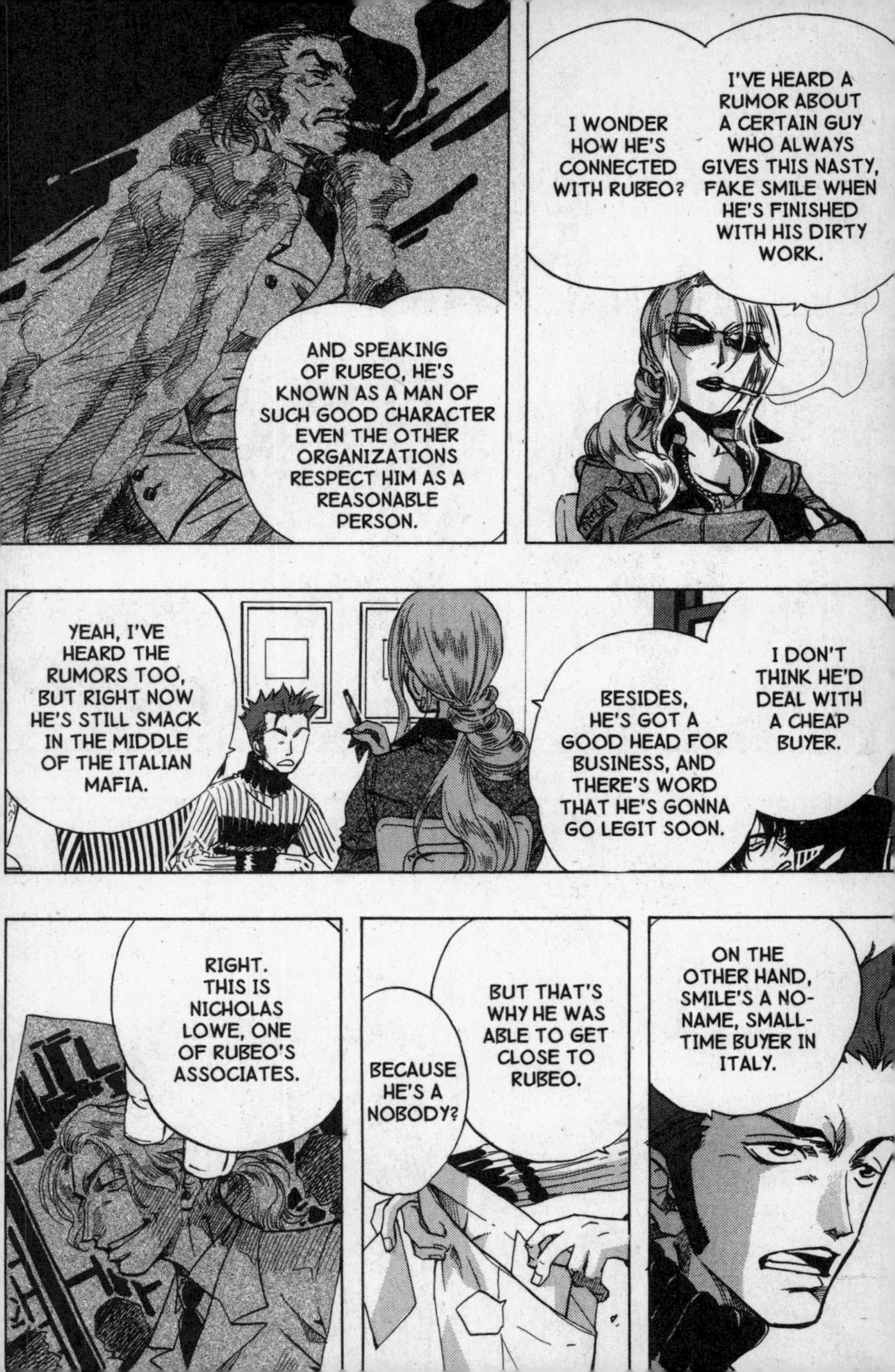
I'VE HEARD A RUMOR ABOUT A CERTAIN GUY WHO ALWAYS GIVES THIS NASTY, FAKE SMILE WHEN HE'S FINISHED WITH HIS DIRTY WORK.
I WONDER HOW HE'S CONNECTED WITH RUBEO?
AND SPEAKING OF RUBEO, HE'S KNOWN AS A MAN OF SUCH GOOD CHARACTER EVEN THE OTHER ORGANIZATIONS RESPECT HIM AS A REASONABLE PERSON.
I DON'T THINK HE'D DEAL WITH A CHEAP BUYER.
BESIDES, HE'S GOT A GOOD HEAD FOR BUSINESS, AND THERE'S WORD THAT HE'S GONNA GO LEGIT SOON.
YEAH, I'VE HEARD THE RUMORS TOO, BUT RIGHT NOW HE'S STILL SMACK IN THE MIDDLE OF THE ITALIAN MAFIA.
ON THE OTHER HAND, SMILE'S A NO-NAME, SMALL-TIME BUYER IN ITALY.
BUT THAT'S WHY HE WAS ABLE TO GET CLOSE TO RUBEO.
BECAUSE HE'S A NOBODY?
RIGHT. THIS IS NICHOLAS LOWE, ONE OF RUBEO'S ASSOCIATES.

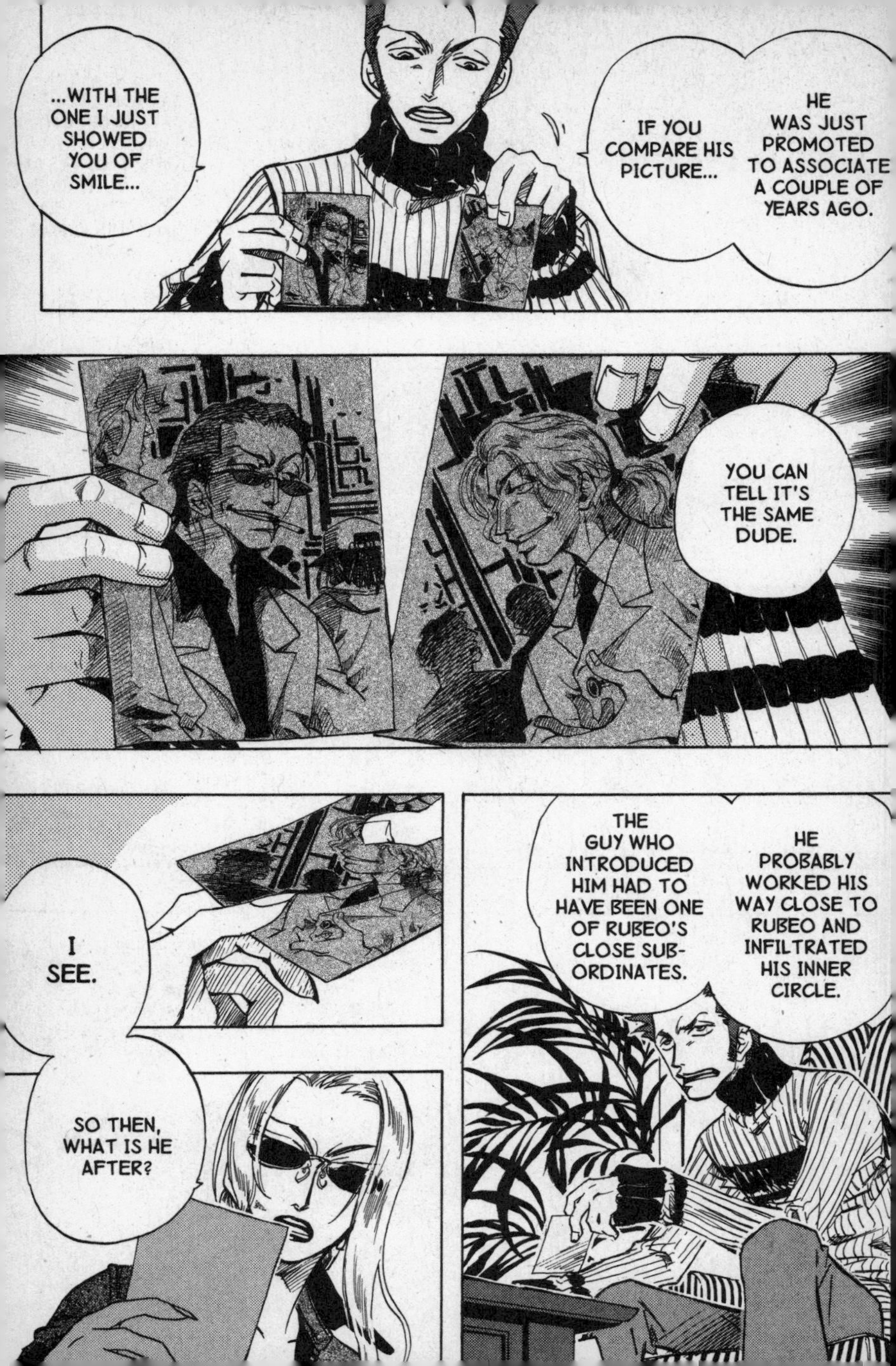
HE WAS JUST PROMOTED TO ASSOCIATE A COUPLE OF YEARS AGO.
IF YOU COMPARE HIS PICTURE...
...WITH THE ONE I JUST SHOWED YOU OF SMILE...
YOU CAN TELL IT'S THE SAME DUDE.
HE PROBABLY WORKED HIS WAY CLOSE TO RUBEO AND INFILTRATED HIS INNER CIRCLE.
THE GUY WHO INTRODUCED HIM HAD TO HAVE BEEN ONE OF RUBEO'S CLOSE SUB-ORDINATES.
I SEE.
SO THEN, WHAT IS HE AFTER?

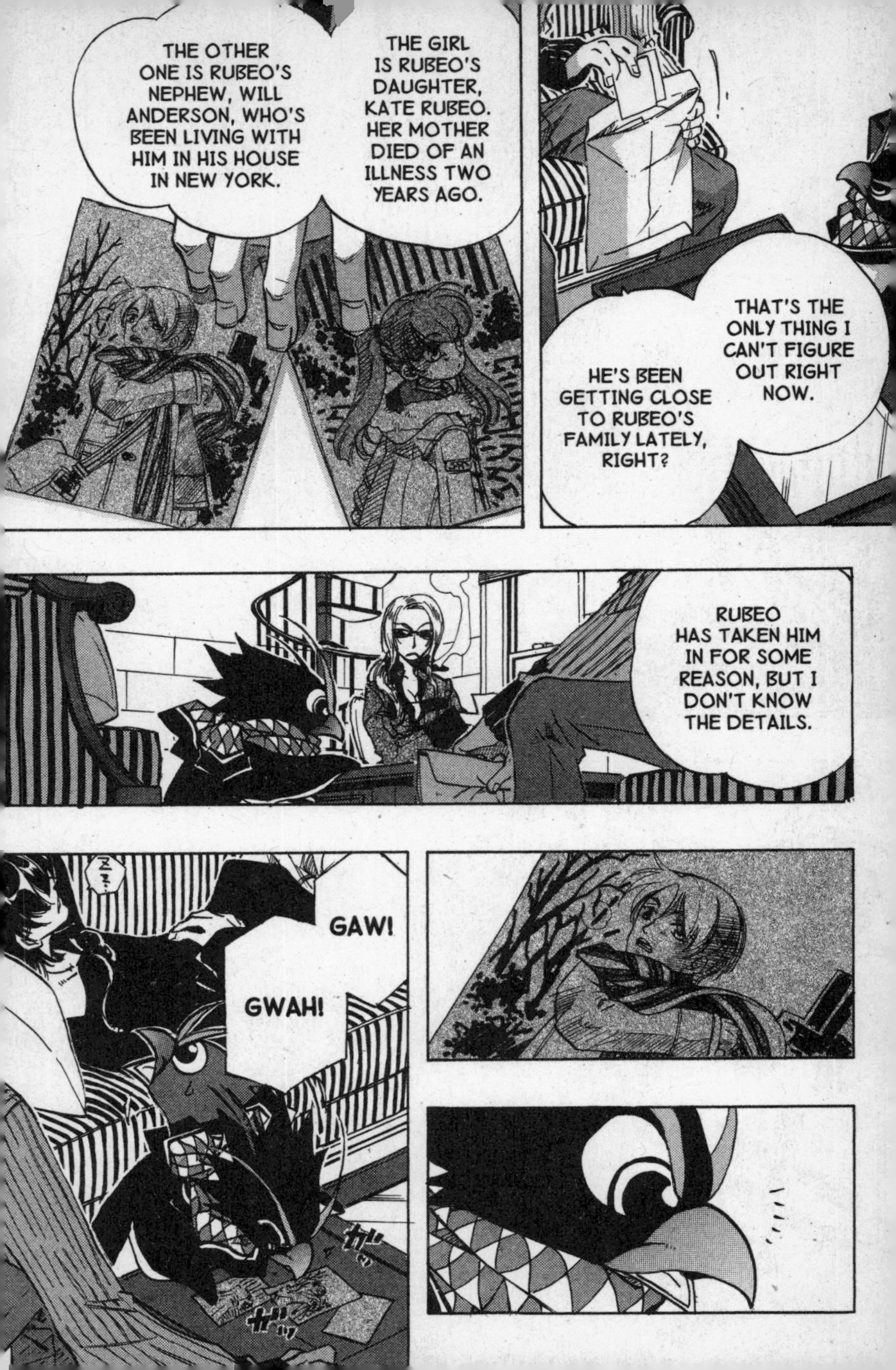
THAT'S THE ONLY THING I CAN'T FIGURE OUT RIGHT NOW.
HE'S BEEN GETTING CLOSE TO RUBEO'S FAMILY LATELY, RIGHT?
THE GIRL IS RUBEO'S DAUGHTER, KATE RUBEO. HER MOTHER DIED OF AN ILLNESS TWO YEARS AGO.
THE OTHER ONE IS RUBEO'S NEPHEW, WILL ANDERSON, WHO'S BEEN LIVING WITH HIM IN HIS HOUSE IN NEW YORK.
RUBEO HAS TAKEN HIM IN FOR SOME REASON, BUT I DON'T KNOW THE DETAILS.
GAW!
GWAH!

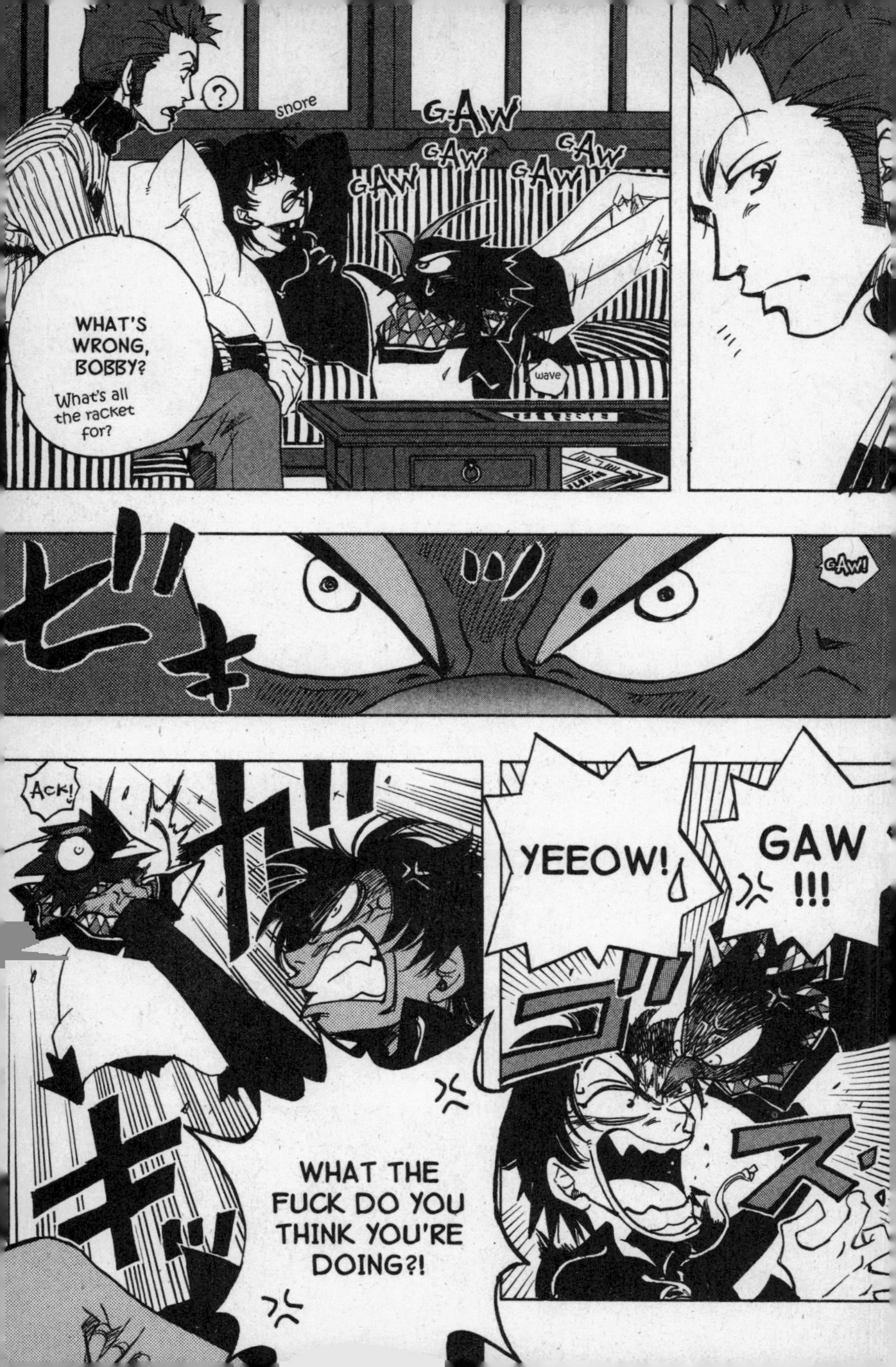

GAW
GAW
GAW
GAW
GAW
snore
?
WHAT'S WRONG, BOBBY?
What's all the racket for?
wave
GAW!
GAW !!!
YEEOW!
Ack!
WHAT THE FUCK DO YOU THINK YOU'RE DOING?!

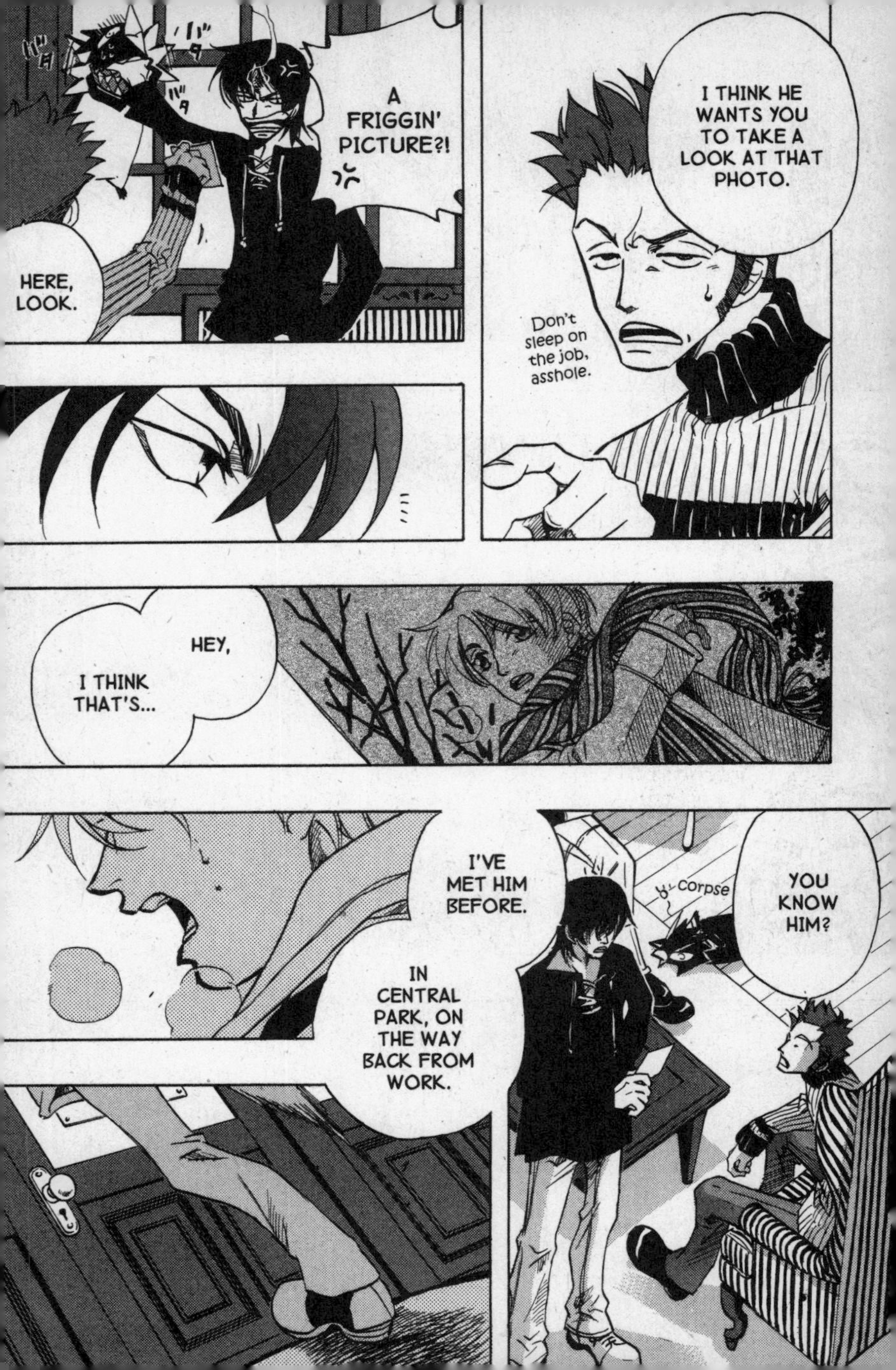

I THINK HE WANTS YOU TO TAKE A LOOK AT THAT PHOTO.
Don't sleep on the job, asshole.
A FRIGGIN' PICTURE?!
HERE, LOOK.
HEY,
I THINK THAT'S...
YOU KNOW HIM?
Corpse
I'VE MET HIM BEFORE.
IN CENTRAL PARK, ON THE WAY BACK FROM WORK.

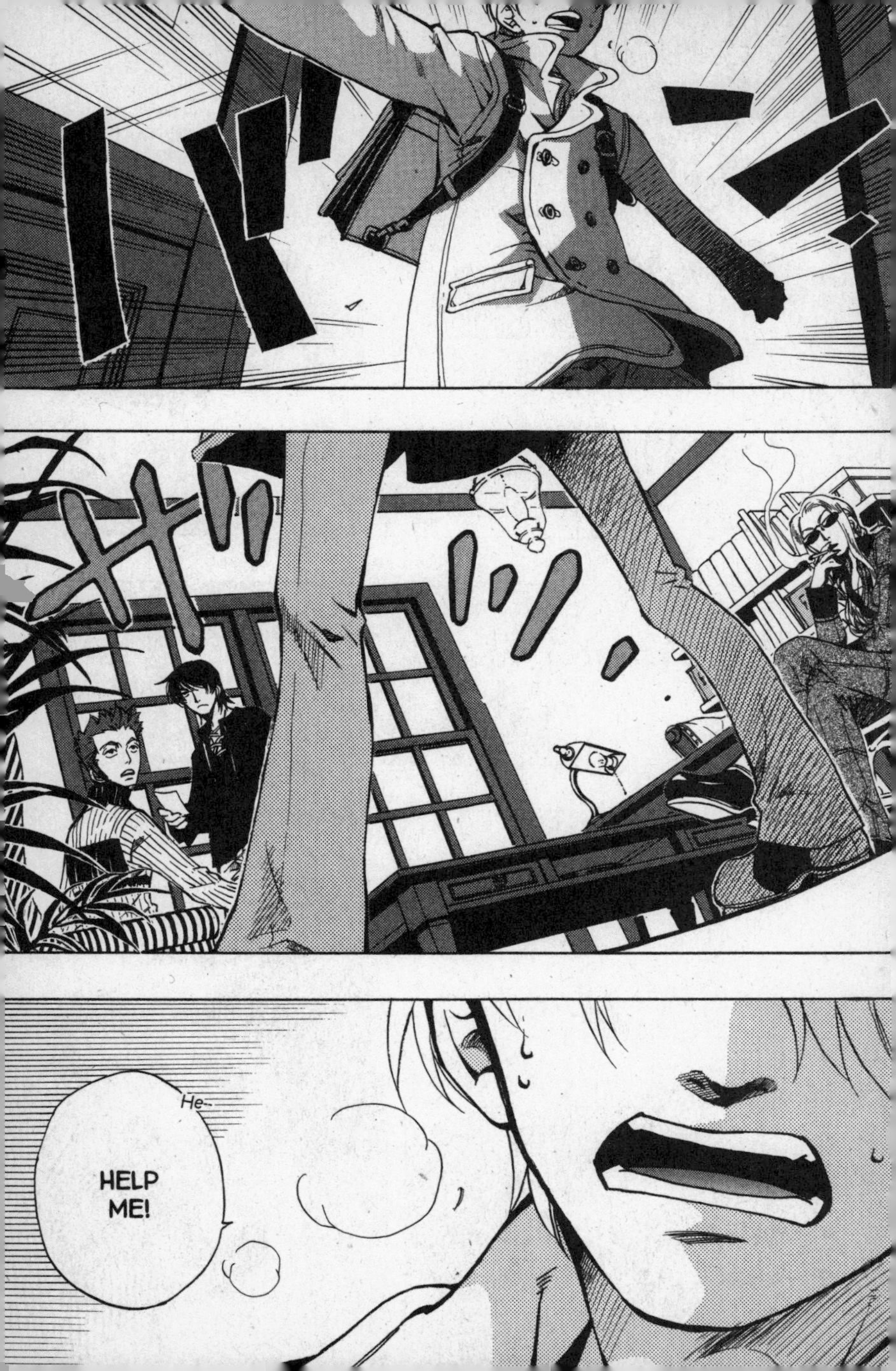
He--
HELP ME!

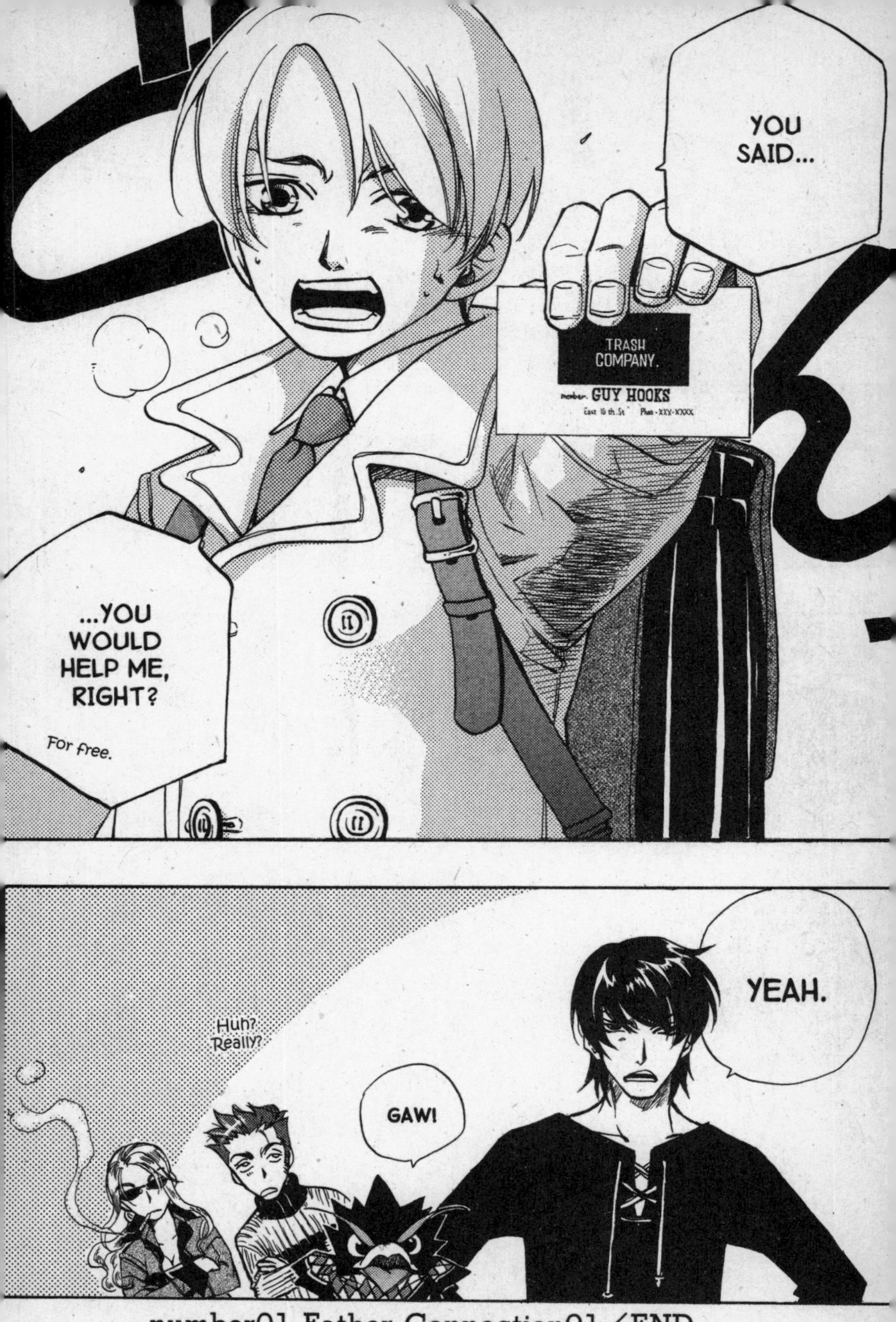
YOU SAID...
TRASH COMPANY.
GUY HOOKS
East 10th.St Phon-XXX-XXXX
...YOU WOULD HELP ME, RIGHT?
For free.
YEAH.
GAW!
Huh? Really?

number01 Father Connection01/END

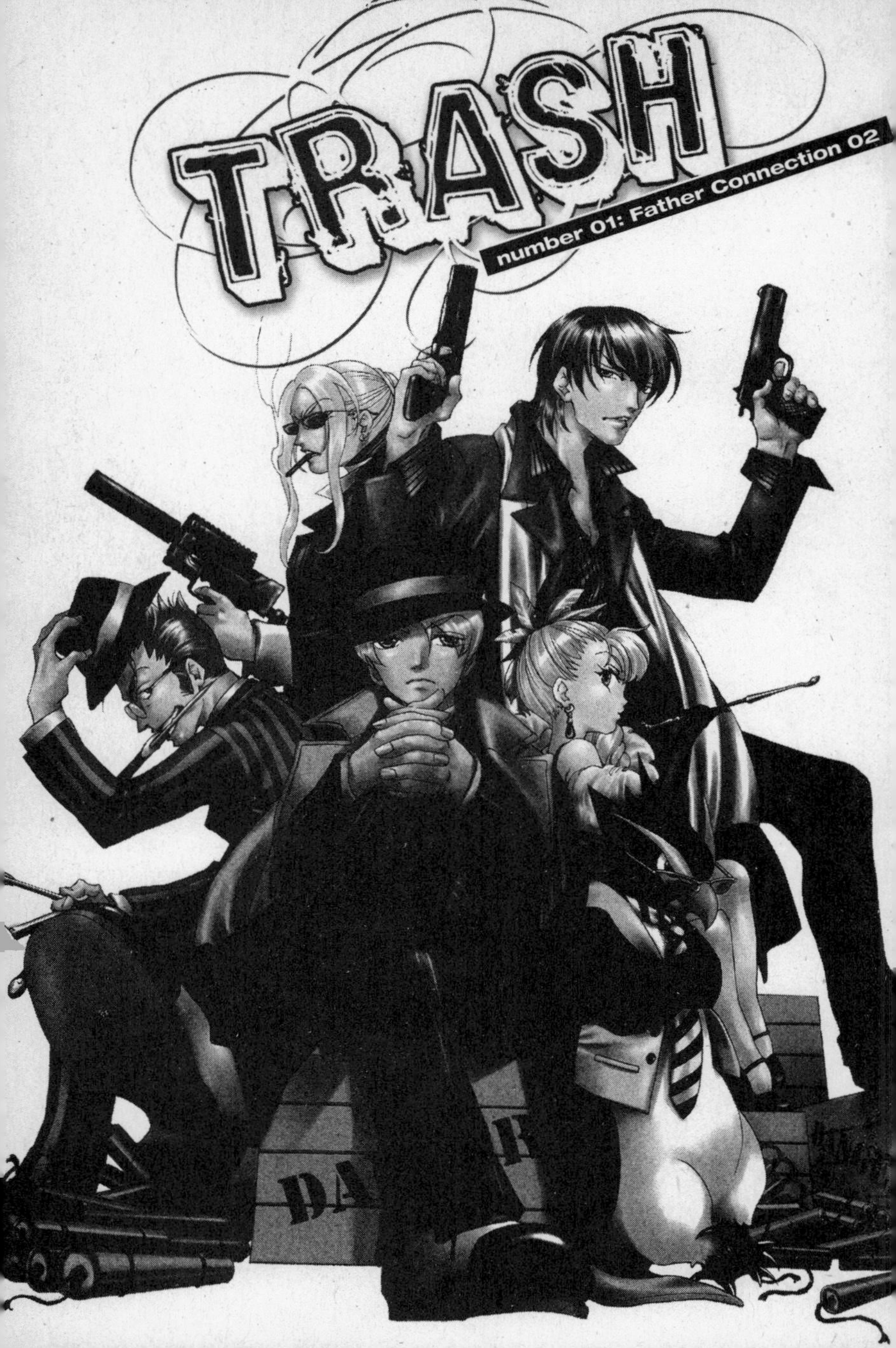
TRASH
number 01: Father Connection 02

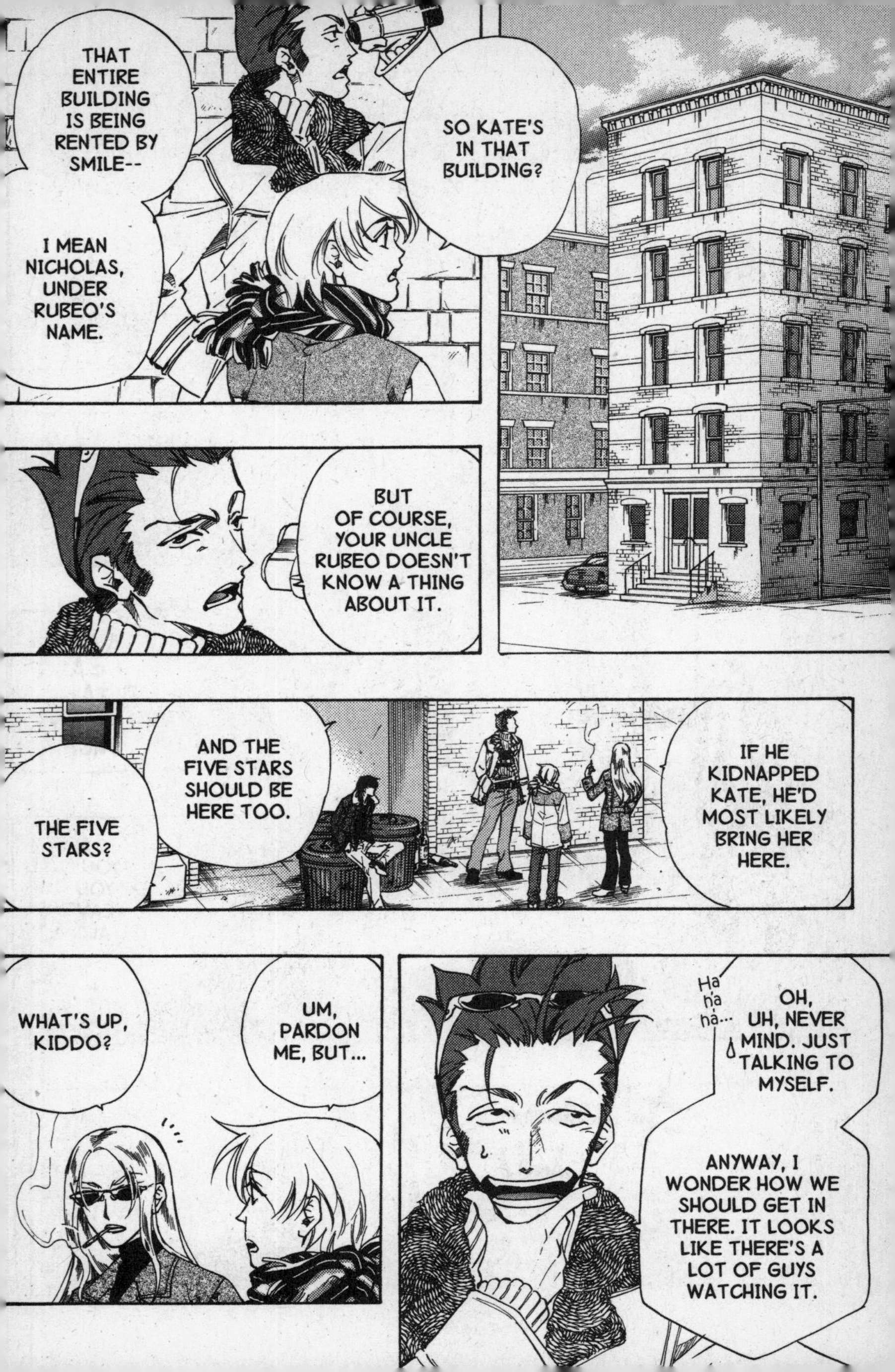
SO KATE'S IN THAT BUILDING?
THAT ENTIRE BUILDING IS BEING RENTED BY SMILE--
I MEAN NICHOLAS, UNDER RUBEO'S NAME.
BUT OF COURSE, YOUR UNCLE RUBEO DOESN'T KNOW A THING ABOUT IT.
IF HE KIDNAPPED KATE, HE'D MOST LIKELY BRING HER HERE.
AND THE FIVE STARS SHOULD BE HERE TOO.
THE FIVE STARS?
Ha ha ha...
OH, UH, NEVER MIND. JUST TALKING TO MYSELF.
ANYWAY, I WONDER HOW WE SHOULD GET IN THERE. IT LOOKS LIKE THERE'S A LOT OF GUYS WATCHING IT.
UM, PARDON ME, BUT...
WHAT'S UP, KIDDO?

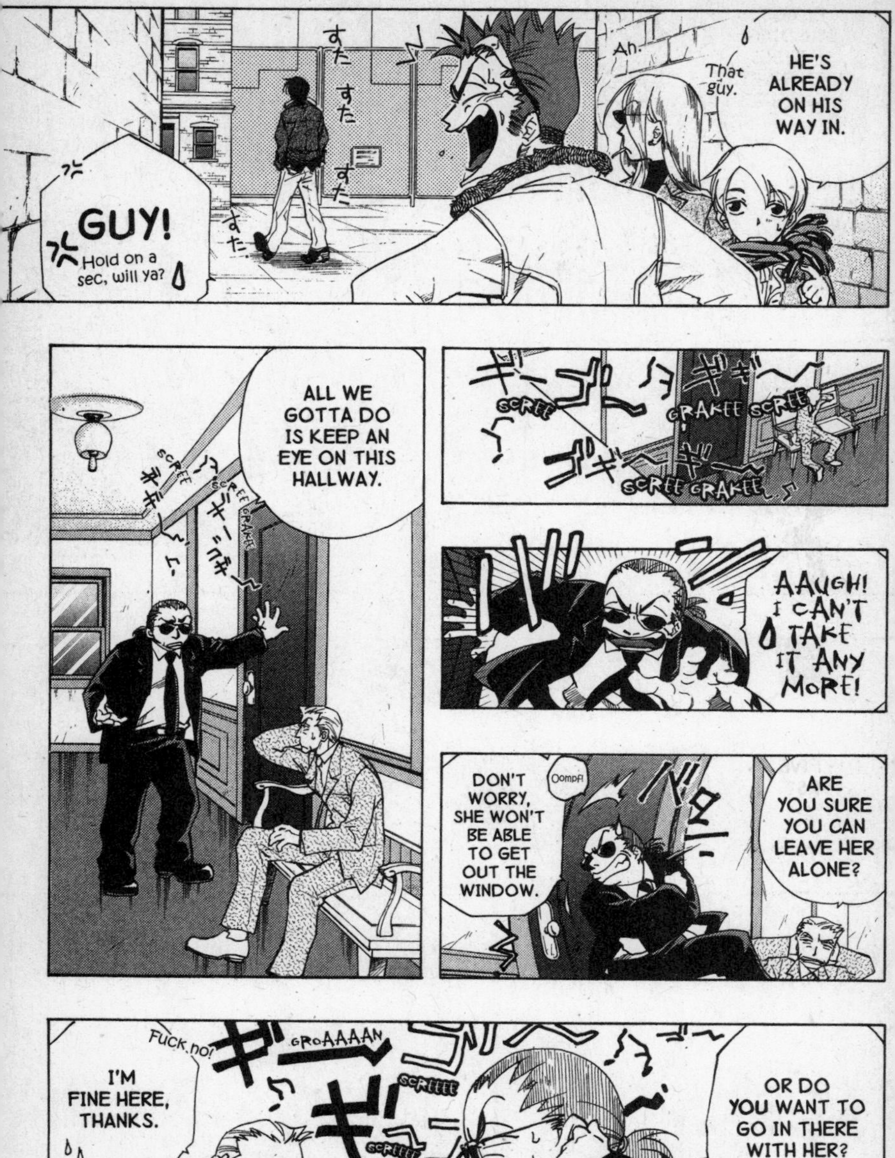
HE'S ALREADY ON HIS WAY IN.
That guy.
Ah.
すた すた すた すた
GUY!
Hold on a sec, will ya?
SCREE GRAKEE SCREE
SCREE GRAKEE
AAUGH! I CAN'T TAKE IT ANY MORE!
ARE YOU SURE YOU CAN LEAVE HER ALONE?
Oompf!
DON'T WORRY, SHE WON'T BE ABLE TO GET OUT THE WINDOW.
ALL WE GOTTA DO IS KEEP AN EYE ON THIS HALLWAY.
SCREE
SCREE
GRAKEE
OR DO YOU WANT TO GO IN THERE WITH HER?
I ain't going back!
SCREEEE
GROAAAAN
SCREEEE
GROAAAAN
I'M FINE HERE, THANKS.
Fuck, no!

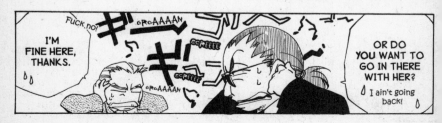

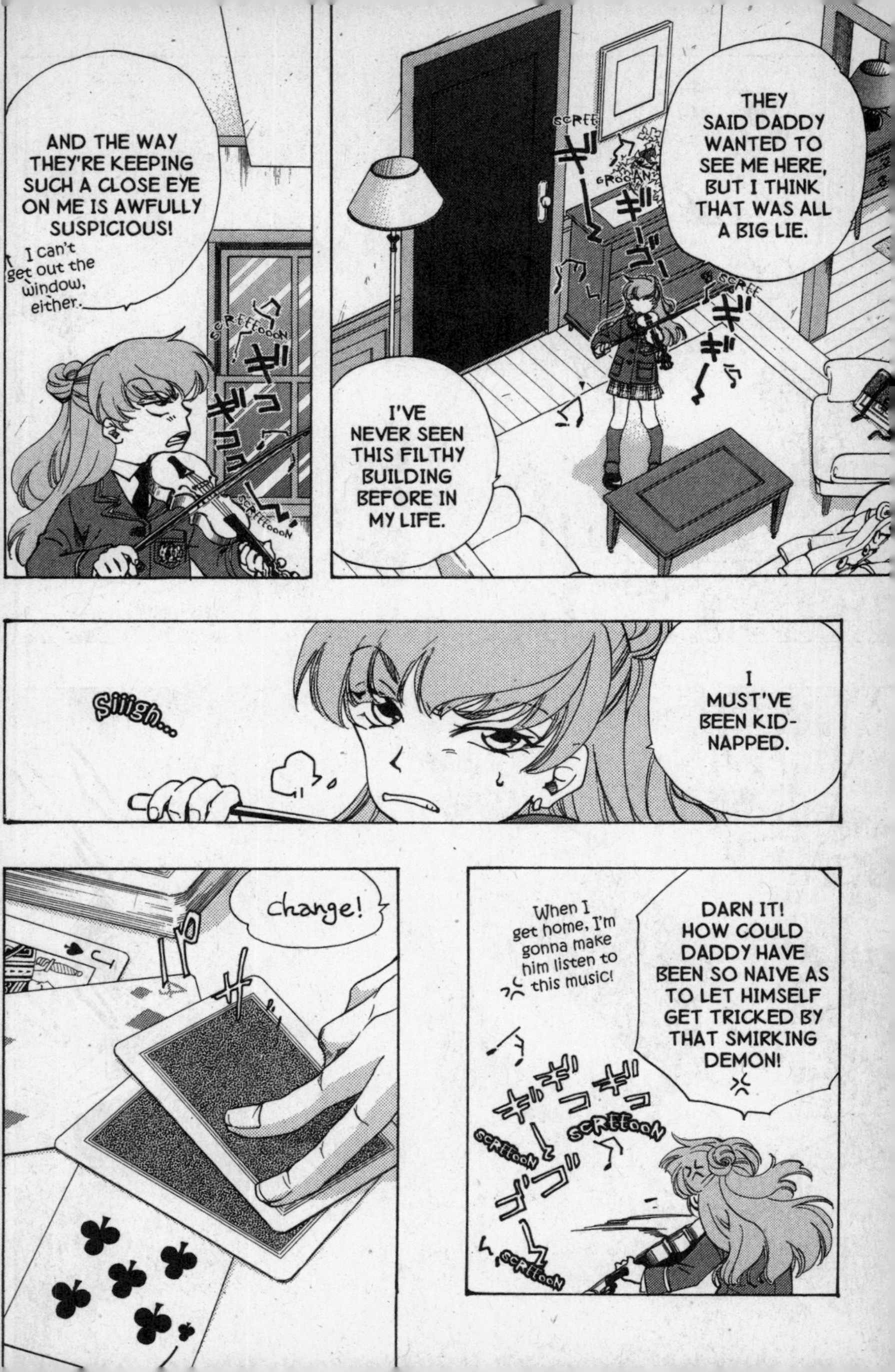
THEY SAID DADDY WANTED TO SEE ME HERE, BUT I THINK THAT WAS ALL A BIG LIE.
SCREE
SCREE
I'VE NEVER SEEN THIS FILTHY BUILDING BEFORE IN MY LIFE.
AND THE WAY THEY'RE KEEPING SUCH A CLOSE EYE ON ME IS AWFULLY SUSPICIOUS!
I can't get out the window, either.
I MUST'VE BEEN KID-NAPPED.
Siiigh...
DARN IT! HOW COULD DADDY HAVE BEEN SO NAIVE AS TO LET HIMSELF GET TRICKED BY THAT SMIRKING DEMON!
When I get home, I'm gonna make him listen to this music!
SCREEOON
SCREEOON
SCREEOON
Change!

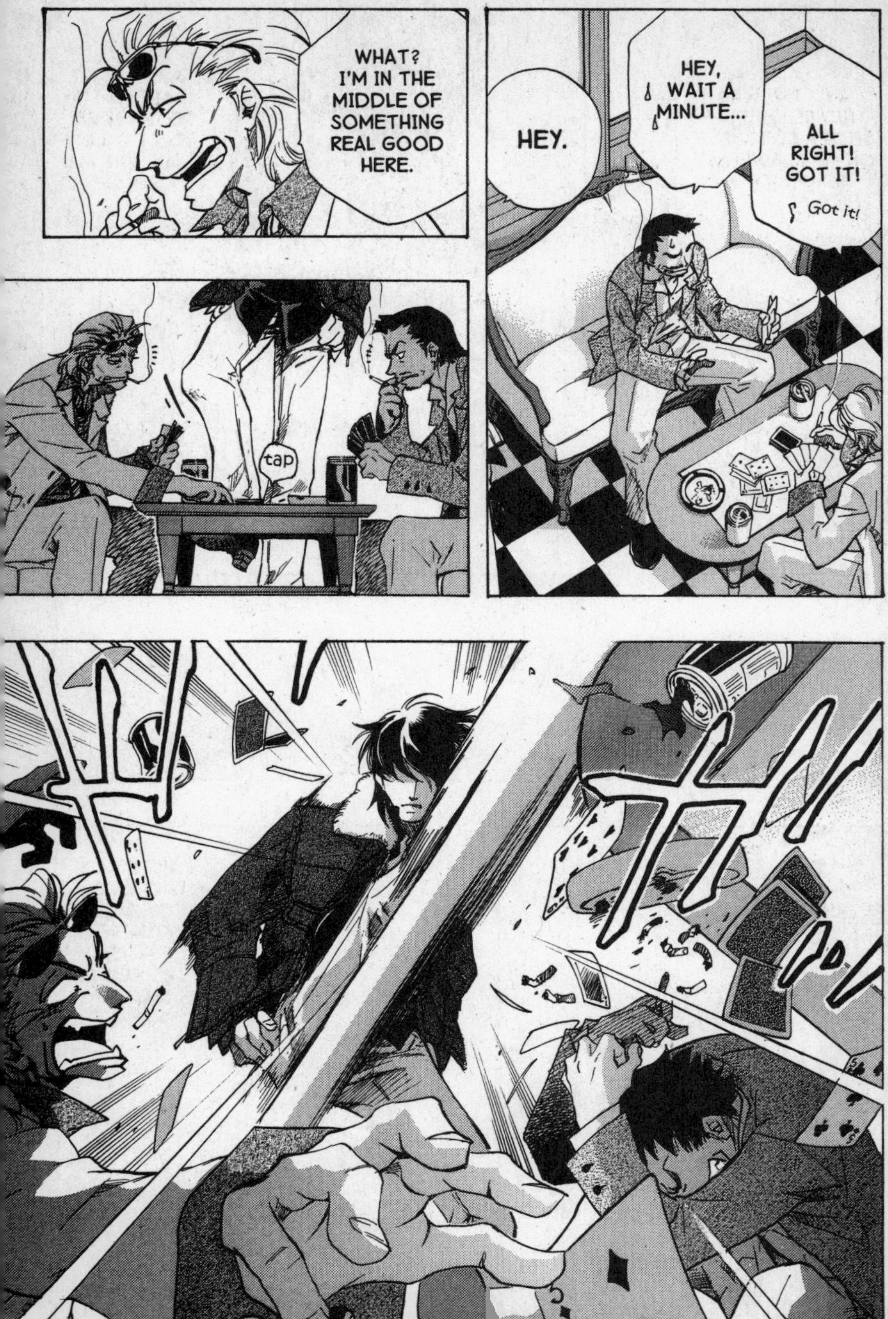
HEY, WAIT A MINUTE...
ALL RIGHT! GOT IT!
Got it!
HEY.
WHAT? I'M IN THE MIDDLE OF SOMETHING REAL GOOD HERE.
tap

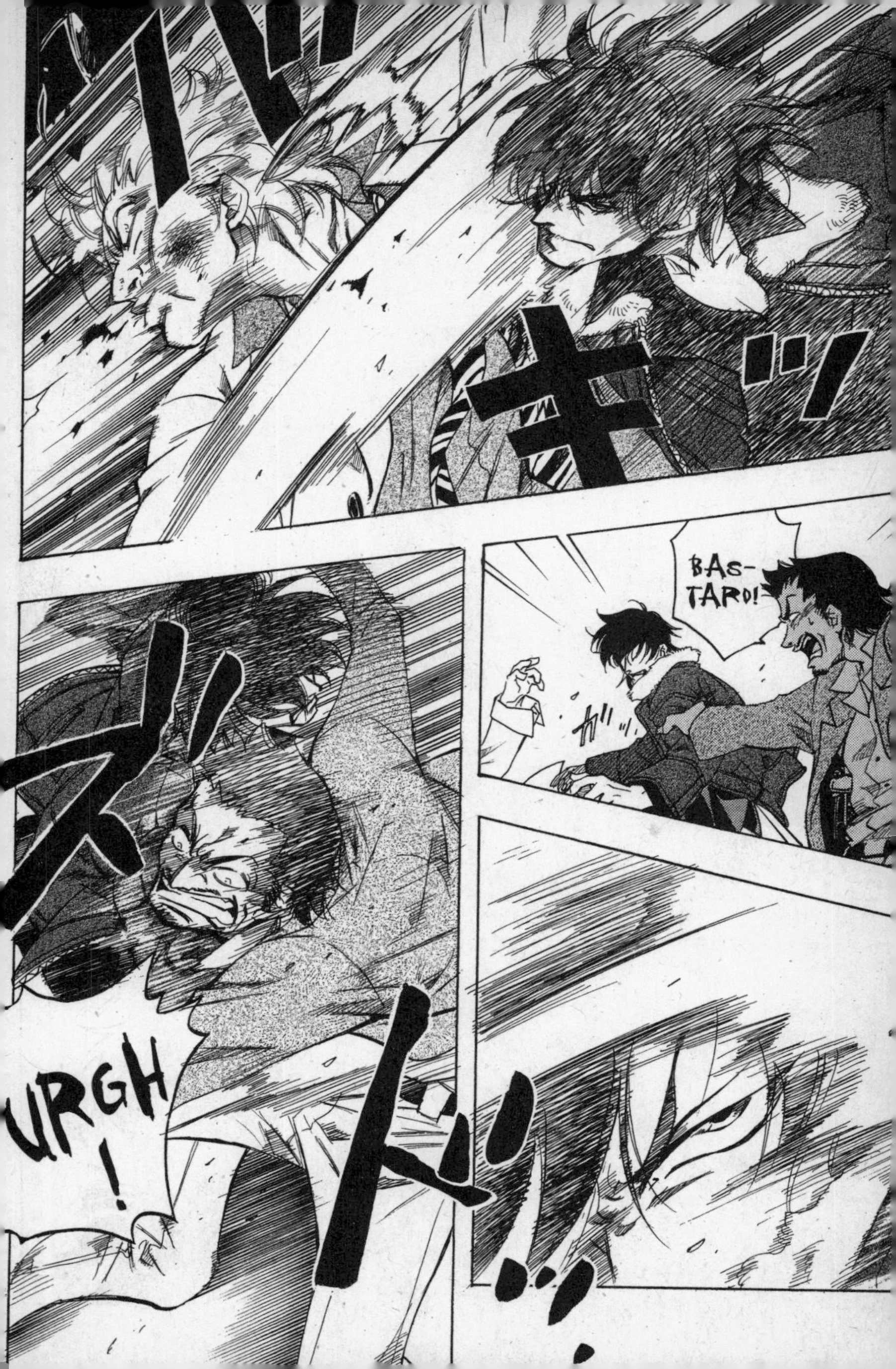

ギッ
BAS-
TARO!
ガッ
URGH
!

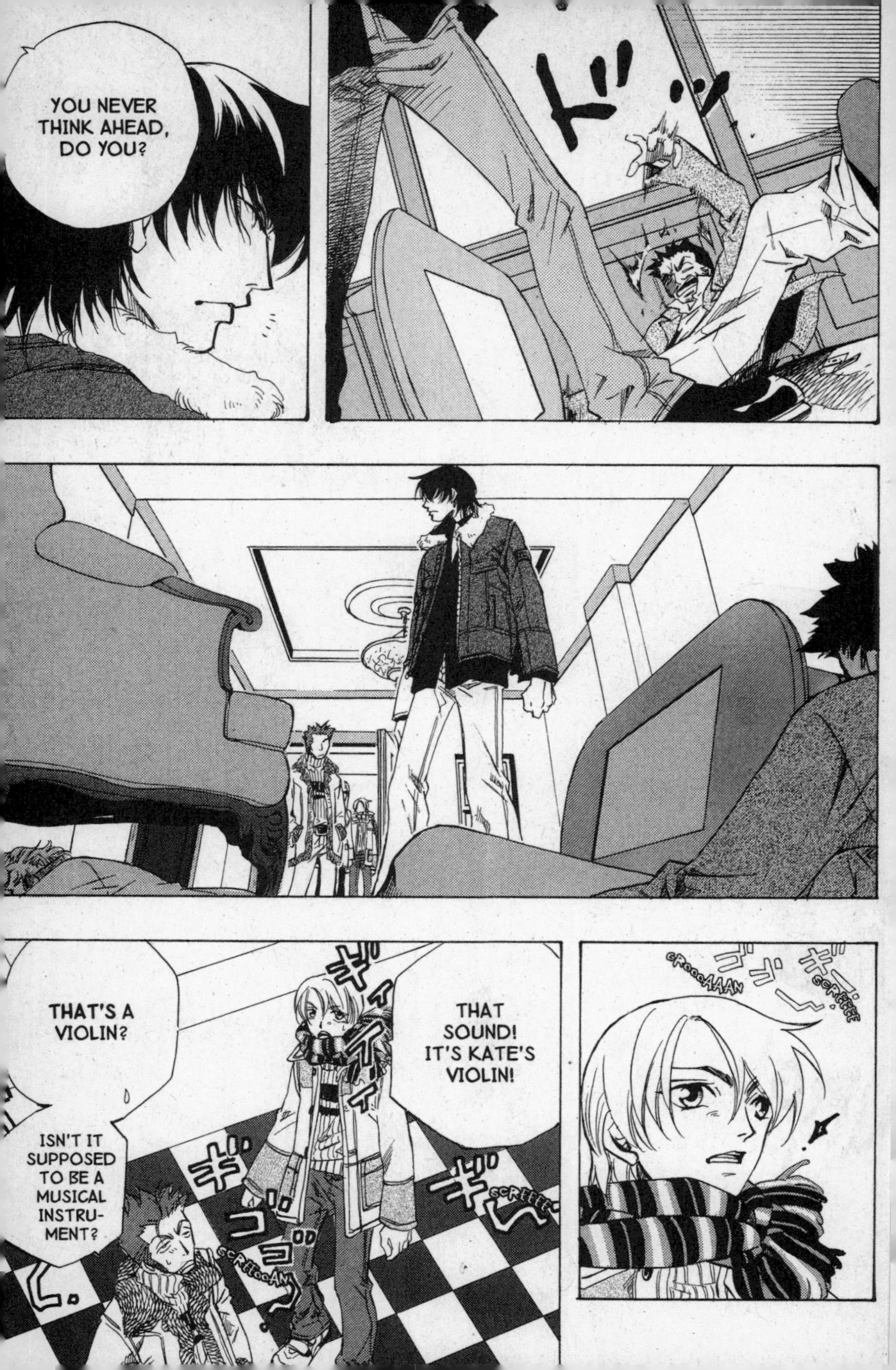

YOU NEVER THINK AHEAD, DO YOU?
GROOOAAAN
SCREEEE
THAT SOUND! IT'S KATE'S VIOLIN!
THAT'S A VIOLIN?
ISN'T IT SUPPOSED TO BE A MUSICAL INSTRU-MENT?
SCREEEE
SCREEOOAN

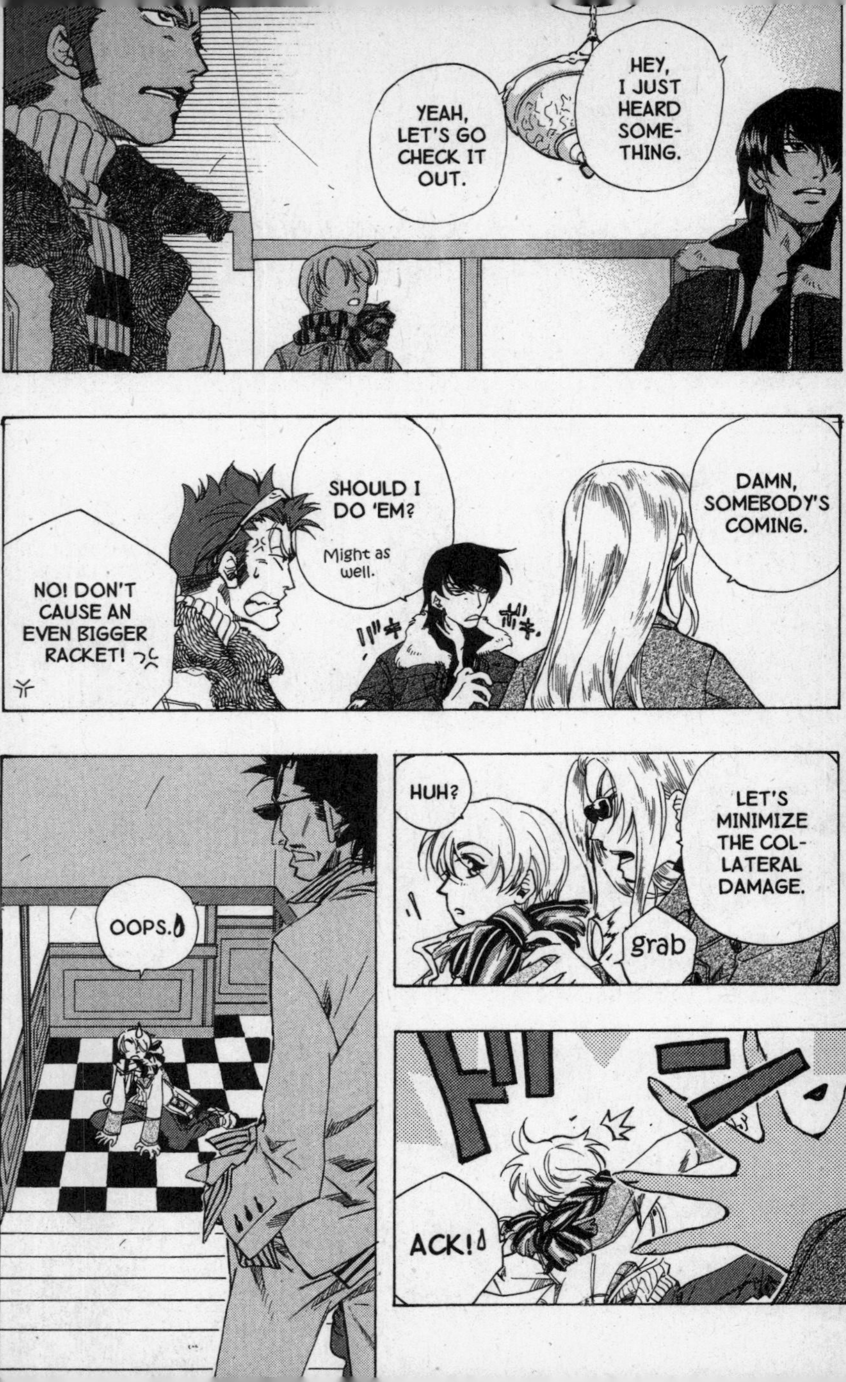
HEY, I JUST HEARD SOME-THING.
YEAH, LET'S GO CHECK IT OUT.
DAMN, SOMEBODY'S COMING.
SHOULD I DO 'EM?
Might as well.
NO! DON'T CAUSE AN EVEN BIGGER RACKET!
LET'S MINIMIZE THE COL-LATERAL DAMAGE.
HUH?
grab
ACK!
OOPS.

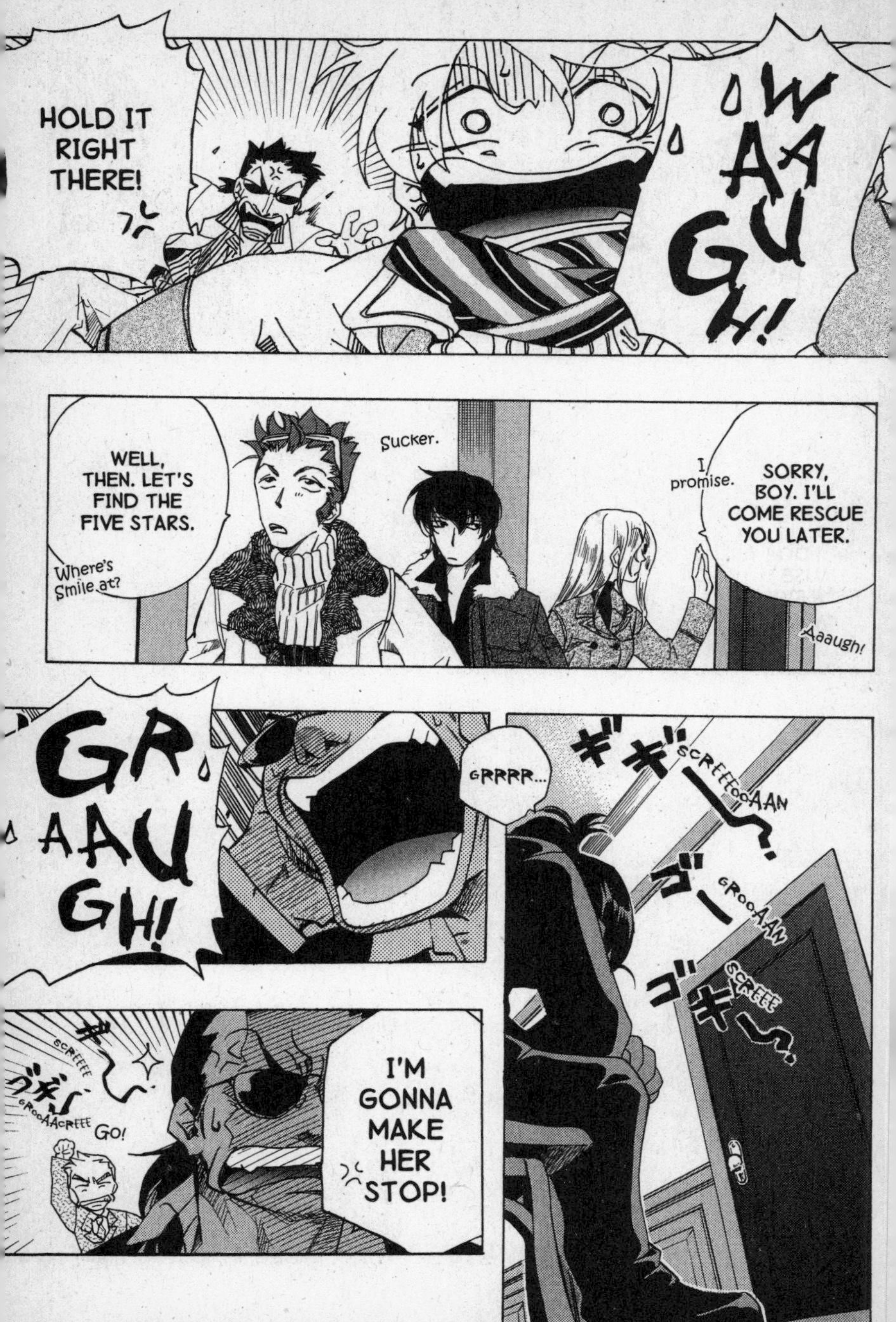
WAAUGH!
HOLD IT RIGHT THERE!
SORRY, BOY. I'LL COME RESCUE YOU LATER.
I promise.
Aaaugh!
Sucker.
WELL, THEN. LET'S FIND THE FIVE STARS.
Where's Smile at?
ギギ～ SCREEEOOAAN
ゴー GROOAAN
ゴキ～ SCREEE
GRRRR...
GRAAUGH!
I'M GONNA MAKE HER STOP!
SCREEEE
GROOAACREEE
GO!

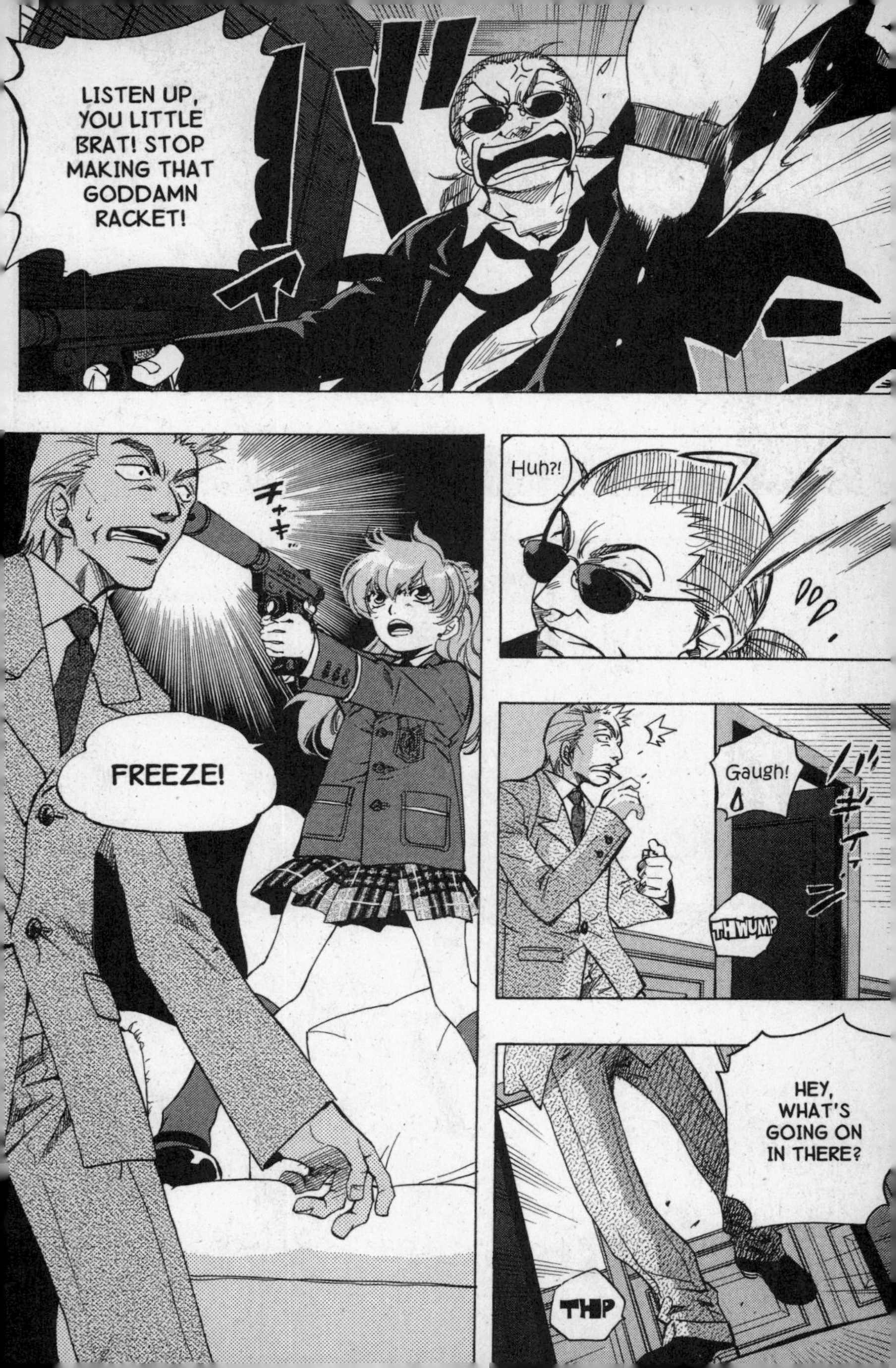
LISTEN UP, YOU LITTLE BRAT! STOP MAKING THAT GODDAMN RACKET!
Huh?!
Gaugh!
THWUMP
HEY, WHAT'S GOING ON IN THERE?
THP
FREEZE!

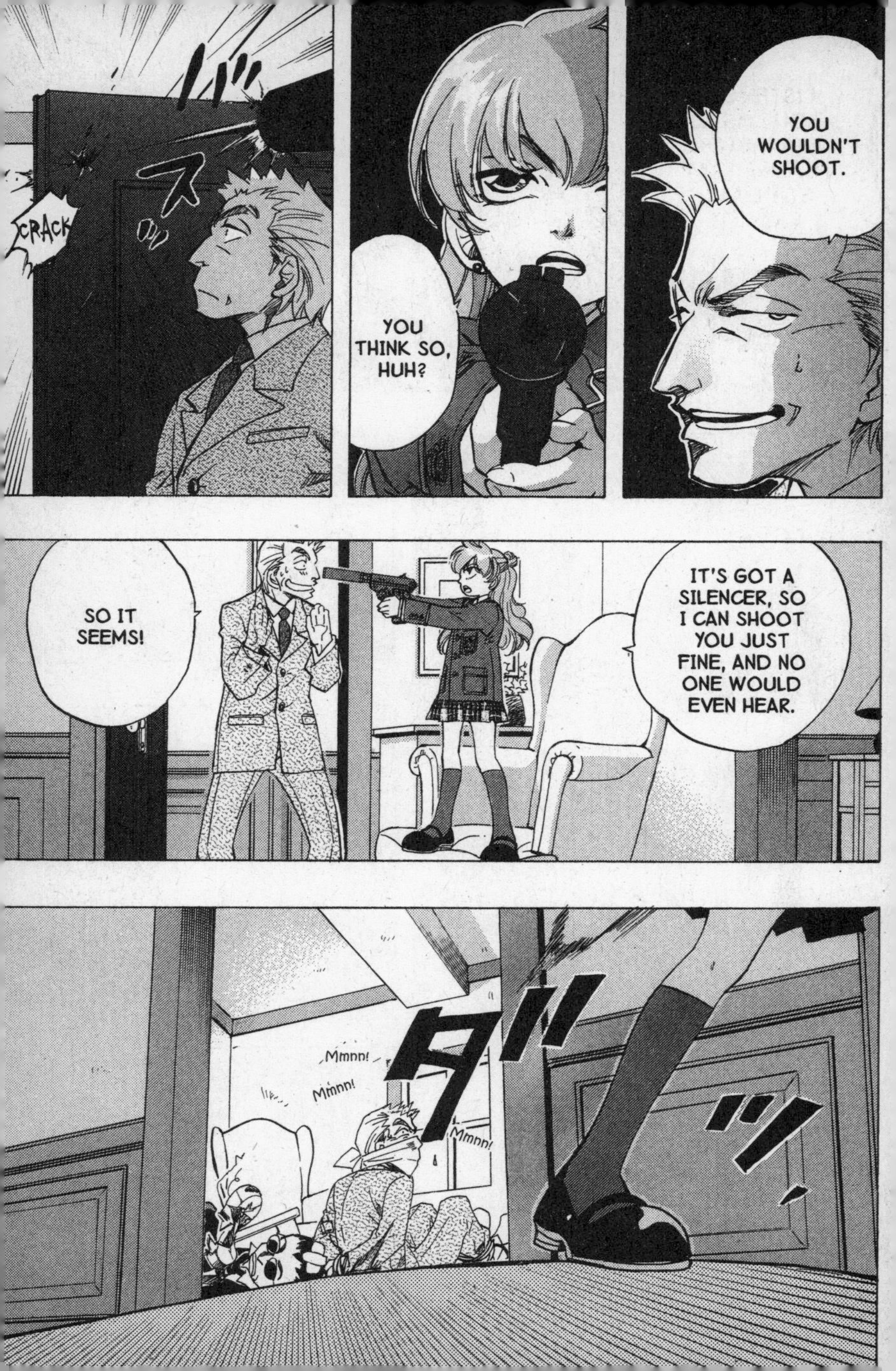
YOU WOULDN'T SHOOT.
YOU THINK SO, HUH?
CRACK
IT'S GOT A SILENCER, SO I CAN SHOOT YOU JUST FINE, AND NO ONE WOULD EVEN HEAR.
SO IT SEEMS!
Mmnn!
Mmnn!
Mmnn!

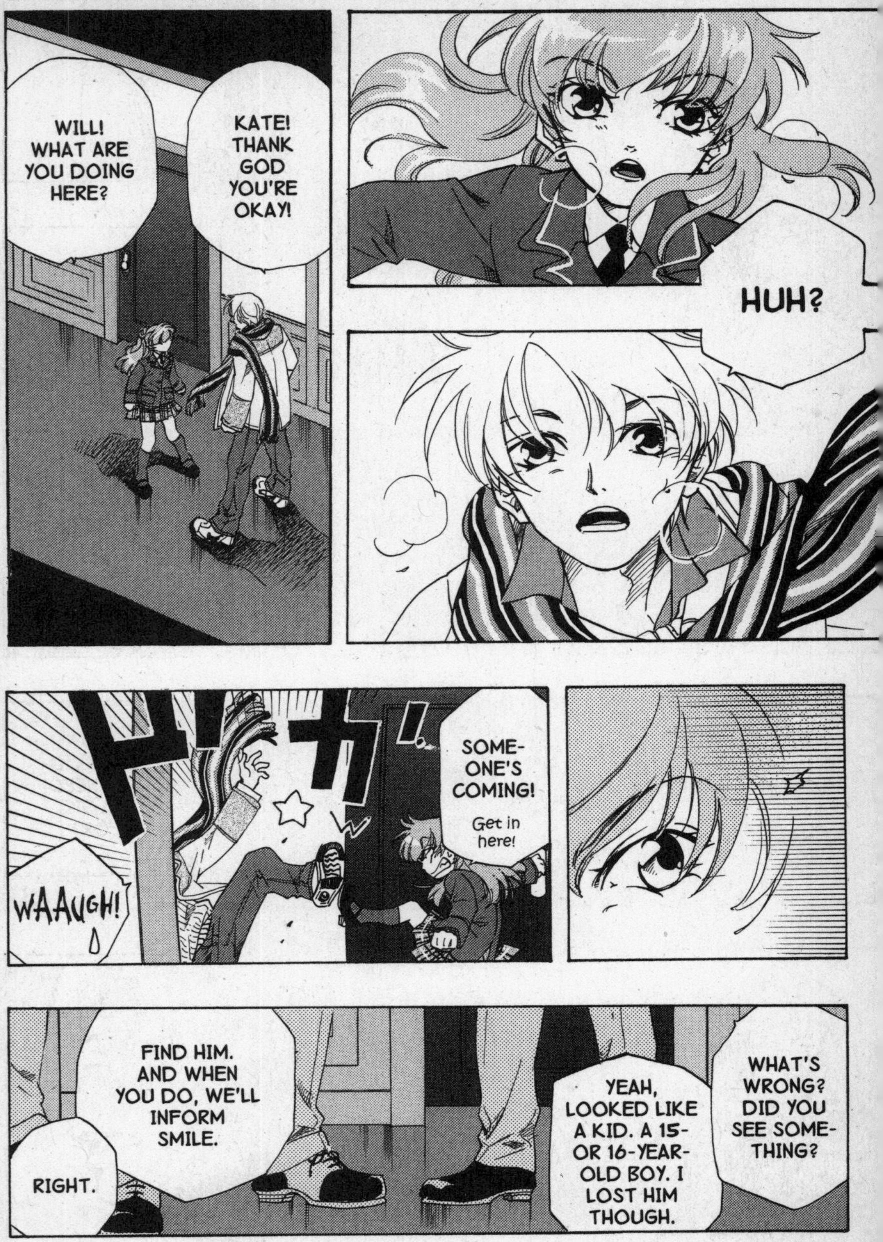
HUH?
KATE! THANK GOD YOU'RE OKAY!
WILL! WHAT ARE YOU DOING HERE?
SOME-ONE'S COMING!
Get in here!
WAAUGH!
WHAT'S WRONG? DID YOU SEE SOME-THING?
YEAH, LOOKED LIKE A KID. A 15- OR 16-YEAR-OLD BOY. I LOST HIM THOUGH.
FIND HIM. AND WHEN YOU DO, WE'LL INFORM SMILE.
RIGHT.

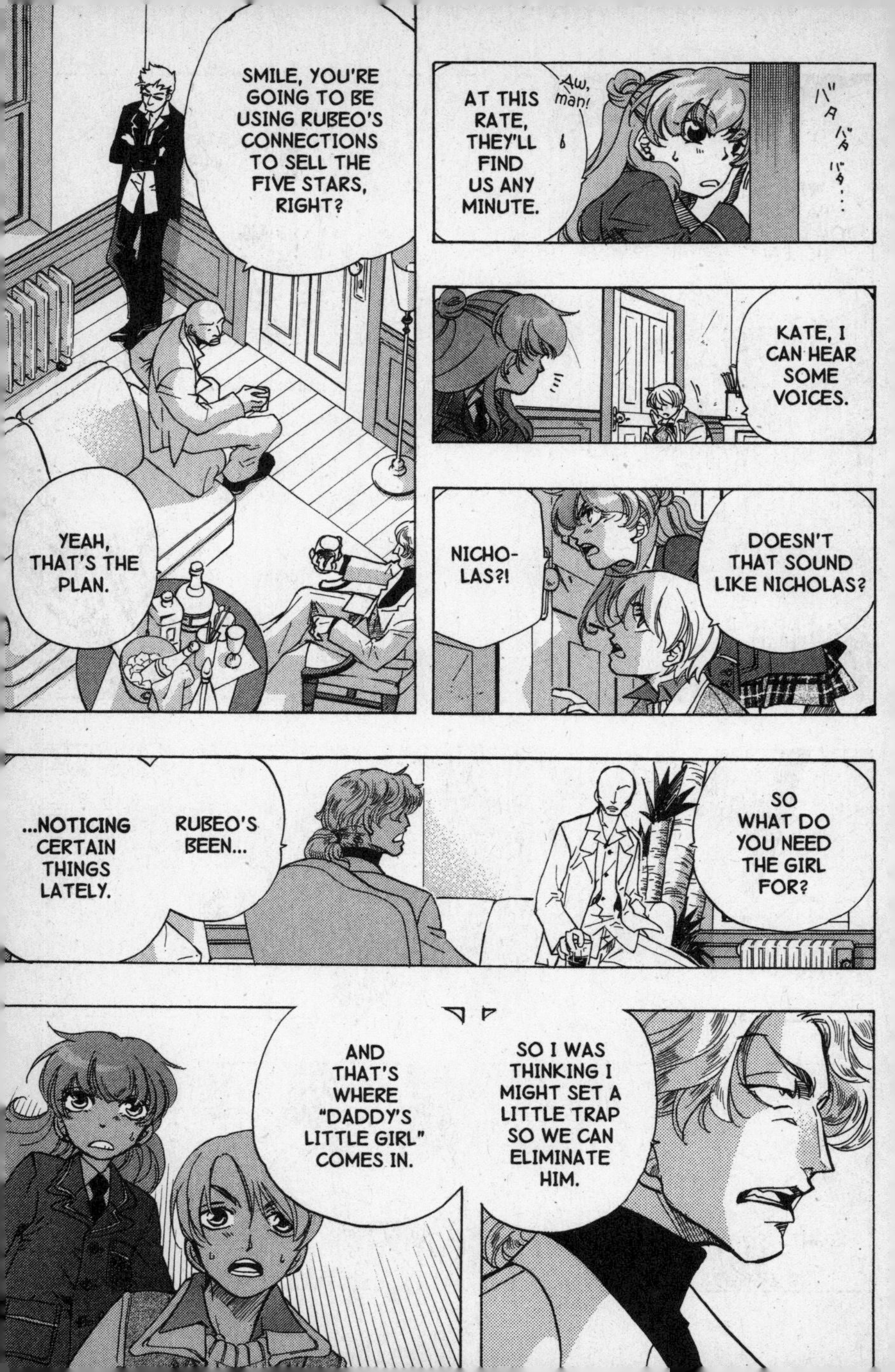

バタ バタ バタ…
Aw, man!
AT THIS RATE, THEY'LL FIND US ANY MINUTE.
KATE, I CAN HEAR SOME VOICES.
DOESN'T THAT SOUND LIKE NICHOLAS?
NICHO-LAS?!
SMILE, YOU'RE GOING TO BE USING RUBEO'S CONNECTIONS TO SELL THE FIVE STARS, RIGHT?
YEAH, THAT'S THE PLAN.
SO WHAT DO YOU NEED THE GIRL FOR?
RUBEO'S BEEN...
...NOTICING CERTAIN THINGS LATELY.
SO I WAS THINKING I MIGHT SET A LITTLE TRAP SO WE CAN ELIMINATE HIM.
AND THAT'S WHERE "DADDY'S LITTLE GIRL" COMES IN.

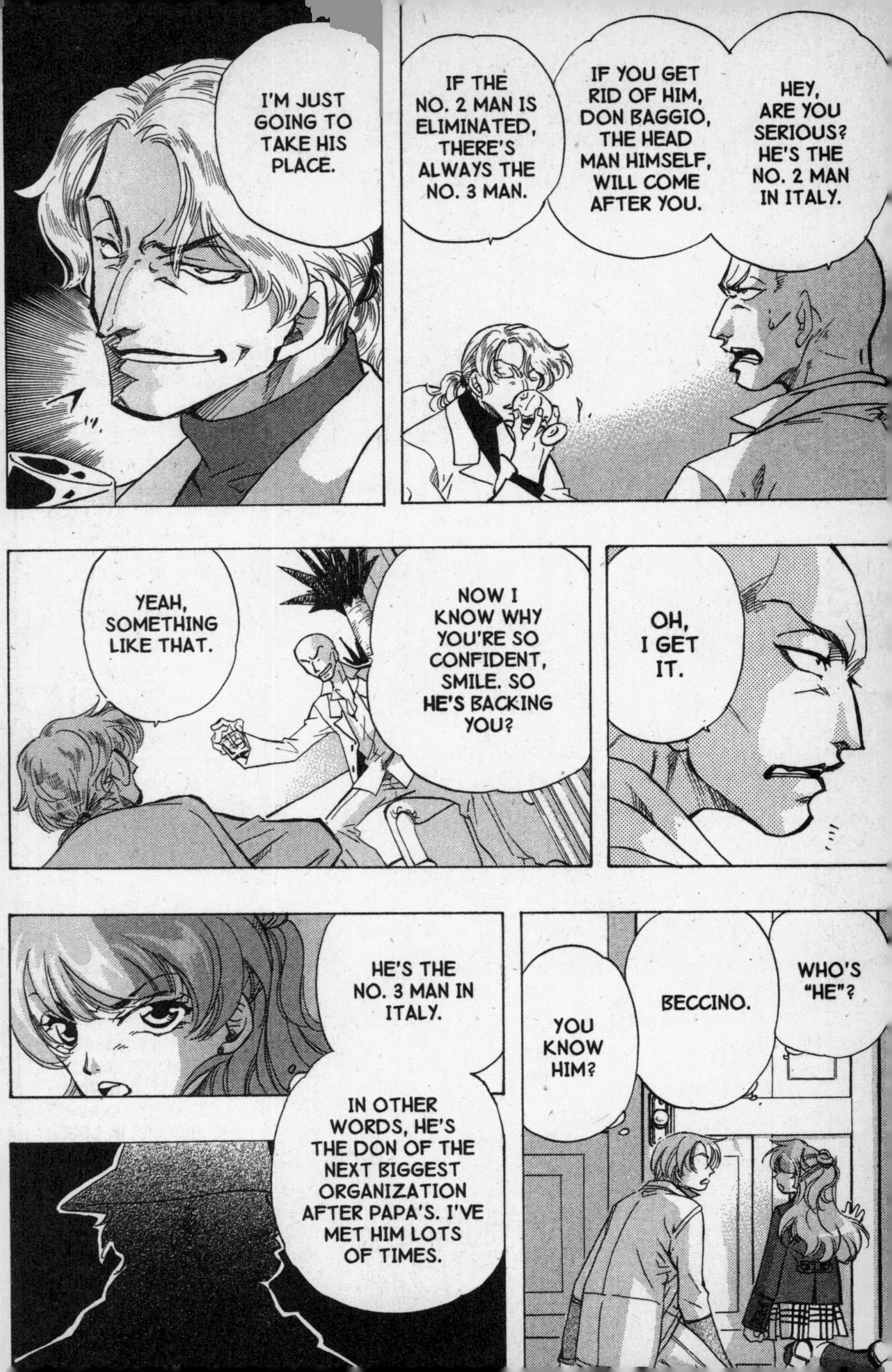
HEY, ARE YOU SERIOUS? HE'S THE NO. 2 MAN IN ITALY.
IF YOU GET RID OF HIM, DON BAGGIO, THE HEAD MAN HIMSELF, WILL COME AFTER YOU.
IF THE NO. 2 MAN IS ELIMINATED, THERE'S ALWAYS THE NO. 3 MAN.
I'M JUST GOING TO TAKE HIS PLACE.
OH, I GET IT.
NOW I KNOW WHY YOU'RE SO CONFIDENT, SMILE. SO HE'S BACKING YOU?
YEAH, SOMETHING LIKE THAT.
WHO'S "HE"?
BECCINO.
YOU KNOW HIM?
HE'S THE NO. 3 MAN IN ITALY.
IN OTHER WORDS, HE'S THE DON OF THE NEXT BIGGEST ORGANIZATION AFTER PAPA'S. I'VE MET HIM LOTS OF TIMES.

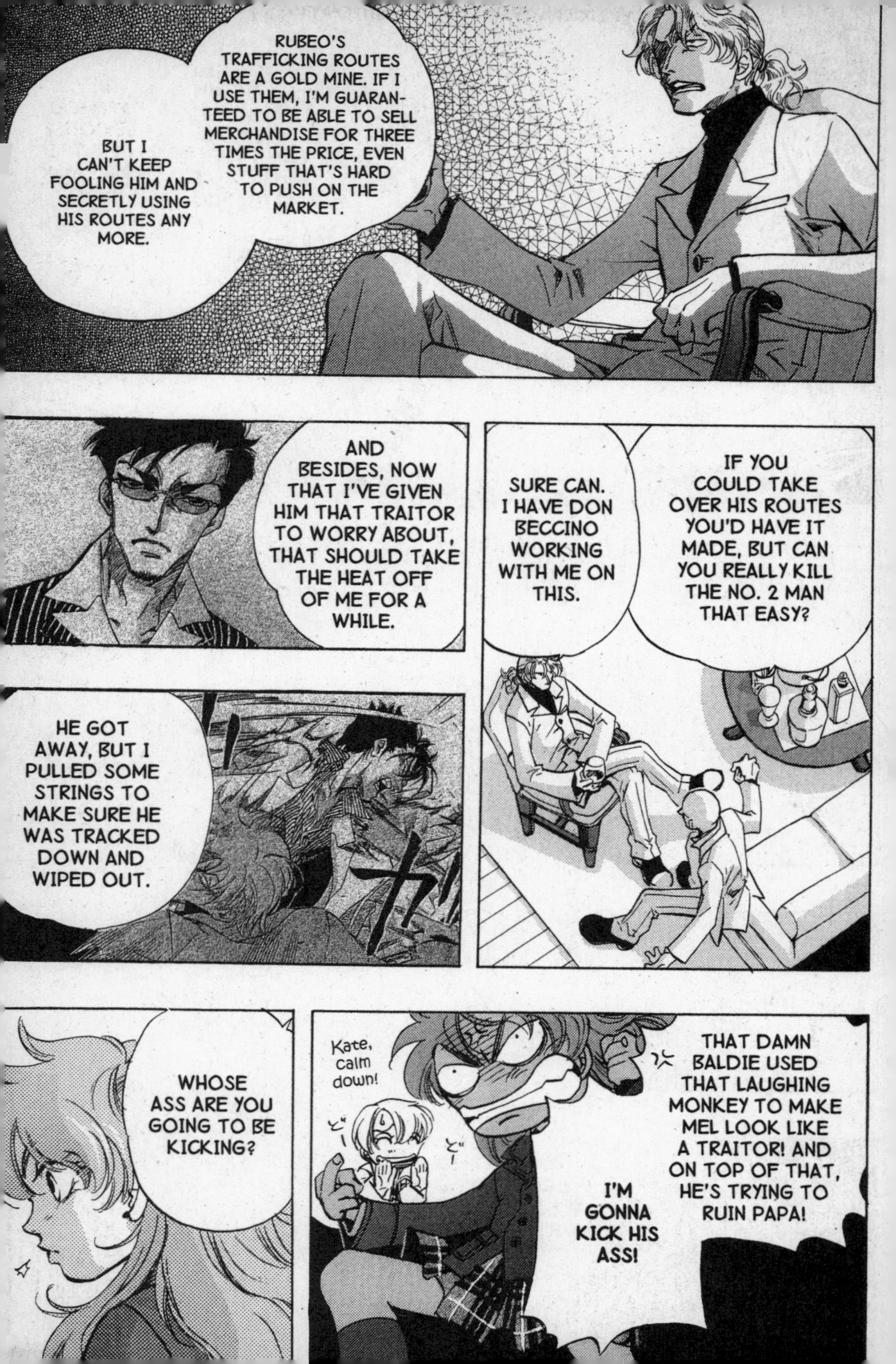
RUBEO'S TRAFFICKING ROUTES ARE A GOLD MINE. IF I USE THEM, I'M GUARANTEED TO BE ABLE TO SELL MERCHANDISE FOR THREE TIMES THE PRICE, EVEN STUFF THAT'S HARD TO PUSH ON THE MARKET.
BUT I CAN'T KEEP FOOLING HIM AND SECRETLY USING HIS ROUTES ANY MORE.
IF YOU COULD TAKE OVER HIS ROUTES YOU'D HAVE IT MADE, BUT CAN YOU REALLY KILL THE NO. 2 MAN THAT EASY?
SURE CAN. I HAVE DON BECCINO WORKING WITH ME ON THIS.
AND BESIDES, NOW THAT I'VE GIVEN HIM THAT TRAITOR TO WORRY ABOUT, THAT SHOULD TAKE THE HEAT OFF OF ME FOR A WHILE.
HE GOT AWAY, BUT I PULLED SOME STRINGS TO MAKE SURE HE WAS TRACKED DOWN AND WIPED OUT.
THAT DAMN BALDIE USED THAT LAUGHING MONKEY TO MAKE MEL LOOK LIKE A TRAITOR! AND ON TOP OF THAT, HE'S TRYING TO RUIN PAPA!
I'M GONNA KICK HIS ASS!
Kate, calm down!
WHOSE ASS ARE YOU GOING TO BE KICKING?

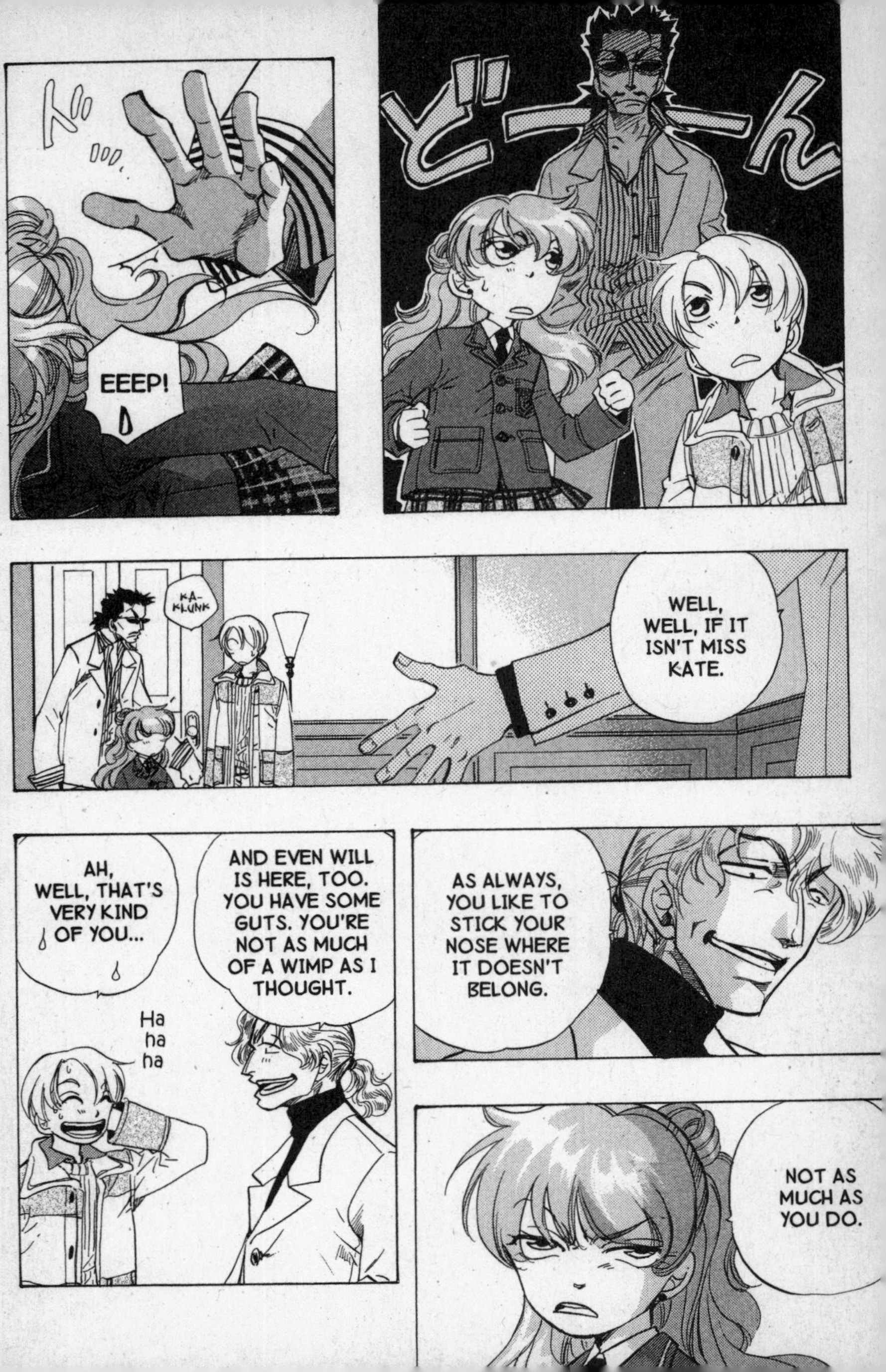
どーん
ドッ
EEEP!
WELL, WELL, IF IT ISN'T MISS KATE.
KA-KLUNK
AS ALWAYS, YOU LIKE TO STICK YOUR NOSE WHERE IT DOESN'T BELONG.
NOT AS MUCH AS YOU DO.
AND EVEN WILL IS HERE, TOO. YOU HAVE SOME GUTS. YOU'RE NOT AS MUCH OF A WIMP AS I THOUGHT.
AH, WELL, THAT'S VERY KIND OF YOU...
Ha ha ha

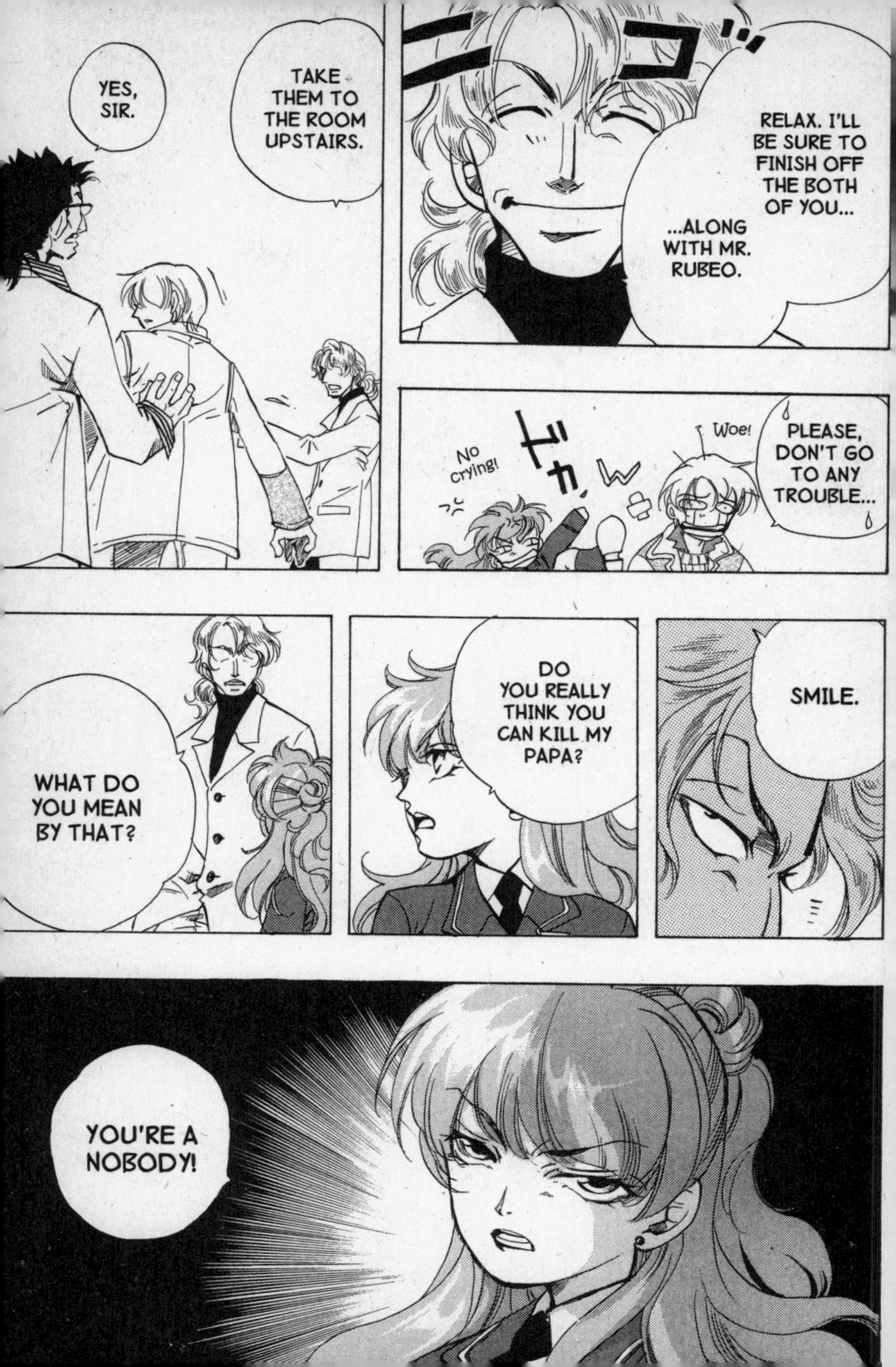
RELAX. I'LL BE SURE TO FINISH OFF THE BOTH OF YOU...
...ALONG WITH MR. RUBEO.
PLEASE, DON'T GO TO ANY TROUBLE...
Woe!
No crying!
TAKE THEM TO THE ROOM UPSTAIRS.
YES, SIR.
SMILE.
DO YOU REALLY THINK YOU CAN KILL MY PAPA?
WHAT DO YOU MEAN BY THAT?
YOU'RE A NOBODY!

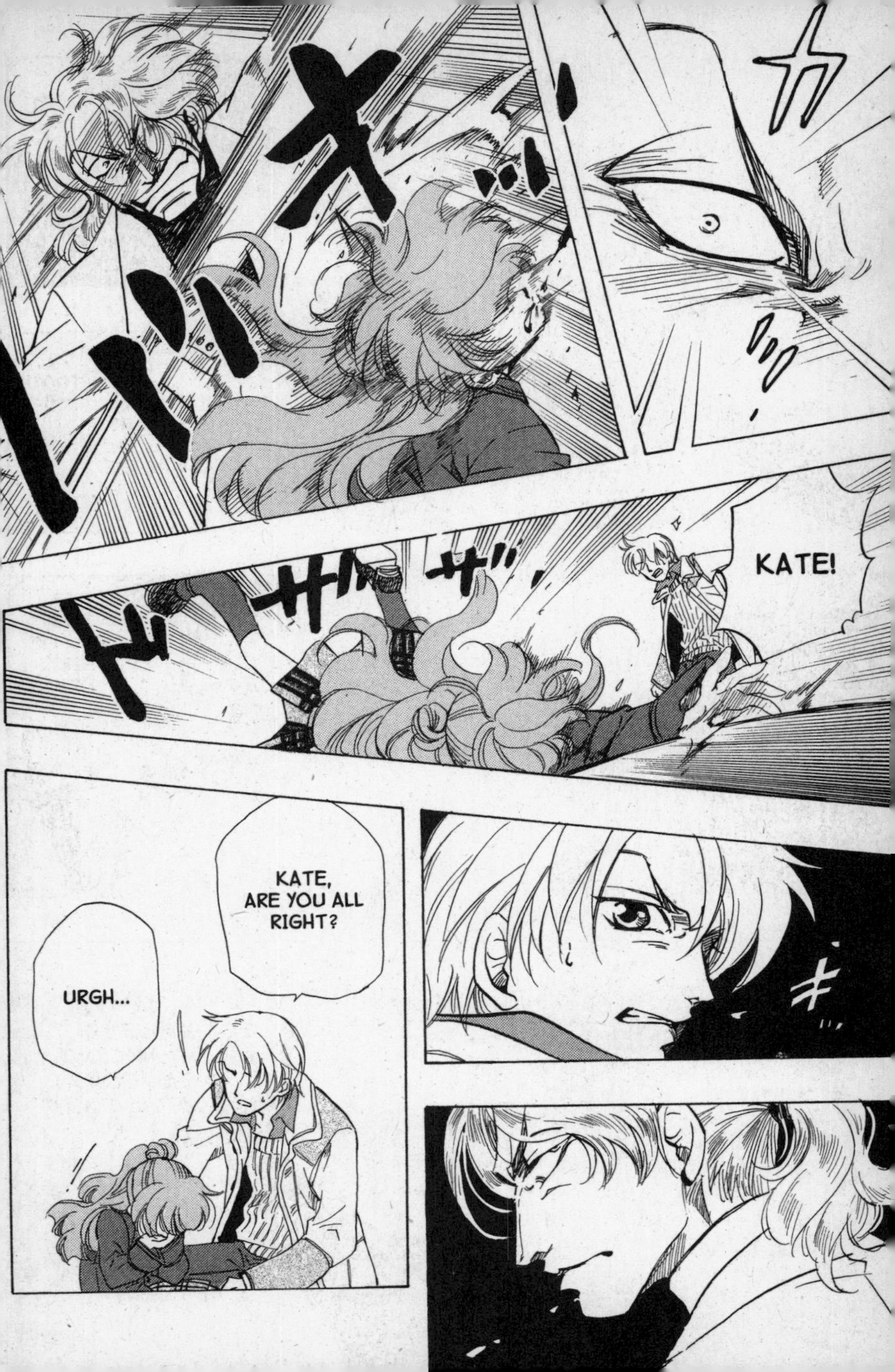
KATE!
KATE, ARE YOU ALL RIGHT?
URGH...

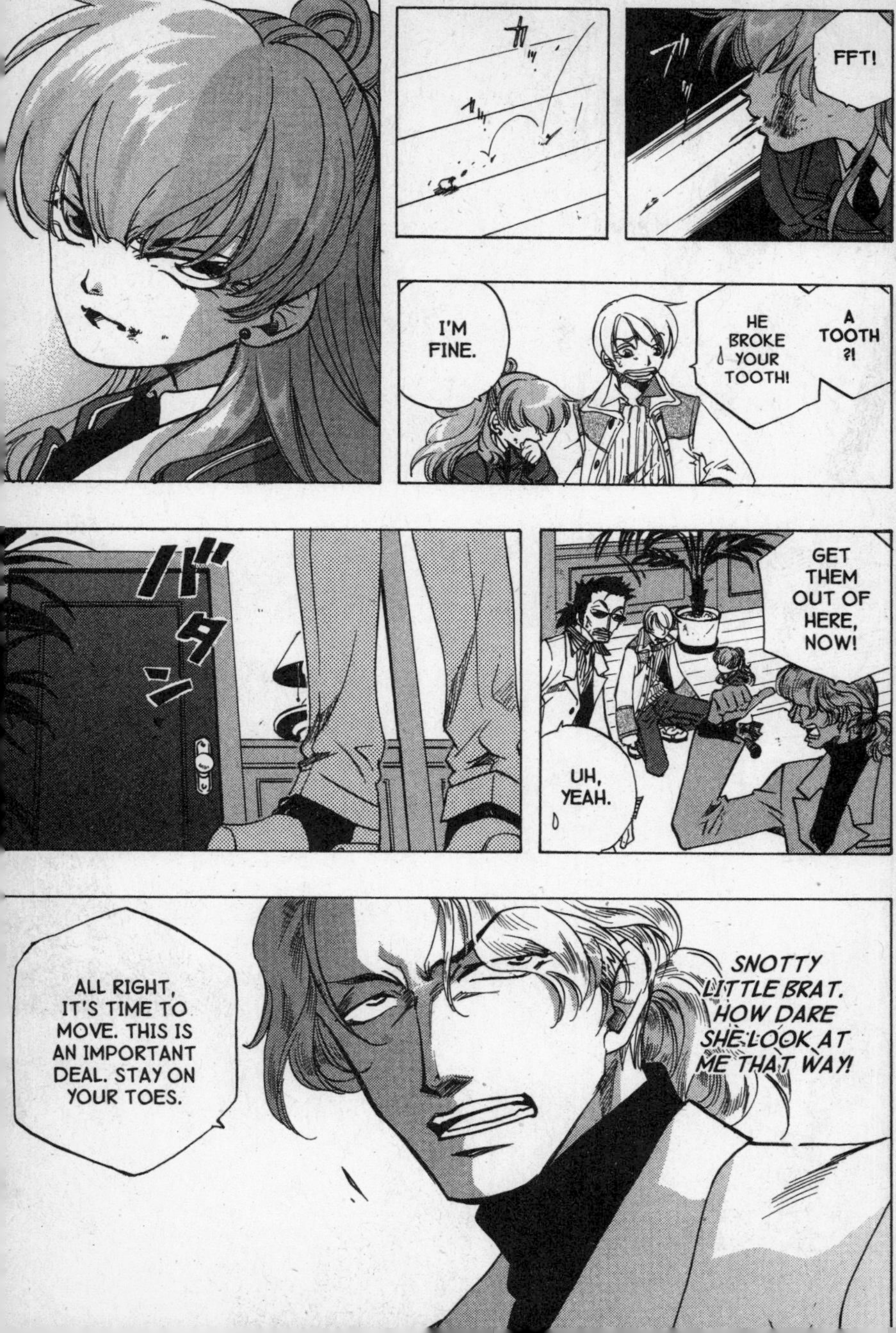
FFT!
A TOOTH ?!
HE BROKE YOUR TOOTH!
I'M FINE.
GET THEM OUT OF HERE, NOW!
UH, YEAH.
バタン
SNOTTY LITTLE BRAT. HOW DARE SHE LOOK AT ME THAT WAY!
ALL RIGHT, IT'S TIME TO MOVE. THIS IS AN IMPORTANT DEAL. STAY ON YOUR TOES.

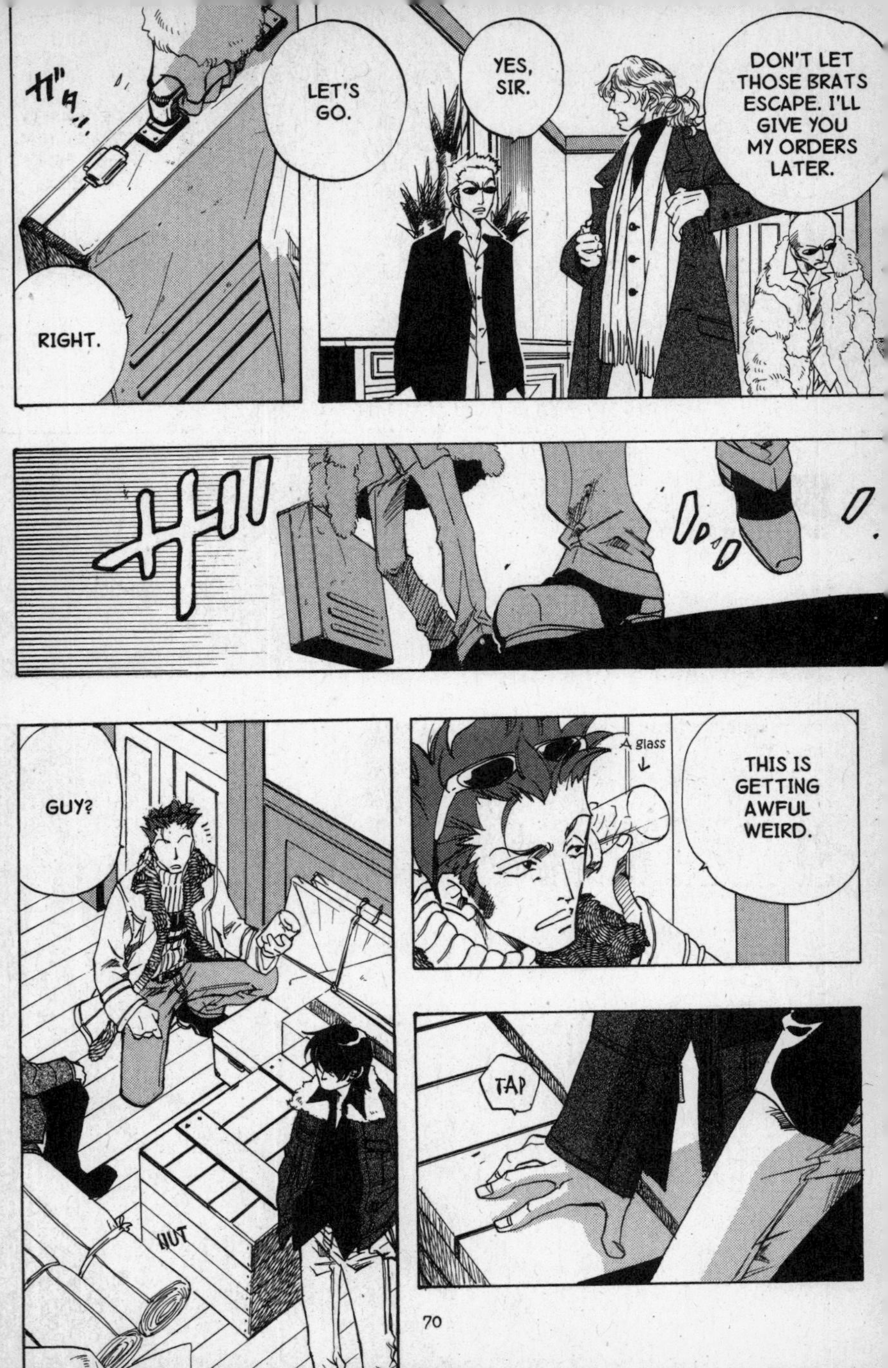
DON'T LET THOSE BRATS ESCAPE. I'LL GIVE YOU MY ORDERS LATER.
YES, SIR.
LET'S GO.
ガタ
RIGHT.
THIS IS GETTING AWFUL WEIRD.
A glass
TAP
GUY?
NUT

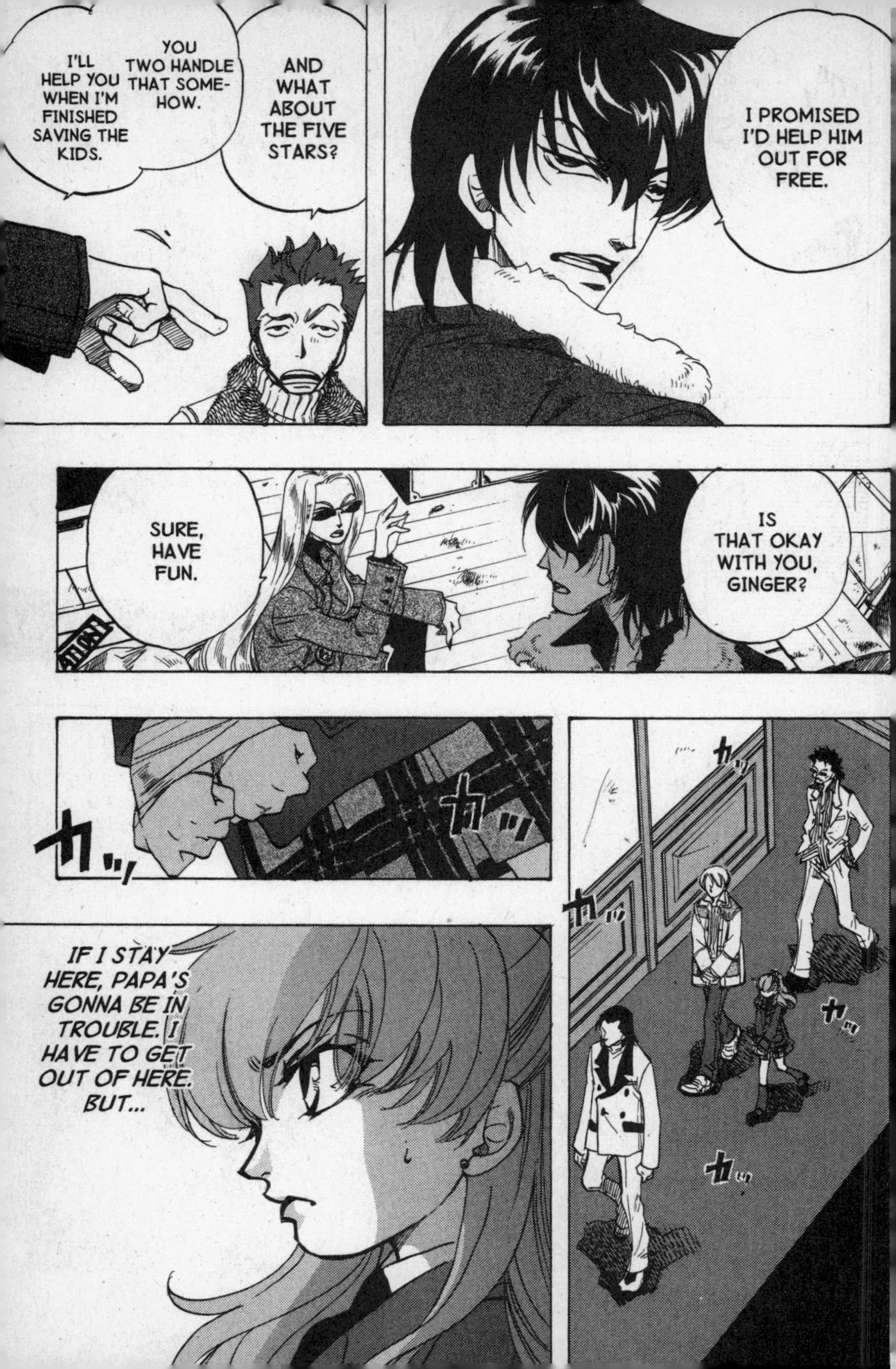

I PROMISED I'D HELP HIM OUT FOR FREE.
AND WHAT ABOUT THE FIVE STARS?
YOU TWO HANDLE THAT SOME-HOW.
I'LL HELP YOU WHEN I'M FINISHED SAVING THE KIDS.
IS THAT OKAY WITH YOU, GINGER?
SURE, HAVE FUN.
カッ
カッ
カッ
カッ
カッ
カッ
IF I STAY HERE, PAPA'S GONNA BE IN TROUBLE. I HAVE TO GET OUT OF HERE. BUT...

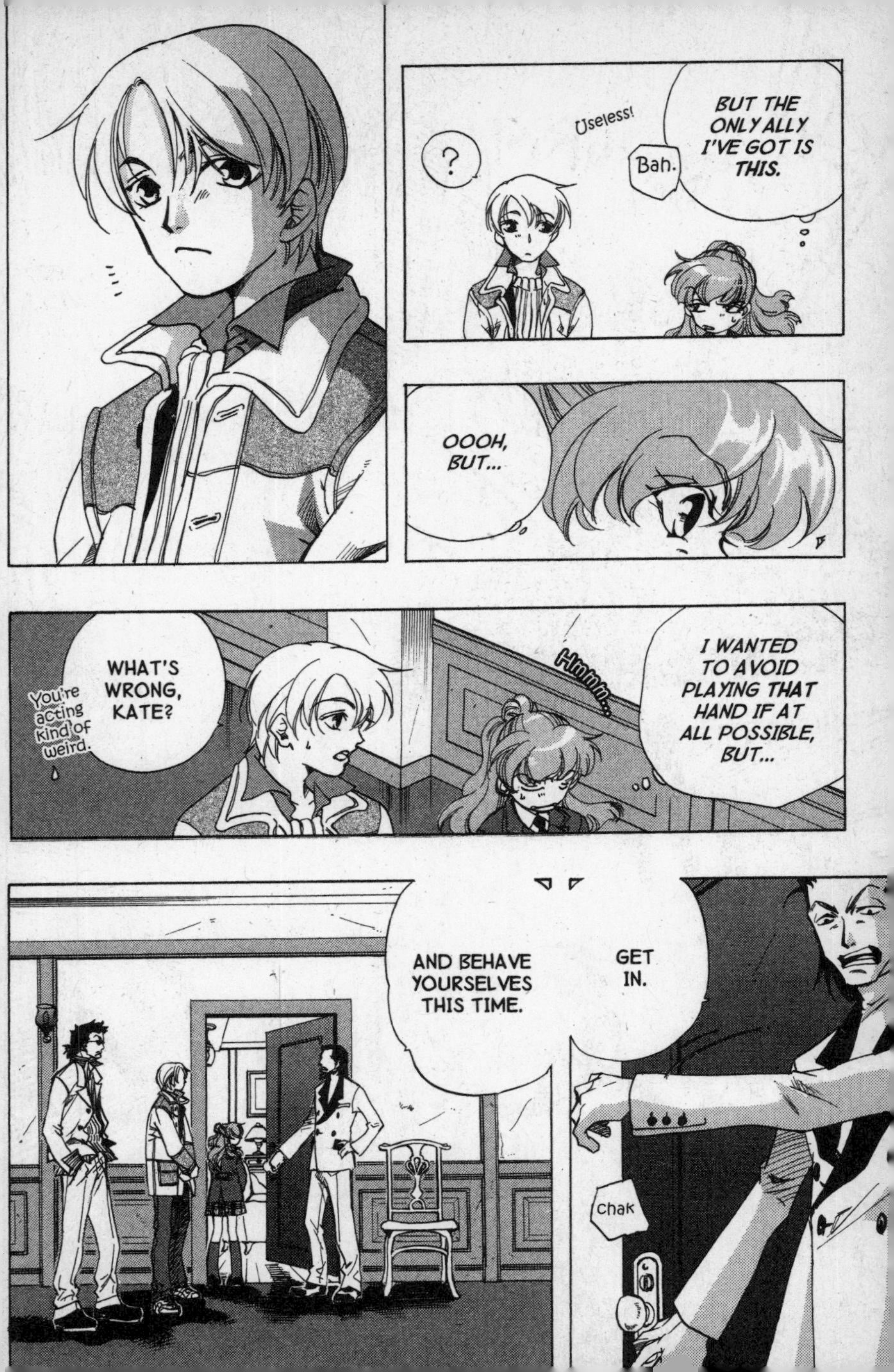
BUT THE ONLY ALLY I'VE GOT IS THIS.
Bah.
Useless!
?
OOOH, BUT...
I WANTED TO AVOID PLAYING THAT HAND IF AT ALL POSSIBLE, BUT...
Hmmm...
WHAT'S WRONG, KATE?
You're acting kind of weird.
GET IN.
AND BEHAVE YOURSELVES THIS TIME.
Chak

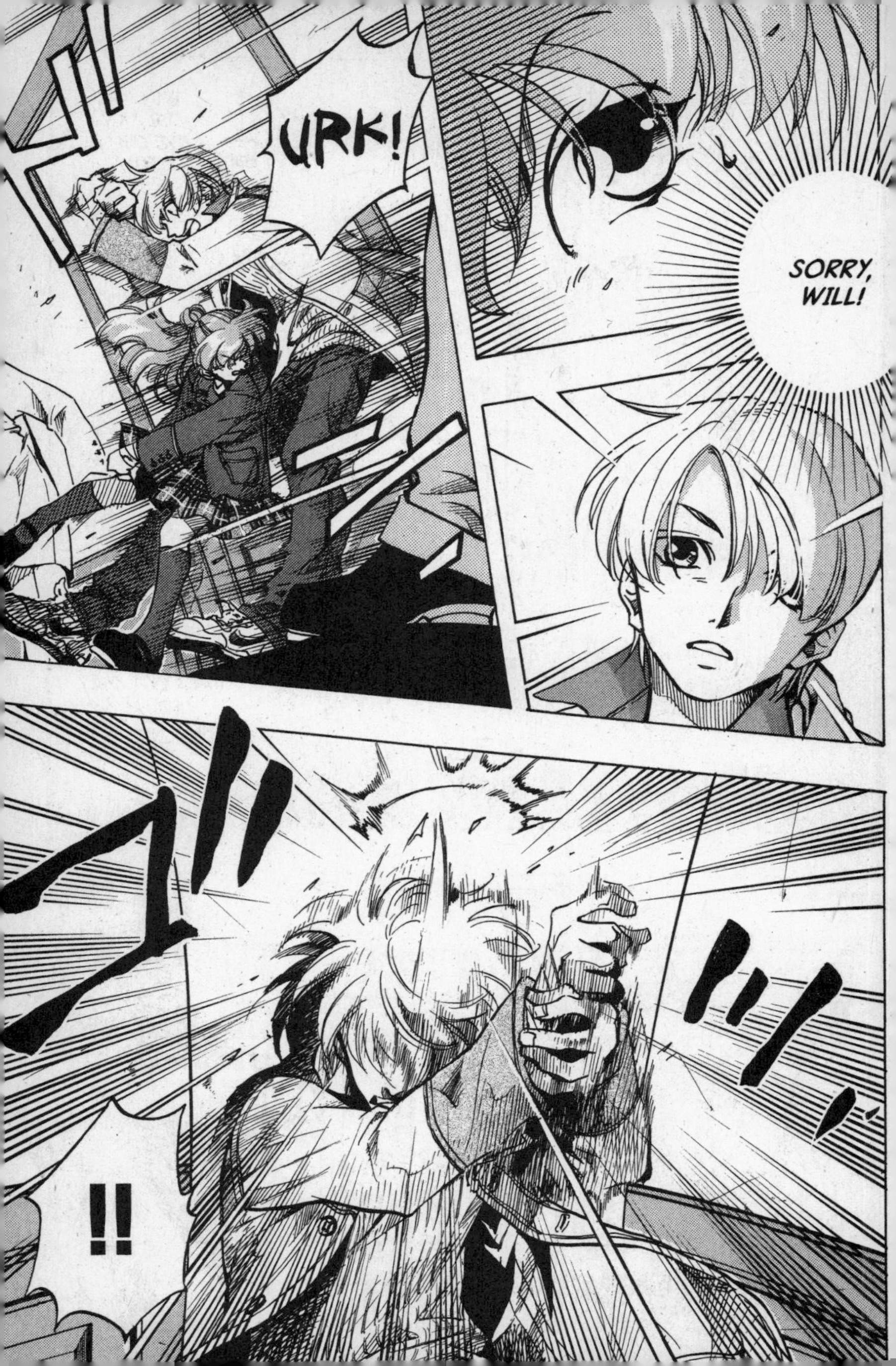
SORRY, WILL!
URK!
!!

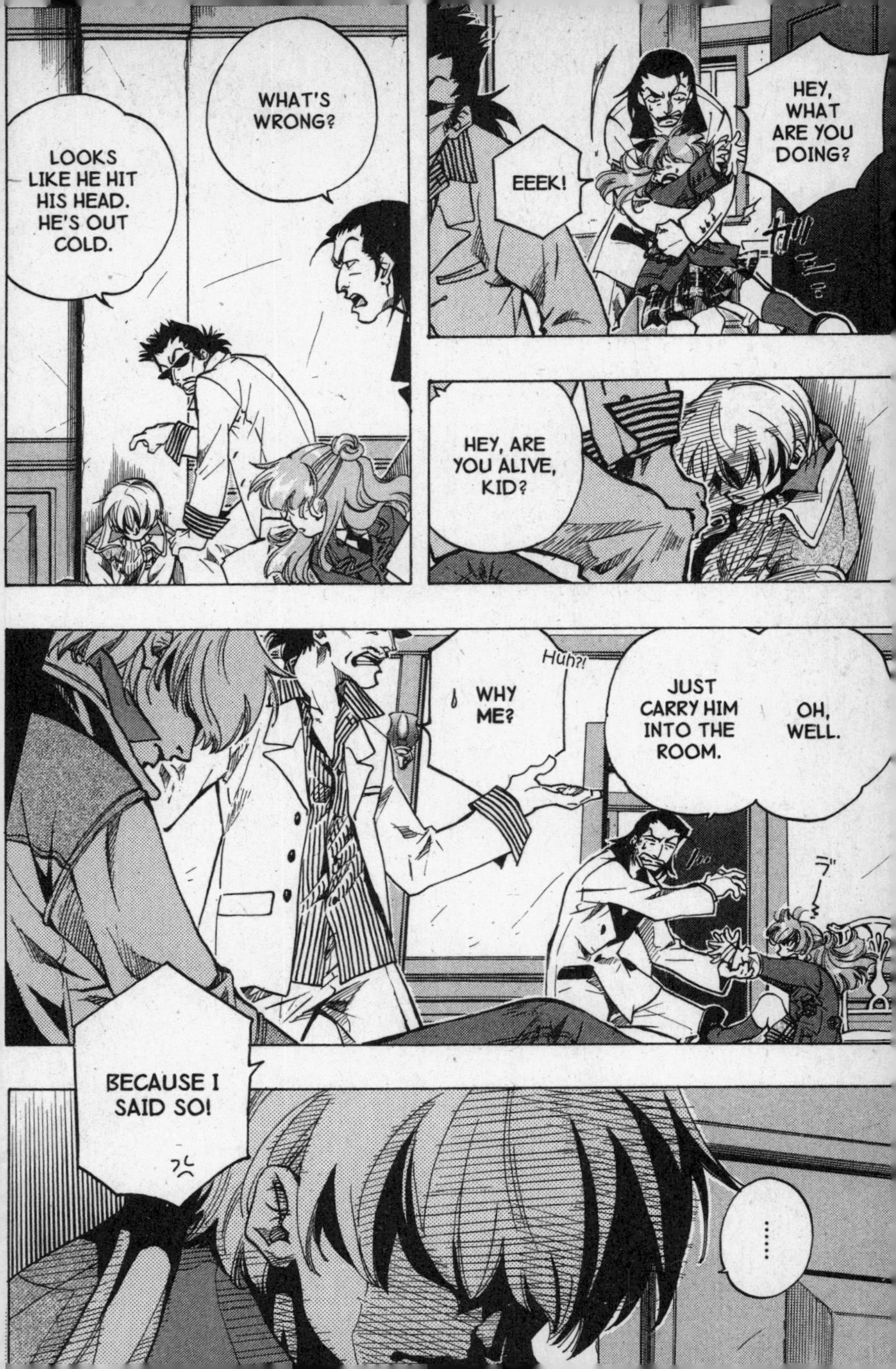
HEY, WHAT ARE YOU DOING?
EEEK!
HEY, ARE YOU ALIVE, KID?
WHAT'S WRONG?
LOOKS LIKE HE HIT HIS HEAD. HE'S OUT COLD.
OH, WELL.
JUST CARRY HIM INTO THE ROOM.
Huh?!
WHY ME?
......
BECAUSE I SAID SO!

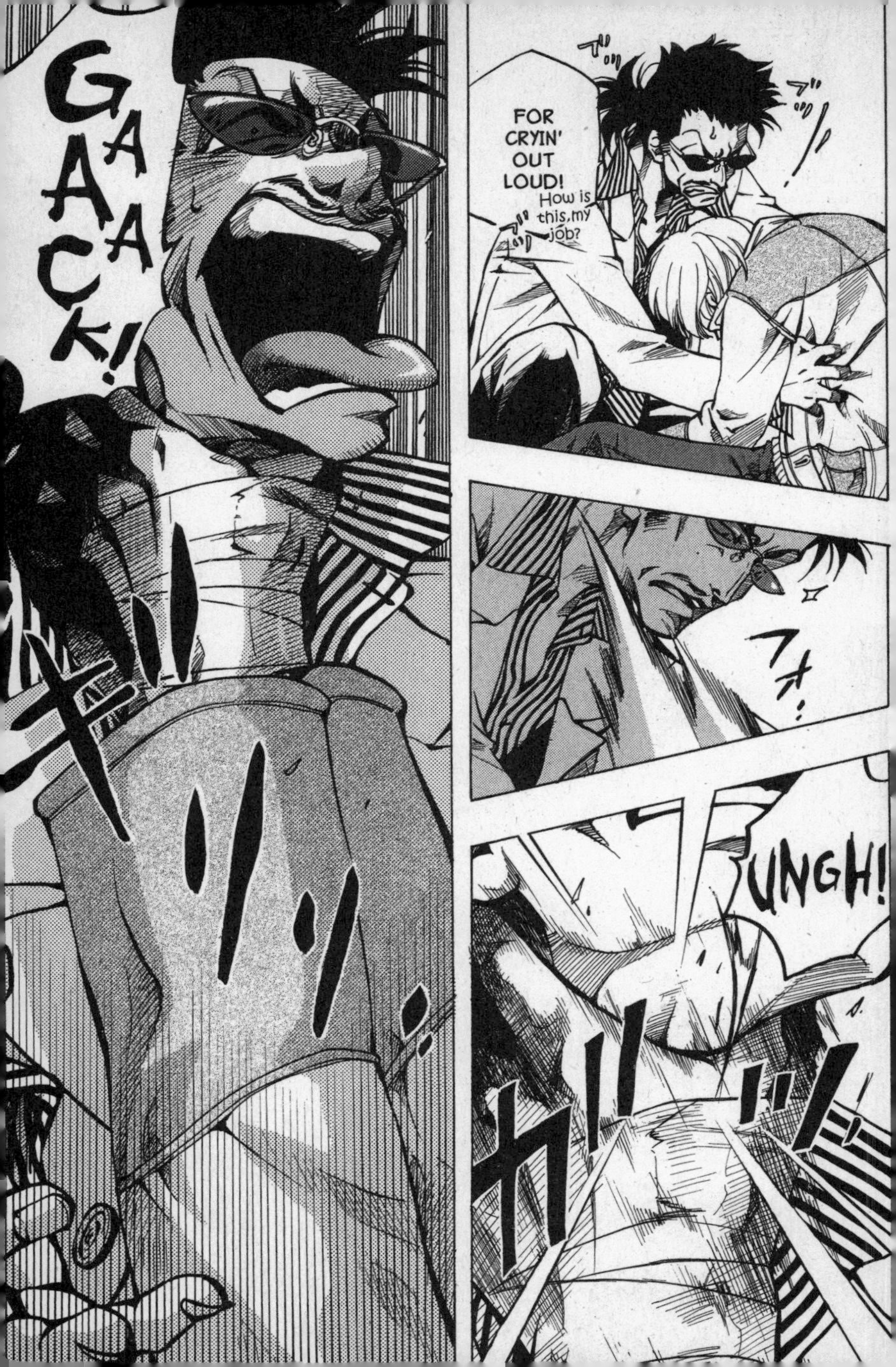
FOR CRYIN' OUT LOUD!
How is this, my job?
UNGH!
GAACK!

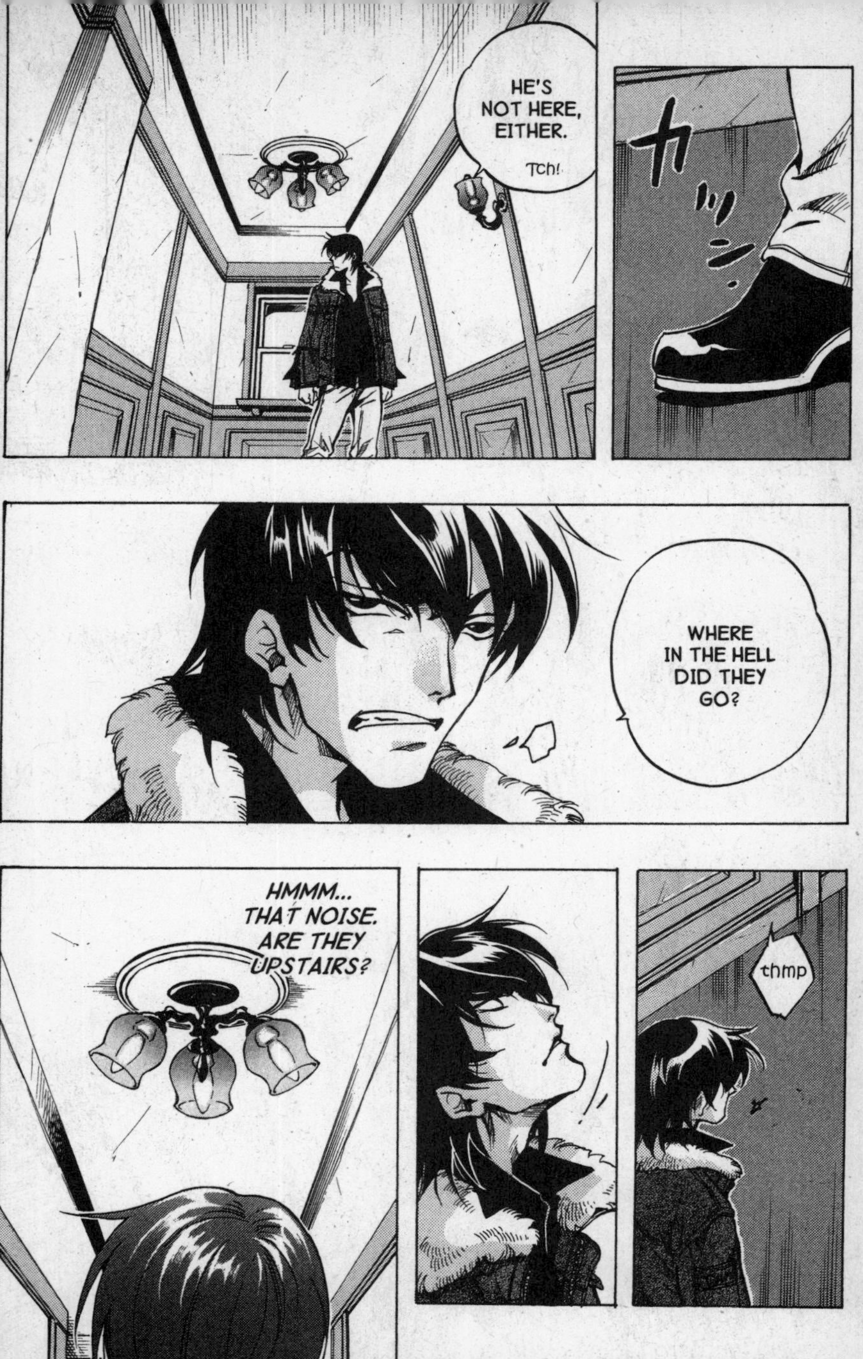
カッ
HE'S NOT HERE, EITHER.
Tch!
WHERE IN THE HELL DID THEY GO?
thmp
HMMM... THAT NOISE. ARE THEY UPSTAIRS?

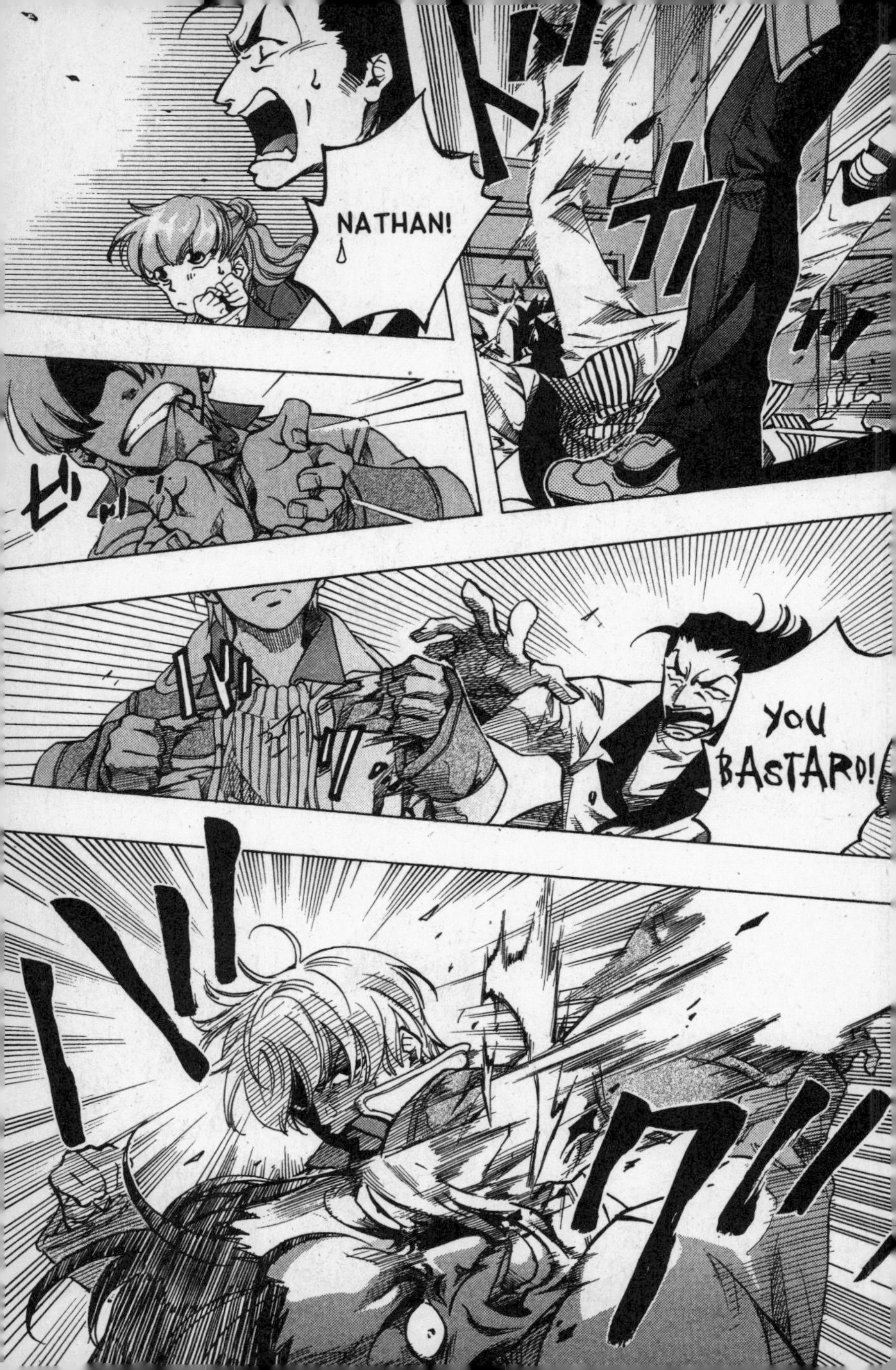
NATHAN!
YOU BASTARD!

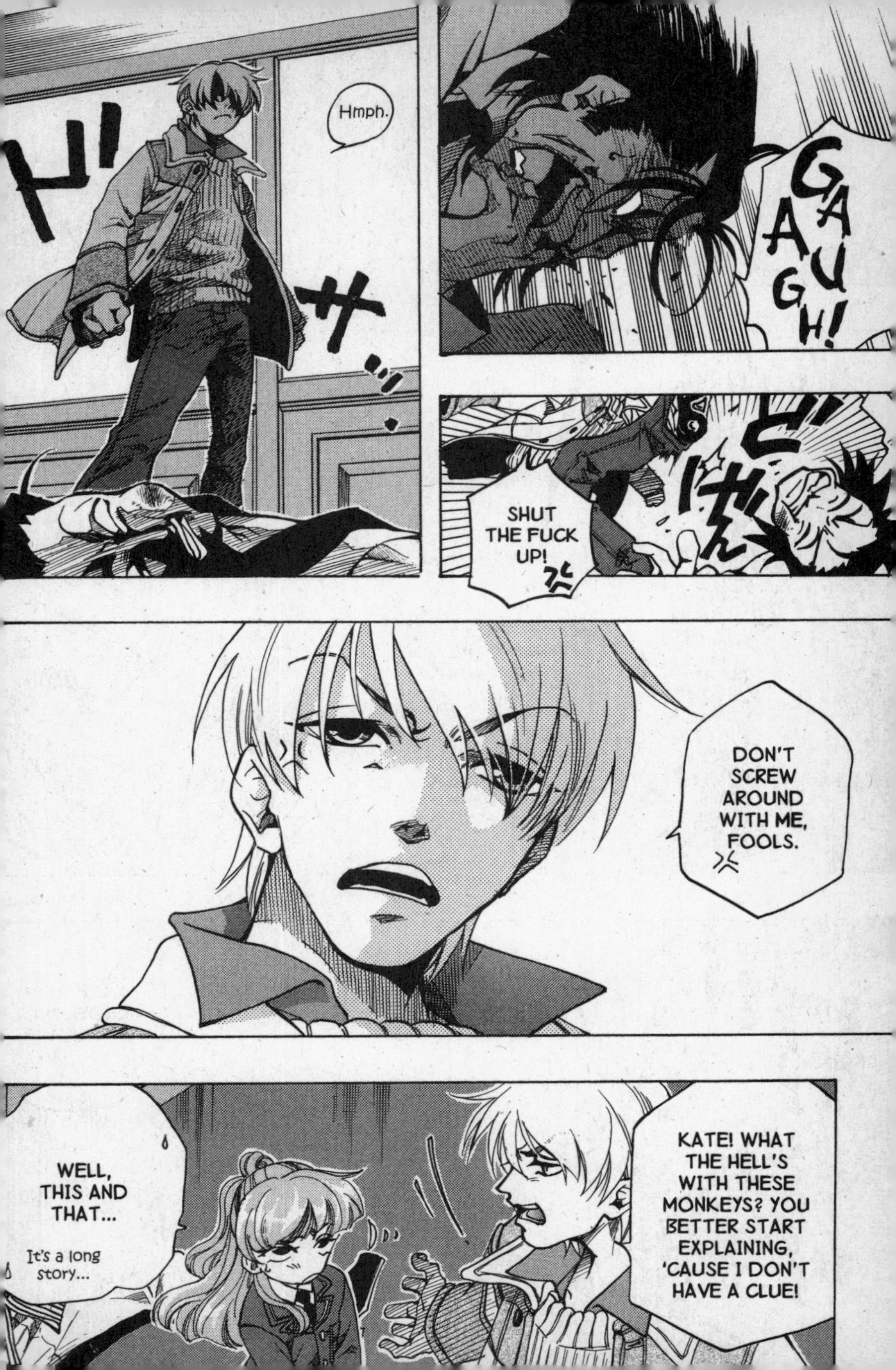
GAAUGH!
SHUT THE FUCK UP!
Hmph.
DON'T SCREW AROUND WITH ME, FOOLS.
KATE! WHAT THE HELL'S WITH THESE MONKEYS? YOU BETTER START EXPLAINING, 'CAUSE I DON'T HAVE A CLUE!
WELL, THIS AND THAT...
It's a long story...

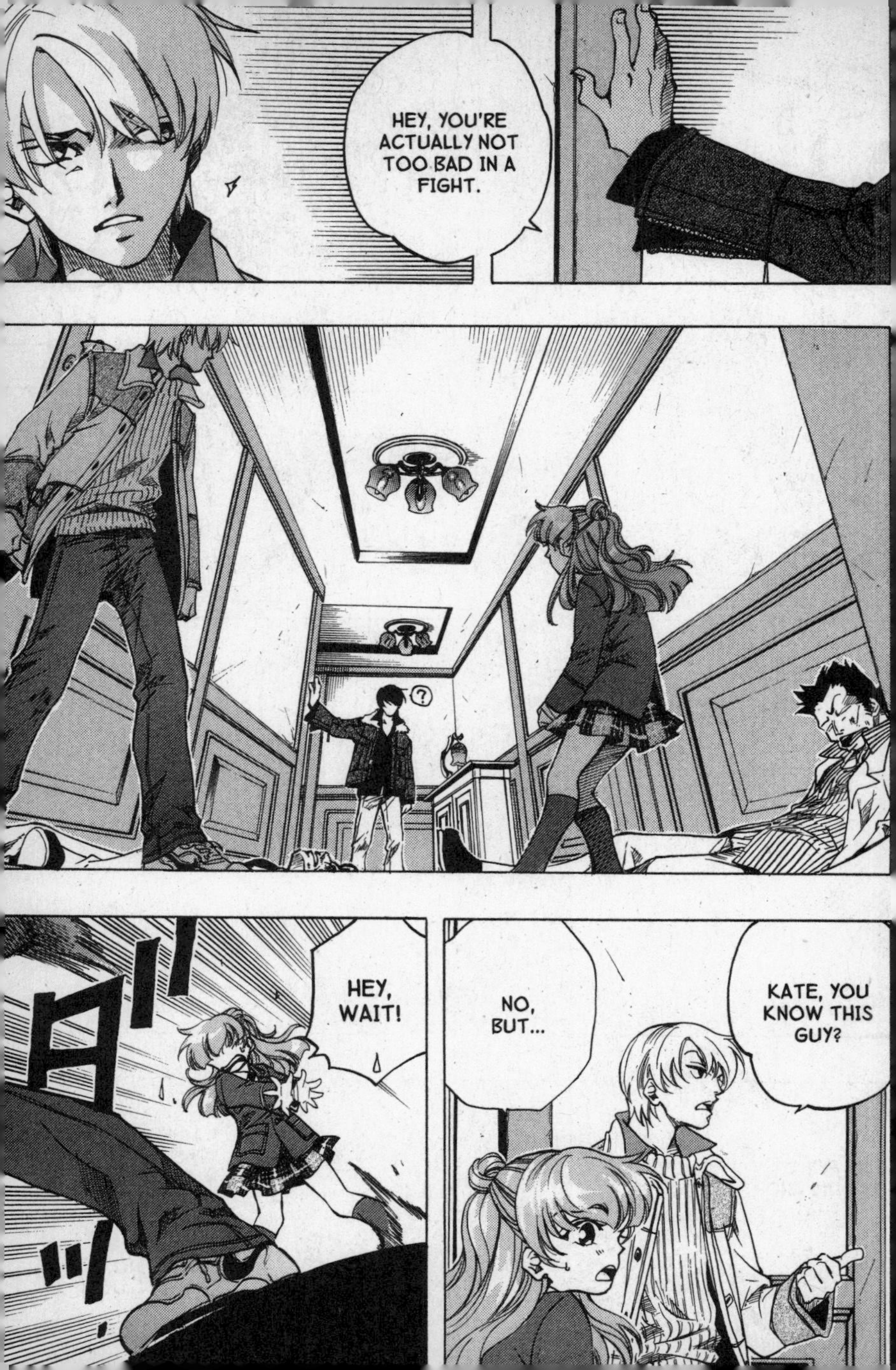
HEY, YOU'RE ACTUALLY NOT TOO BAD IN A FIGHT.
?
KATE, YOU KNOW THIS GUY?
NO, BUT...
HEY, WAIT!

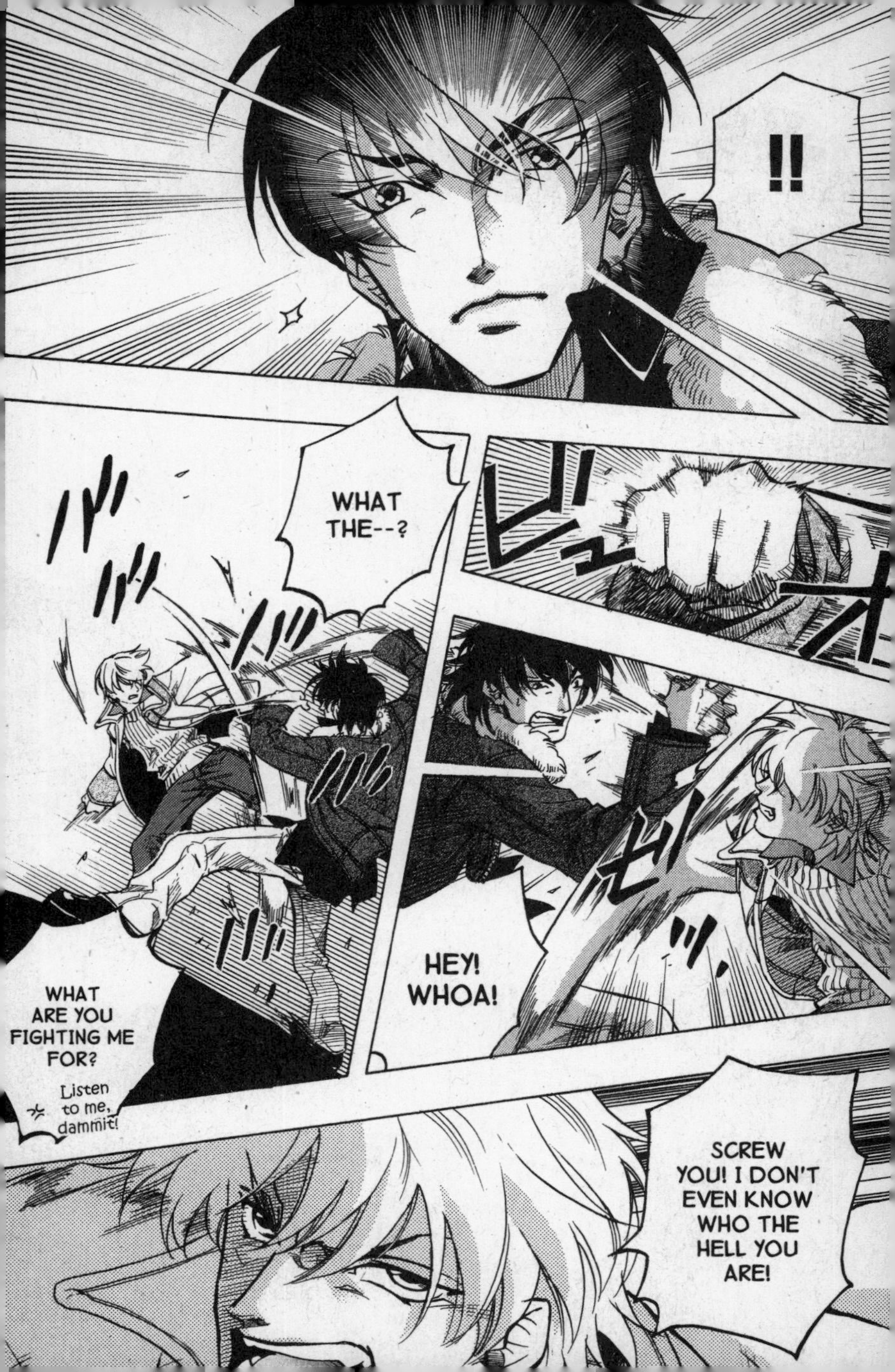
!!
HEY! WHOA!
WHAT THE--?
WHAT ARE YOU FIGHTING ME FOR?
Listen to me, dammit!
SCREW YOU! I DON'T EVEN KNOW WHO THE HELL YOU ARE!

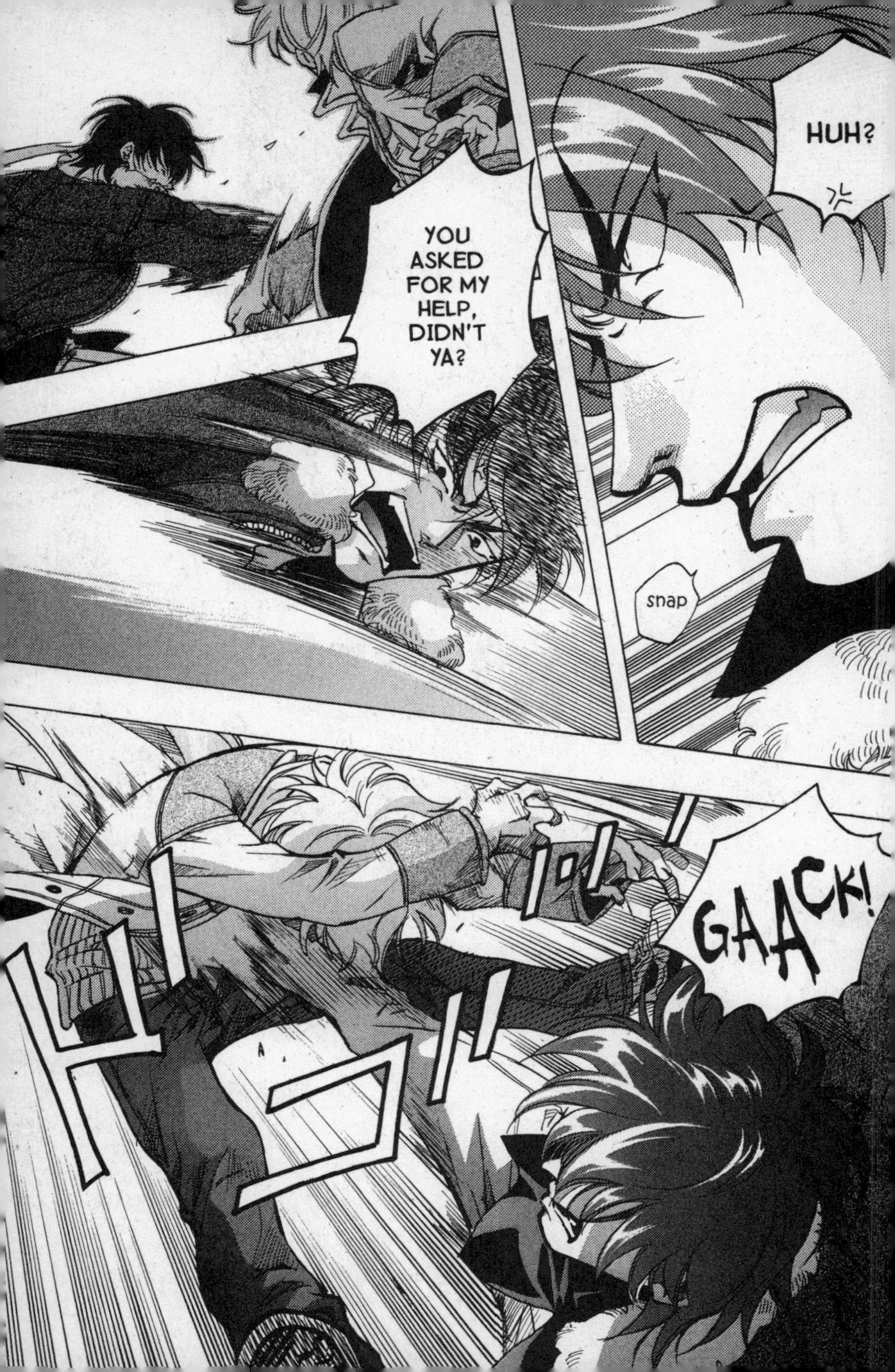
HUH?
snap
YOU ASKED FOR MY HELP, DIDN'T YA?
GAACK!

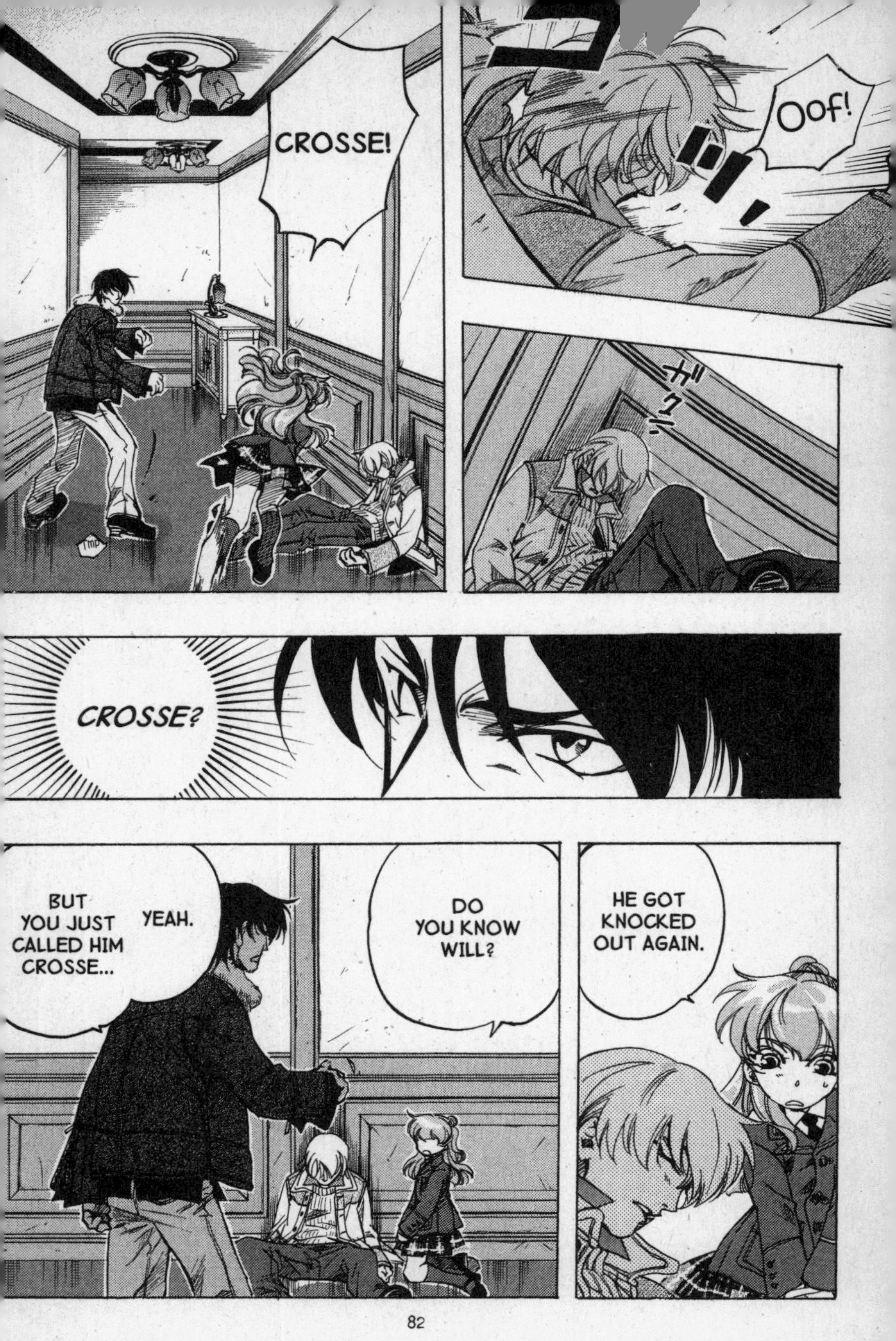
Oof!
CROSSE!
CROSSE?
HE GOT KNOCKED OUT AGAIN.
DO YOU KNOW WILL?
YEAH.
BUT YOU JUST CALLED HIM CROSSE...

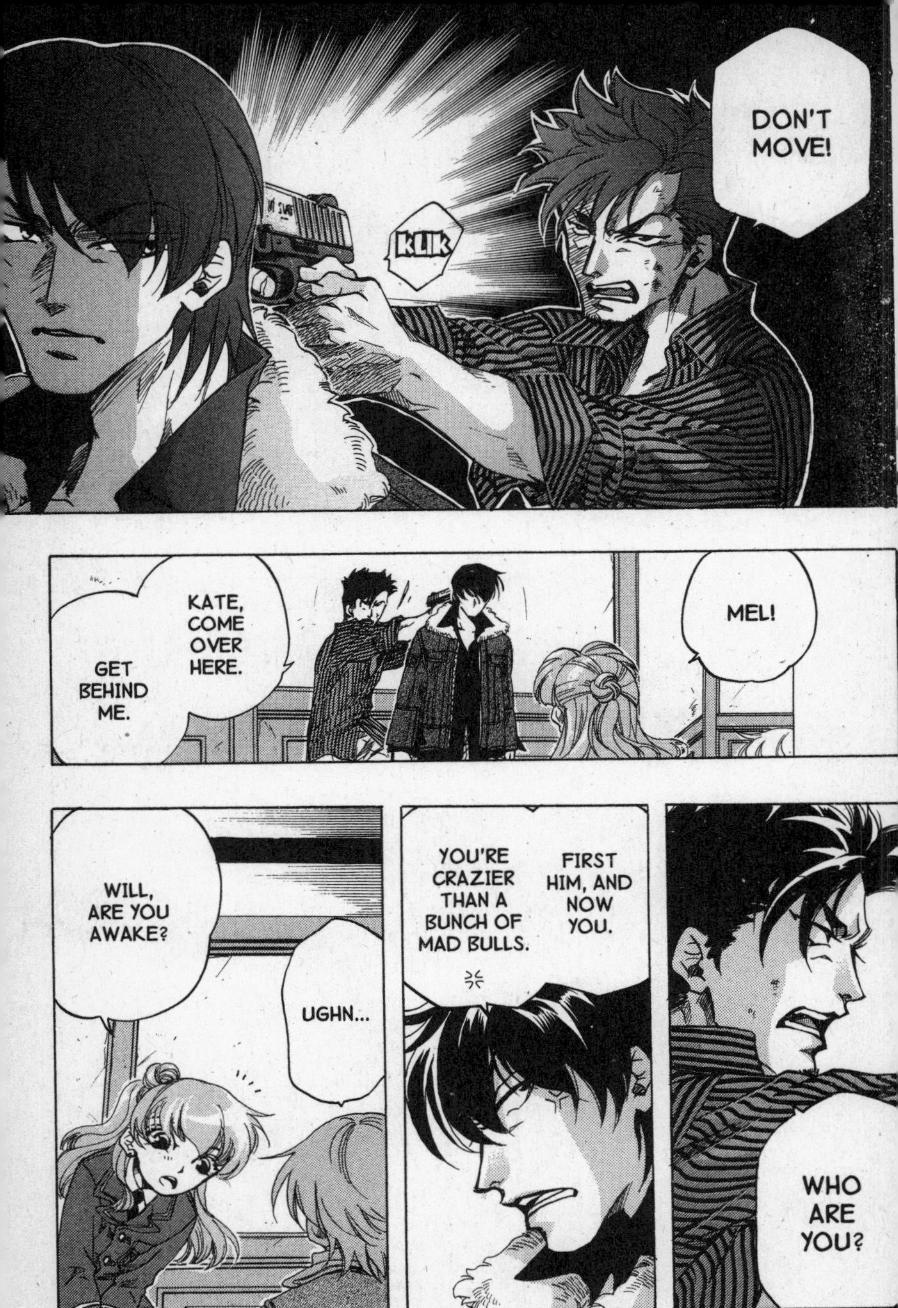
DON'T MOVE!
KLIK
MEL!
KATE, COME OVER HERE.
GET BEHIND ME.
WHO ARE YOU?
FIRST HIM, AND NOW YOU.
YOU'RE CRAZIER THAN A BUNCH OF MAD BULLS.
WILL, ARE YOU AWAKE?
UGHN...

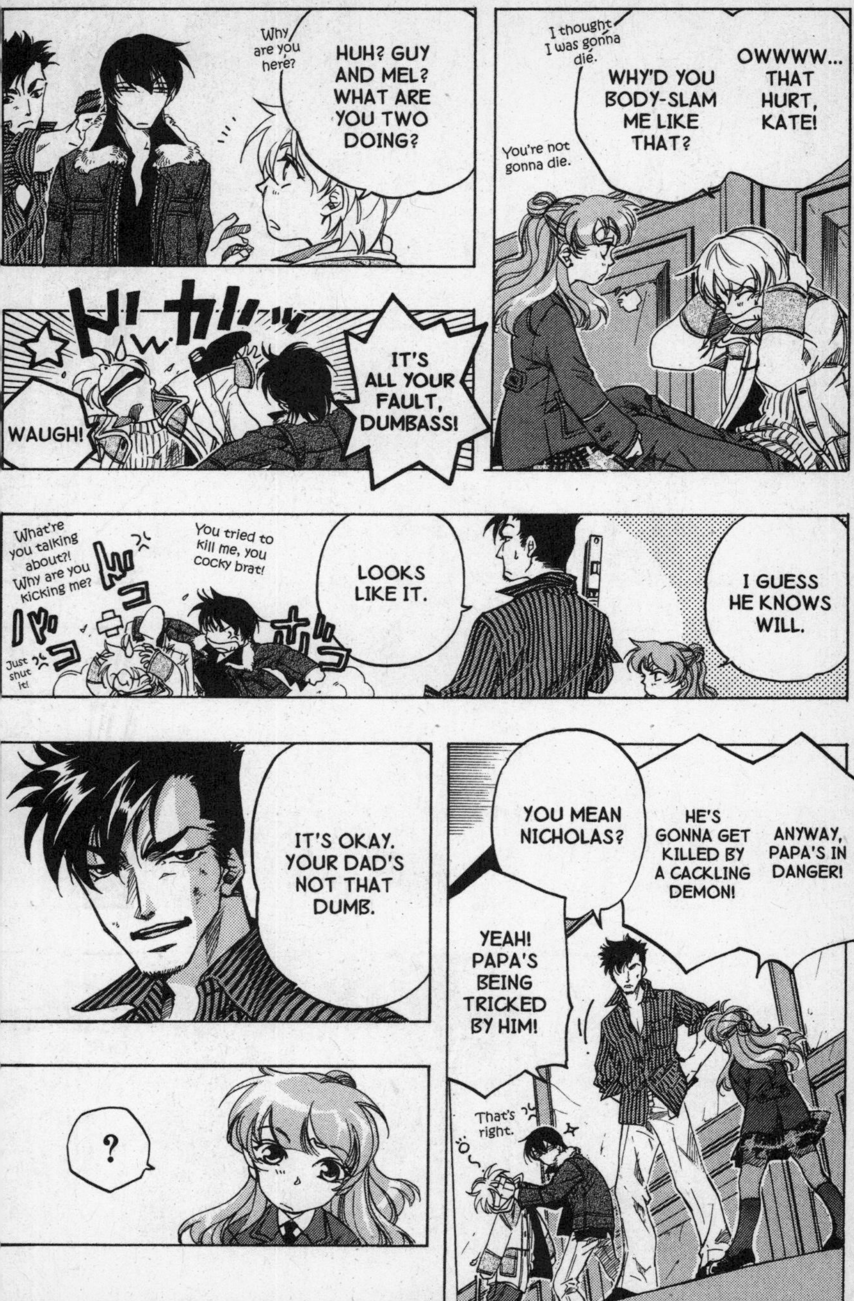
OWWWW... THAT HURT, KATE!
WHY'D YOU BODY-SLAM ME LIKE THAT?
I thought I was gonna die.
You're not gonna die.
HUH? GUY AND MEL? WHAT ARE YOU TWO DOING?
Why are you here?
IT'S ALL YOUR FAULT, DUMBASS!
WAUGH!
I GUESS HE KNOWS WILL.
LOOKS LIKE IT.
You tried to kill me, you cocky brat!
What're you talking about?! Why are you kicking me?
Just shut it!
ANYWAY, PAPA'S IN DANGER!
HE'S GONNA GET KILLED BY A CACKLING DEMON!
YOU MEAN NICHOLAS?
YEAH! PAPA'S BEING TRICKED BY HIM!
That's right.
IT'S OKAY. YOUR DAD'S NOT THAT DUMB.
?

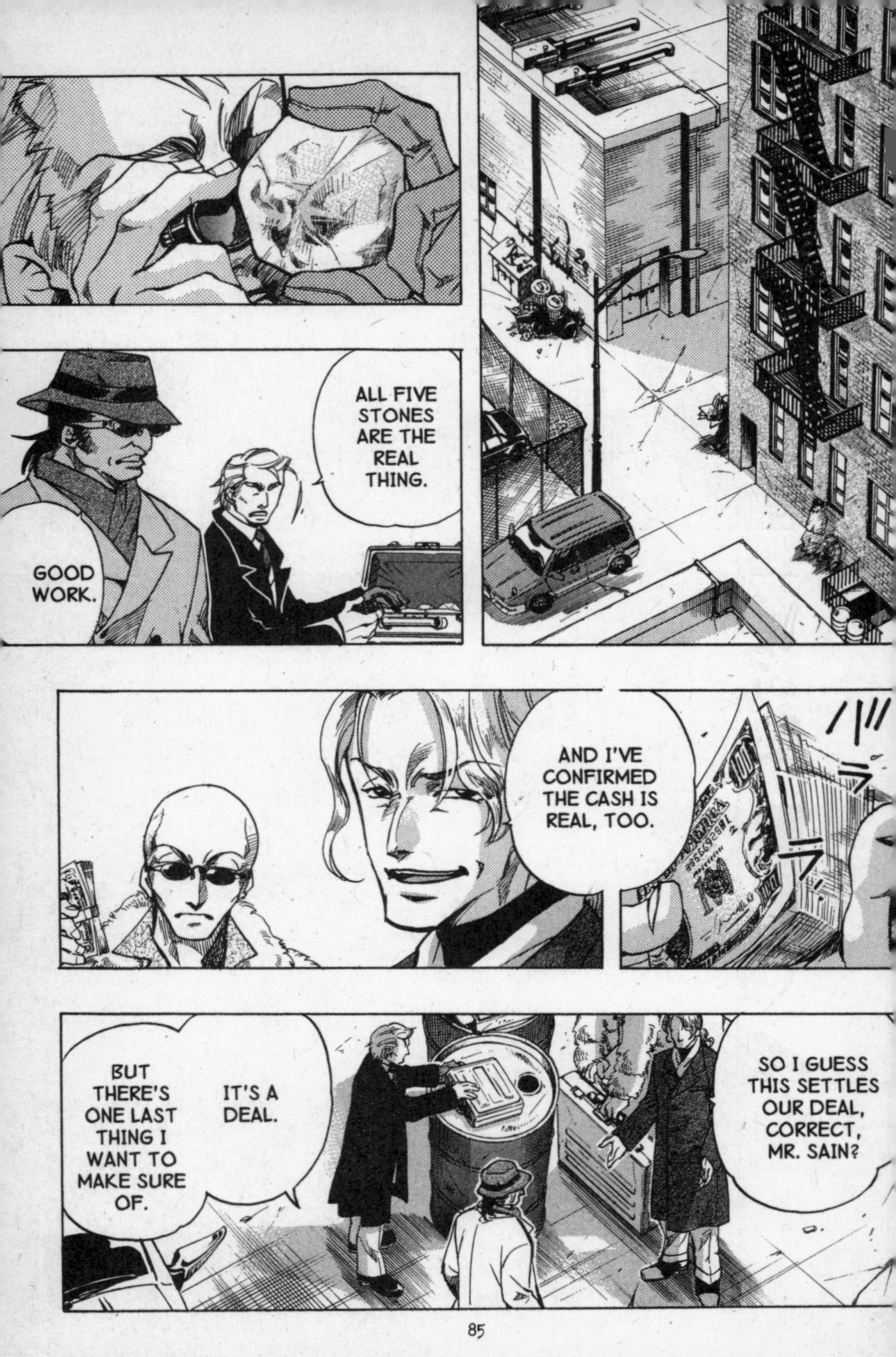
ALL FIVE STONES ARE THE REAL THING.
GOOD WORK.
AND I'VE CONFIRMED THE CASH IS REAL, TOO.
SO I GUESS THIS SETTLES OUR DEAL, CORRECT, MR. SAIN?
IT'S A DEAL.
BUT THERE'S ONE LAST THING I WANT TO MAKE SURE OF.

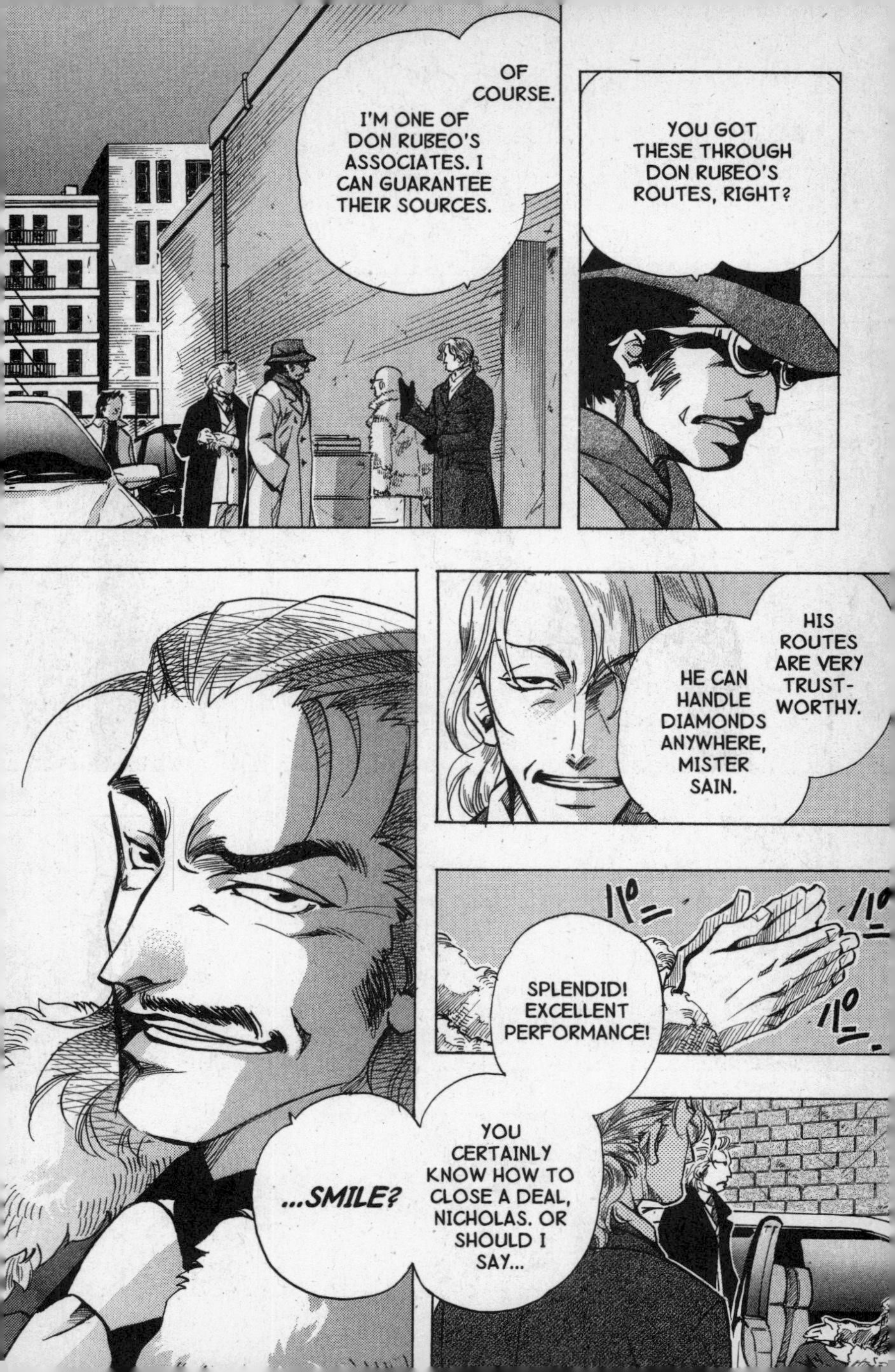
YOU GOT THESE THROUGH DON RUBEO'S ROUTES, RIGHT?
OF COURSE.
I'M ONE OF DON RUBEO'S ASSOCIATES. I CAN GUARANTEE THEIR SOURCES.
HIS ROUTES ARE VERY TRUST-WORTHY.
HE CAN HANDLE DIAMONDS ANYWHERE, MISTER SAIN.
SPLENDID! EXCELLENT PERFORMANCE!
YOU CERTAINLY KNOW HOW TO CLOSE A DEAL, NICHOLAS. OR SHOULD I SAY...
...SMILE?

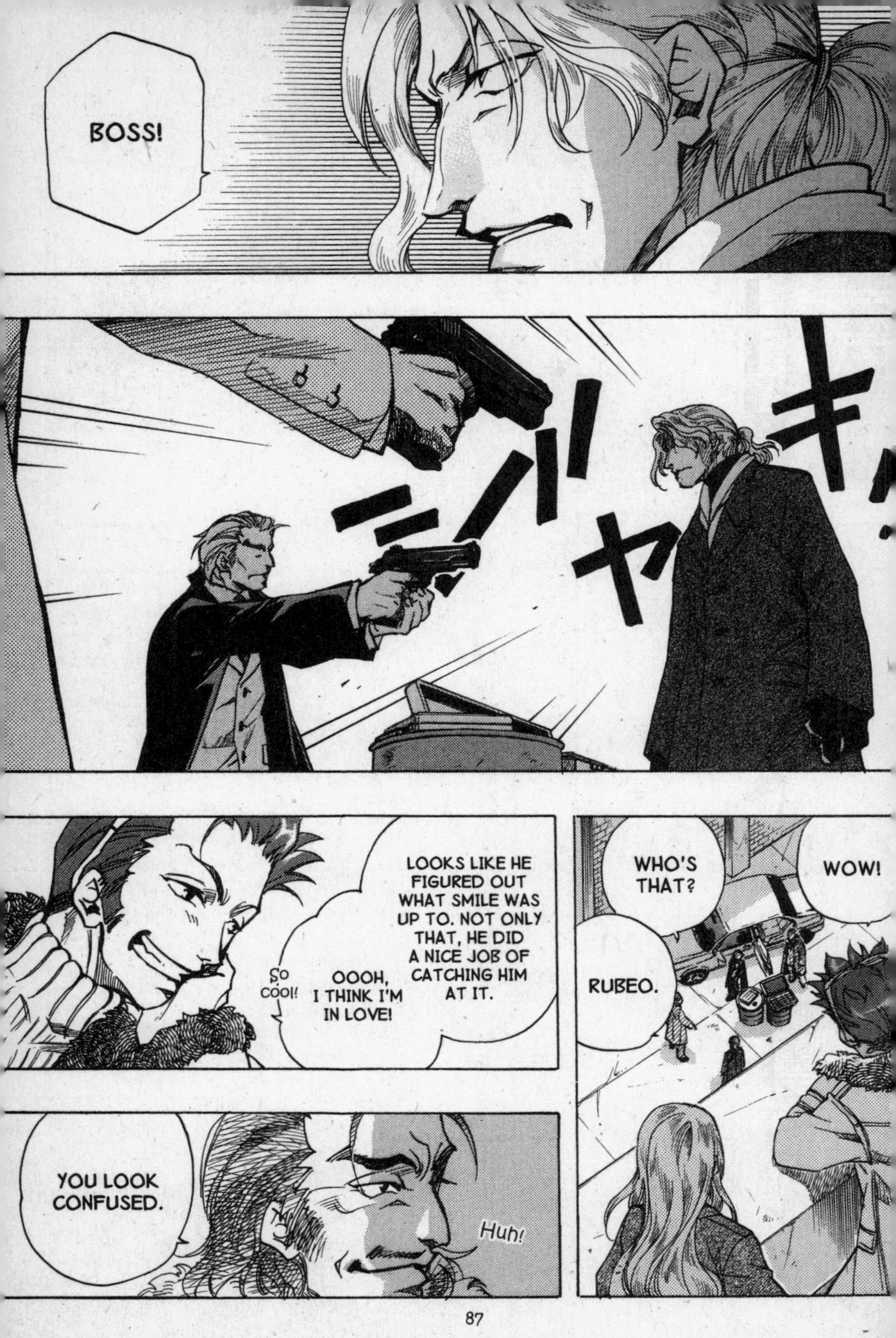
BOSS!
ジャキ
WOW!
WHO'S THAT?
RUBEO.
LOOKS LIKE HE FIGURED OUT WHAT SMILE WAS UP TO. NOT ONLY THAT, HE DID A NICE JOB OF CATCHING HIM AT IT.
OOOH, I THINK I'M IN LOVE!
So cool!
YOU LOOK CONFUSED.
Huh!

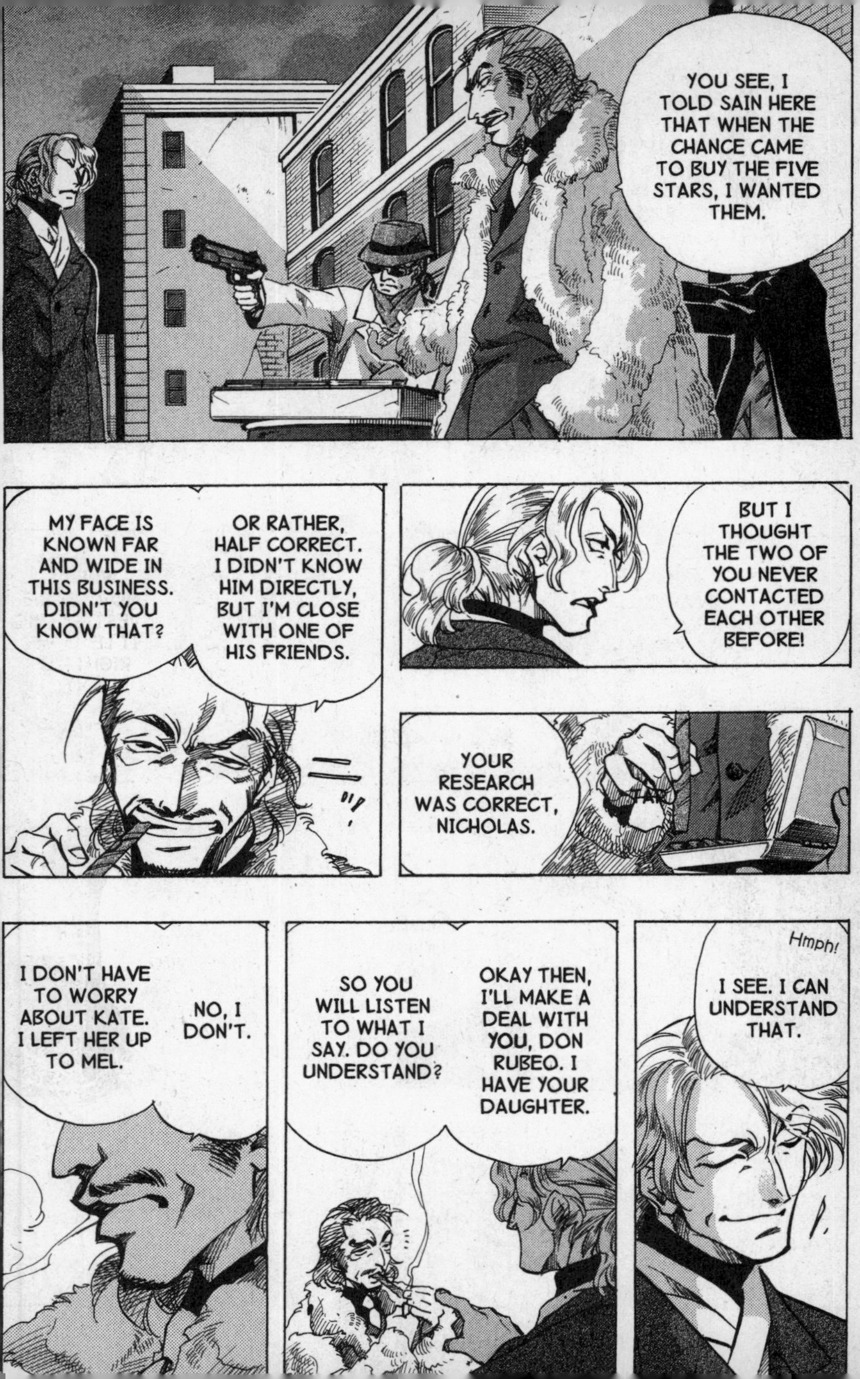
YOU SEE, I TOLD SAIN HERE THAT WHEN THE CHANCE CAME TO BUY THE FIVE STARS, I WANTED THEM.
BUT I THOUGHT THE TWO OF YOU NEVER CONTACTED EACH OTHER BEFORE!
YOUR RESEARCH WAS CORRECT, NICHOLAS.
OR RATHER, HALF CORRECT. I DIDN'T KNOW HIM DIRECTLY, BUT I'M CLOSE WITH ONE OF HIS FRIENDS.
MY FACE IS KNOWN FAR AND WIDE IN THIS BUSINESS. DIDN'T YOU KNOW THAT?
Hmph!
I SEE. I CAN UNDERSTAND THAT.
OKAY THEN, I'LL MAKE A DEAL WITH YOU, DON RUBEO. I HAVE YOUR DAUGHTER.
SO YOU WILL LISTEN TO WHAT I SAY. DO YOU UNDERSTAND?
NO, I DON'T.
I DON'T HAVE TO WORRY ABOUT KATE. I LEFT HER UP TO MEL.

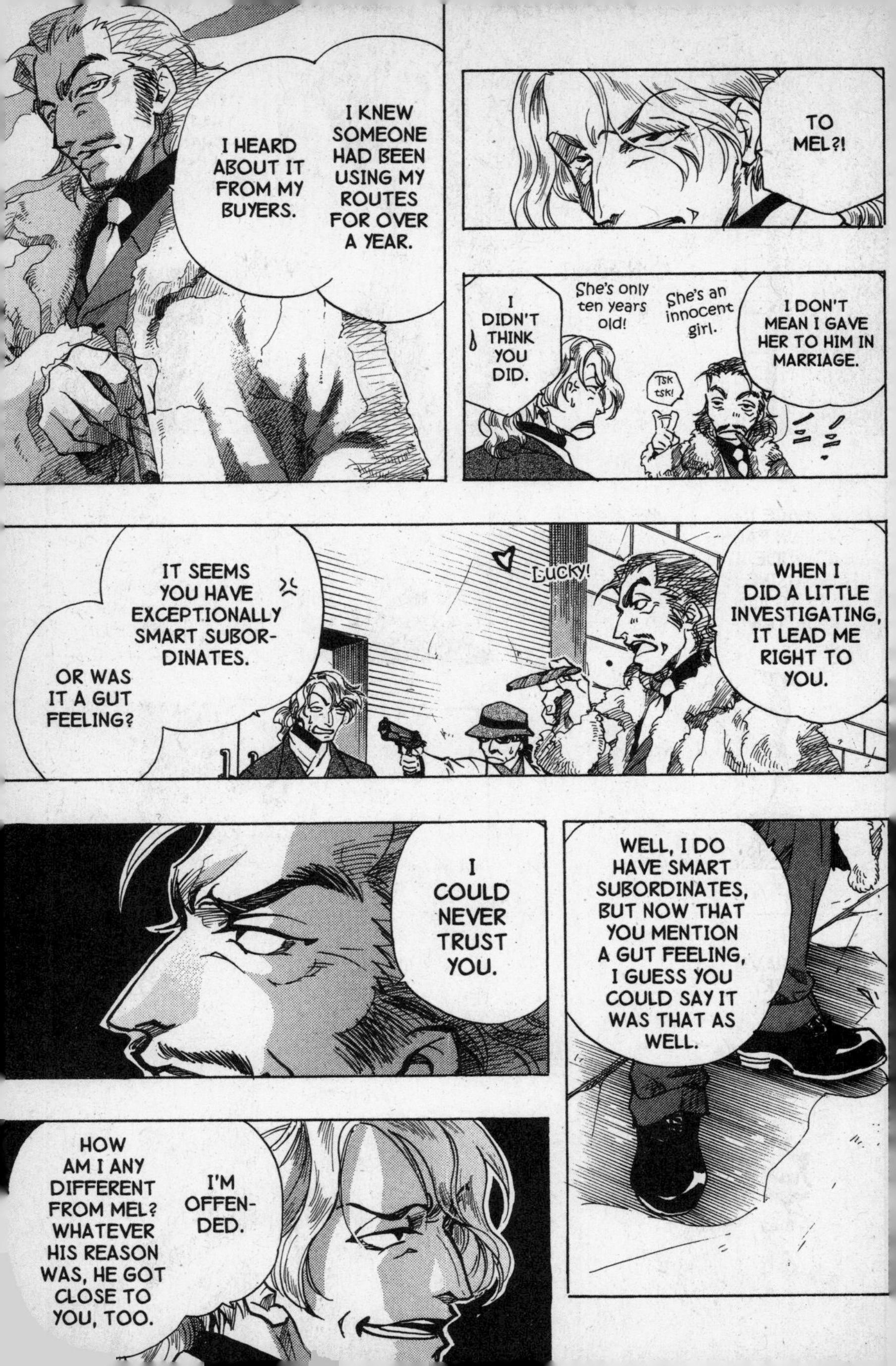
TO MEL?!
I DON'T MEAN I GAVE HER TO HIM IN MARRIAGE.
She's an innocent girl.
TSK tsk!
She's only ten years old!
I DIDN'T THINK YOU DID.
I KNEW SOMEONE HAD BEEN USING MY ROUTES FOR OVER A YEAR.
I HEARD ABOUT IT FROM MY BUYERS.
WHEN I DID A LITTLE INVESTIGATING, IT LEAD ME RIGHT TO YOU.
Lucky!
IT SEEMS YOU HAVE EXCEPTIONALLY SMART SUBOR-DINATES.
OR WAS IT A GUT FEELING?
WELL, I DO HAVE SMART SUBORDINATES, BUT NOW THAT YOU MENTION A GUT FEELING, I GUESS YOU COULD SAY IT WAS THAT AS WELL.
I COULD NEVER TRUST YOU.
I'M OFFEN-DED.
HOW AM I ANY DIFFERENT FROM MEL? WHATEVER HIS REASON WAS, HE GOT CLOSE TO YOU, TOO.

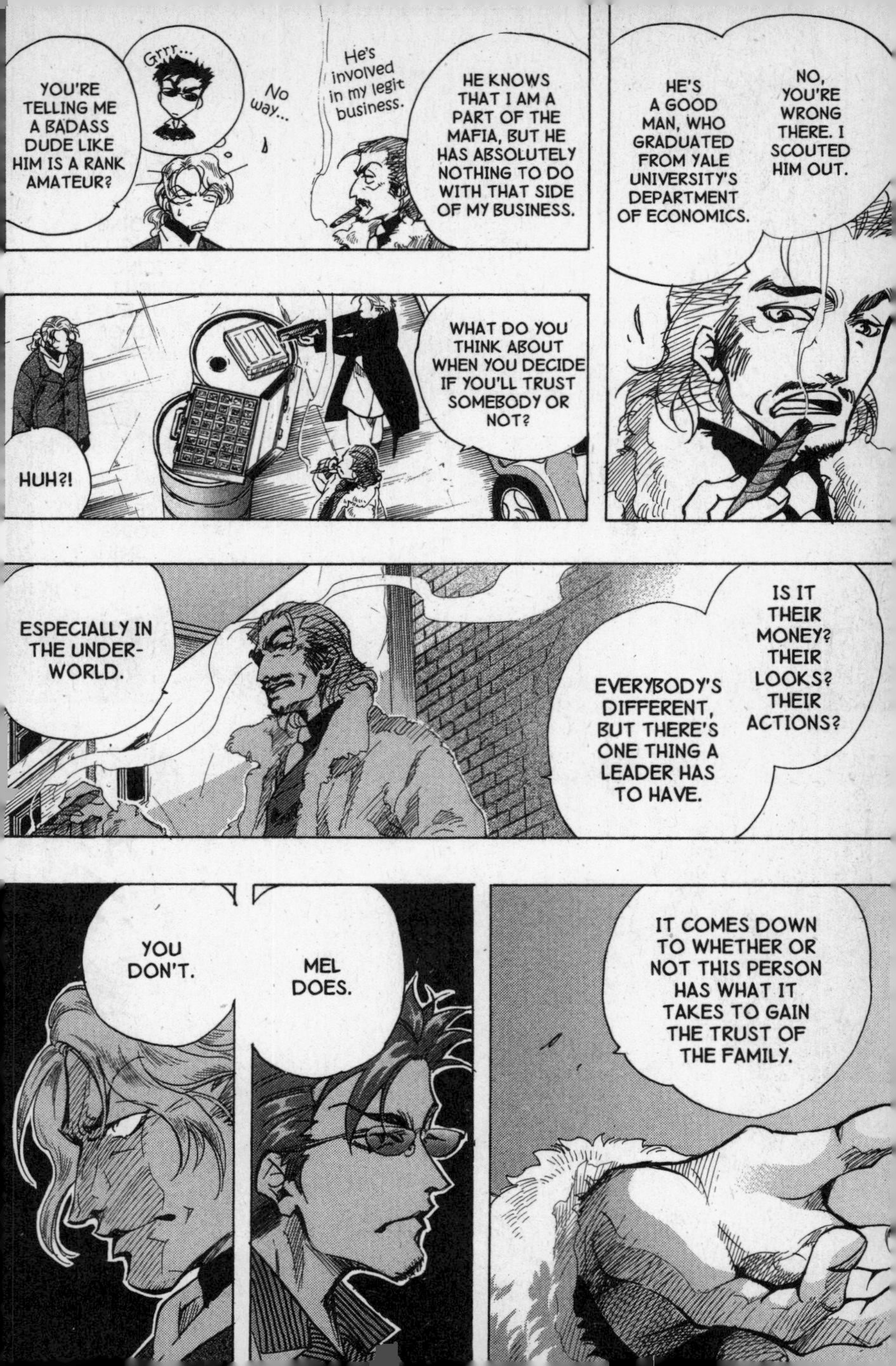
NO, YOU'RE WRONG THERE. I SCOUTED HIM OUT.
HE'S A GOOD MAN, WHO GRADUATED FROM YALE UNIVERSITY'S DEPARTMENT OF ECONOMICS.
HE KNOWS THAT I AM A PART OF THE MAFIA, BUT HE HAS ABSOLUTELY NOTHING TO DO WITH THAT SIDE OF MY BUSINESS.
He's involved in my legit business.
No way...
Grrr...
YOU'RE TELLING ME A BADASS DUDE LIKE HIM IS A RANK AMATEUR?
WHAT DO YOU THINK ABOUT WHEN YOU DECIDE IF YOU'LL TRUST SOMEBODY OR NOT?
HUH?!
IS IT THEIR MONEY? THEIR LOOKS? THEIR ACTIONS?
EVERYBODY'S DIFFERENT, BUT THERE'S ONE THING A LEADER HAS TO HAVE.
ESPECIALLY IN THE UNDER-WORLD.
IT COMES DOWN TO WHETHER OR NOT THIS PERSON HAS WHAT IT TAKES TO GAIN THE TRUST OF THE FAMILY.
MEL DOES.
YOU DON'T.

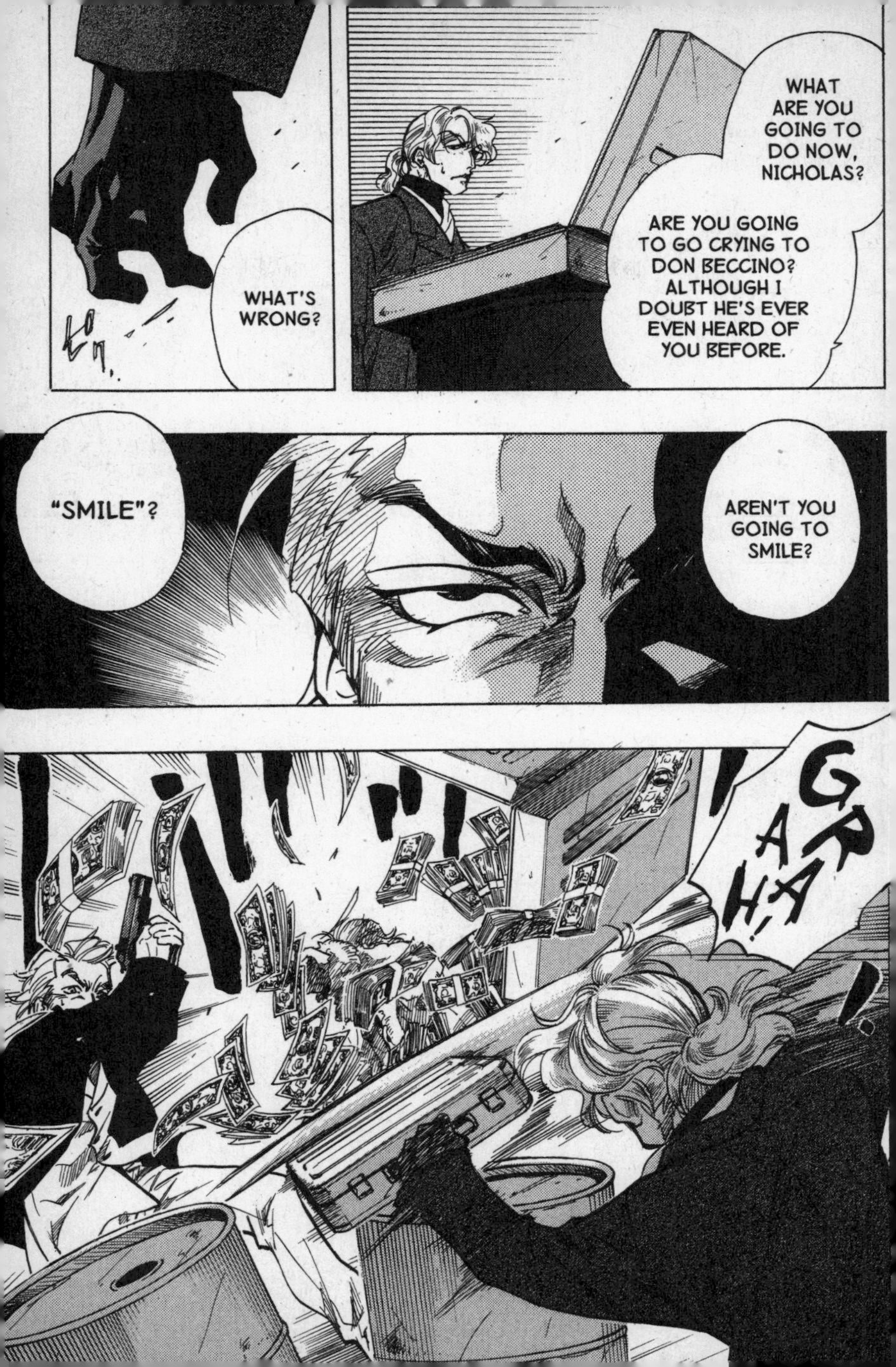
WHAT ARE YOU GOING TO DO NOW, NICHOLAS?
ARE YOU GOING TO GO CRYING TO DON BECCINO? ALTHOUGH I DOUBT HE'S EVER EVEN HEARD OF YOU BEFORE.
WHAT'S WRONG?
AREN'T YOU GOING TO SMILE?
"SMILE"?
GRAAH!

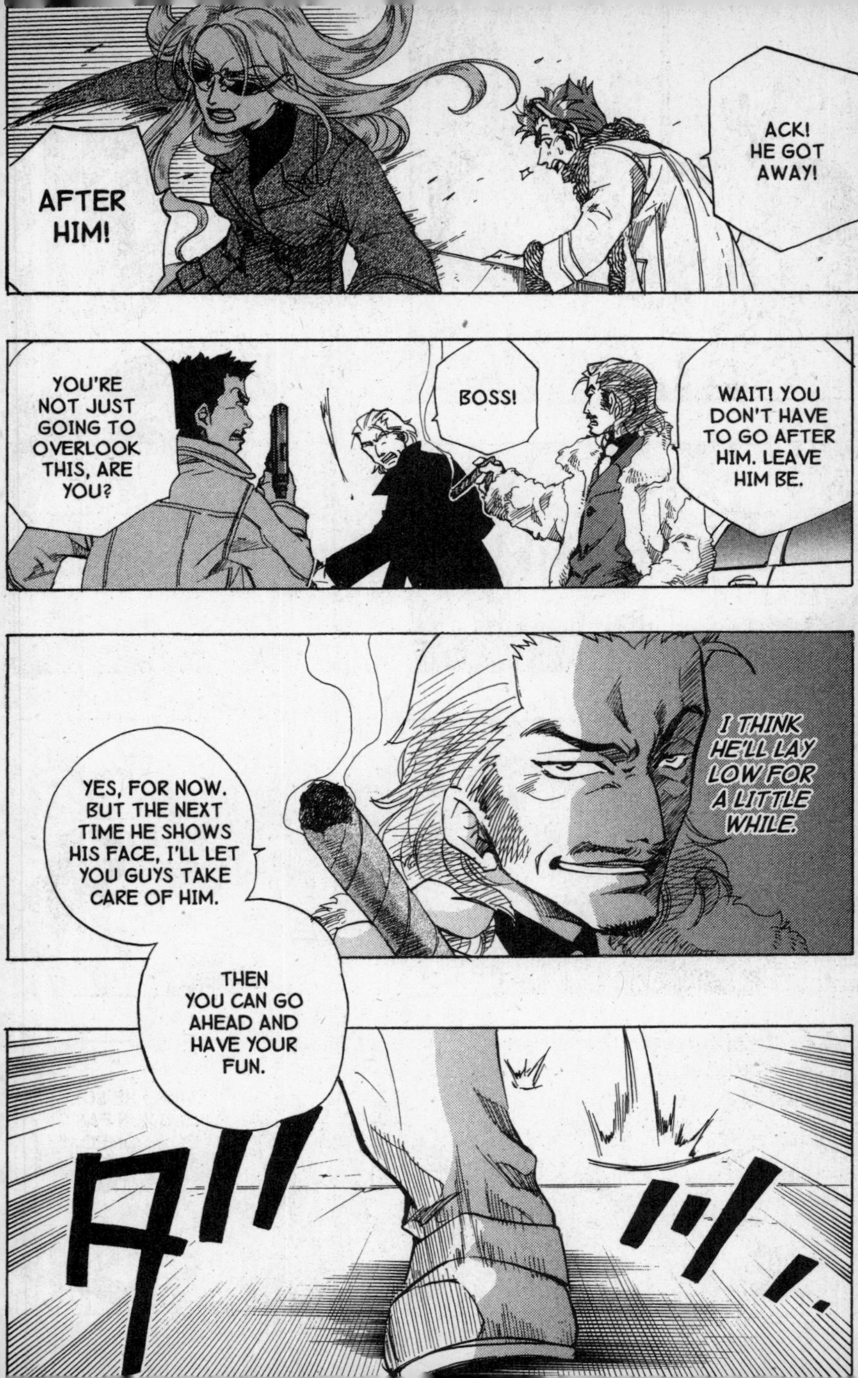
ACK! HE GOT AWAY!
AFTER HIM!
WAIT! YOU DON'T HAVE TO GO AFTER HIM. LEAVE HIM BE.
BOSS!
YOU'RE NOT JUST GOING TO OVERLOOK THIS, ARE YOU?
I THINK HE'LL LAY LOW FOR A LITTLE WHILE.
YES, FOR NOW. BUT THE NEXT TIME HE SHOWS HIS FACE, I'LL LET YOU GUYS TAKE CARE OF HIM.
THEN YOU CAN GO AHEAD AND HAVE YOUR FUN.
ダッ!

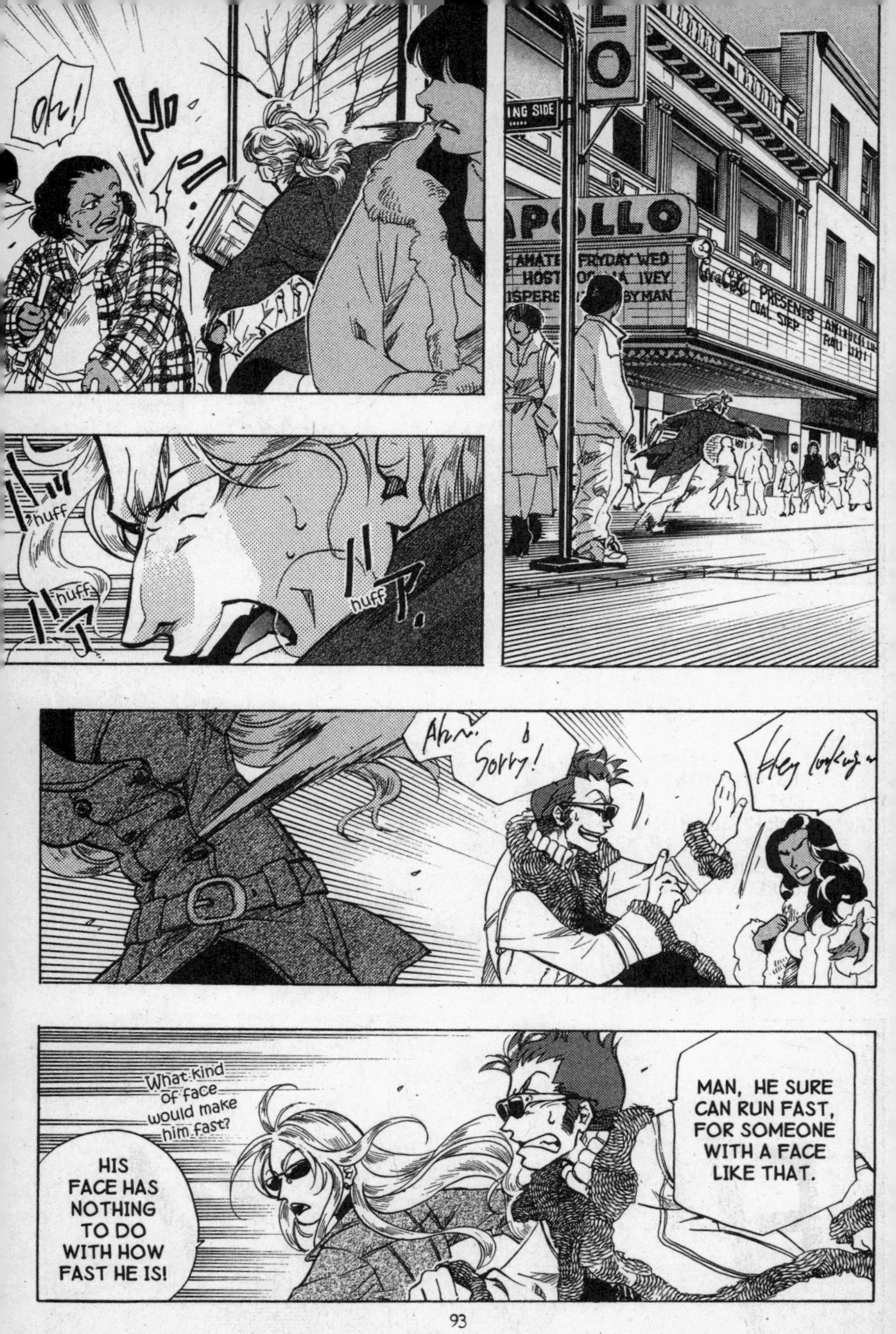
APOLLO
PRESENTS
Oh!
huff
huff
huff
Ah… Sorry!
MAN, HE SURE CAN RUN FAST, FOR SOMEONE WITH A FACE LIKE THAT.
What kind of face would make him fast?
HIS FACE HAS NOTHING TO DO WITH HOW FAST HE IS!

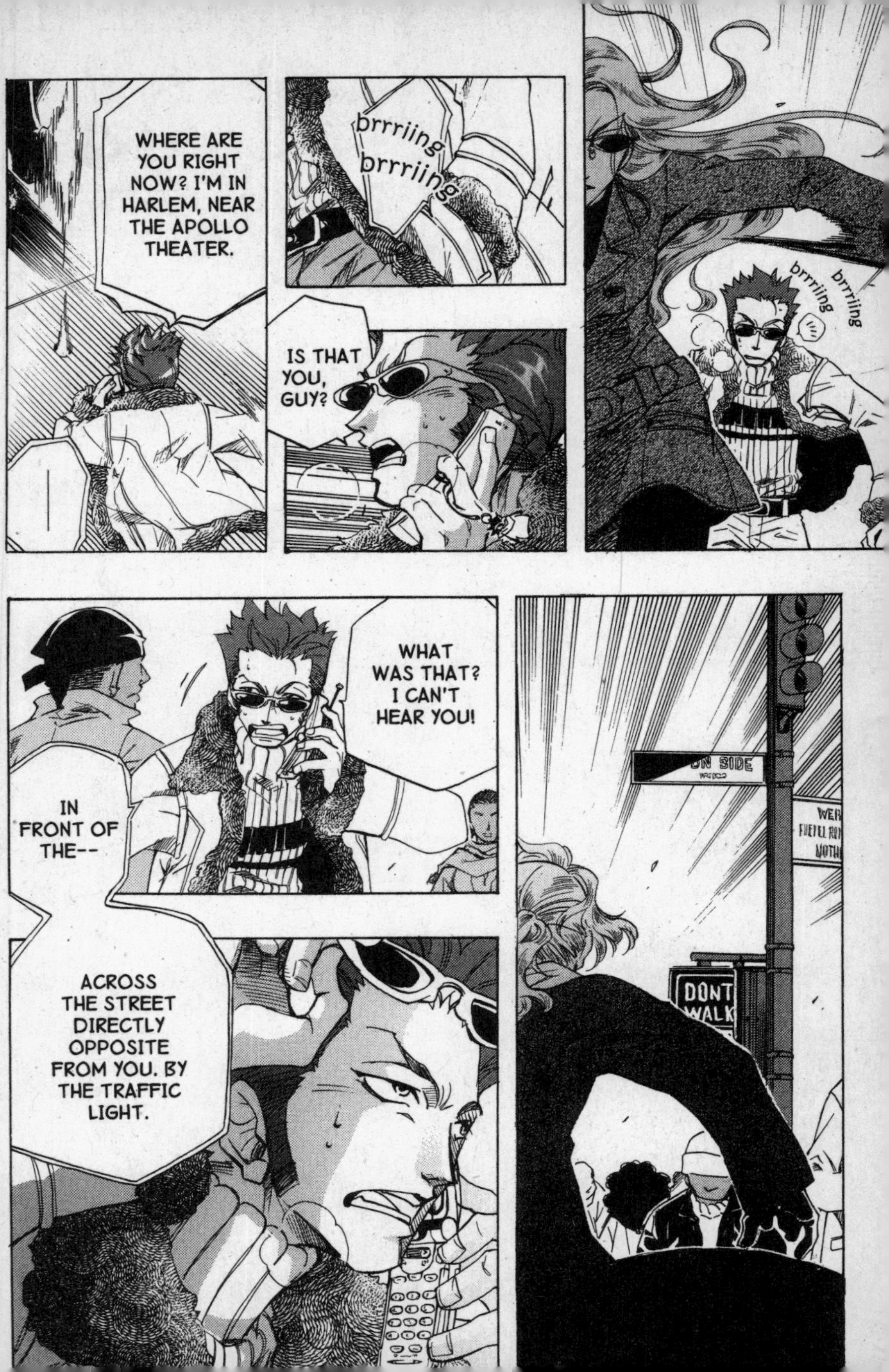
brrriing brrriing
brrriing brrriing
IS THAT YOU, GUY?
WHERE ARE YOU RIGHT NOW? I'M IN HARLEM, NEAR THE APOLLO THEATER.
ON SIDE
DONT WALK
WHAT WAS THAT? I CAN'T HEAR YOU!
IN FRONT OF THE--
ACROSS THE STREET DIRECTLY OPPOSITE FROM YOU. BY THE TRAFFIC LIGHT.

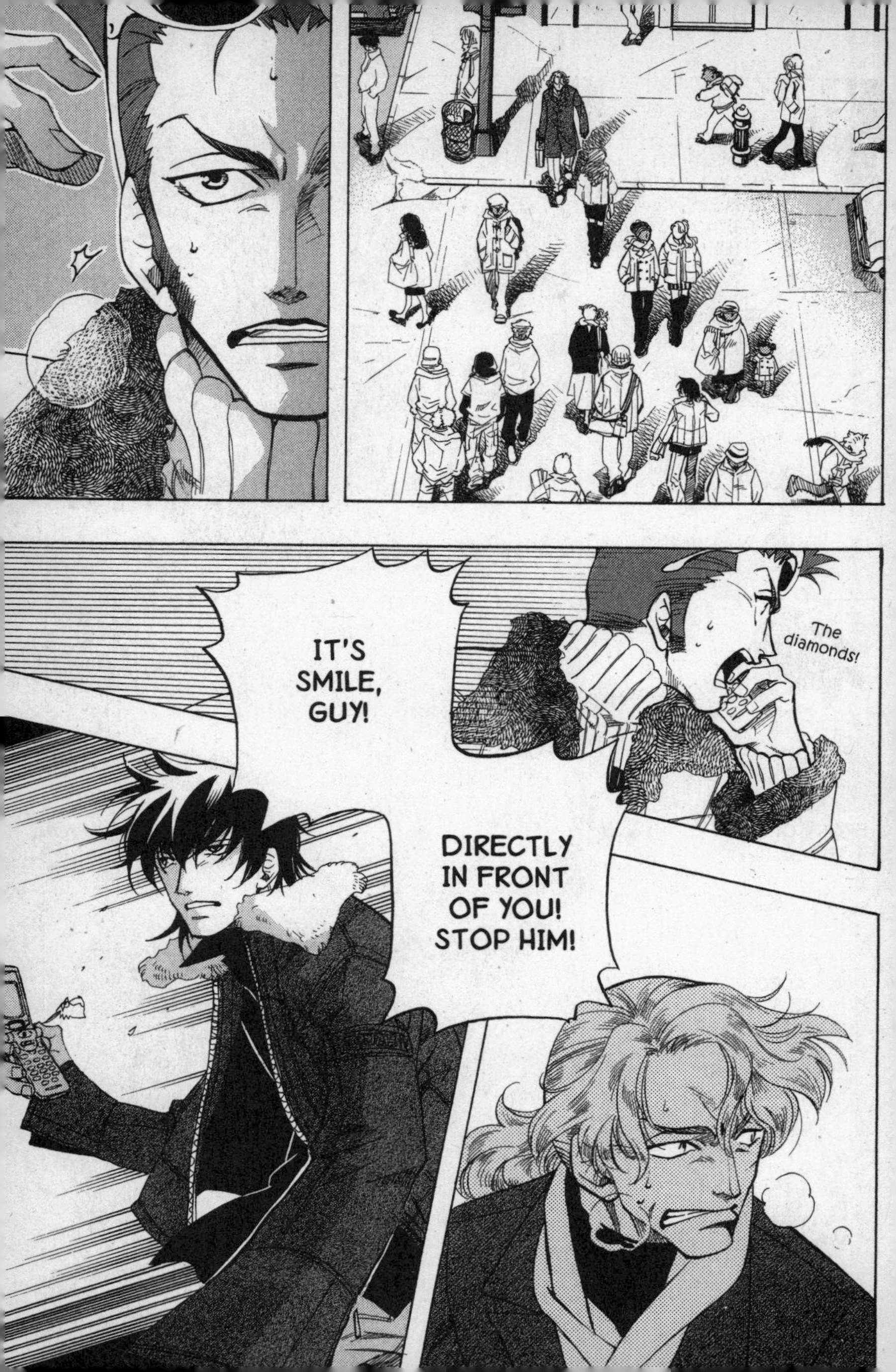
The diamonds!
IT'S SMILE, GUY!
DIRECTLY IN FRONT OF YOU! STOP HIM!

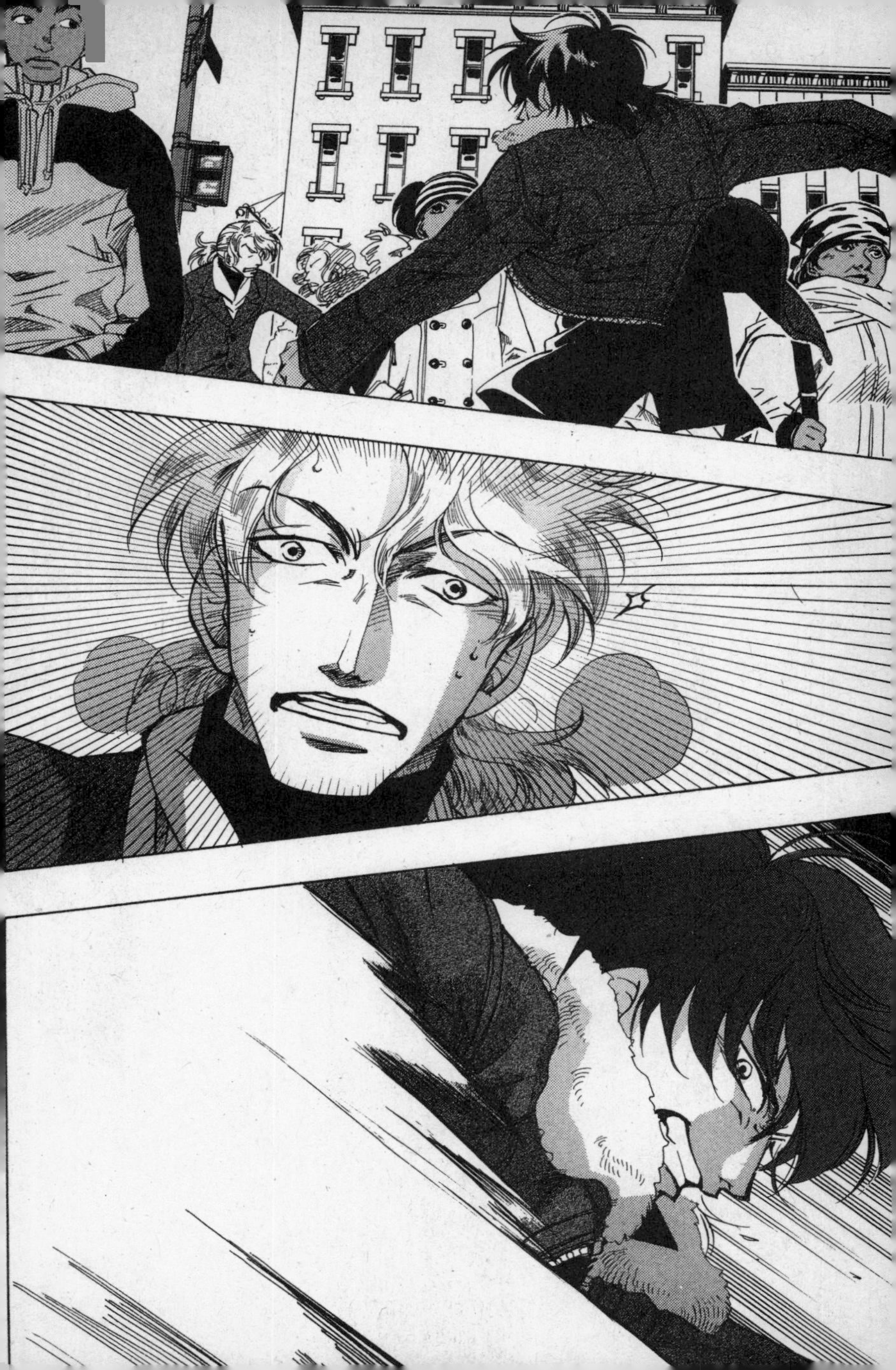

WELL, I DID SAY TO STOP HIM...

klunk

GAACK!

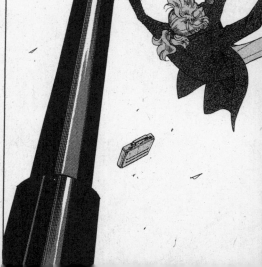

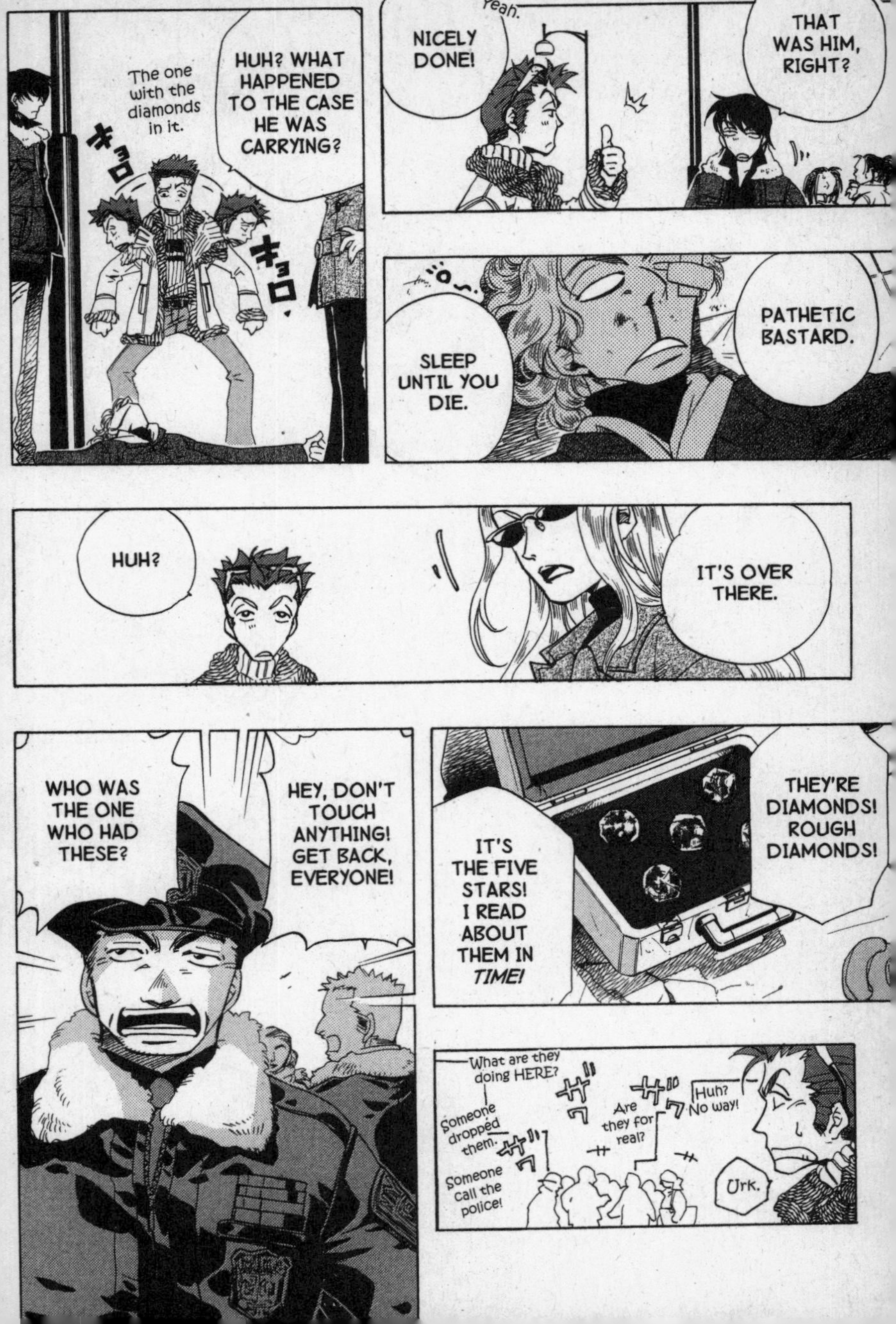
Yo!
THAT WAS HIM, RIGHT?
Yeah.
NICELY DONE!
PATHETIC BASTARD.
SLEEP UNTIL YOU DIE.
HUH? WHAT HAPPENED TO THE CASE HE WAS CARRYING?
The one with the diamonds in it.
キョロ
キョロ
IT'S OVER THERE.
HUH?
THEY'RE DIAMONDS! ROUGH DIAMONDS!
IT'S THE FIVE STARS! I READ ABOUT THEM IN *TIME!*
Huh? No way!
Urk.
Are they for real?
What are they doing HERE?
Someone dropped them.
Someone call the police!
HEY, DON'T TOUCH ANYTHING! GET BACK, EVERYONE!
WHO WAS THE ONE WHO HAD THESE?

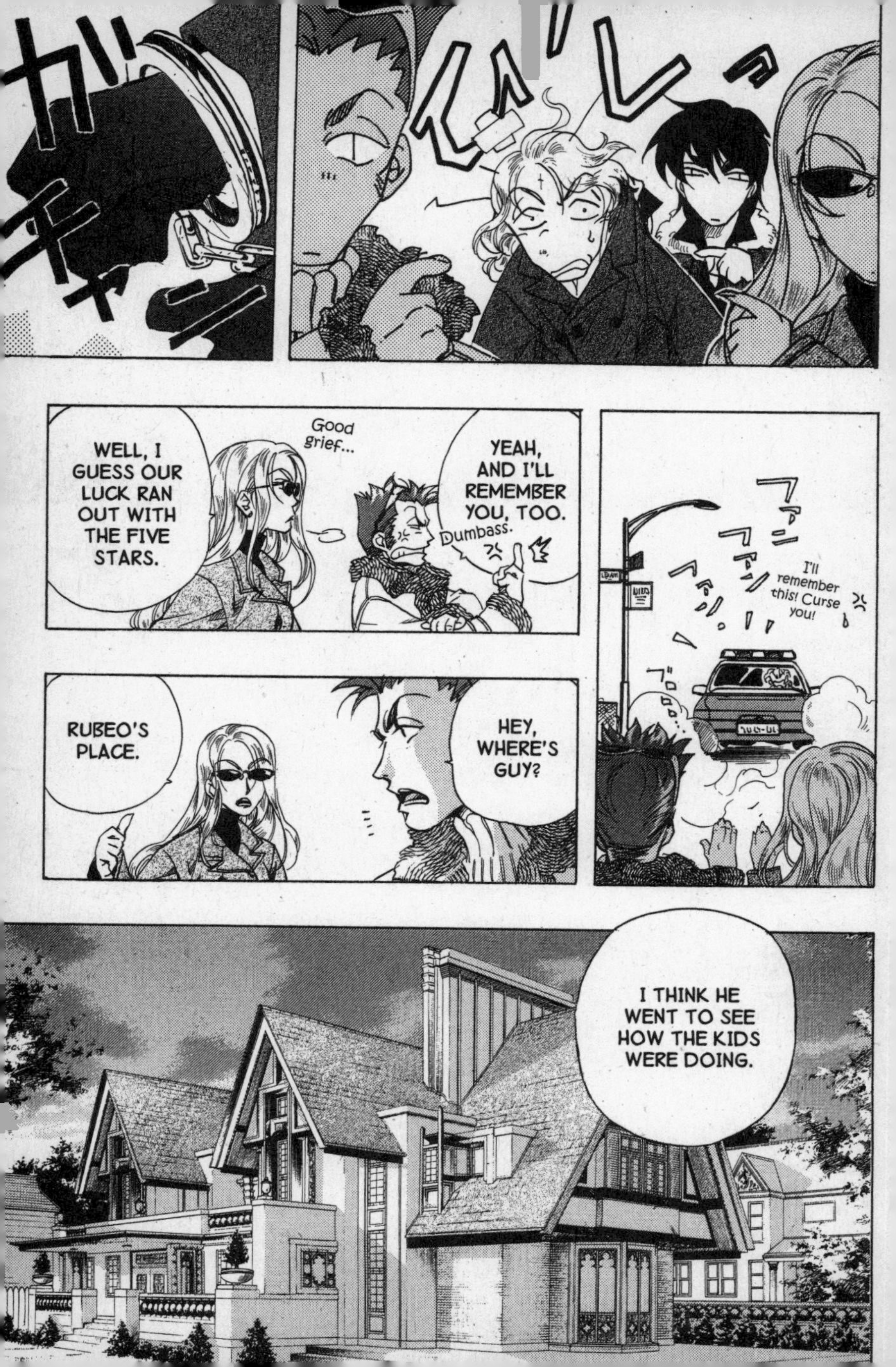
I'll remember this! Curse you!
YEAH, AND I'LL REMEMBER YOU, TOO.
Dumbass.
Good grief...
WELL, I GUESS OUR LUCK RAN OUT WITH THE FIVE STARS.
HEY, WHERE'S GUY?
RUBEO'S PLACE.
I THINK HE WENT TO SEE HOW THE KIDS WERE DOING.

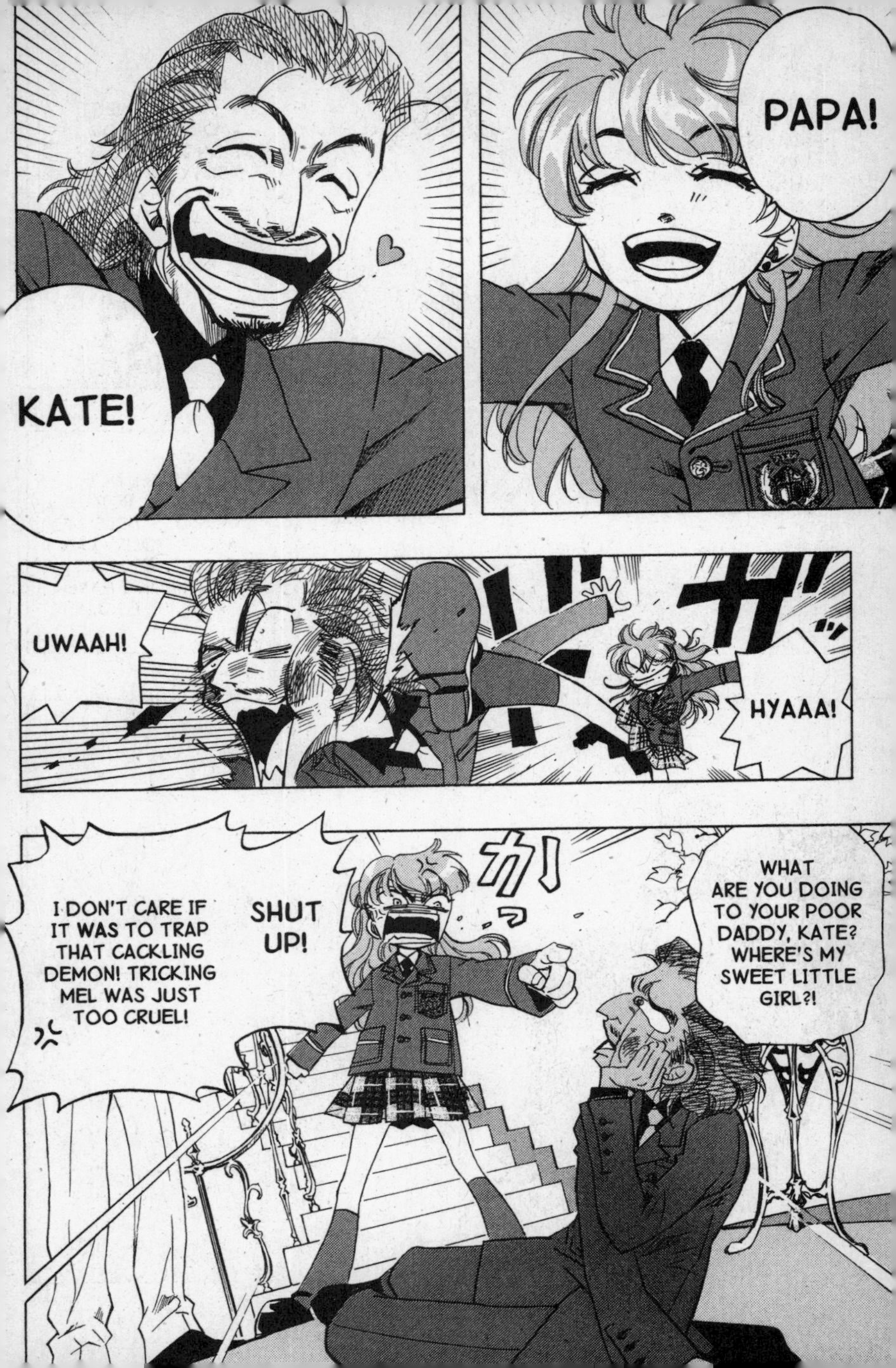
PAPA!
KATE!
ガッ
HYAAA!
UWAAH!
WHAT ARE YOU DOING TO YOUR POOR DADDY, KATE? WHERE'S MY SWEET LITTLE GIRL?!
カッ
SHUT UP!
I DON'T CARE IF IT WAS TO TRAP THAT CACKLING DEMON! TRICKING MEL WAS JUST TOO CRUEL!

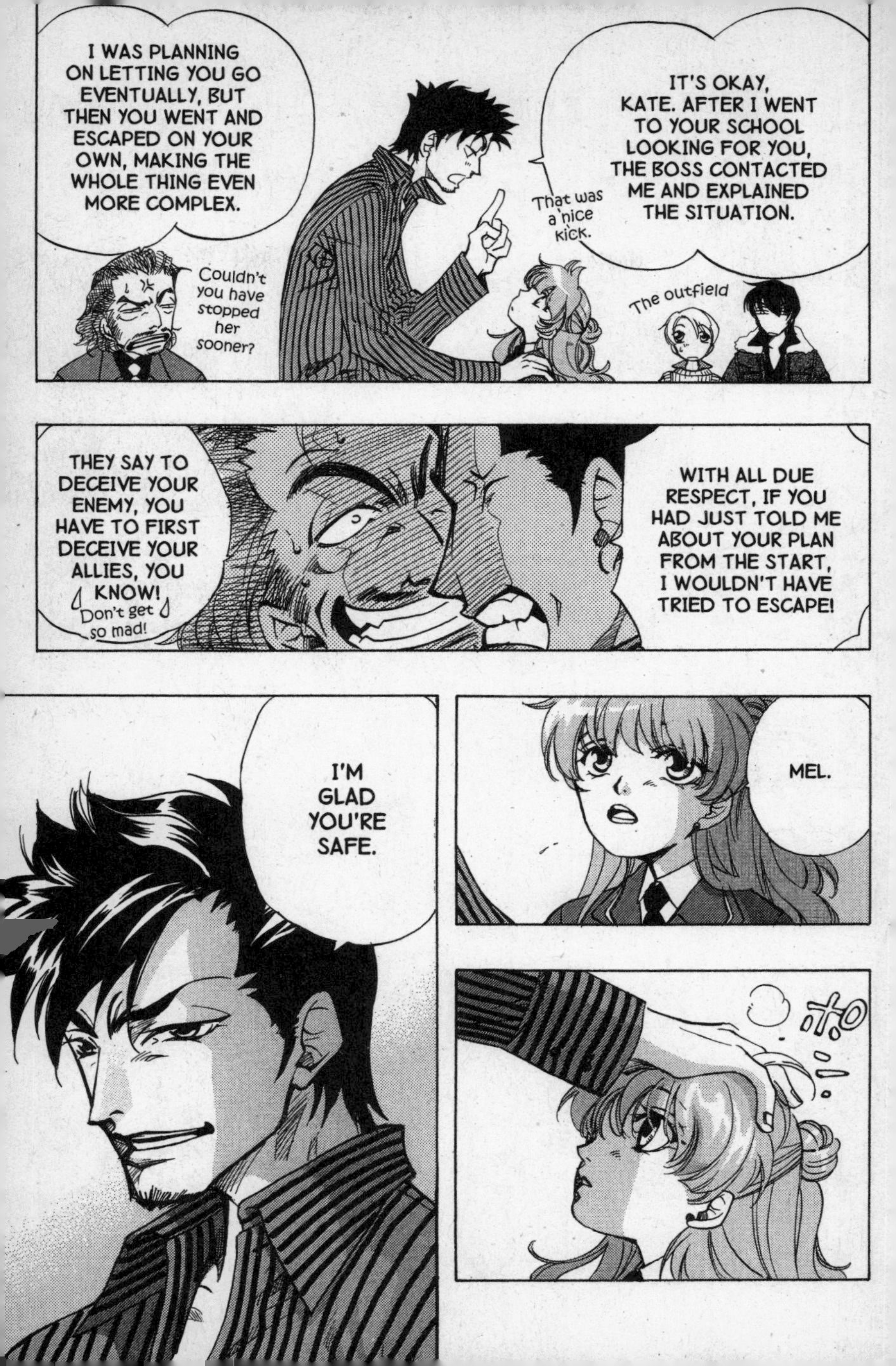
IT'S OKAY, KATE. AFTER I WENT TO YOUR SCHOOL LOOKING FOR YOU, THE BOSS CONTACTED ME AND EXPLAINED THE SITUATION.
That was a nice kick.
The outfield
I WAS PLANNING ON LETTING YOU GO EVENTUALLY, BUT THEN YOU WENT AND ESCAPED ON YOUR OWN, MAKING THE WHOLE THING EVEN MORE COMPLEX.
Couldn't you have stopped her sooner?
WITH ALL DUE RESPECT, IF YOU HAD JUST TOLD ME ABOUT YOUR PLAN FROM THE START, I WOULDN'T HAVE TRIED TO ESCAPE!
THEY SAY TO DECEIVE YOUR ENEMY, YOU HAVE TO FIRST DECEIVE YOUR ALLIES, YOU KNOW!
Don't get so mad!
MEL.
I'M GLAD YOU'RE SAFE.

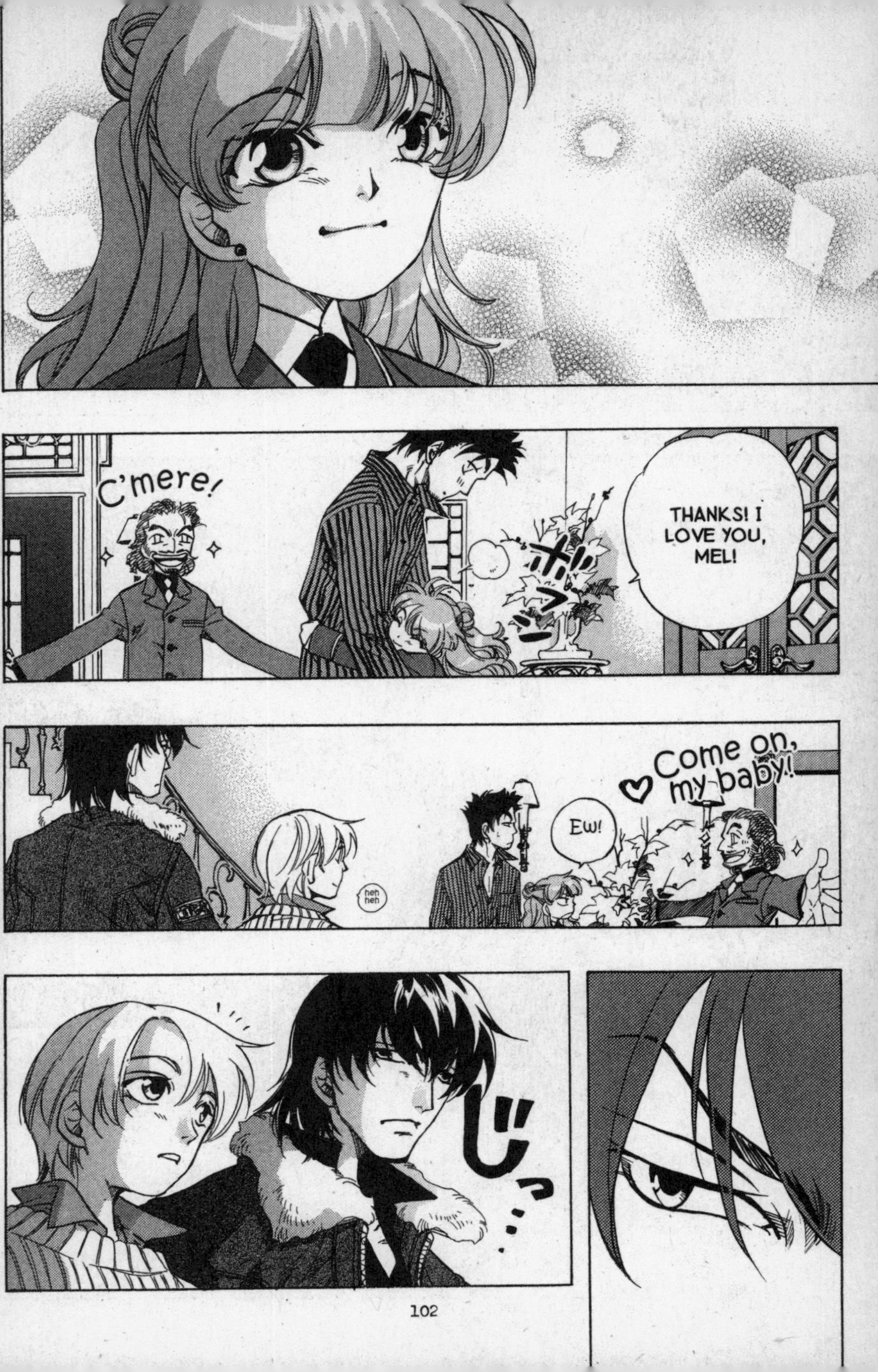
THANKS! I LOVE YOU, MEL!
C'mere!
Come on, my baby!
Ew!
heh heh
じっ

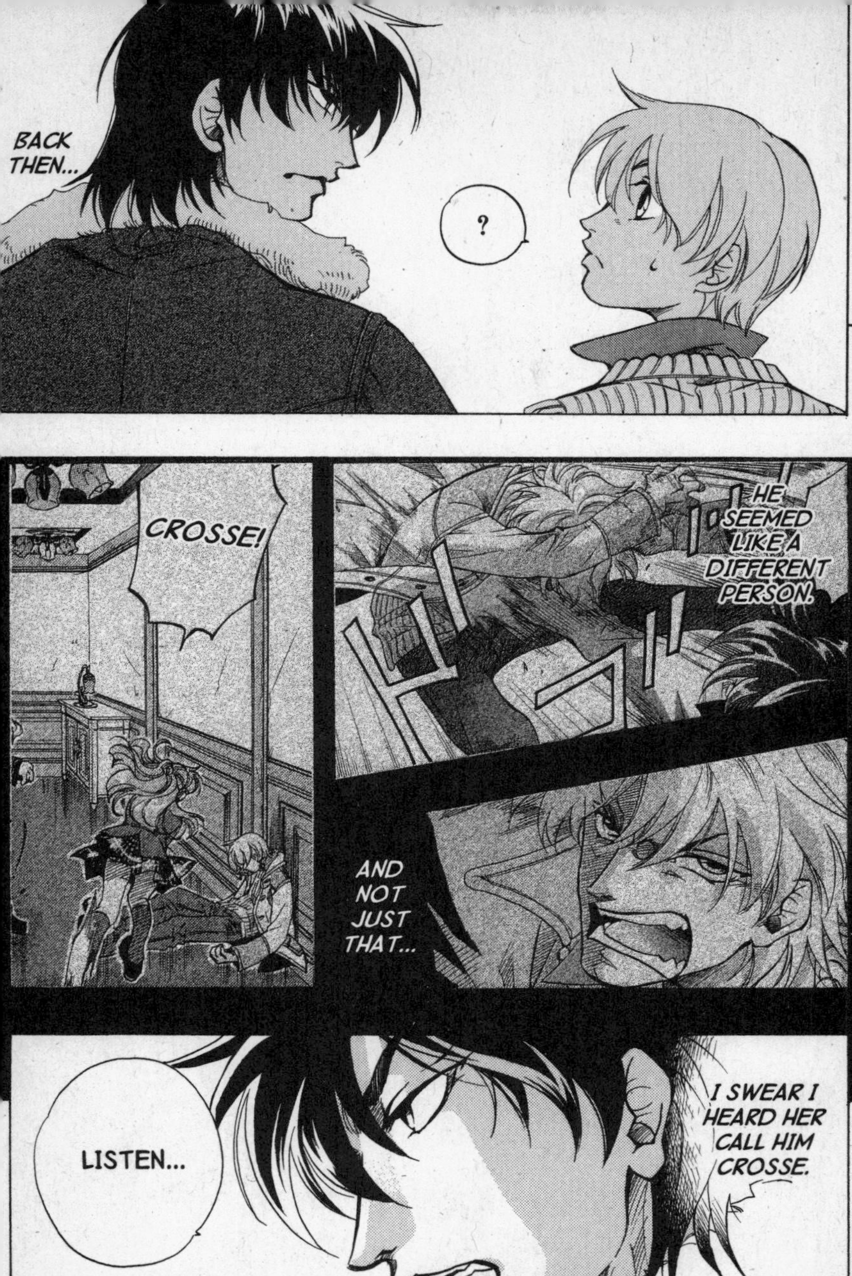
BACK THEN...
?
HE SEEMED LIKE A DIFFERENT PERSON.
AND NOT JUST THAT...
CROSSE!
I SWEAR I HEARD HER CALL HIM CROSSE.
LISTEN...

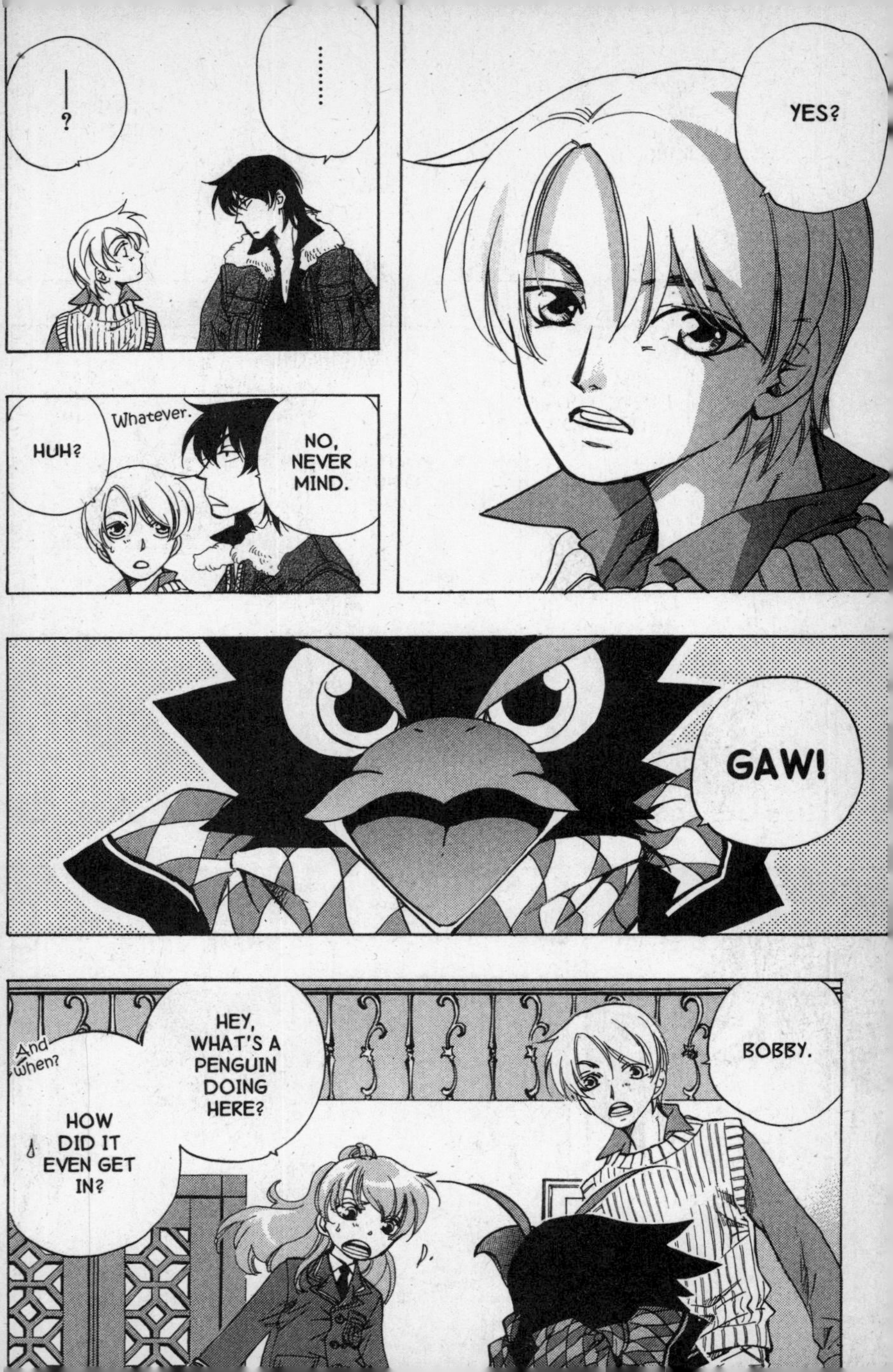
YES?
......
—?
NO, NEVER MIND.
Whatever.
HUH?
GAW!
BOBBY.
HEY, WHAT'S A PENGUIN DOING HERE?
And when?
HOW DID IT EVEN GET IN?

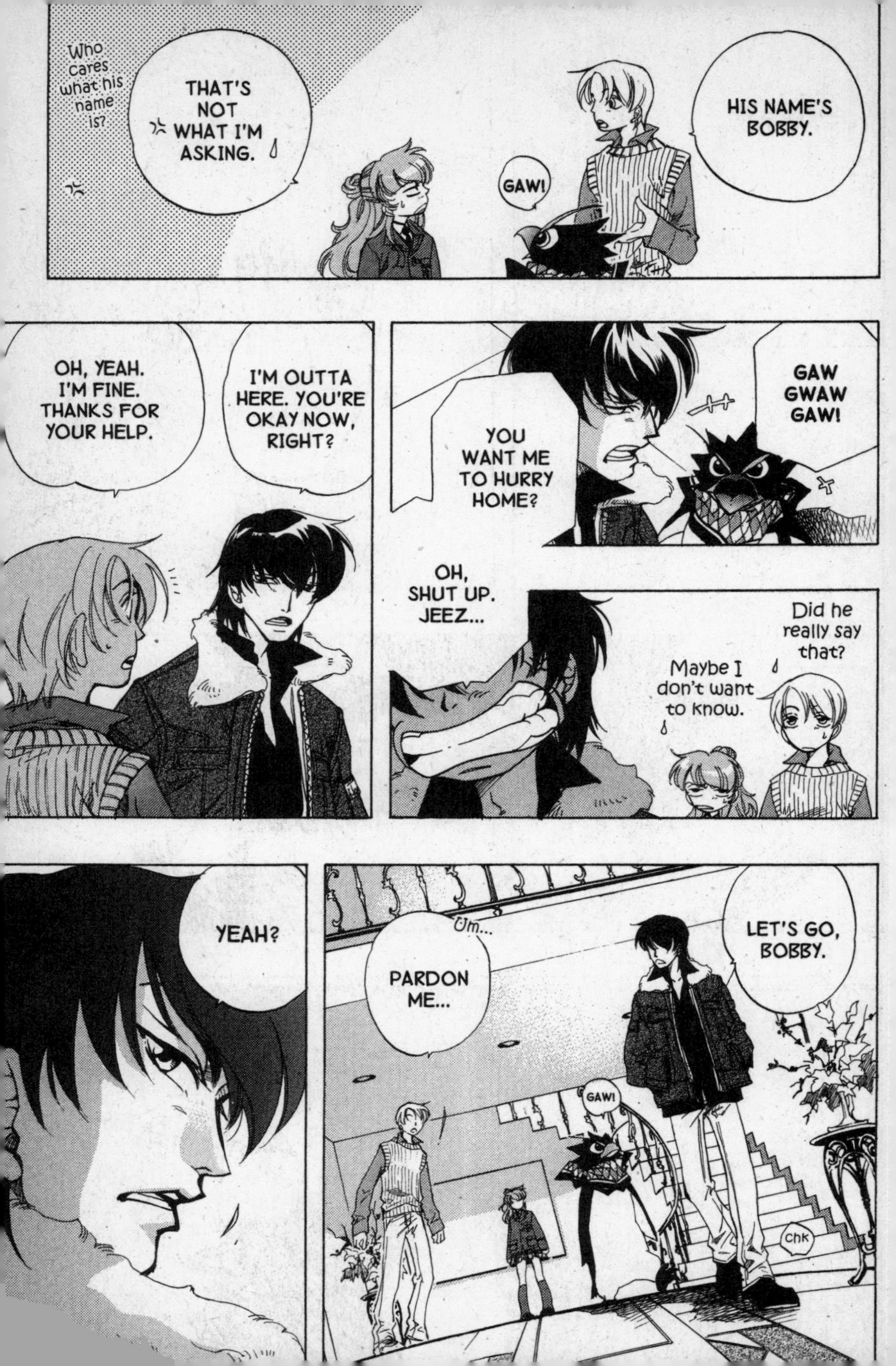
HIS NAME'S BOBBY.
GAW!
THAT'S NOT WHAT I'M ASKING.
Who cares what his name is?
GAW GWAW GAW!
YOU WANT ME TO HURRY HOME?
OH, SHUT UP. JEEZ...
Did he really say that?
Maybe I don't want to know.
I'M OUTTA HERE. YOU'RE OKAY NOW, RIGHT?
OH, YEAH. I'M FINE. THANKS FOR YOUR HELP.
LET'S GO, BOBBY.
Um...
PARDON ME...
GAW!
Chk
YEAH?

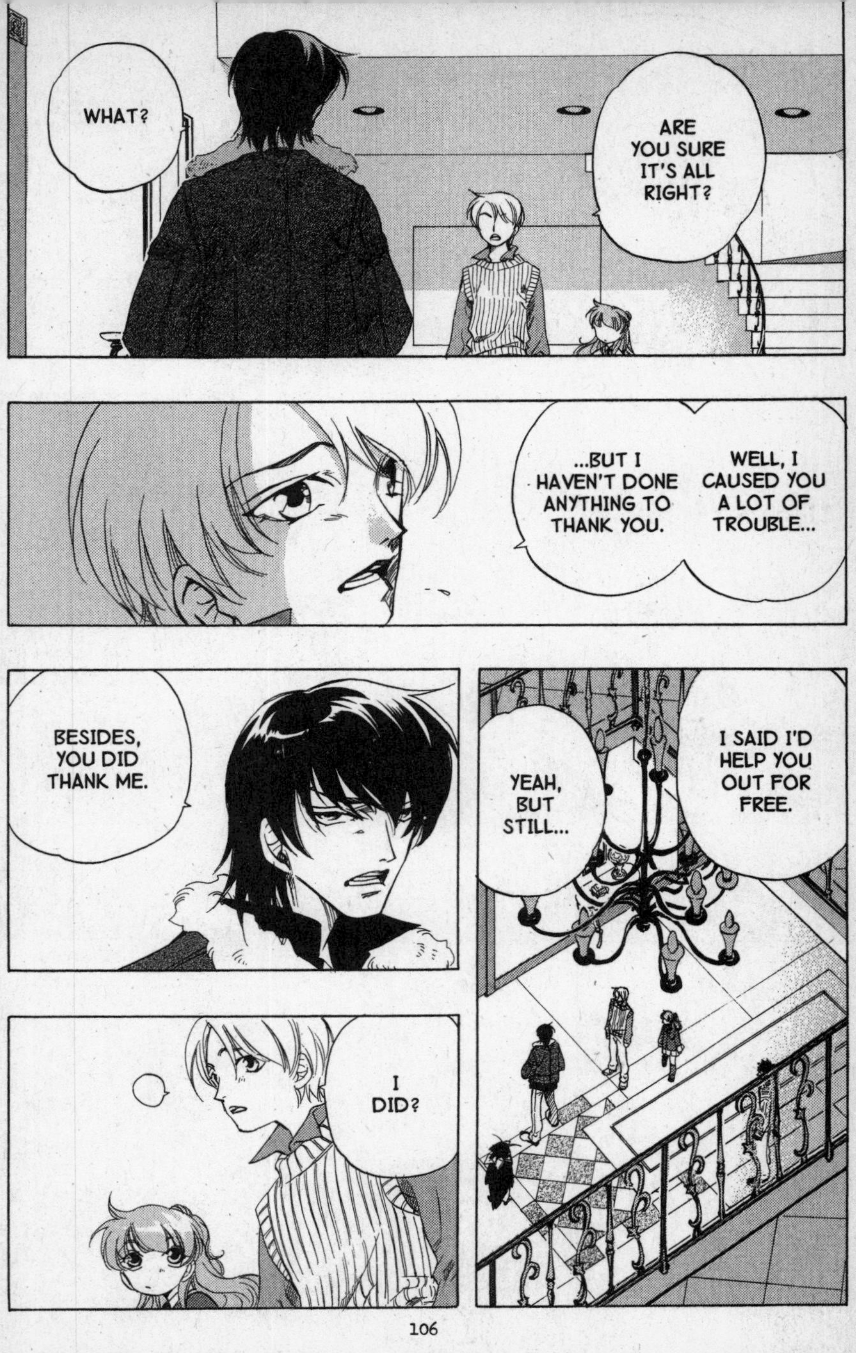
ARE YOU SURE IT'S ALL RIGHT?
WHAT?
WELL, I CAUSED YOU A LOT OF TROUBLE...
...BUT I HAVEN'T DONE ANYTHING TO THANK YOU.
I SAID I'D HELP YOU OUT FOR FREE.
YEAH, BUT STILL...
BESIDES, YOU DID THANK ME.
I DID?

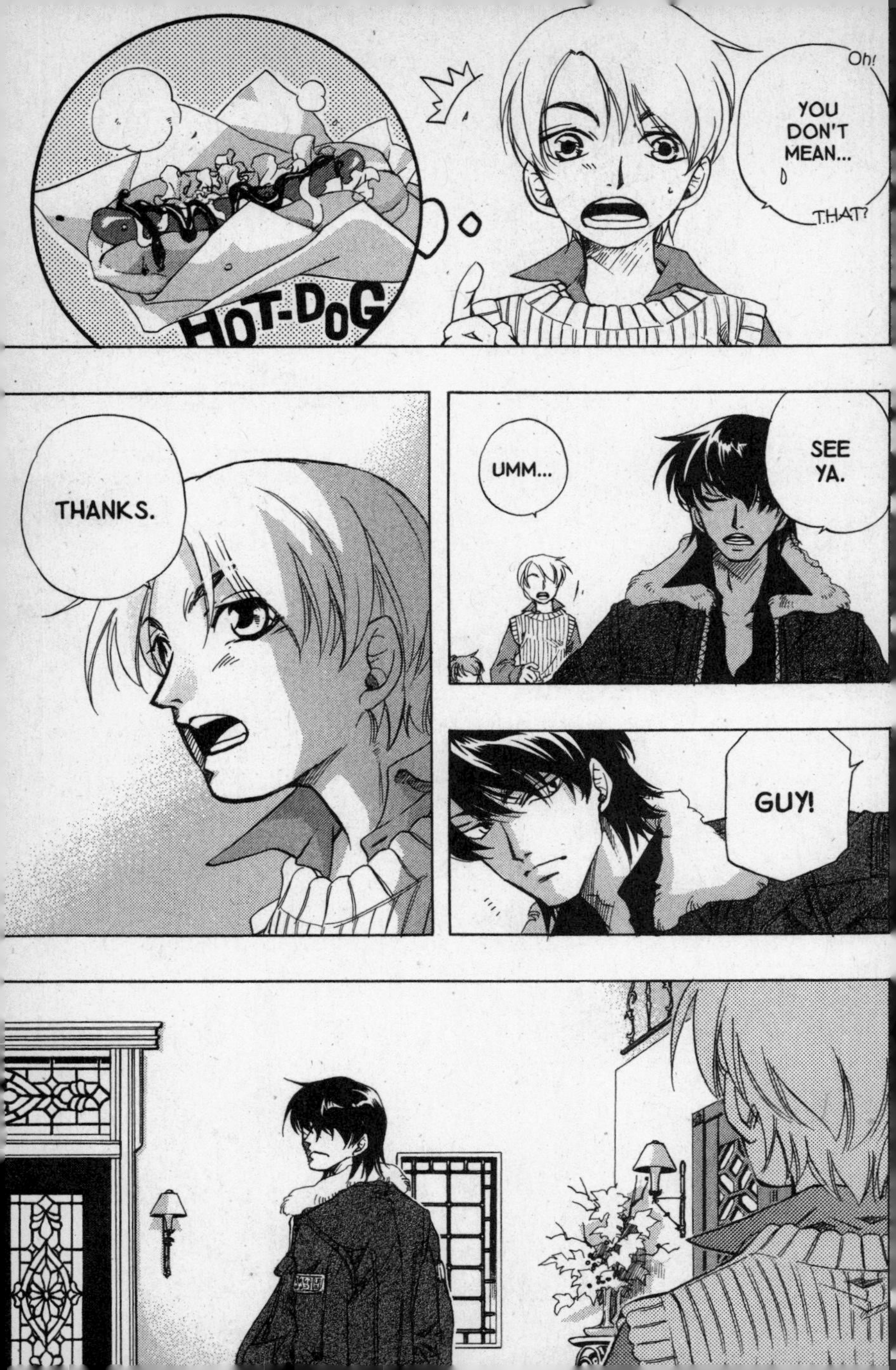
Oh!
YOU DON'T MEAN... THAT?
HOT-DOG
SEE YA.
UMM...
GUY!
THANKS.

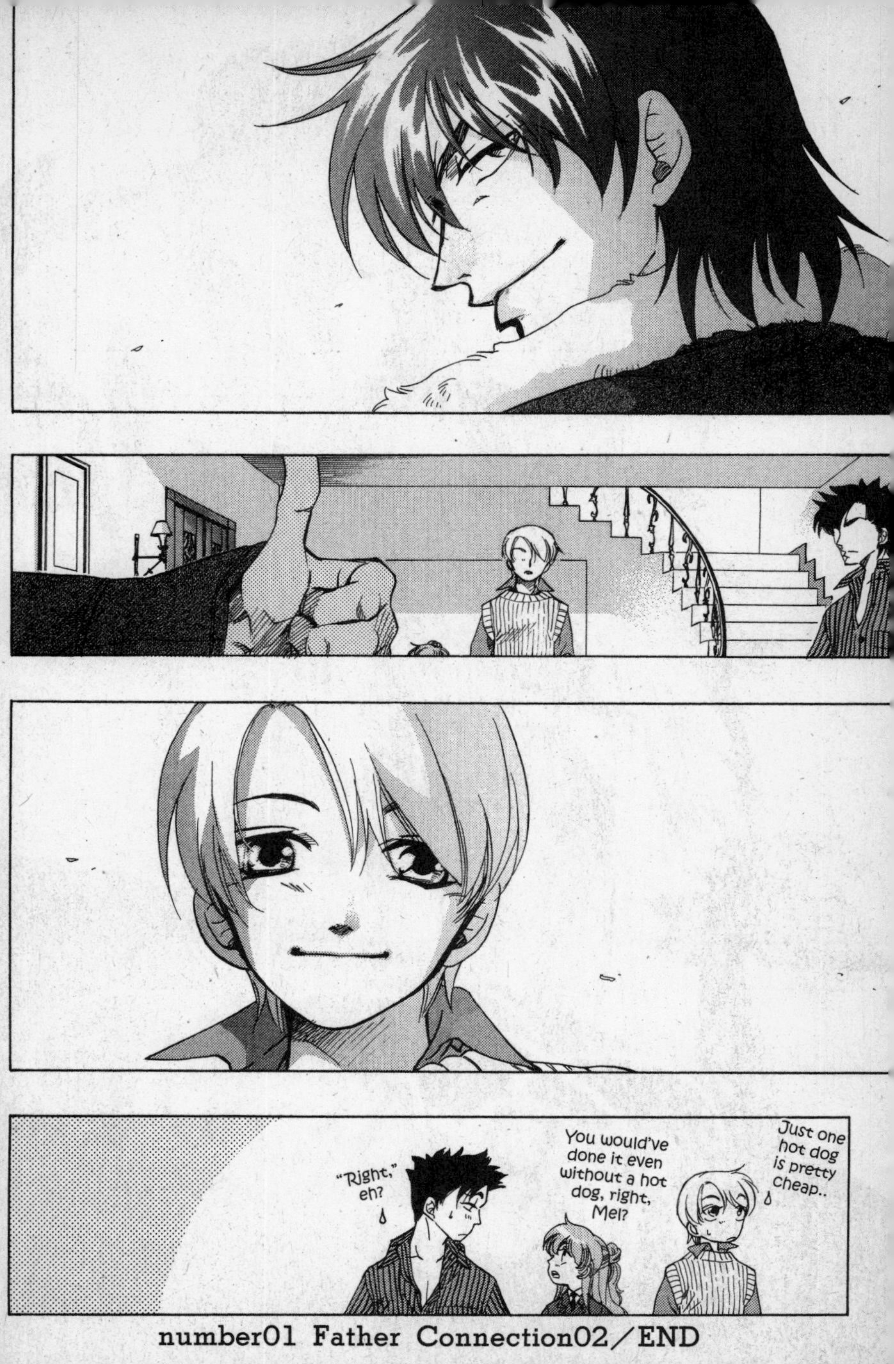
Just one hot dog is pretty cheap..
You would've done it even without a hot dog, right, Mel?
"Right," eh?

number01 Father Connection02/END

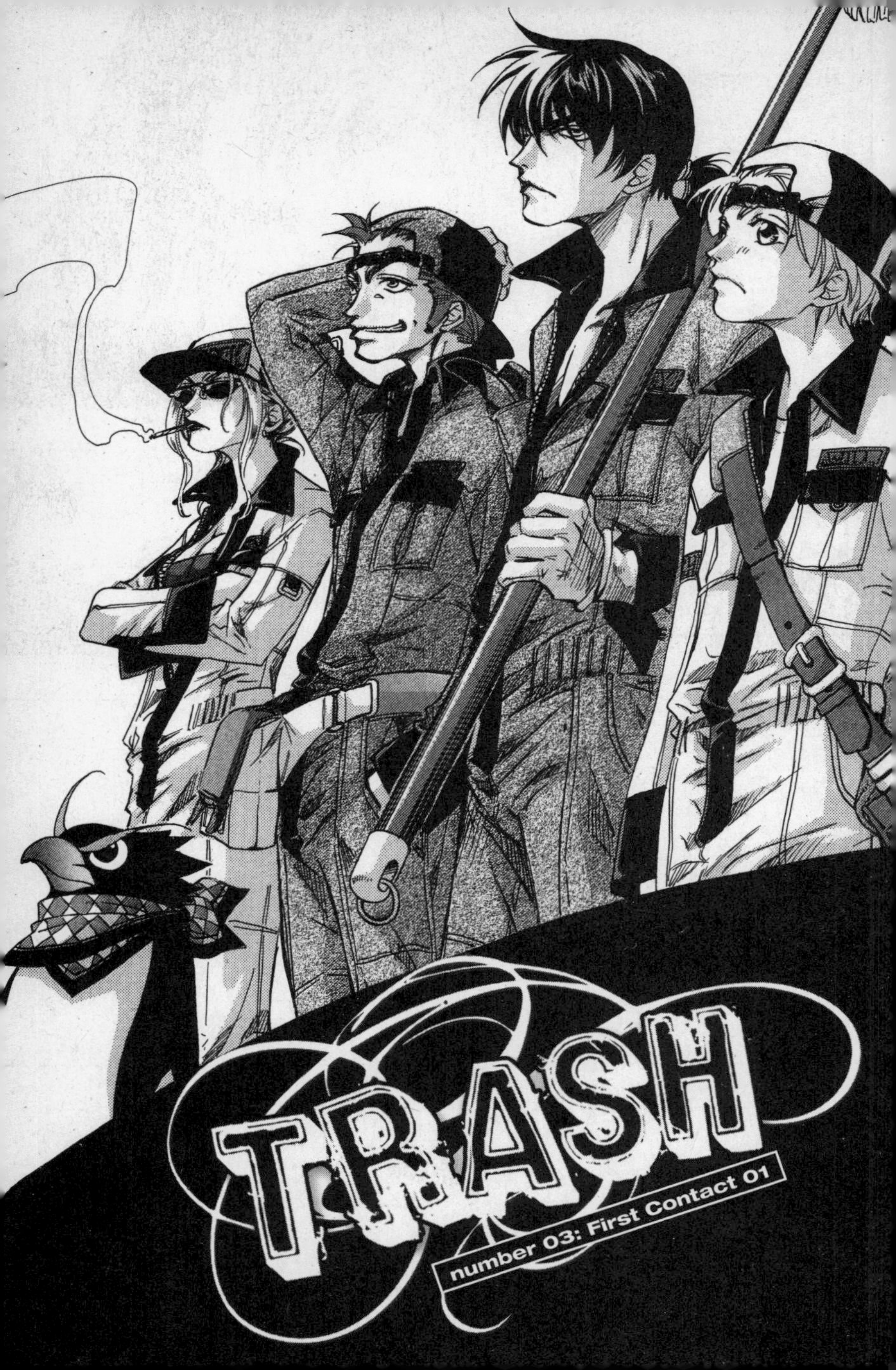
TRASH
number 03: First Contact 01

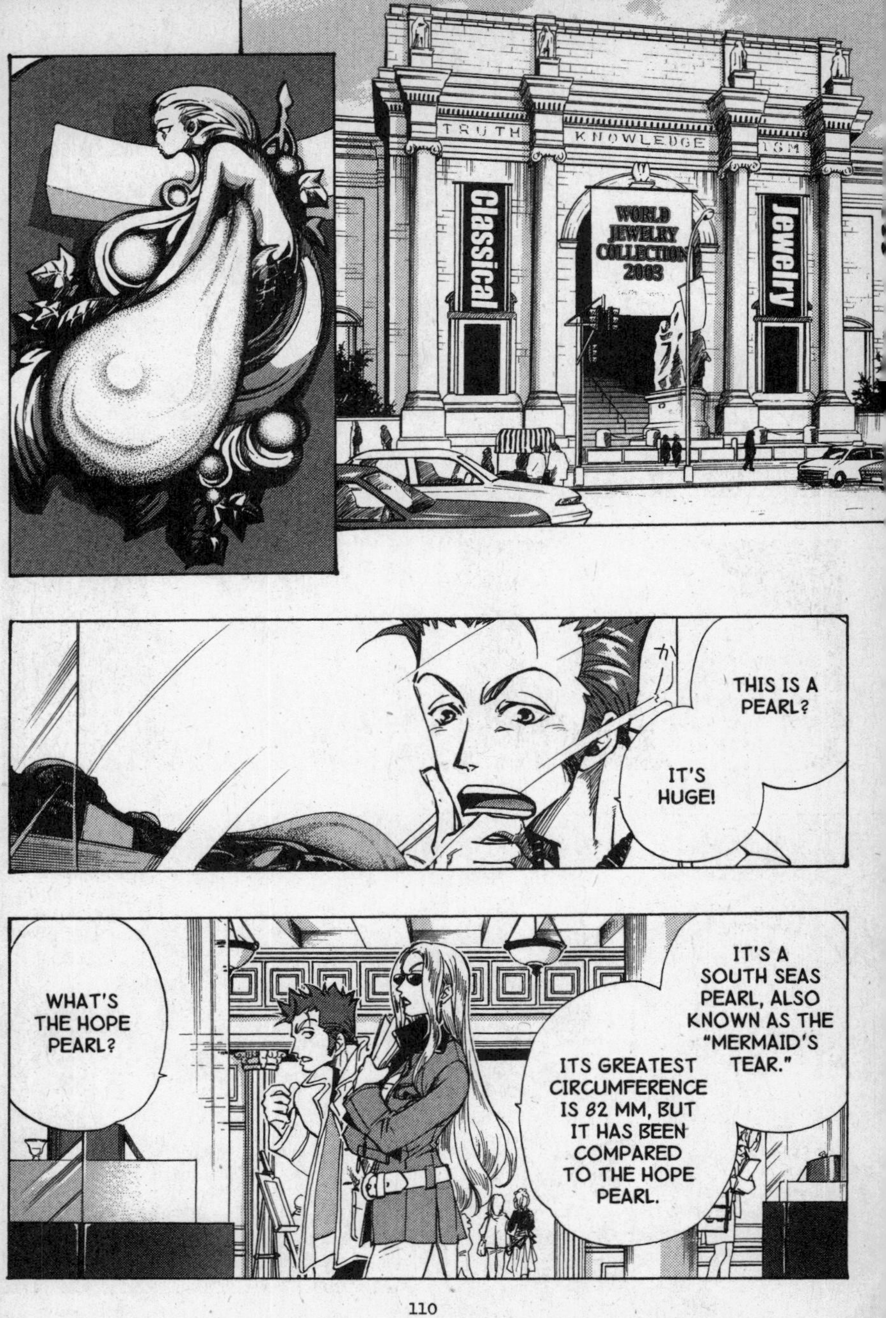

TRUTH KNOWLEDGE ISM
Jewelry
WORLD JEWELRY COLLECTION 2003
Classical
THIS IS A PEARL?
IT'S HUGE!
IT'S A SOUTH SEAS PEARL, ALSO KNOWN AS THE "MERMAID'S TEAR."
ITS GREATEST CIRCUMFERENCE IS 82 MM, BUT IT HAS BEEN COMPARED TO THE HOPE PEARL.
WHAT'S THE HOPE PEARL?

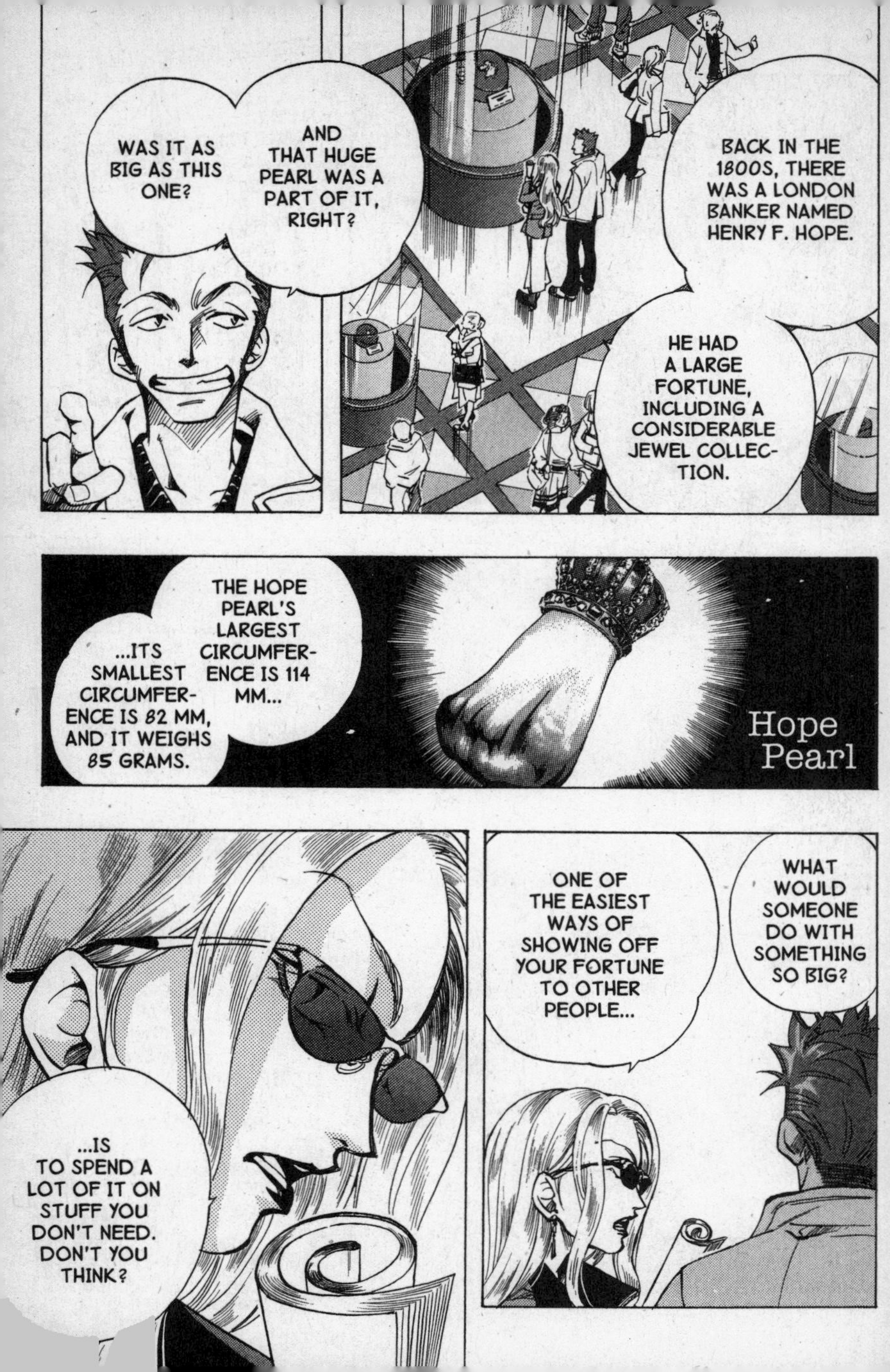
BACK IN THE 1800S, THERE WAS A LONDON BANKER NAMED HENRY F. HOPE.
HE HAD A LARGE FORTUNE, INCLUDING A CONSIDERABLE JEWEL COLLECTION.
AND THAT HUGE PEARL WAS A PART OF IT, RIGHT?
WAS IT AS BIG AS THIS ONE?
THE HOPE PEARL'S LARGEST CIRCUMFERENCE IS 114 MM...
...ITS SMALLEST CIRCUMFERENCE IS 82 MM, AND IT WEIGHS 85 GRAMS.
Hope Pearl
WHAT WOULD SOMEONE DO WITH SOMETHING SO BIG?
ONE OF THE EASIEST WAYS OF SHOWING OFF YOUR FORTUNE TO OTHER PEOPLE...
...IS TO SPEND A LOT OF IT ON STUFF YOU DON'T NEED. DON'T YOU THINK?

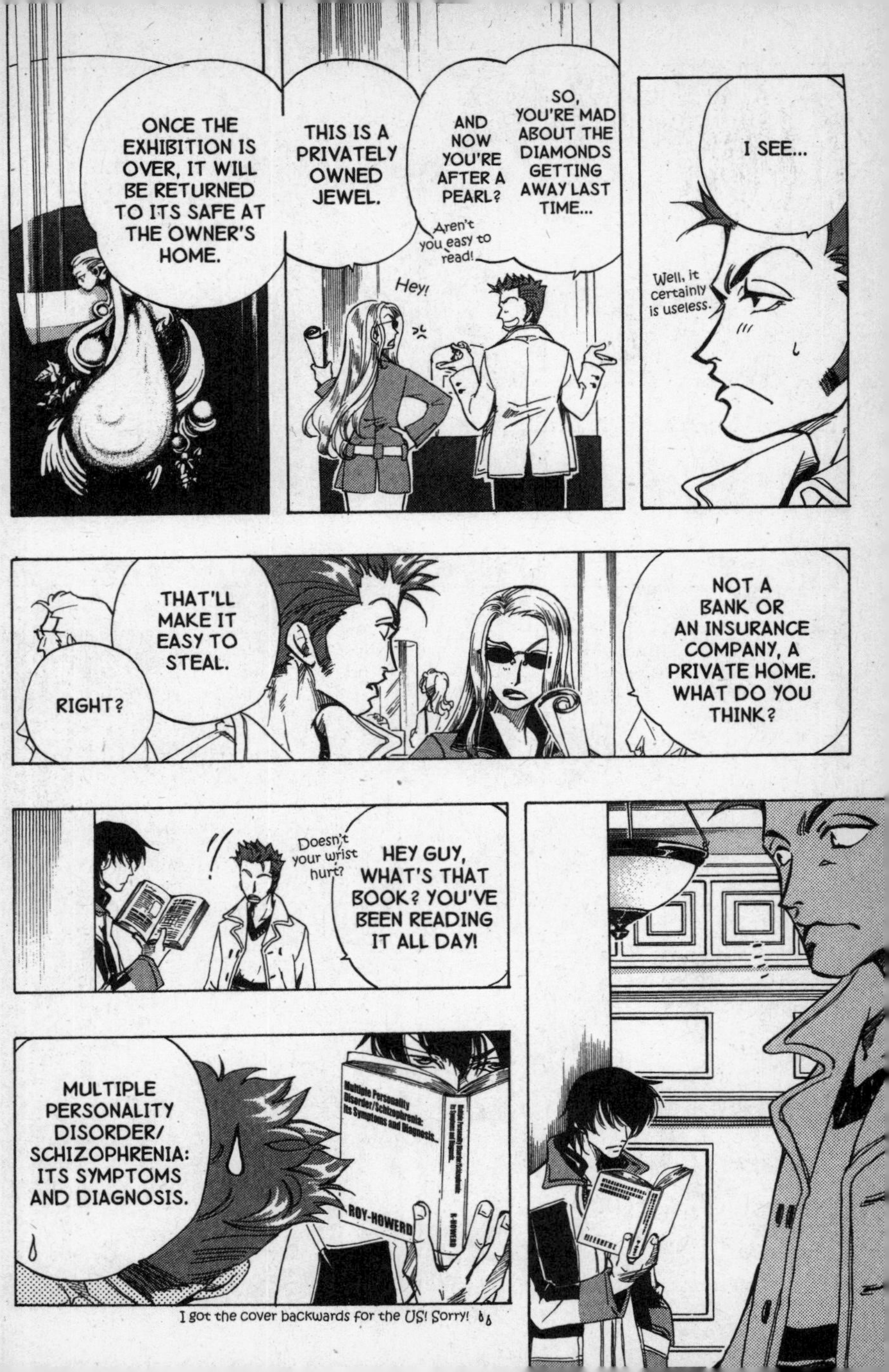
I SEE...
Well, it certainly is useless.
SO, YOU'RE MAD ABOUT THE DIAMONDS GETTING AWAY LAST TIME...
AND NOW YOU'RE AFTER A PEARL?
Aren't you easy to read!
Hey!
THIS IS A PRIVATELY OWNED JEWEL.
ONCE THE EXHIBITION IS OVER, IT WILL BE RETURNED TO ITS SAFE AT THE OWNER'S HOME.
NOT A BANK OR AN INSURANCE COMPANY, A PRIVATE HOME. WHAT DO YOU THINK?
THAT'LL MAKE IT EASY TO STEAL.
RIGHT?
HEY GUY, WHAT'S THAT BOOK? YOU'VE BEEN READING IT ALL DAY!
Doesn't your wrist hurt?
MULTIPLE PERSONALITY DISORDER/ SCHIZOPHRENIA: ITS SYMPTOMS AND DIAGNOSIS.
Multiple Personality Disorder/Schizophrenia: Its Symptoms and Diagnosis
ROY-HOWERD
I got the cover backwards for the US! Sorry!

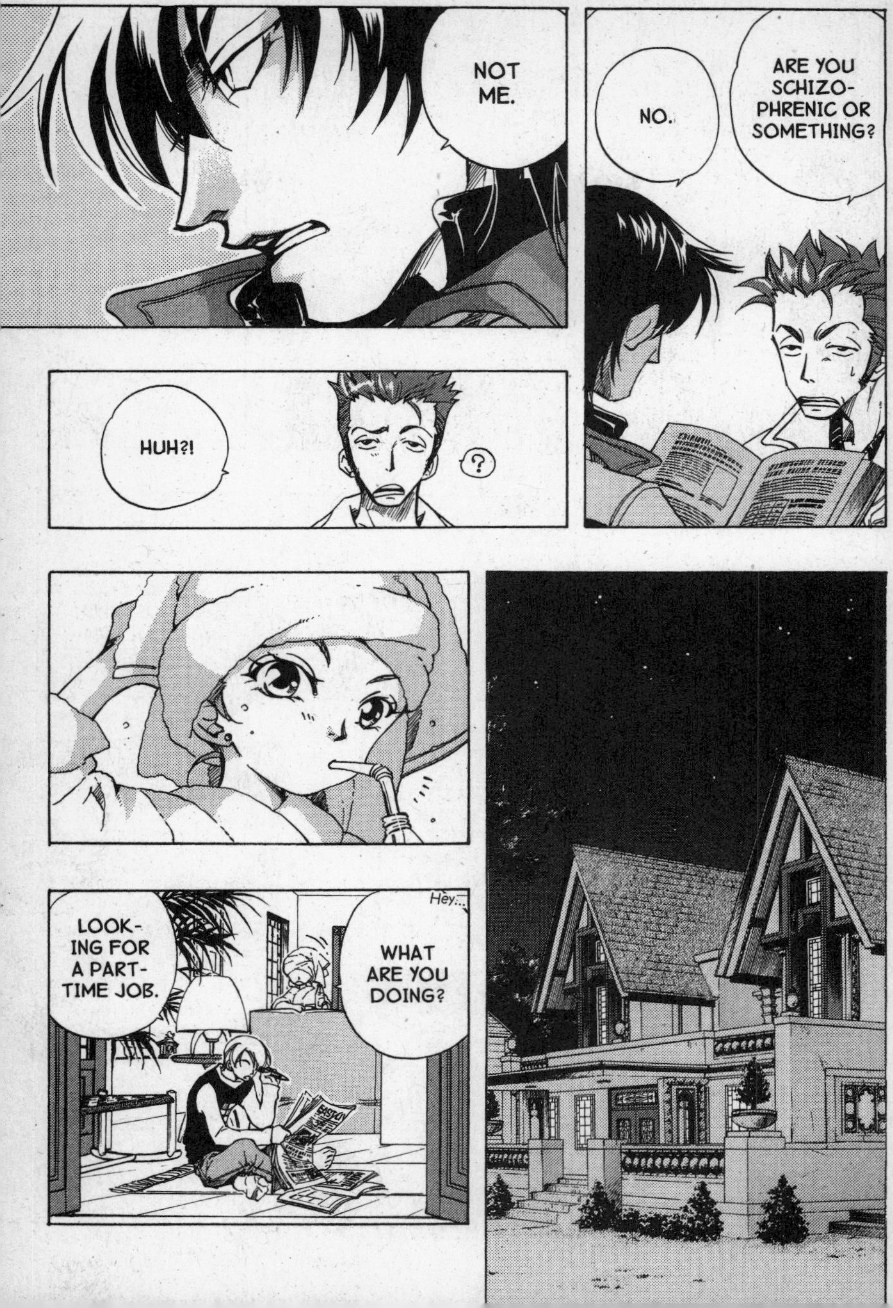
ARE YOU SCHIZO-PHRENIC OR SOMETHING?
NO.
NOT ME.
HUH?!
?
Hey...
WHAT ARE YOU DOING?
LOOK-ING FOR A PART-TIME JOB.

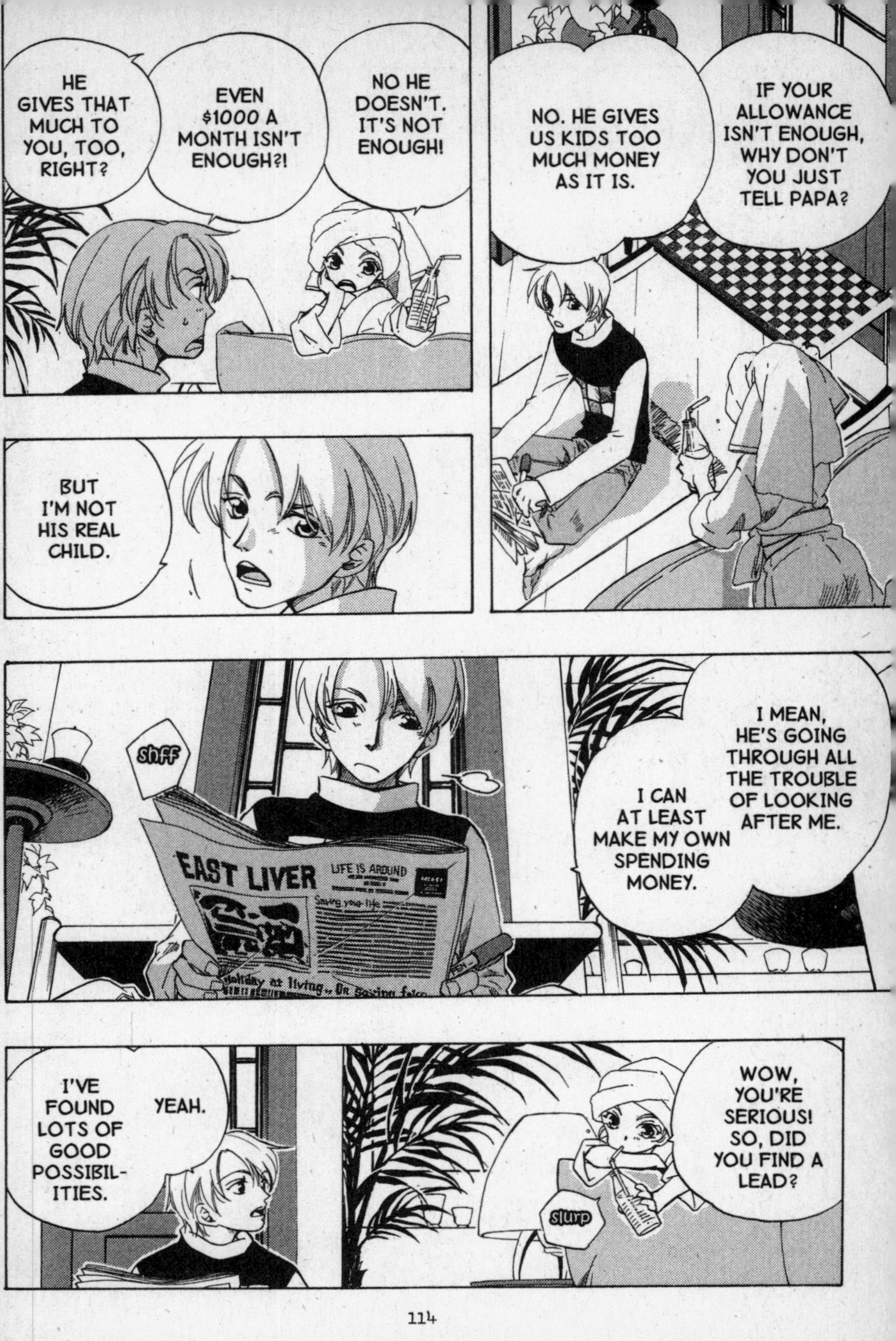
IF YOUR ALLOWANCE ISN'T ENOUGH, WHY DON'T YOU JUST TELL PAPA?
NO. HE GIVES US KIDS TOO MUCH MONEY AS IT IS.
NO HE DOESN'T. IT'S NOT ENOUGH!
EVEN $1000 A MONTH ISN'T ENOUGH?!
HE GIVES THAT MUCH TO YOU, TOO, RIGHT?
BUT I'M NOT HIS REAL CHILD.
I MEAN, HE'S GOING THROUGH ALL THE TROUBLE OF LOOKING AFTER ME.
I CAN AT LEAST MAKE MY OWN SPENDING MONEY.
shff
EAST LIVER
LIFE IS AROUND
Saving your life
Holiday at living
WOW, YOU'RE SERIOUS! SO, DID YOU FIND A LEAD?
slurp
YEAH.
I'VE FOUND LOTS OF GOOD POSSIBIL-ITIES.

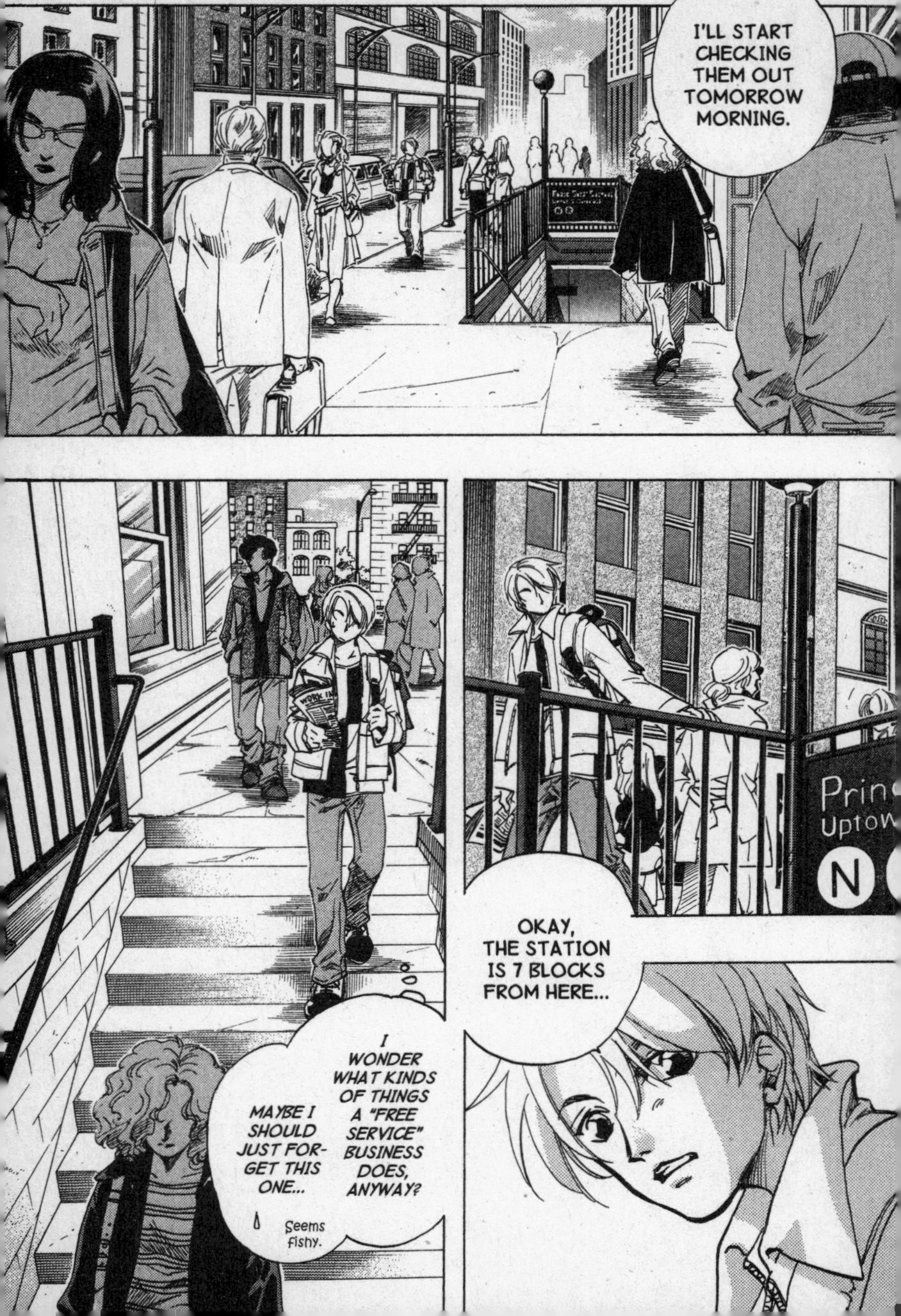
I'LL START CHECKING THEM OUT TOMORROW MORNING.
OKAY, THE STATION IS 7 BLOCKS FROM HERE...
I WONDER WHAT KINDS OF THINGS A "FREE SERVICE" BUSINESS DOES, ANYWAY?
MAYBE I SHOULD JUST FORGET THIS ONE...
Seems fishy.

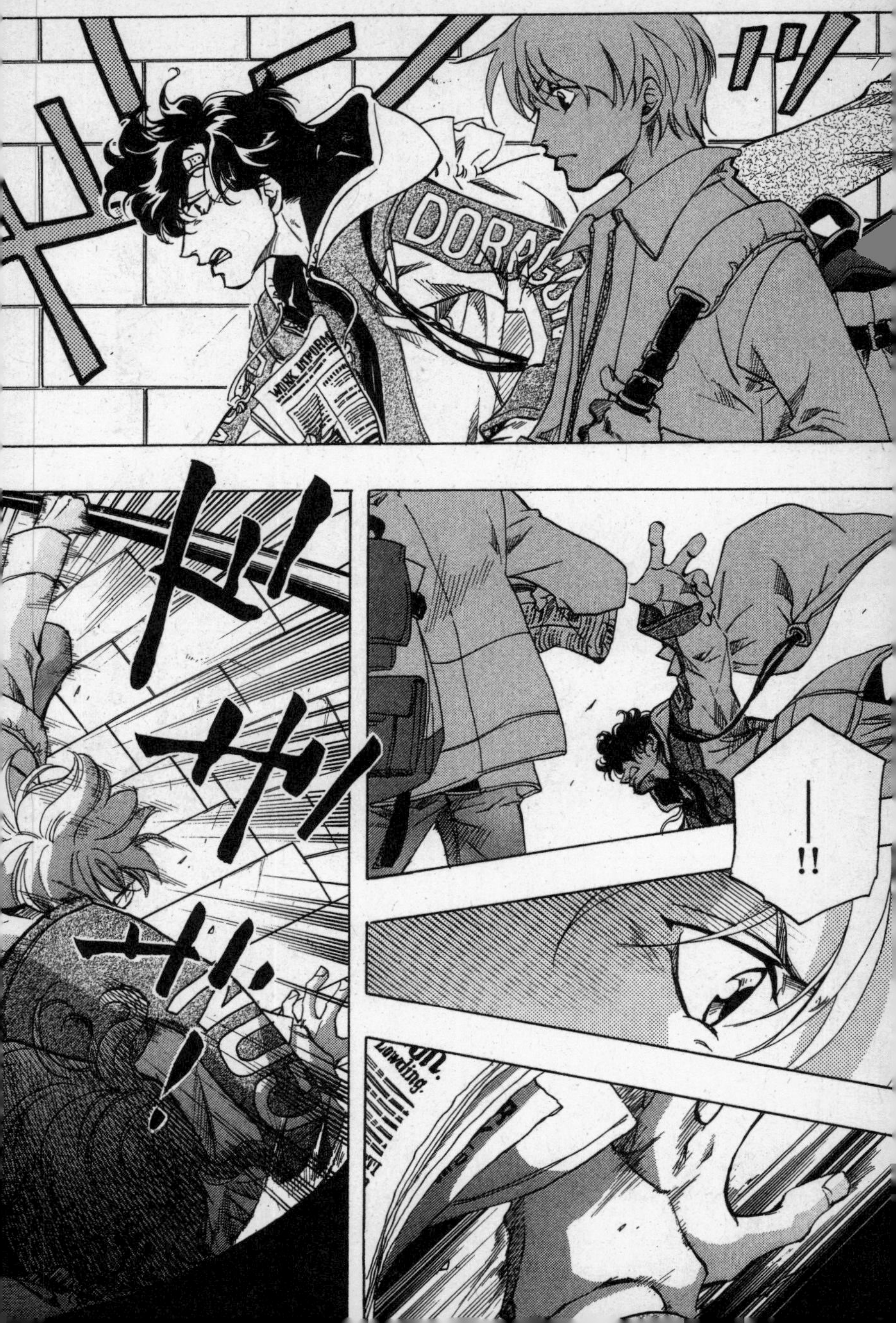
—!!

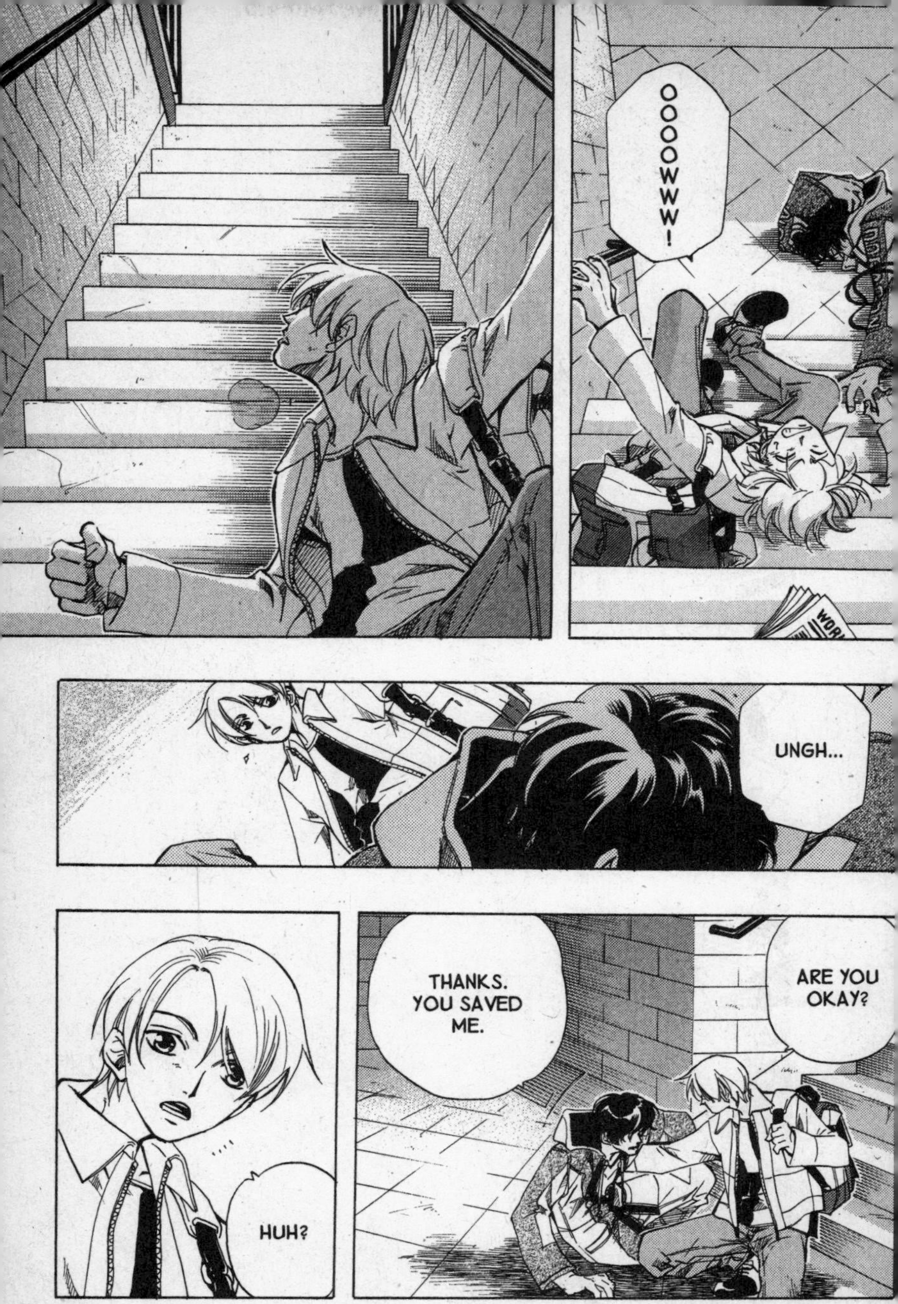
OOOOWWW!
UNGH...
ARE YOU OKAY?
THANKS. YOU SAVED ME.
HUH?

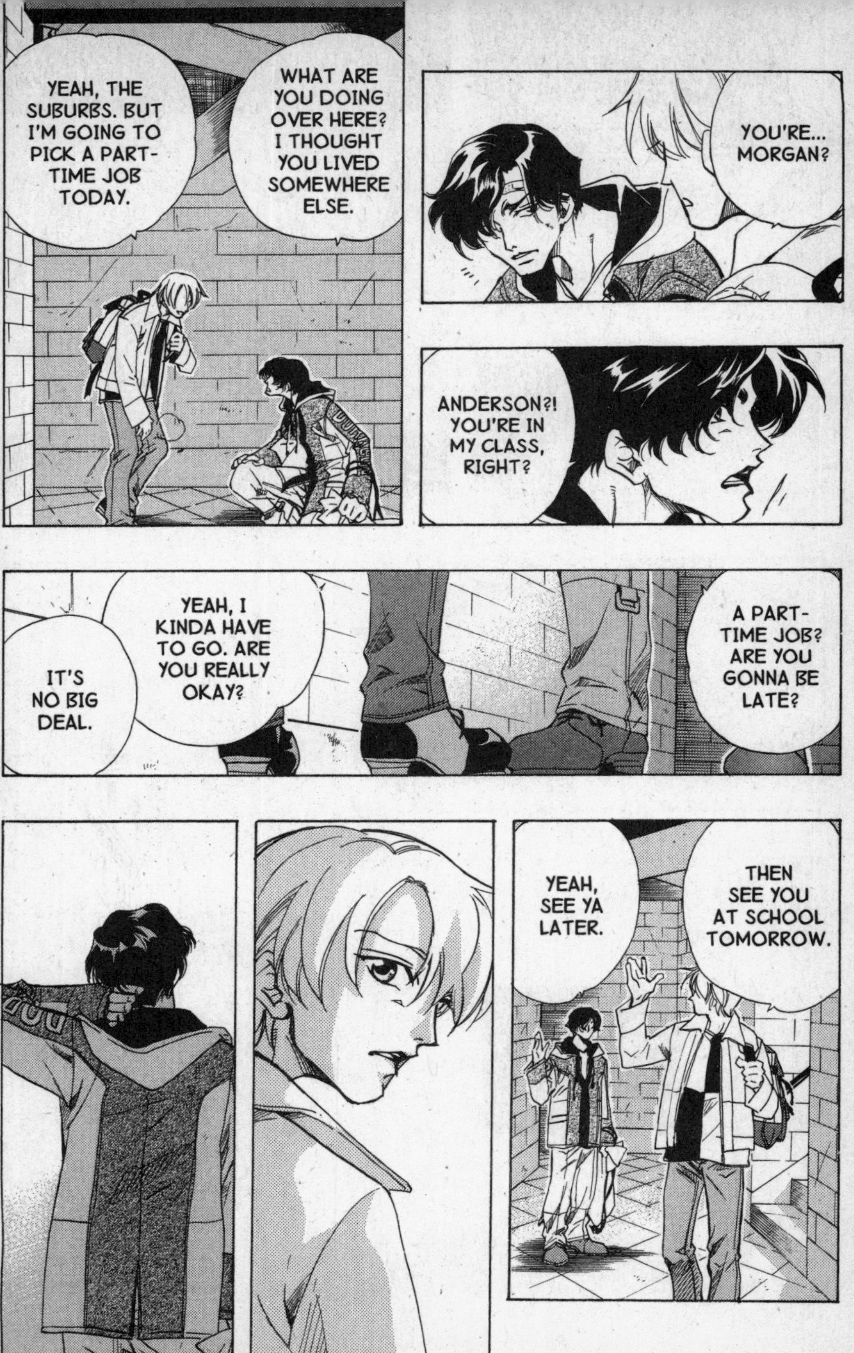
YOU'RE... MORGAN?
ANDERSON?! YOU'RE IN MY CLASS, RIGHT?
WHAT ARE YOU DOING OVER HERE? I THOUGHT YOU LIVED SOMEWHERE ELSE.
YEAH, THE SUBURBS. BUT I'M GOING TO PICK A PART-TIME JOB TODAY.
A PART-TIME JOB? ARE YOU GONNA BE LATE?
YEAH, I KINDA HAVE TO GO. ARE YOU REALLY OKAY?
IT'S NO BIG DEAL.
THEN SEE YOU AT SCHOOL TOMORROW.
YEAH, SEE YA LATER.

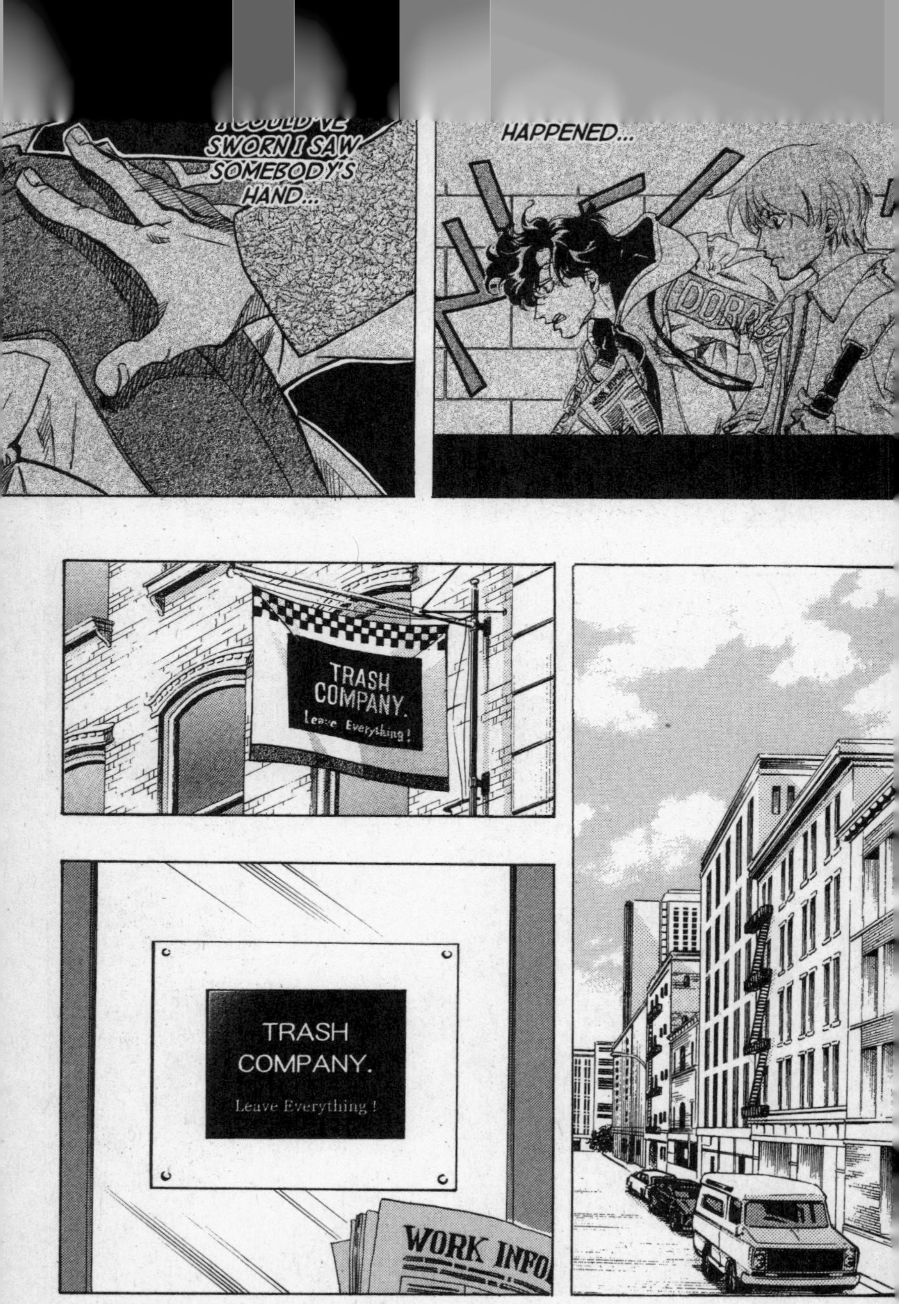
[redacted] HAPPENED...
DORA
WORK INFO
[redacted] SWORN I SAW SOMEBODY'S HAND...
TRASH COMPANY. Leave Everything!
TRASH COMPANY. Leave Everything !
WORK INFO

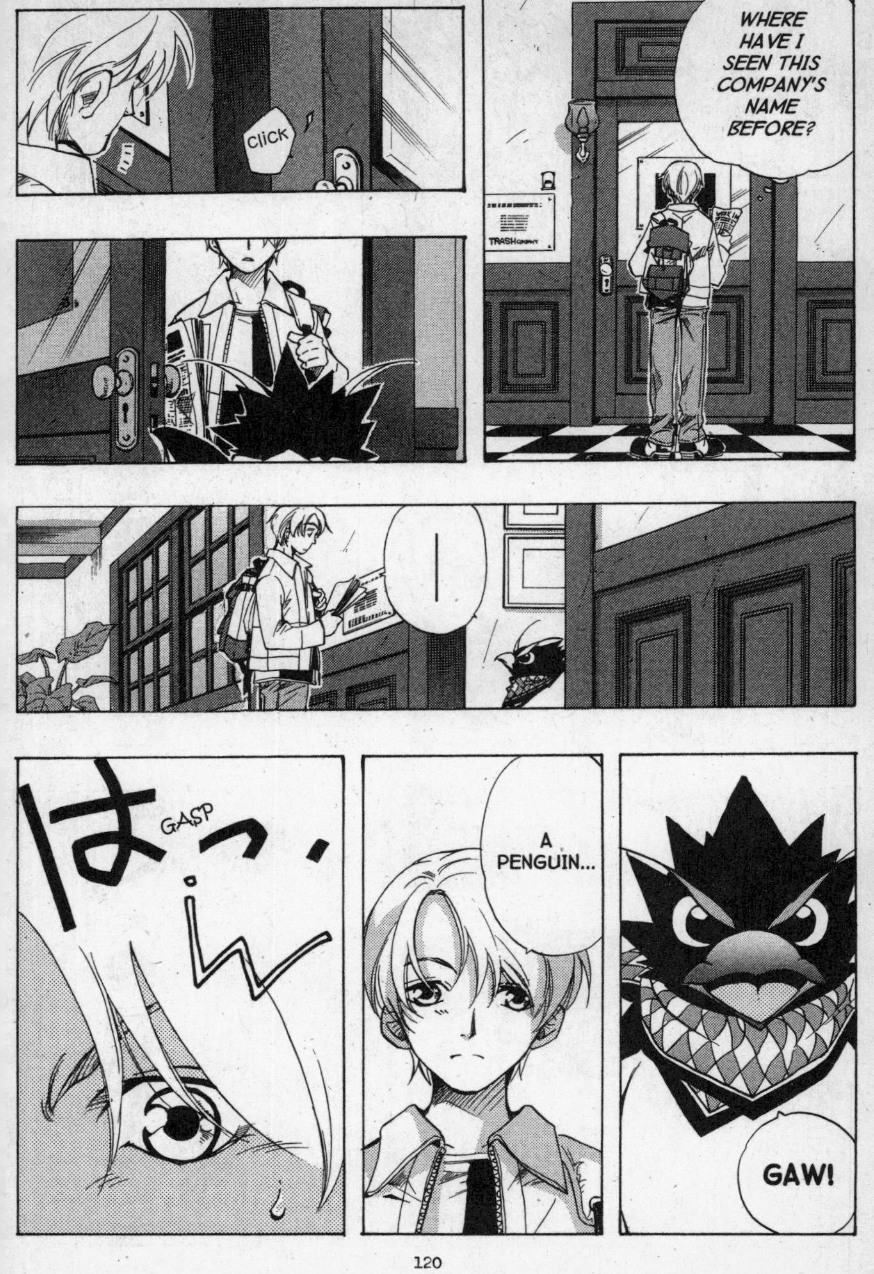
WHERE HAVE I SEEN THIS COMPANY'S NAME BEFORE?
TRASH COMPANY
Click
GAW!
A PENGUIN...
はっ
GASP

THAT'S IT! IT WAS THEM!

TRASH COMPANY.

GUY-HOOKS

WHY DIDN'T I REALIZE IT BEFORE? I'M SUCH A MORON!

Well, there are a lot of places called "So-and-so Company."

OOMPH!

I THINK I'M GONNA PASS ON THIS PLACE!

twirl

ACK.

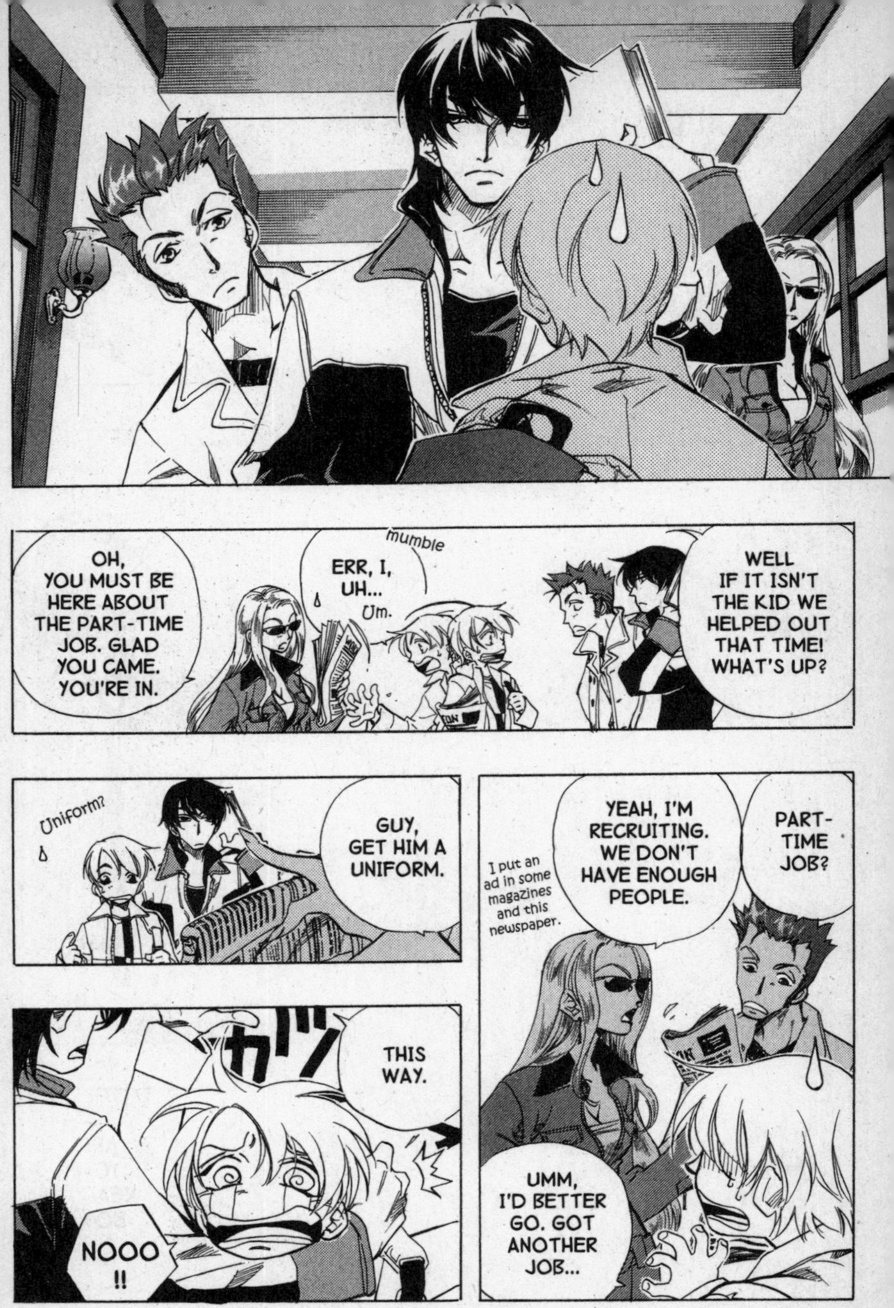
WELL IF IT ISN'T THE KID WE HELPED OUT THAT TIME! WHAT'S UP?
mumble
ERR, I, UH...
Um.
OH, YOU MUST BE HERE ABOUT THE PART-TIME JOB. GLAD YOU CAME. YOU'RE IN.
PART-TIME JOB?
YEAH, I'M RECRUITING. WE DON'T HAVE ENOUGH PEOPLE.
I put an ad in some magazines and this newspaper.
UMM, I'D BETTER GO. GOT ANOTHER JOB...
GUY, GET HIM A UNIFORM.
Uniform?
THIS WAY.
NOOO !!

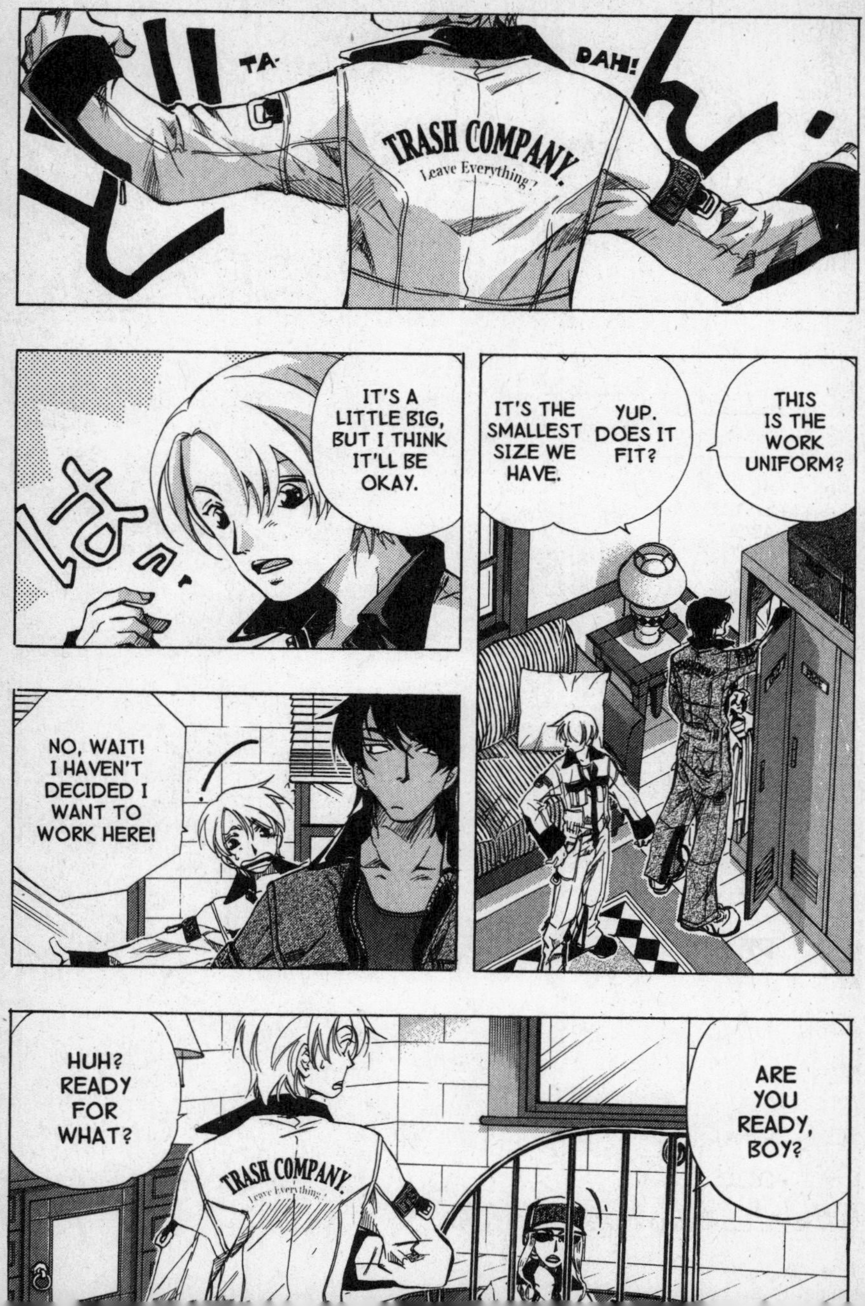
TA-
DAH!
TRASH COMPANY.
Leave Everything?
THIS IS THE WORK UNIFORM?
YUP. DOES IT FIT?
IT'S THE SMALLEST SIZE WE HAVE.
IT'S A LITTLE BIG, BUT I THINK IT'LL BE OKAY.
NO, WAIT! I HAVEN'T DECIDED I WANT TO WORK HERE!
ARE YOU READY, BOY?
HUH? READY FOR WHAT?
TRASH COMPANY.
Leave Everything?

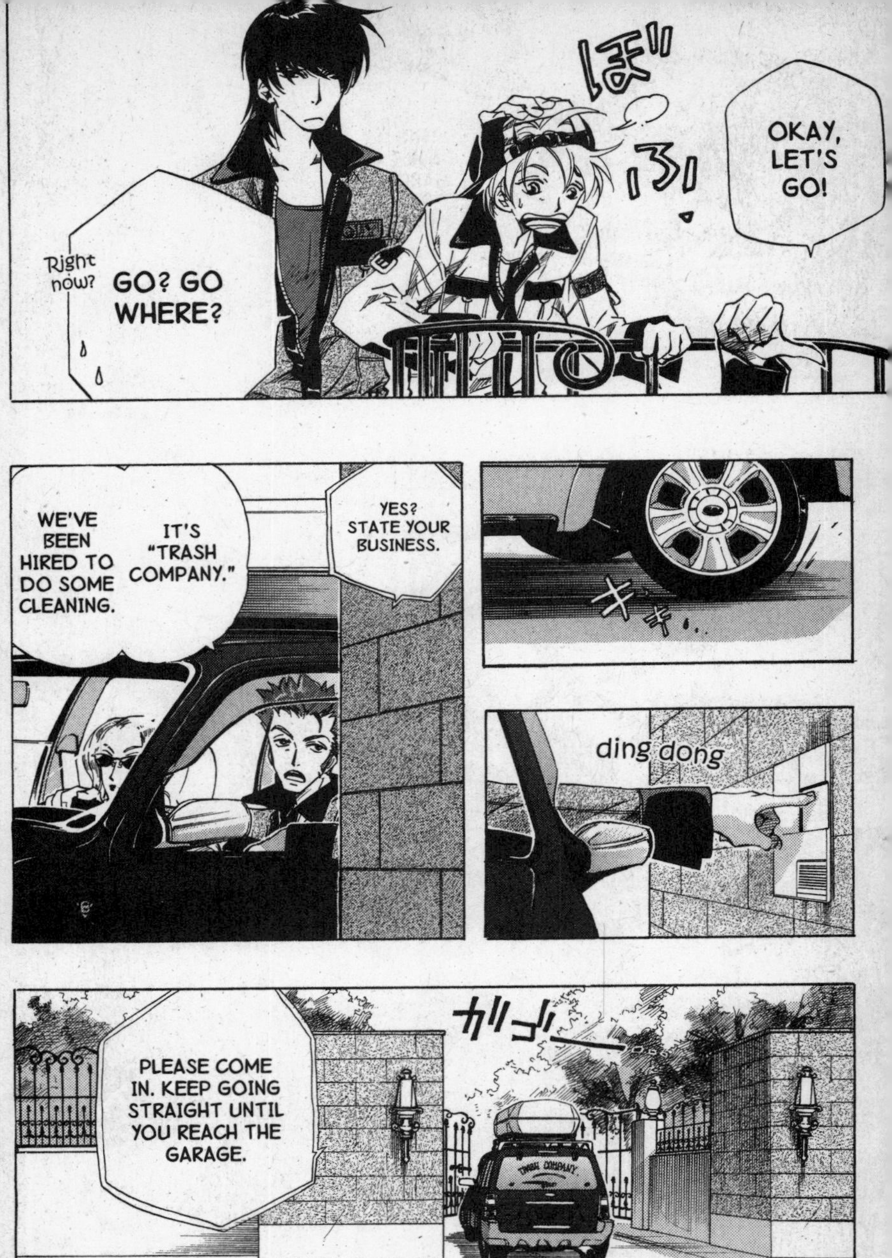
OKAY, LET'S GO!
ぼふ
GO? GO WHERE?
Right now?
キキ
ding dong
YES? STATE YOUR BUSINESS.
IT'S "TRASH COMPANY."
WE'VE BEEN HIRED TO DO SOME CLEANING.
カリゴー
PLEASE COME IN. KEEP GOING STRAIGHT UNTIL YOU REACH THE GARAGE.
TRASH COMPANY

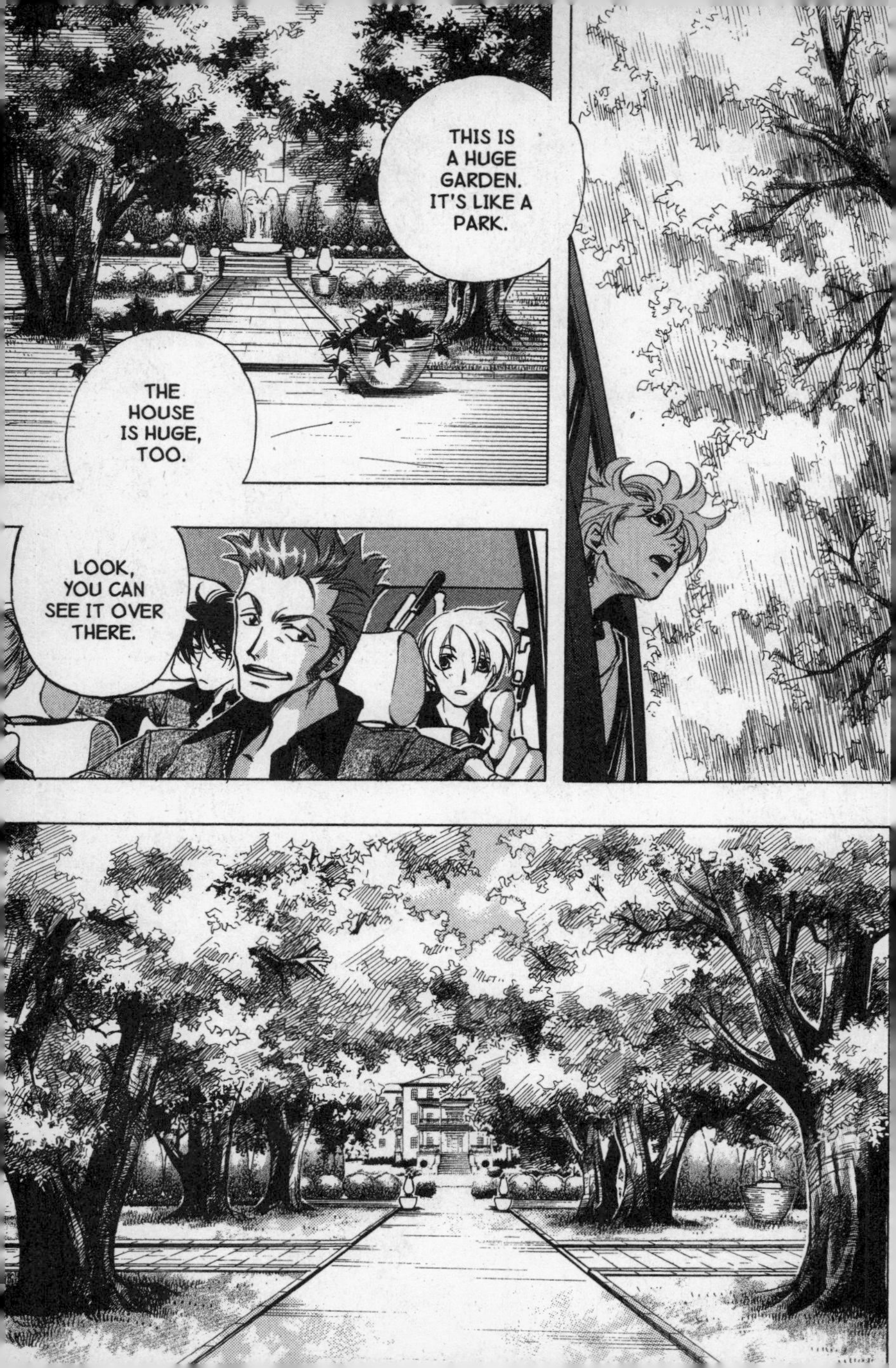
THIS IS A HUGE GARDEN. IT'S LIKE A PARK.
THE HOUSE IS HUGE, TOO.
LOOK, YOU CAN SEE IT OVER THERE.

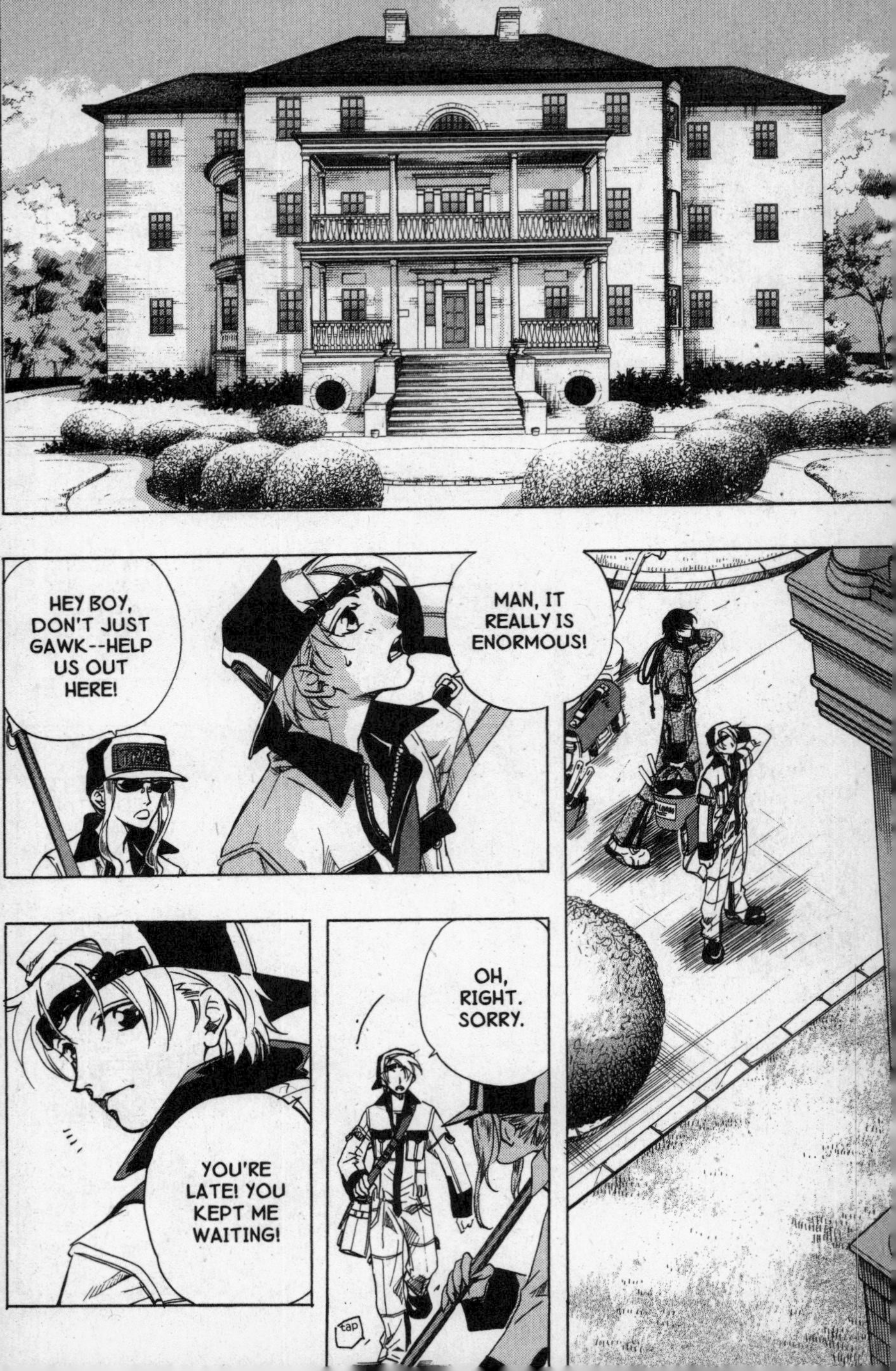
MAN, IT REALLY IS ENORMOUS!
HEY BOY, DON'T JUST GAWK--HELP US OUT HERE!
OH, RIGHT. SORRY.
tap
YOU'RE LATE! YOU KEPT ME WAITING!

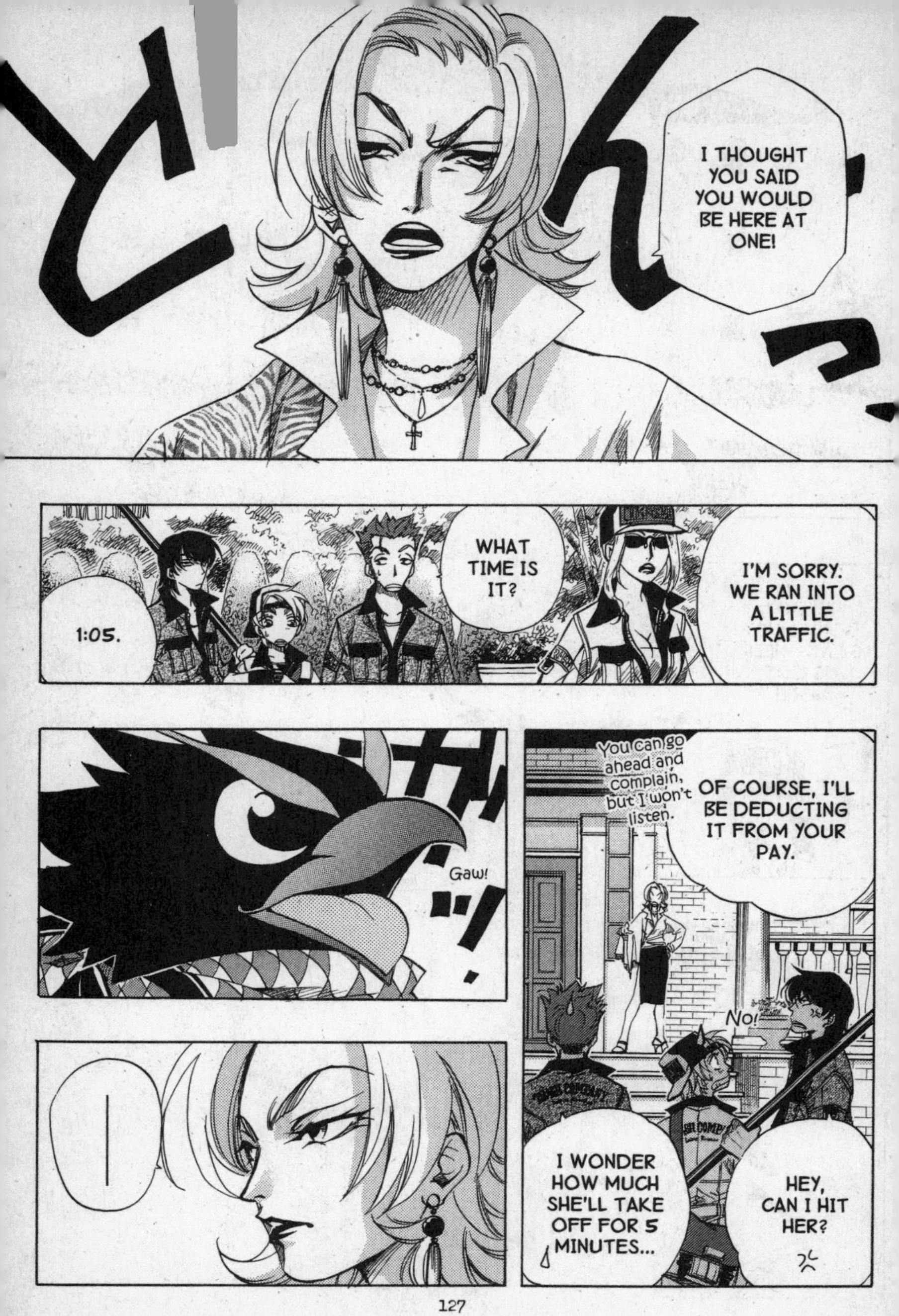
I THOUGHT YOU SAID YOU WOULD BE HERE AT ONE!
I'M SORRY. WE RAN INTO A LITTLE TRAFFIC.
WHAT TIME IS IT?
1:05.
OF COURSE, I'LL BE DEDUCTING IT FROM YOUR PAY.
You can go ahead and complain, but I won't listen.
No!
HEY, CAN I HIT HER?
I WONDER HOW MUCH SHE'LL TAKE OFF FOR 5 MINUTES...
Gaw!

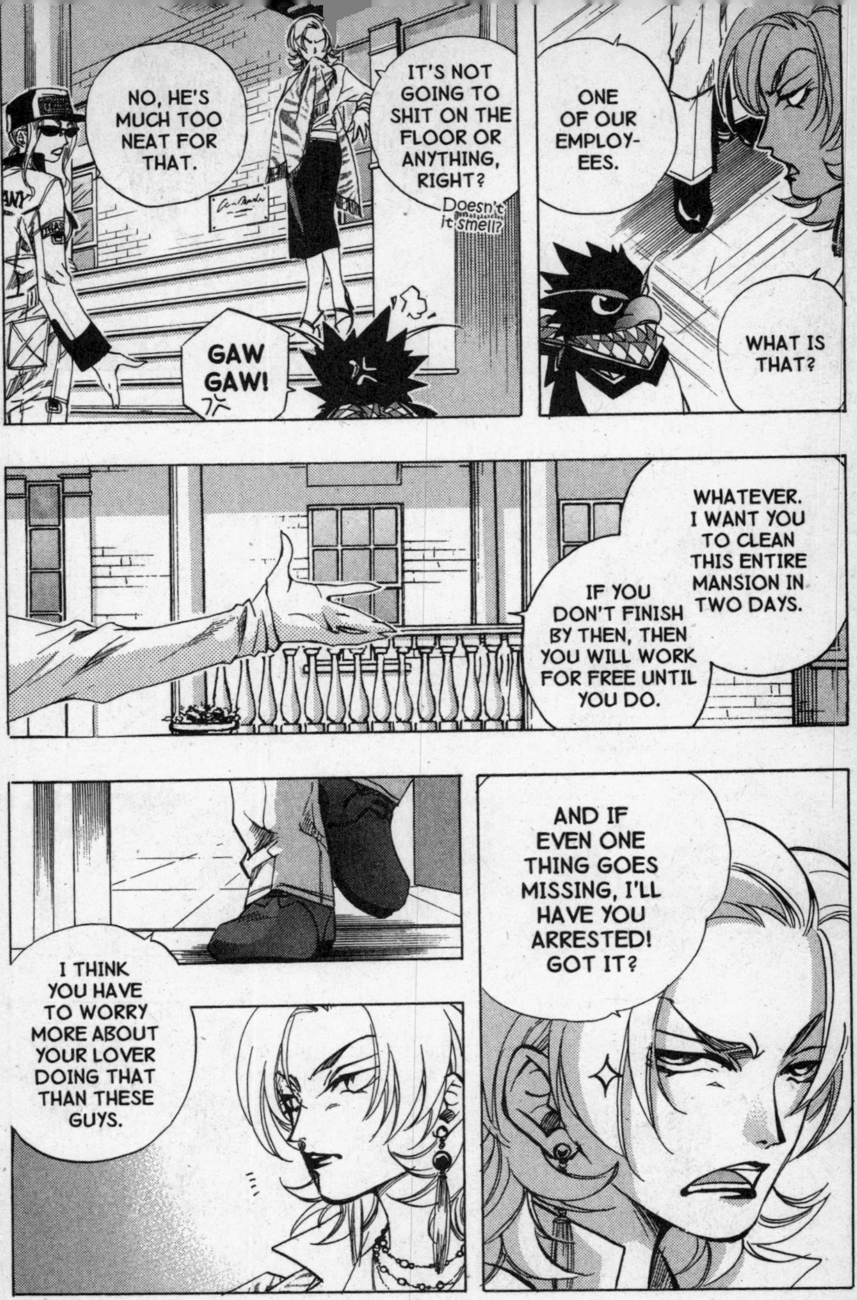
WHAT IS THAT?
ONE OF OUR EMPLOY-EES.
IT'S NOT GOING TO SHIT ON THE FLOOR OR ANYTHING, RIGHT?
Doesn't it smell?
NO, HE'S MUCH TOO NEAT FOR THAT.
GAW GAW!
WHATEVER. I WANT YOU TO CLEAN THIS ENTIRE MANSION IN TWO DAYS.
IF YOU DON'T FINISH BY THEN, THEN YOU WILL WORK FOR FREE UNTIL YOU DO.
AND IF EVEN ONE THING GOES MISSING, I'LL HAVE YOU ARRESTED! GOT IT?
I THINK YOU HAVE TO WORRY MORE ABOUT YOUR LOVER DOING THAT THAN THESE GUYS.

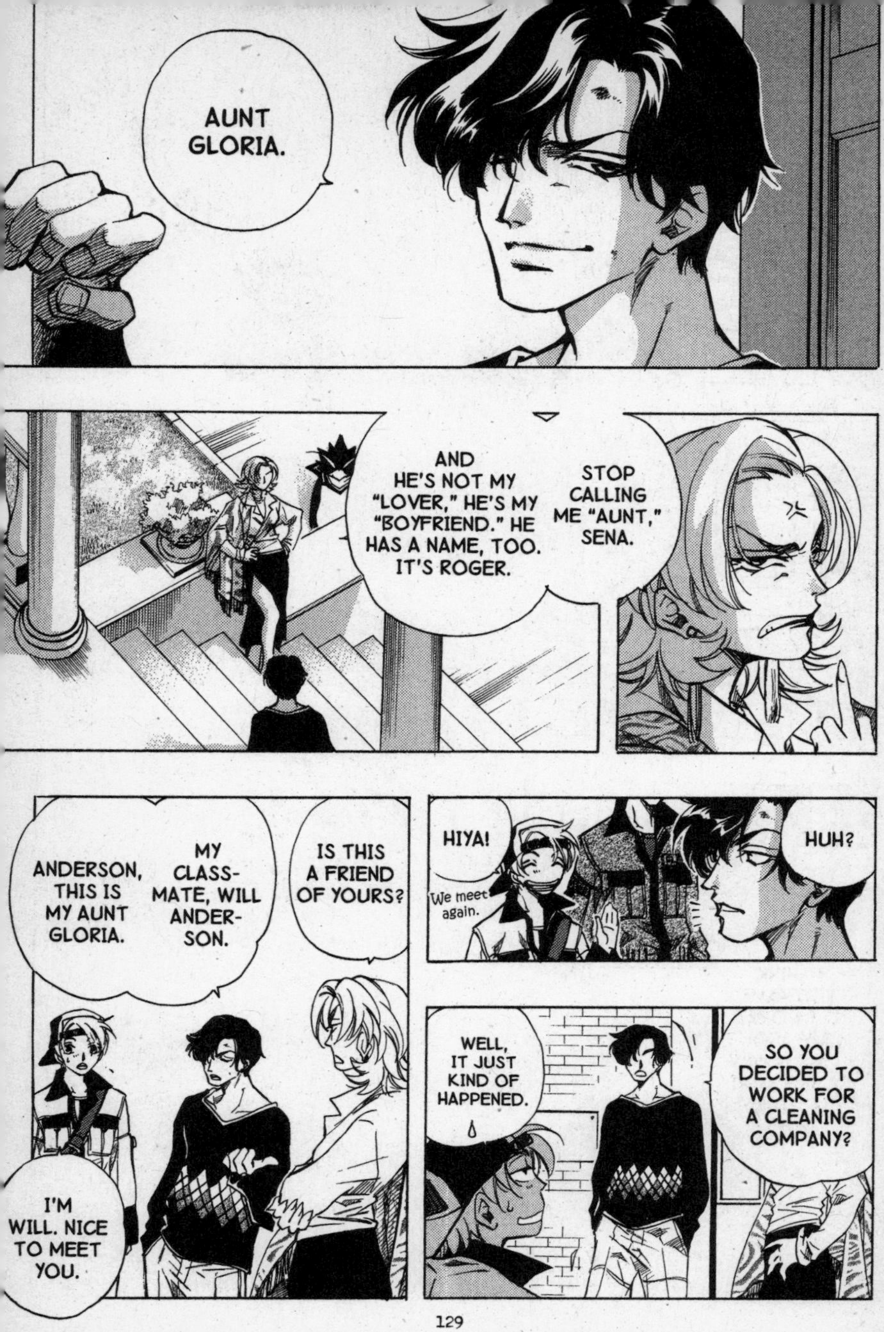
AUNT GLORIA.
STOP CALLING ME "AUNT," SENA.
AND HE'S NOT MY "LOVER," HE'S MY "BOYFRIEND." HE HAS A NAME, TOO. IT'S ROGER.
HUH?
HIYA!
We meet again.
SO YOU DECIDED TO WORK FOR A CLEANING COMPANY?
WELL, IT JUST KIND OF HAPPENED.
IS THIS A FRIEND OF YOURS?
MY CLASS-MATE, WILL ANDER-SON.
ANDERSON, THIS IS MY AUNT GLORIA.
I'M WILL. NICE TO MEET YOU.

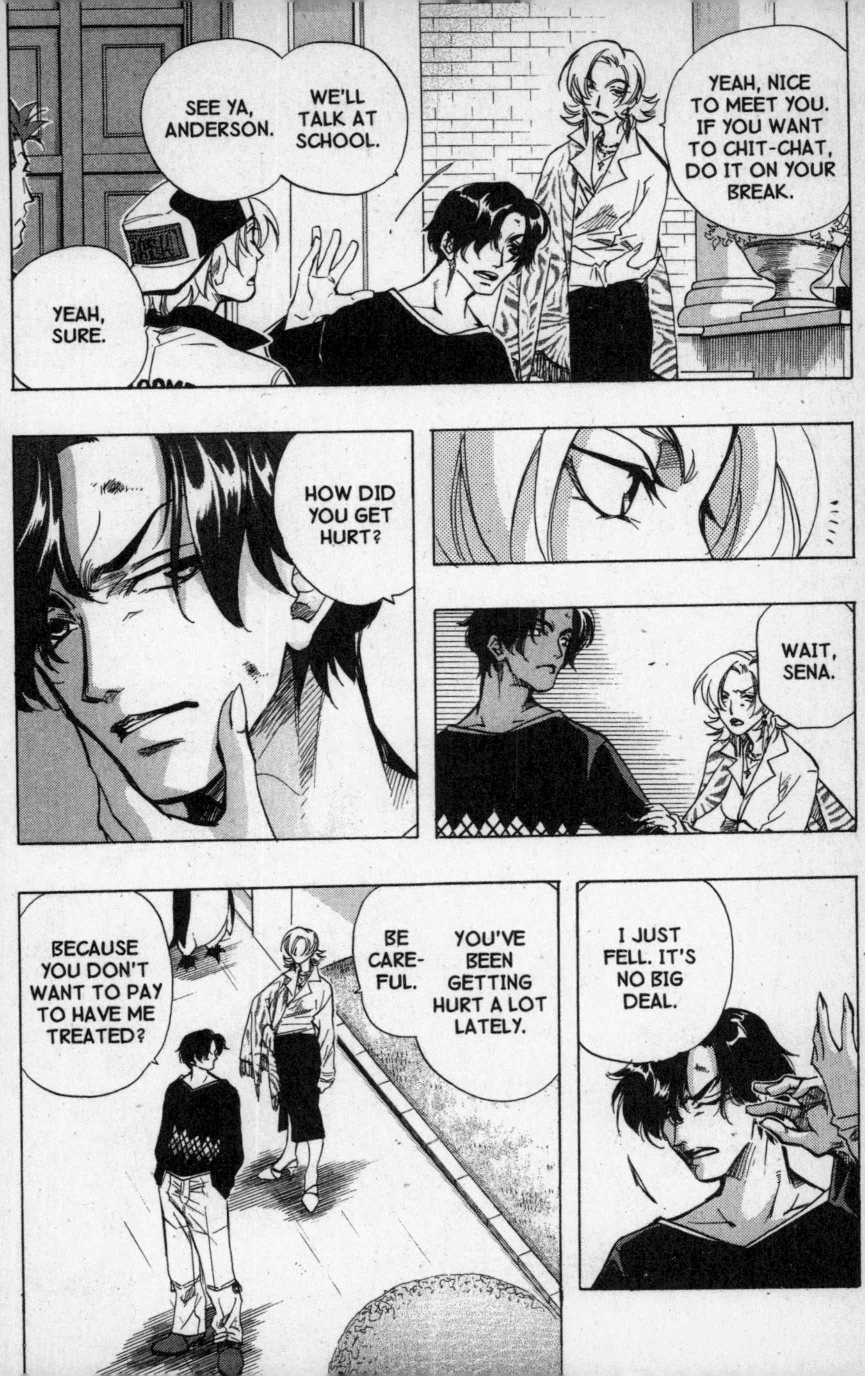
YEAH, NICE TO MEET YOU. IF YOU WANT TO CHIT-CHAT, DO IT ON YOUR BREAK.
WE'LL TALK AT SCHOOL.
SEE YA, ANDERSON.
YEAH, SURE.
WAIT, SENA.
HOW DID YOU GET HURT?
I JUST FELL. IT'S NO BIG DEAL.
YOU'VE BEEN GETTING HURT A LOT LATELY.
BE CARE-FUL.
BECAUSE YOU DON'T WANT TO PAY TO HAVE ME TREATED?

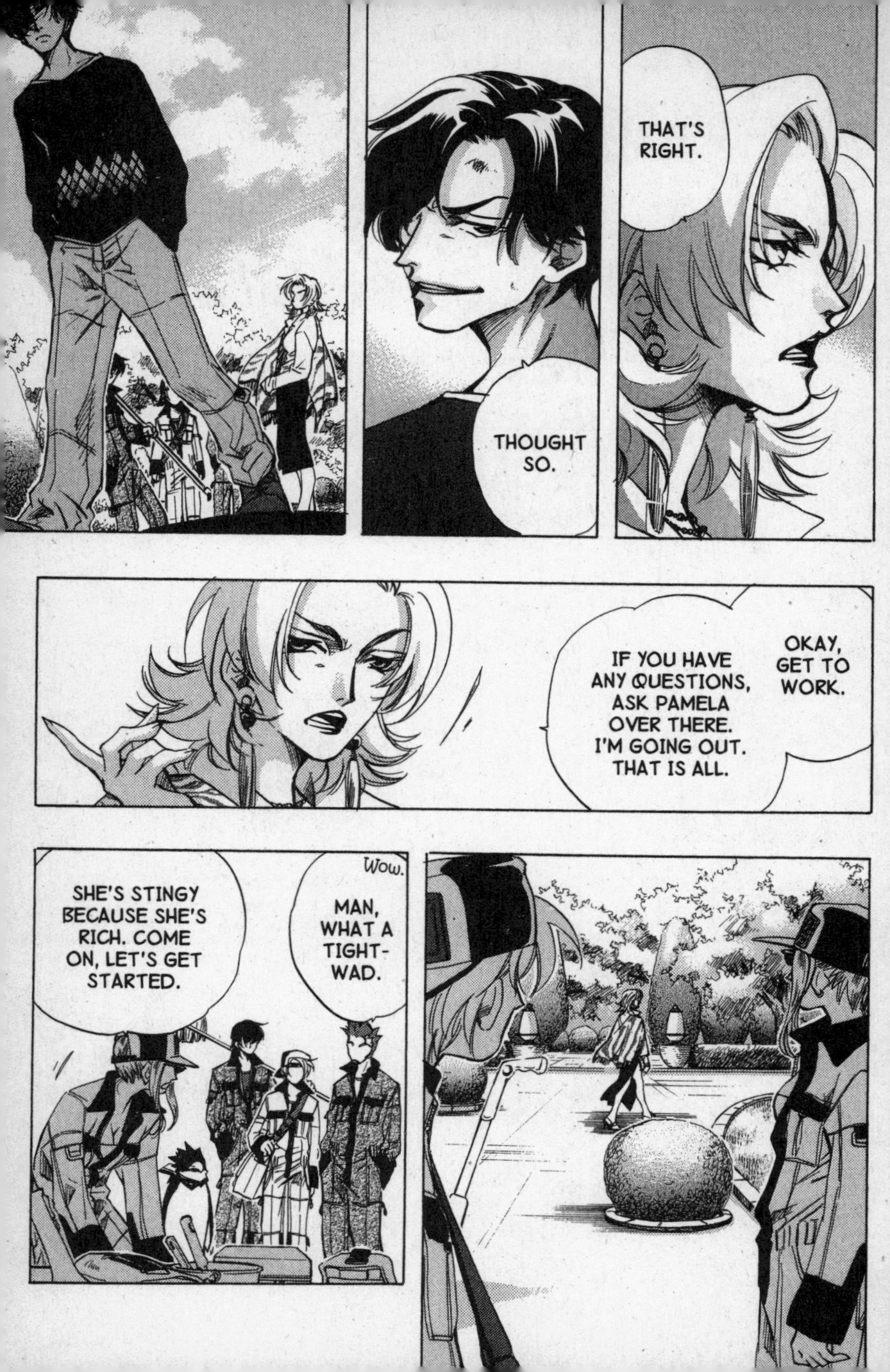
THAT'S RIGHT.
THOUGHT SO.
OKAY, GET TO WORK.
IF YOU HAVE ANY QUESTIONS, ASK PAMELA OVER THERE. I'M GOING OUT. THAT IS ALL.
Wow.
MAN, WHAT A TIGHT-WAD.
SHE'S STINGY BECAUSE SHE'S RICH. COME ON, LET'S GET STARTED.

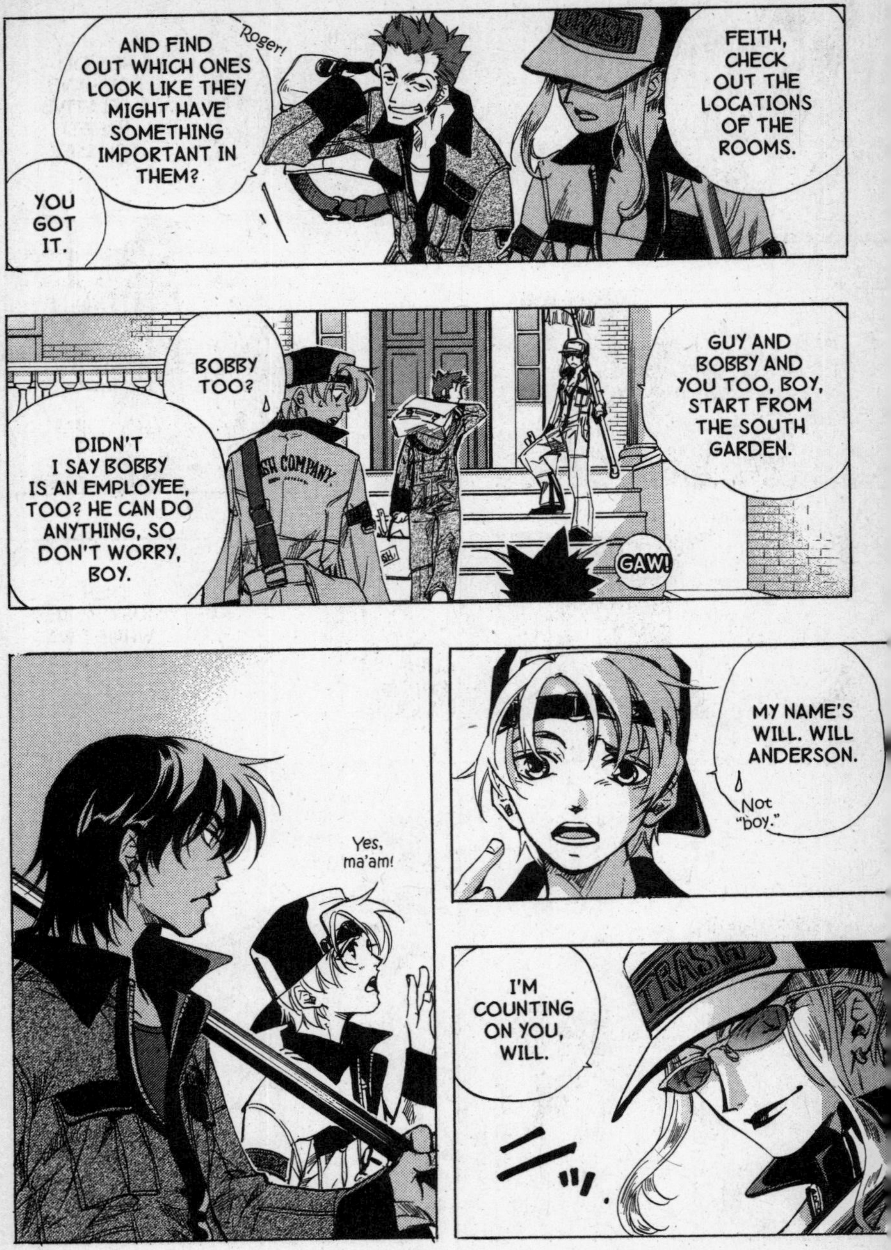
FEITH, CHECK OUT THE LOCATIONS OF THE ROOMS.
Roger!
AND FIND OUT WHICH ONES LOOK LIKE THEY MIGHT HAVE SOMETHING IMPORTANT IN THEM?
YOU GOT IT.
GUY AND BOBBY AND YOU TOO, BOY, START FROM THE SOUTH GARDEN.
GAW!
BOBBY TOO?
DIDN'T I SAY BOBBY IS AN EMPLOYEE, TOO? HE CAN DO ANYTHING, SO DON'T WORRY, BOY.
MY NAME'S WILL. WILL ANDERSON.
Not "boy."
I'M COUNTING ON YOU, WILL.
Yes, ma'am!

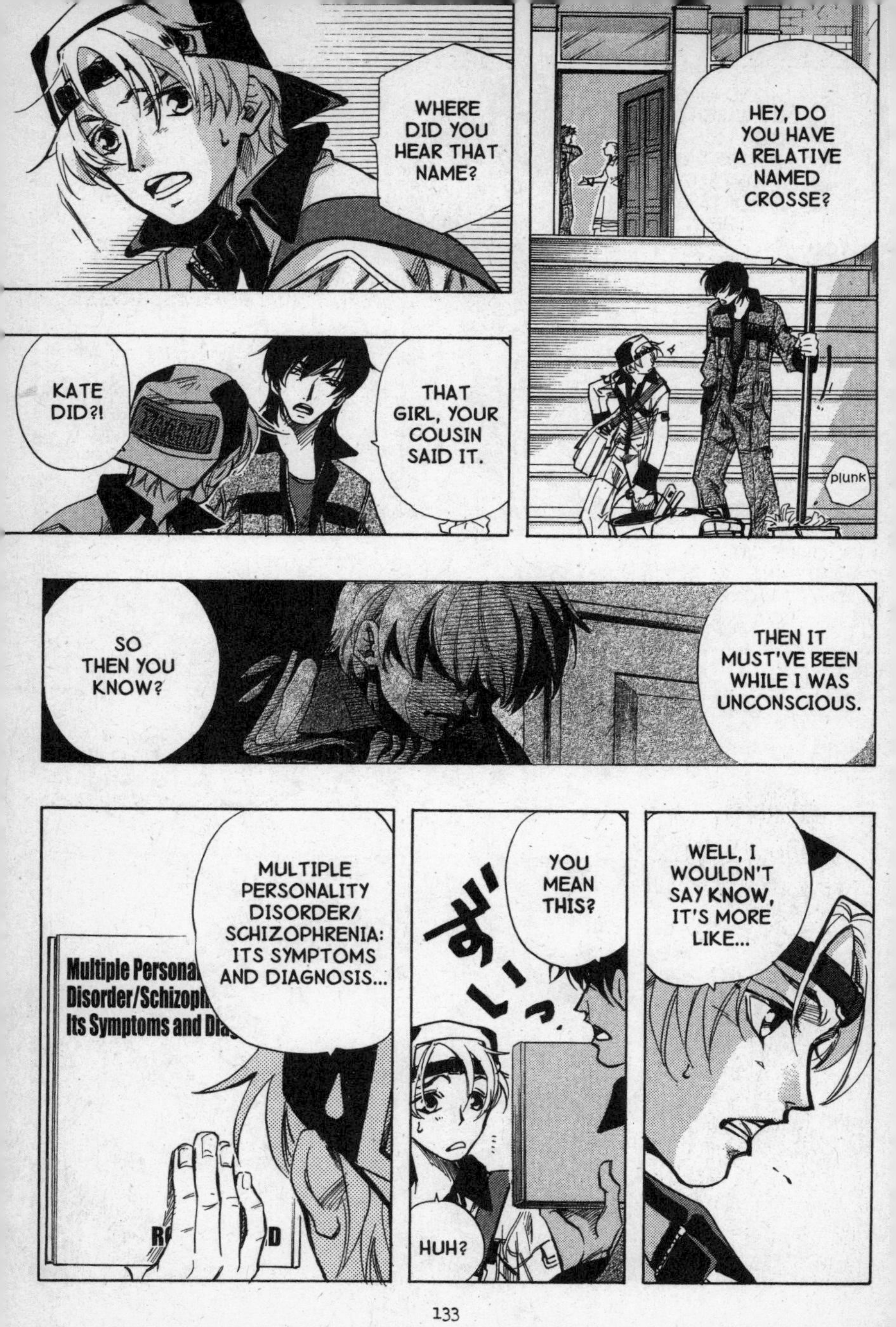
HEY, DO YOU HAVE A RELATIVE NAMED CROSSE?
plunk
WHERE DID YOU HEAR THAT NAME?
THAT GIRL, YOUR COUSIN SAID IT.
KATE DID?!
THEN IT MUST'VE BEEN WHILE I WAS UNCONSCIOUS.
SO THEN YOU KNOW?
WELL, I WOULDN'T SAY KNOW, IT'S MORE LIKE...
YOU MEAN THIS?
ずいっ
HUH?
MULTIPLE PERSONALITY DISORDER/ SCHIZOPHRENIA: ITS SYMPTOMS AND DIAGNOSIS...

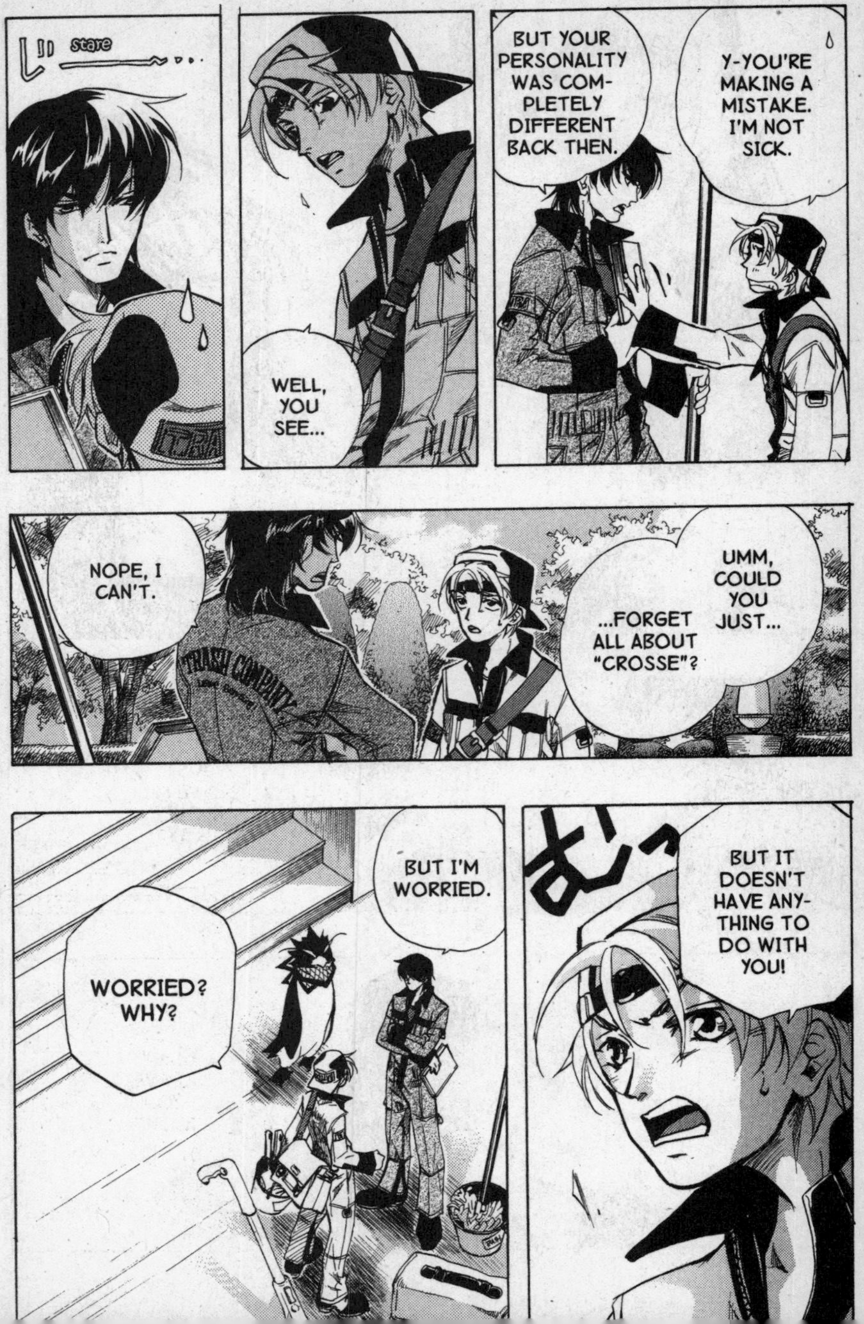
Y-YOU'RE MAKING A MISTAKE. I'M NOT SICK.
BUT YOUR PERSONALITY WAS COM-PLETELY DIFFERENT BACK THEN.
WELL, YOU SEE...
stare
UMM, COULD YOU JUST...
...FORGET ALL ABOUT "CROSSE"?
NOPE, I CAN'T.
BUT IT DOESN'T HAVE ANY-THING TO DO WITH YOU!
BUT I'M WORRIED.
WORRIED? WHY?

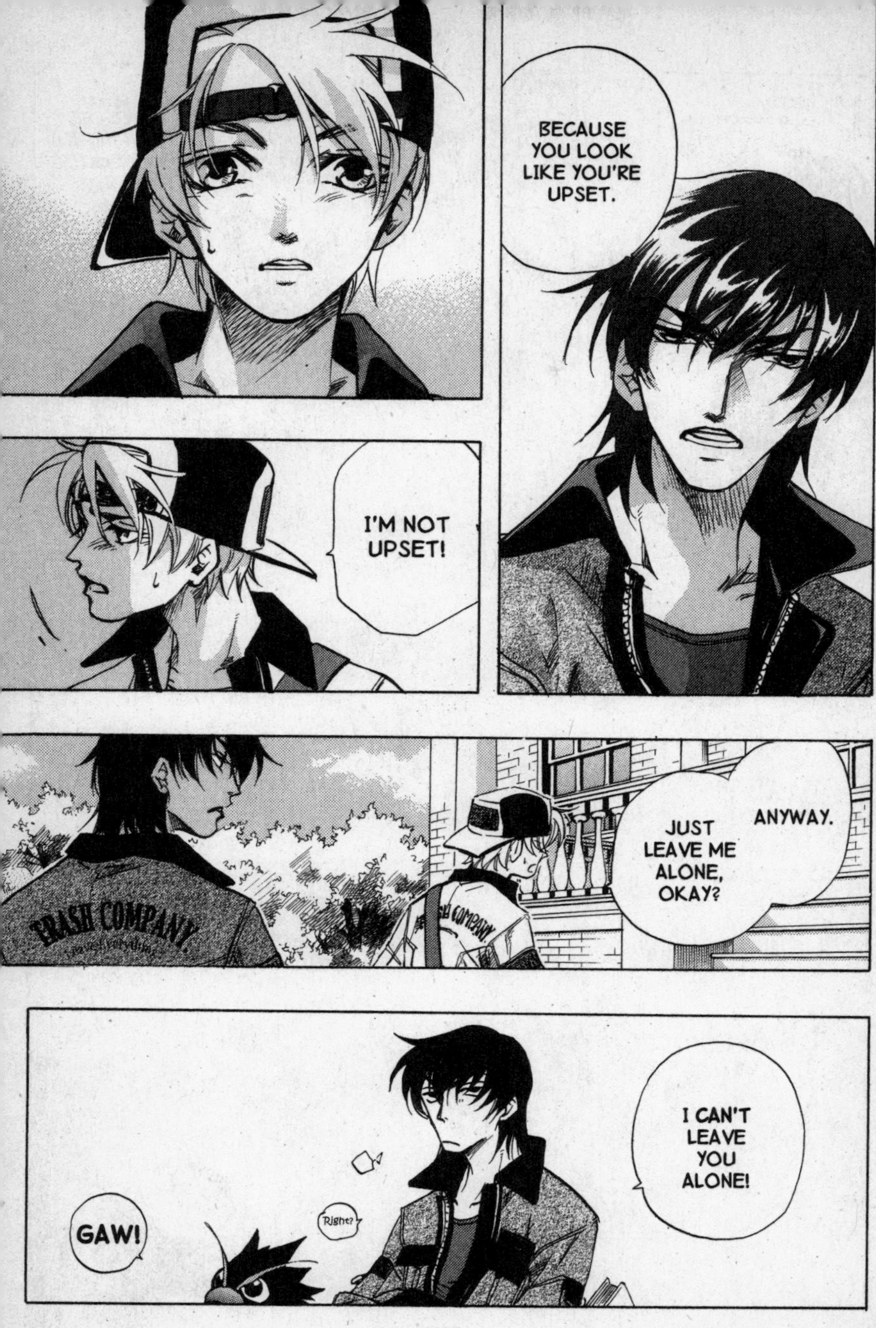
BECAUSE YOU LOOK LIKE YOU'RE UPSET.
I'M NOT UPSET!
ANYWAY.
JUST LEAVE ME ALONE, OKAY?
ERASH COMPANY.
I CAN'T LEAVE YOU ALONE!
Right?
GAW!

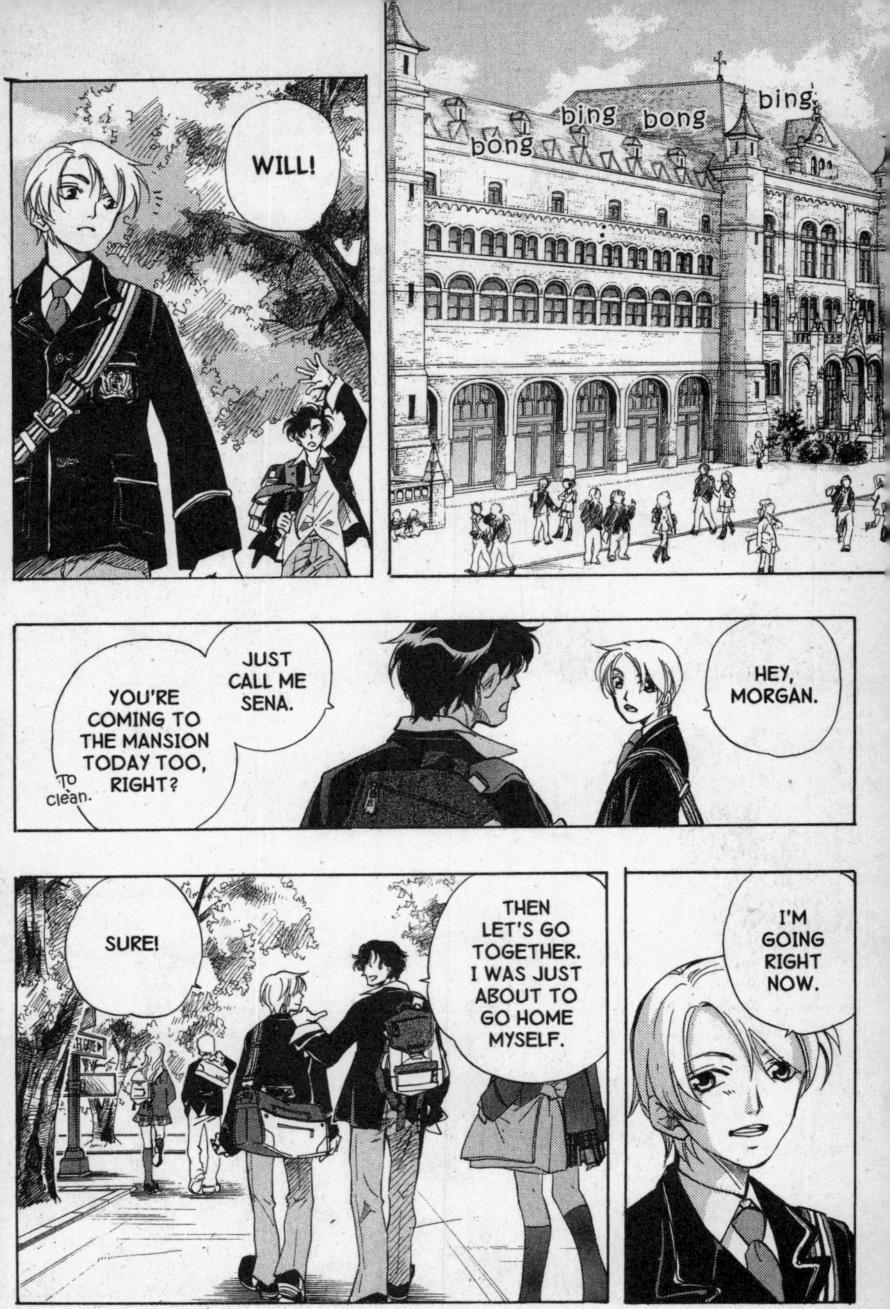
bong
bing
bong
bing
WILL!
HEY, MORGAN.
JUST CALL ME SENA.
YOU'RE COMING TO THE MANSION TODAY TOO, RIGHT?
TO clean.
I'M GOING RIGHT NOW.
THEN LET'S GO TOGETHER. I WAS JUST ABOUT TO GO HOME MYSELF.
SURE!

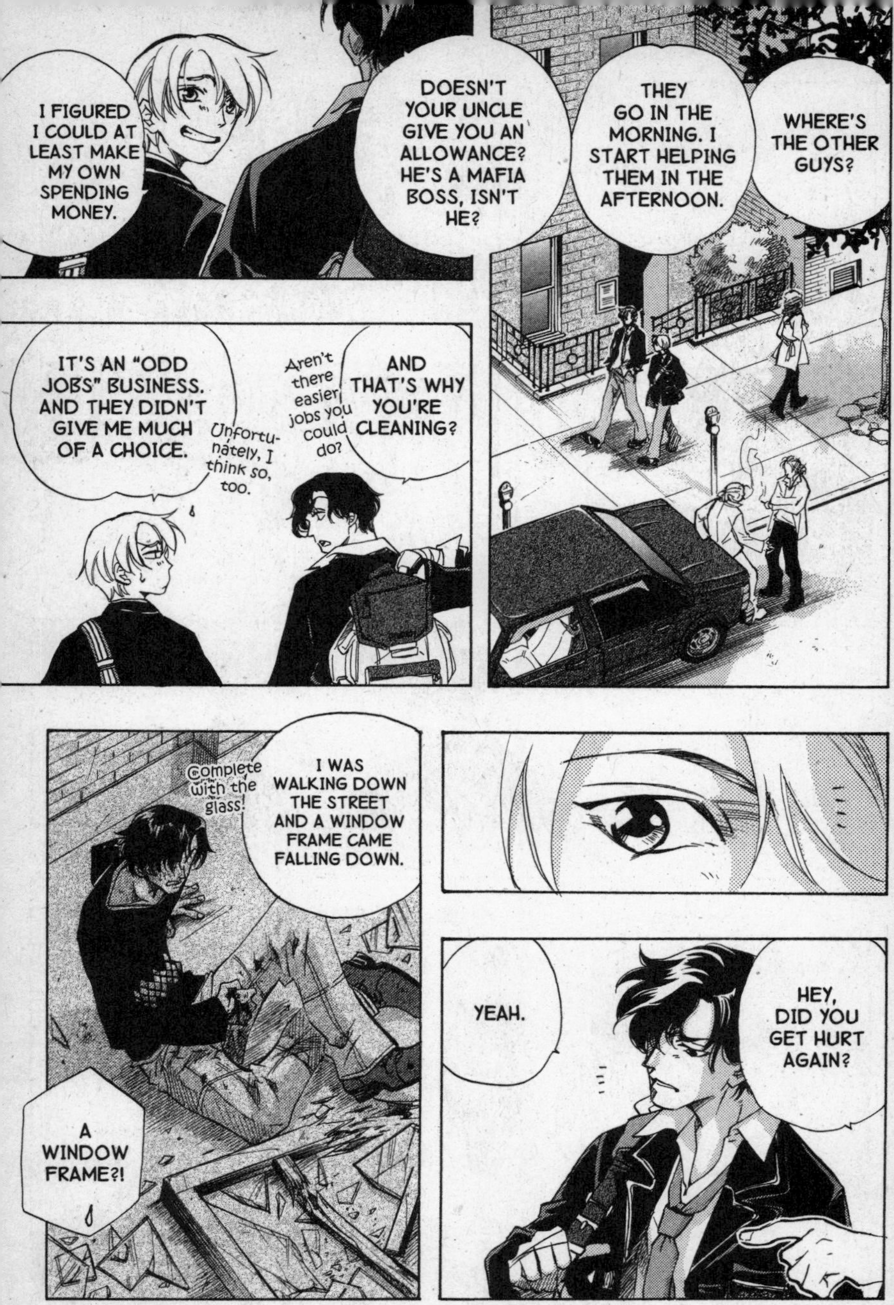
WHERE'S THE OTHER GUYS?
THEY GO IN THE MORNING. I START HELPING THEM IN THE AFTERNOON.
DOESN'T YOUR UNCLE GIVE YOU AN ALLOWANCE? HE'S A MAFIA BOSS, ISN'T HE?
I FIGURED I COULD AT LEAST MAKE MY OWN SPENDING MONEY.
AND THAT'S WHY YOU'RE CLEANING?
Aren't there easier jobs you could do?
IT'S AN "ODD JOBS" BUSINESS. AND THEY DIDN'T GIVE ME MUCH OF A CHOICE.
Unfortunately, I think so, too.
HEY, DID YOU GET HURT AGAIN?
YEAH.
I WAS WALKING DOWN THE STREET AND A WINDOW FRAME CAME FALLING DOWN.
Complete with the glass!
A WINDOW FRAME?!

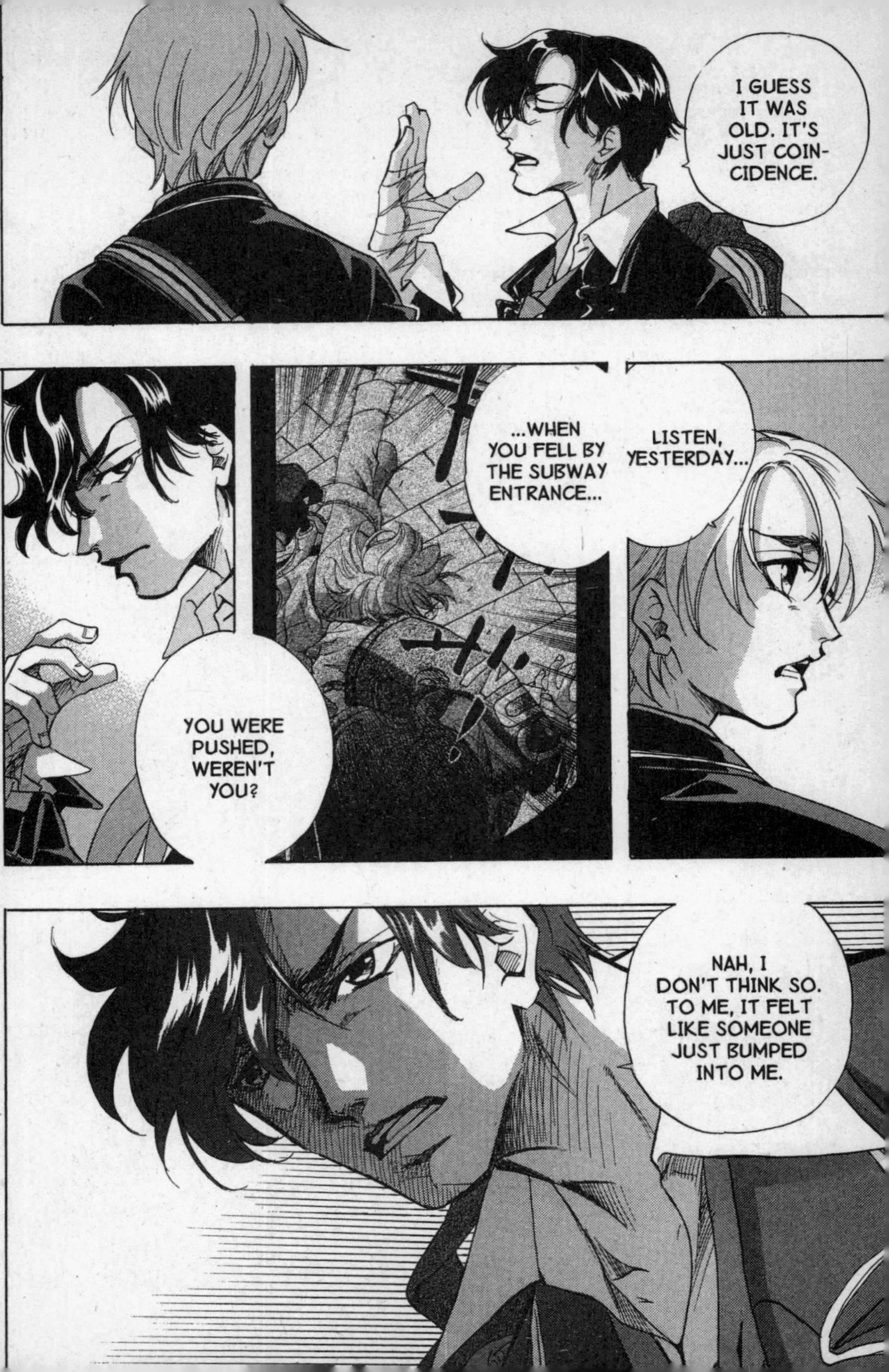
I GUESS IT WAS OLD. IT'S JUST COIN-CIDENCE.
LISTEN, YESTERDAY...
...WHEN YOU FELL BY THE SUBWAY ENTRANCE...
YOU WERE PUSHED, WEREN'T YOU?
NAH, I DON'T THINK SO. TO ME, IT FELT LIKE SOMEONE JUST BUMPED INTO ME.

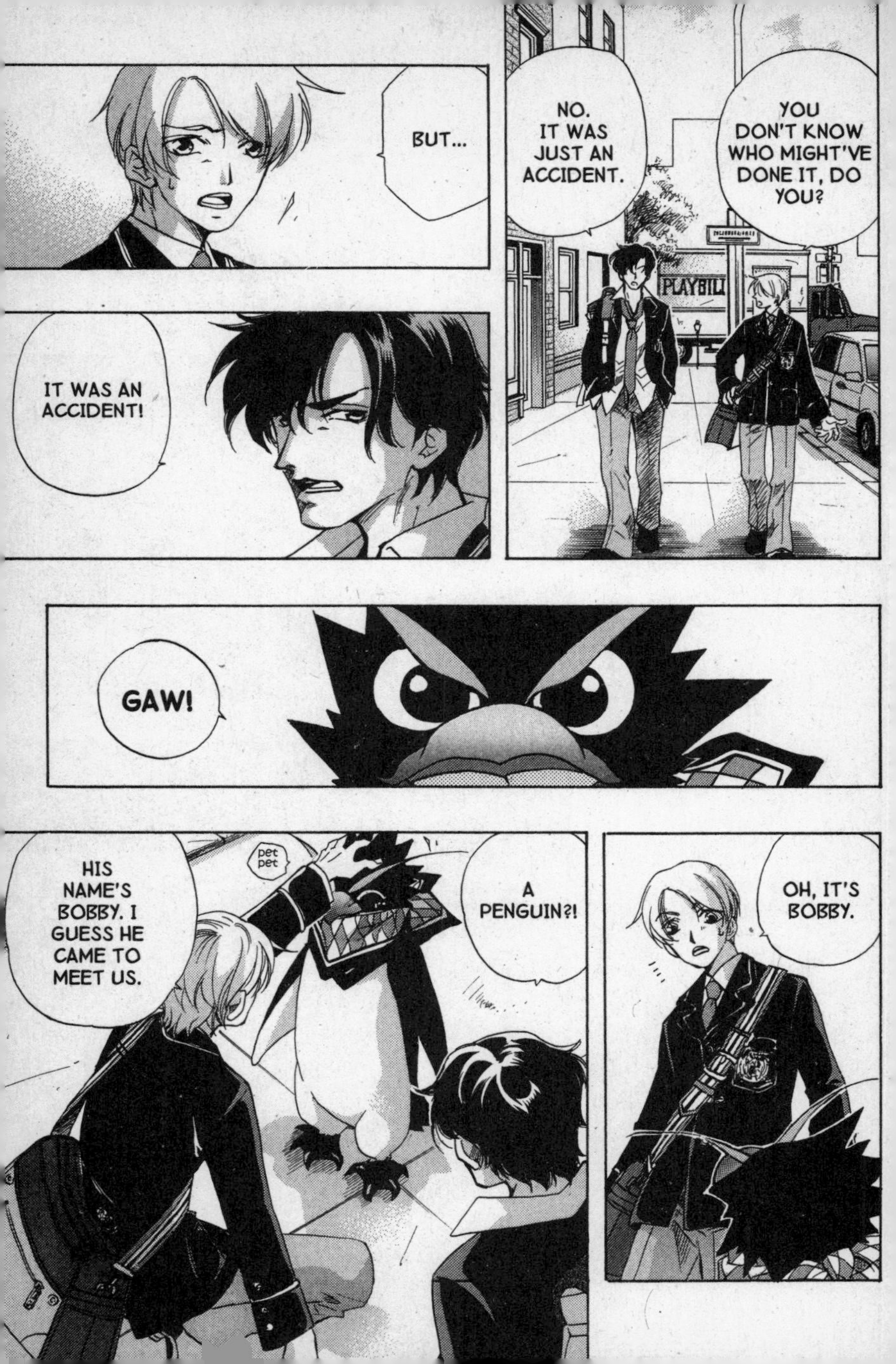
YOU DON'T KNOW WHO MIGHT'VE DONE IT, DO YOU?
NO. IT WAS JUST AN ACCIDENT.
PLAYBILL
BUT...
IT WAS AN ACCIDENT!
GAW!
OH, IT'S BOBBY.
A PENGUIN?!
pet pet
HIS NAME'S BOBBY. I GUESS HE CAME TO MEET US.

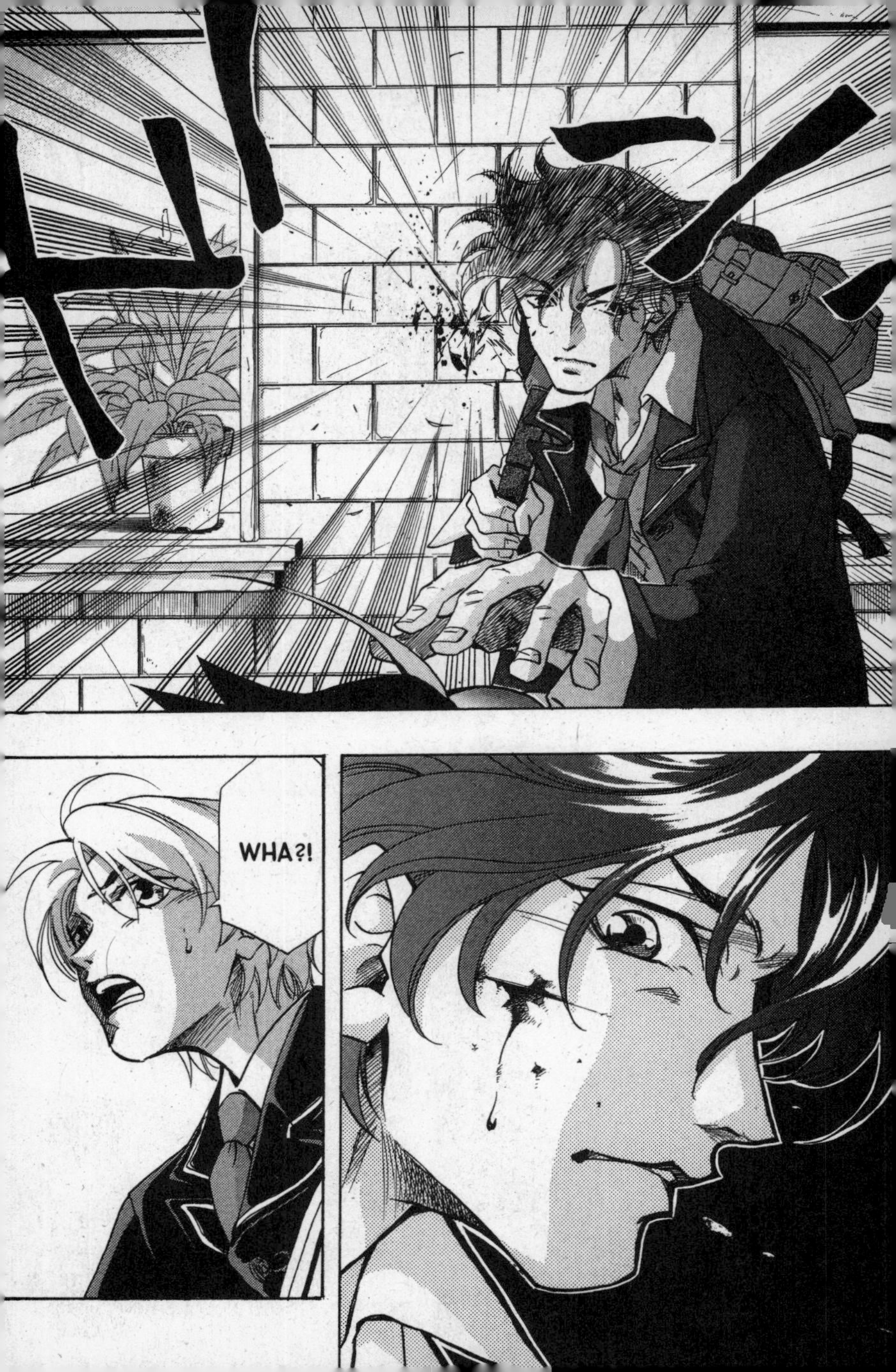
WHA?!

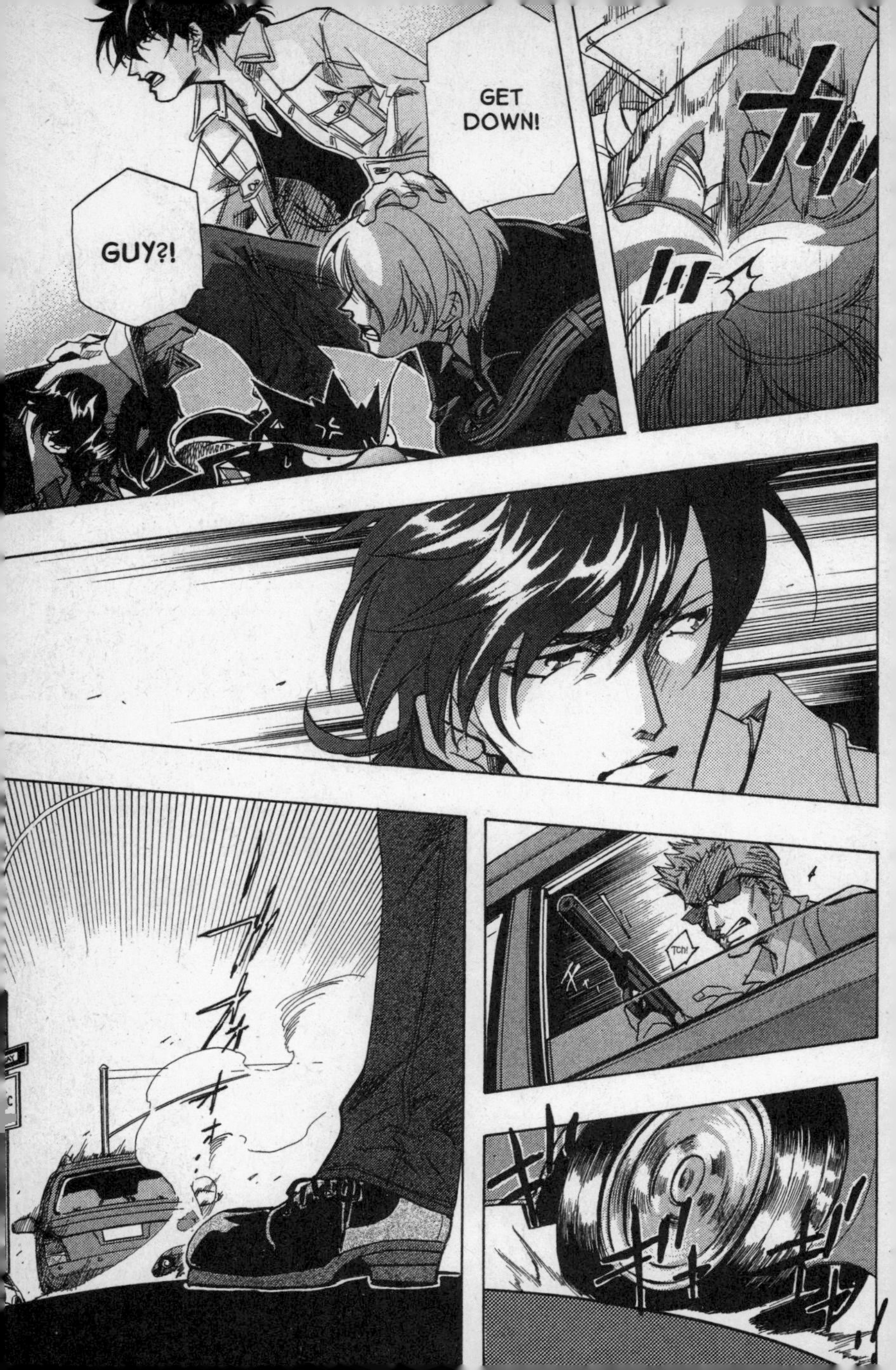
GET DOWN!
GUY?!
TCH!

A GUNSHOT.

A GUN-SHOT?!

BUT WHAT WAS THAT SOUND?

YEAH.

YOU OKAY?

TAKE A LOOK AT THE WALL BEHIND YOU.

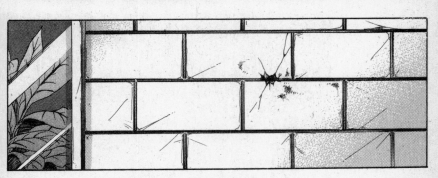

LOOKS LIKE THEY WERE AIMING AT YOUR FRIEND FROM AROUND THE CORNER.

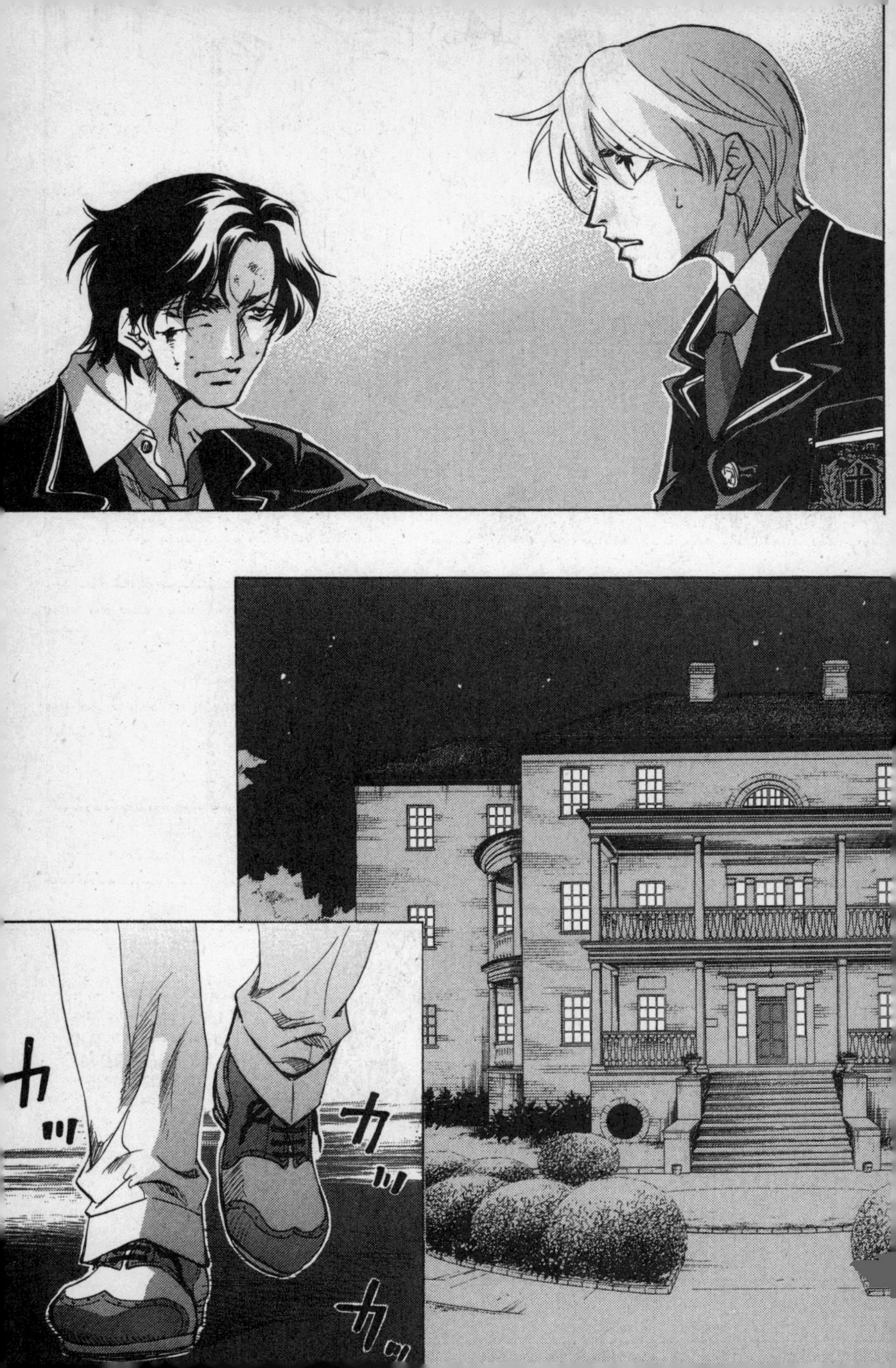
カッ
カッ
カッ

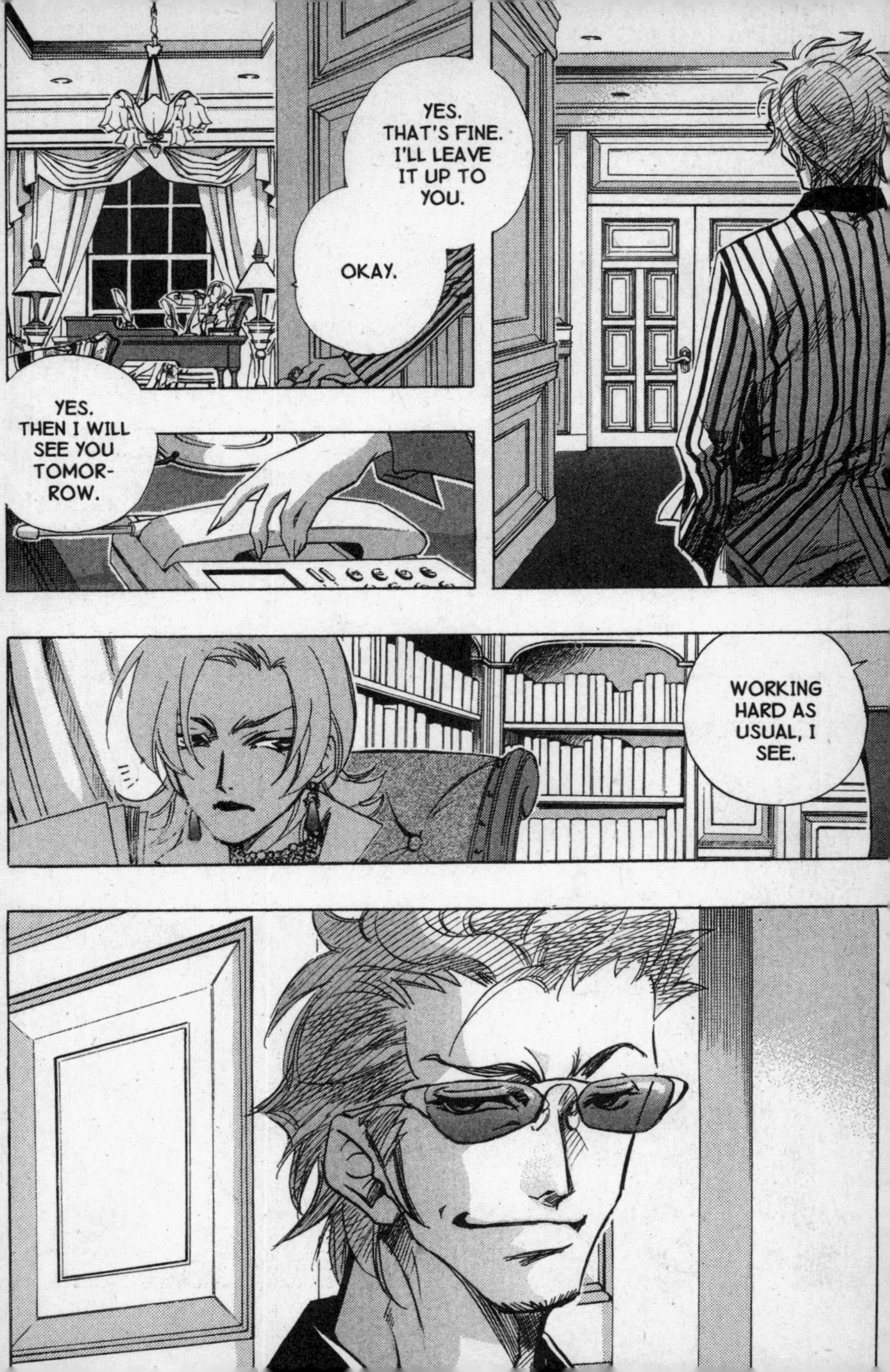
YES. THAT'S FINE. I'LL LEAVE IT UP TO YOU.
OKAY.
YES. THEN I WILL SEE YOU TOMORROW.
WORKING HARD AS USUAL, I SEE.

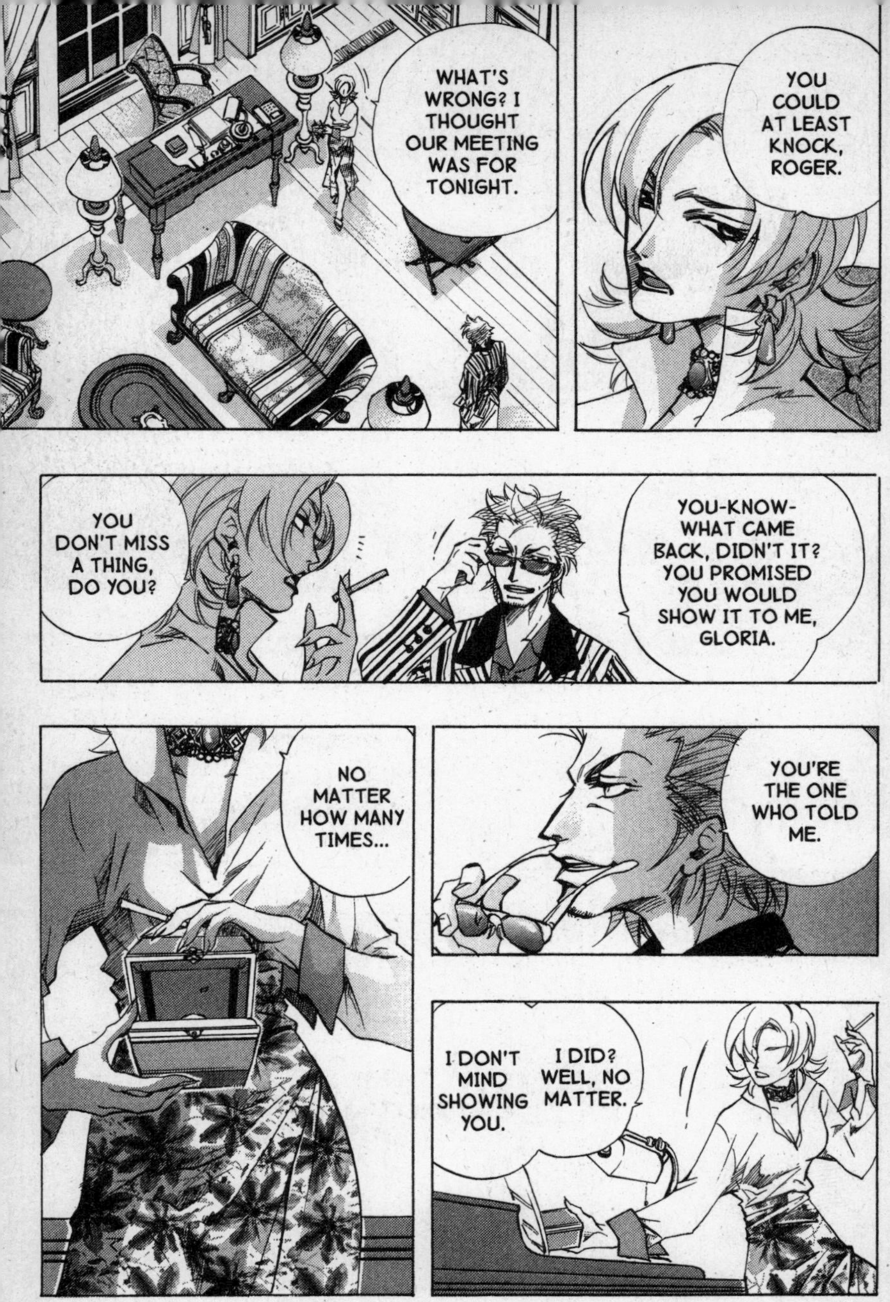
YOU COULD AT LEAST KNOCK, ROGER.
WHAT'S WRONG? I THOUGHT OUR MEETING WAS FOR TONIGHT.
YOU-KNOW-WHAT CAME BACK, DIDN'T IT? YOU PROMISED YOU WOULD SHOW IT TO ME, GLORIA.
YOU DON'T MISS A THING, DO YOU?
YOU'RE THE ONE WHO TOLD ME.
I DID? WELL, NO MATTER.
I DON'T MIND SHOWING YOU.
NO MATTER HOW MANY TIMES...

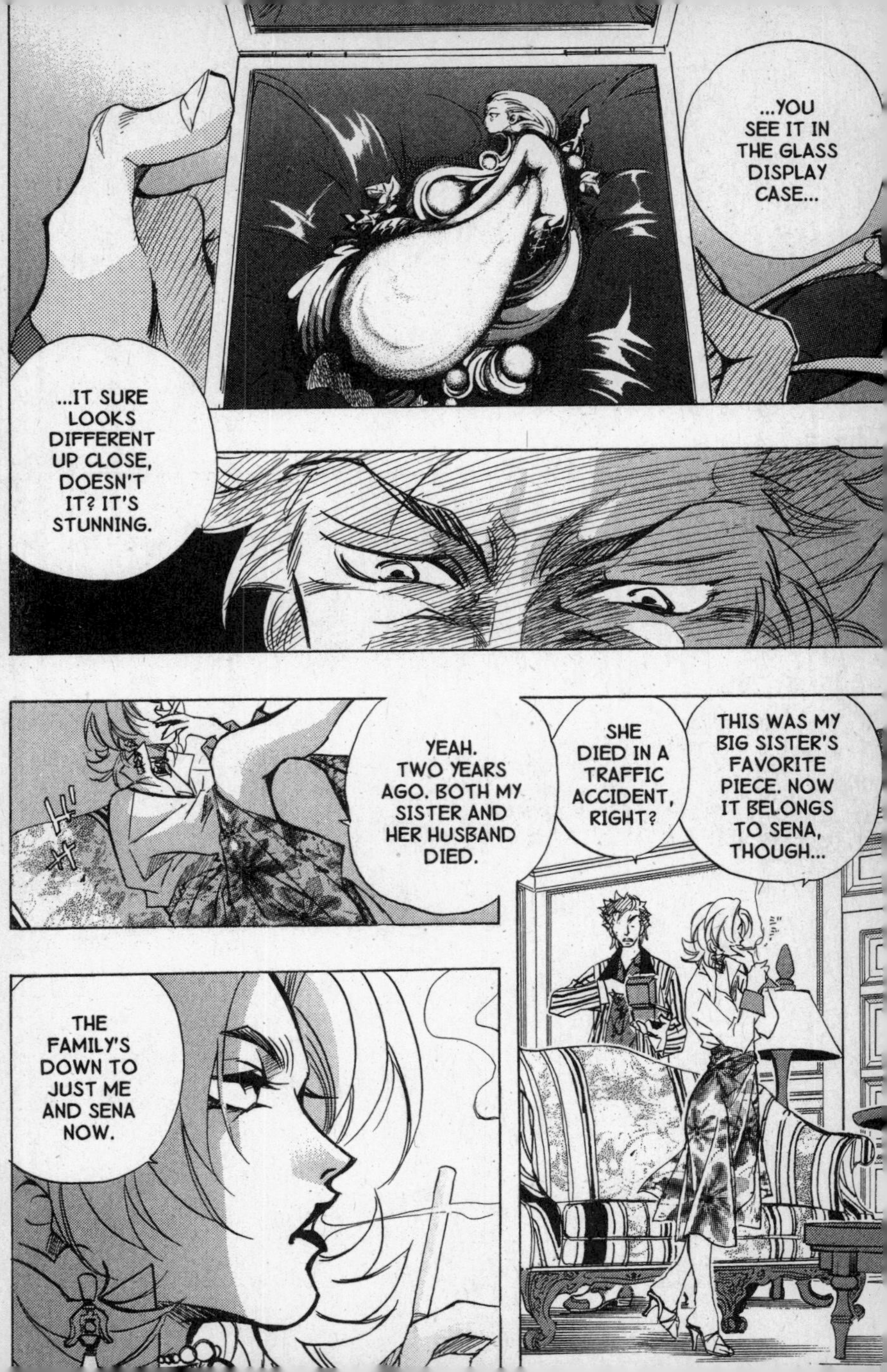
...YOU SEE IT IN THE GLASS DISPLAY CASE...
...IT SURE LOOKS DIFFERENT UP CLOSE, DOESN'T IT? IT'S STUNNING.
THIS WAS MY BIG SISTER'S FAVORITE PIECE. NOW IT BELONGS TO SENA, THOUGH...
SHE DIED IN A TRAFFIC ACCIDENT, RIGHT?
YEAH. TWO YEARS AGO. BOTH MY SISTER AND HER HUSBAND DIED.
THE FAMILY'S DOWN TO JUST ME AND SENA NOW.

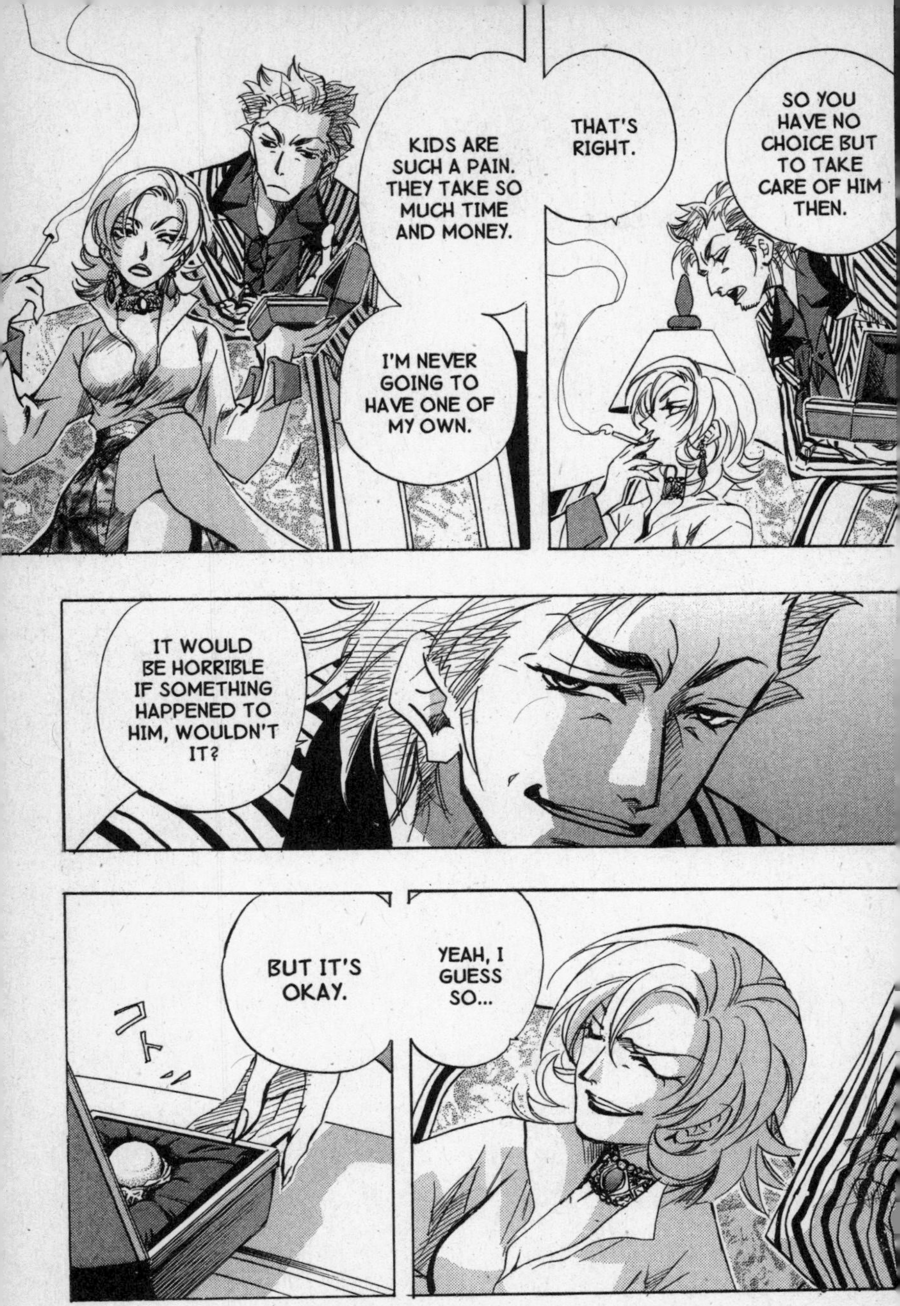
SO YOU HAVE NO CHOICE BUT TO TAKE CARE OF HIM THEN.
THAT'S RIGHT.
KIDS ARE SUCH A PAIN. THEY TAKE SO MUCH TIME AND MONEY.
I'M NEVER GOING TO HAVE ONE OF MY OWN.
IT WOULD BE HORRIBLE IF SOMETHING HAPPENED TO HIM, WOULDN'T IT?
YEAH, I GUESS SO...
BUT IT'S OKAY.
コトッ

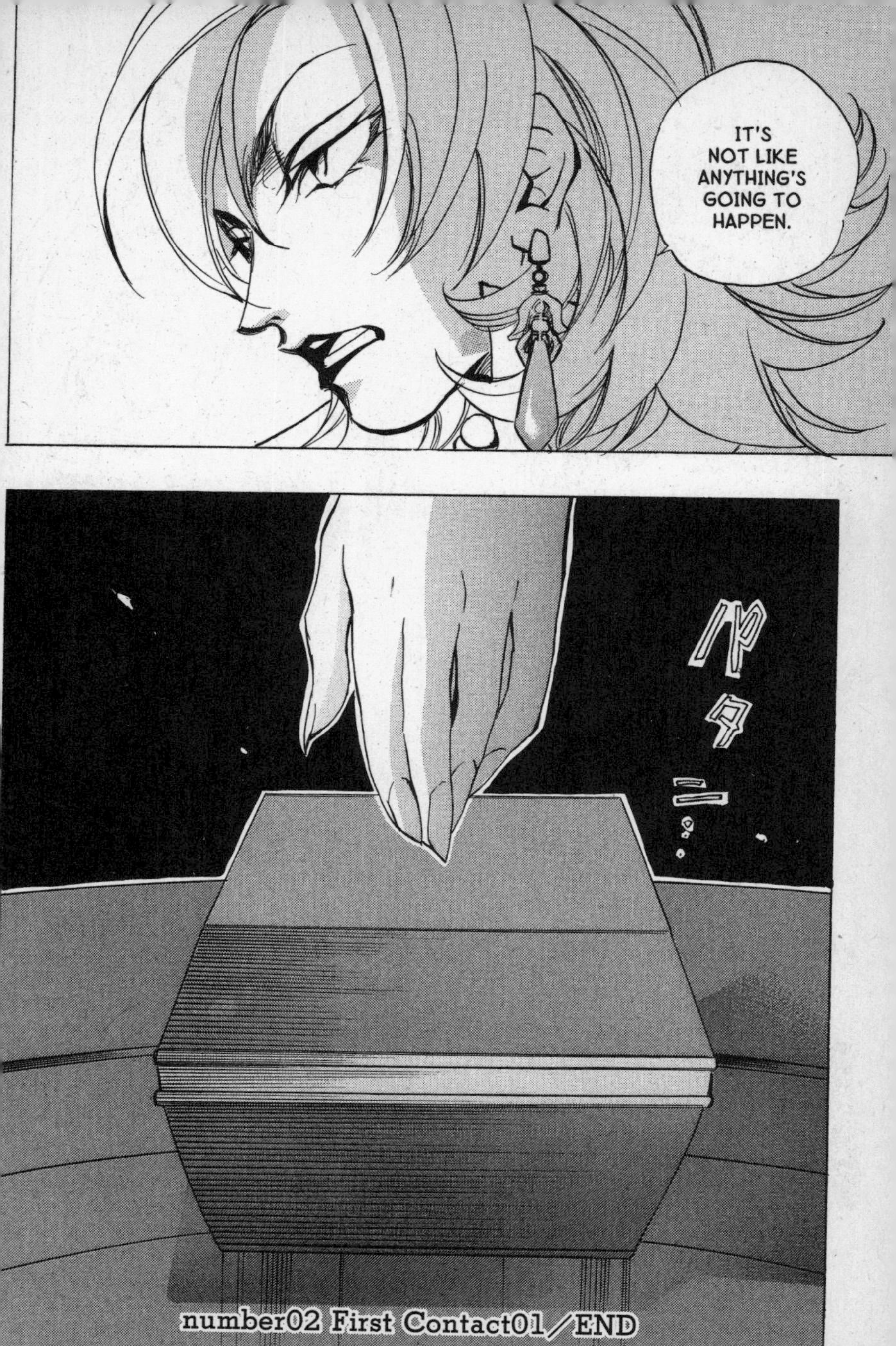
IT'S NOT LIKE ANYTHING'S GOING TO HAPPEN.
number02 First Contact01／END

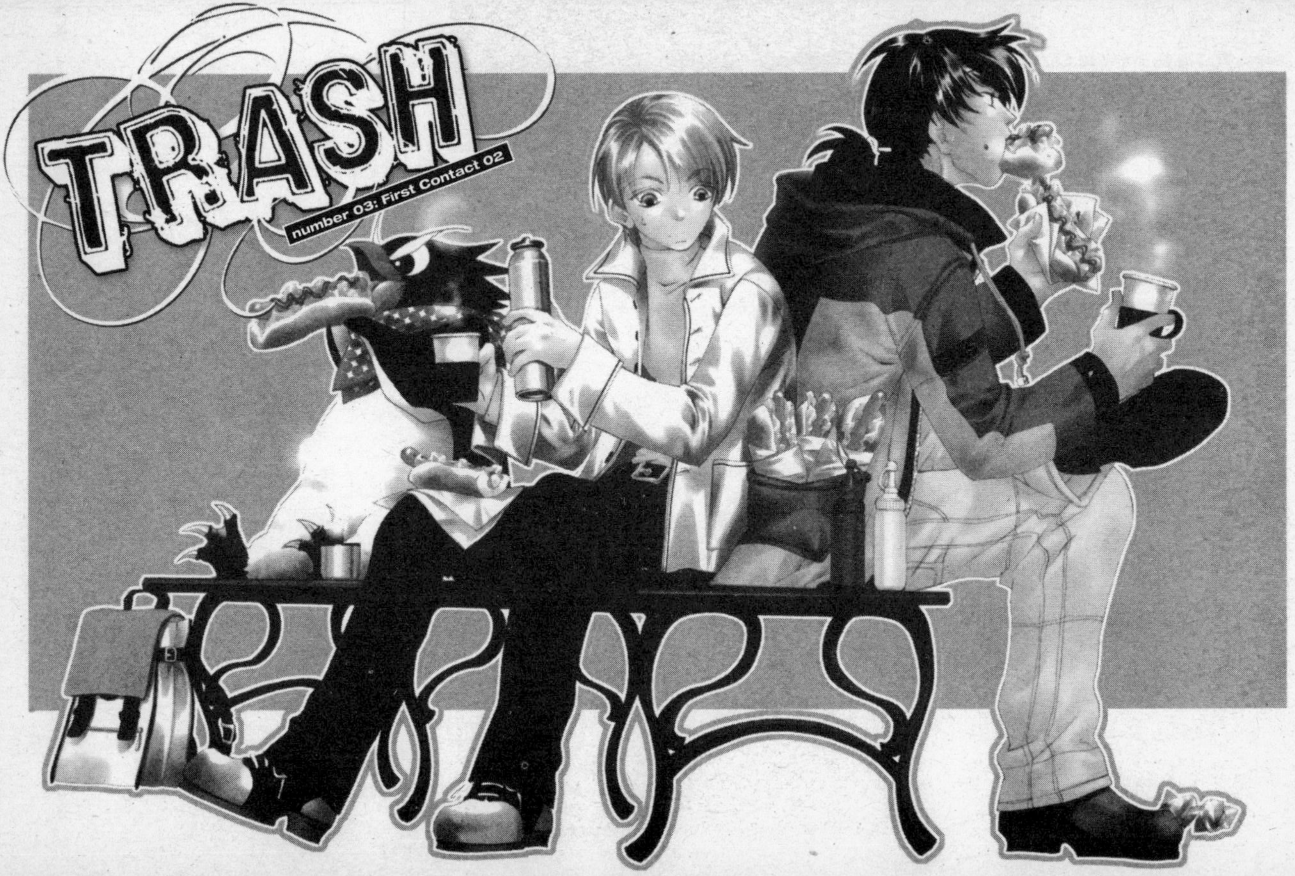
TRASH
number 03: First Contact 02

Father Connection
&
First Contact

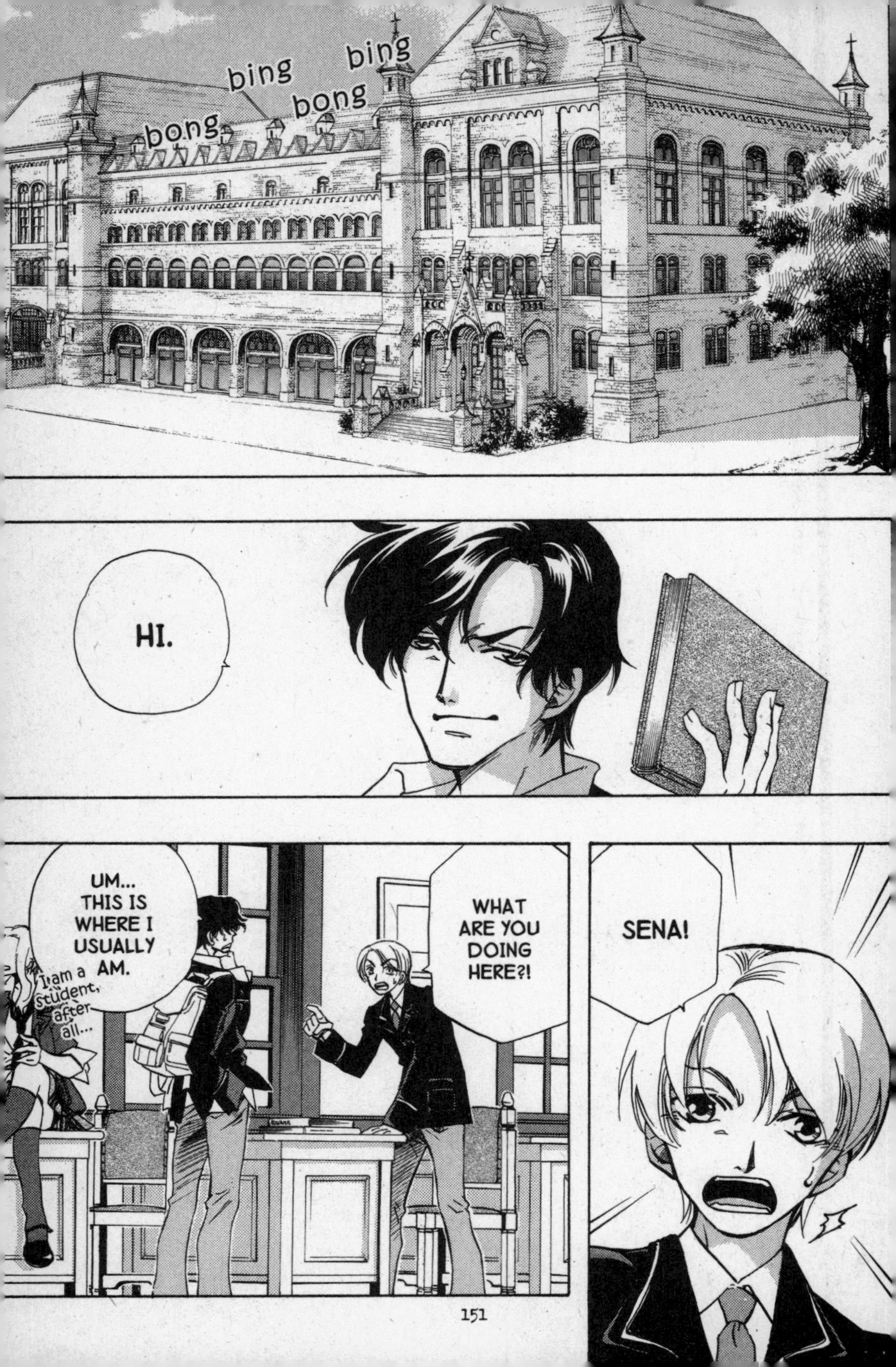
bing
bong
bing
bong
HI.
SENA!
WHAT ARE YOU DOING HERE?!
UM... THIS IS WHERE I USUALLY AM.
I am a student, after all...

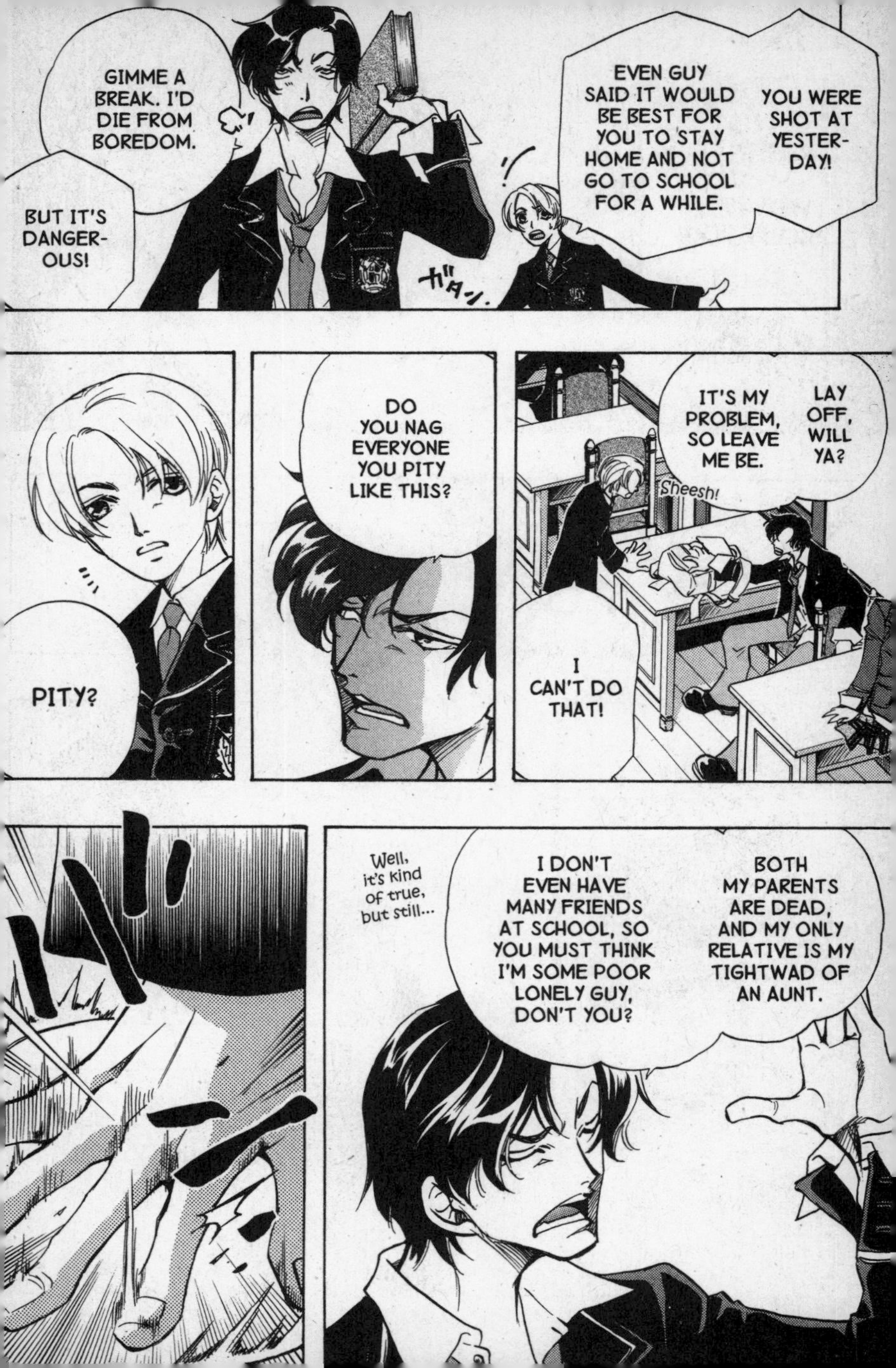
YOU WERE SHOT AT YESTER-DAY!
EVEN GUY SAID IT WOULD BE BEST FOR YOU TO STAY HOME AND NOT GO TO SCHOOL FOR A WHILE.
GIMME A BREAK. I'D DIE FROM BOREDOM.
BUT IT'S DANGER-OUS!
LAY OFF, WILL YA?
IT'S MY PROBLEM, SO LEAVE ME BE.
Sheesh!
I CAN'T DO THAT!
DO YOU NAG EVERYONE YOU PITY LIKE THIS?
PITY?
BOTH MY PARENTS ARE DEAD, AND MY ONLY RELATIVE IS MY TIGHTWAD OF AN AUNT.
I DON'T EVEN HAVE MANY FRIENDS AT SCHOOL, SO YOU MUST THINK I'M SOME POOR LONELY GUY, DON'T YOU?
Well, it's kind of true, but still...

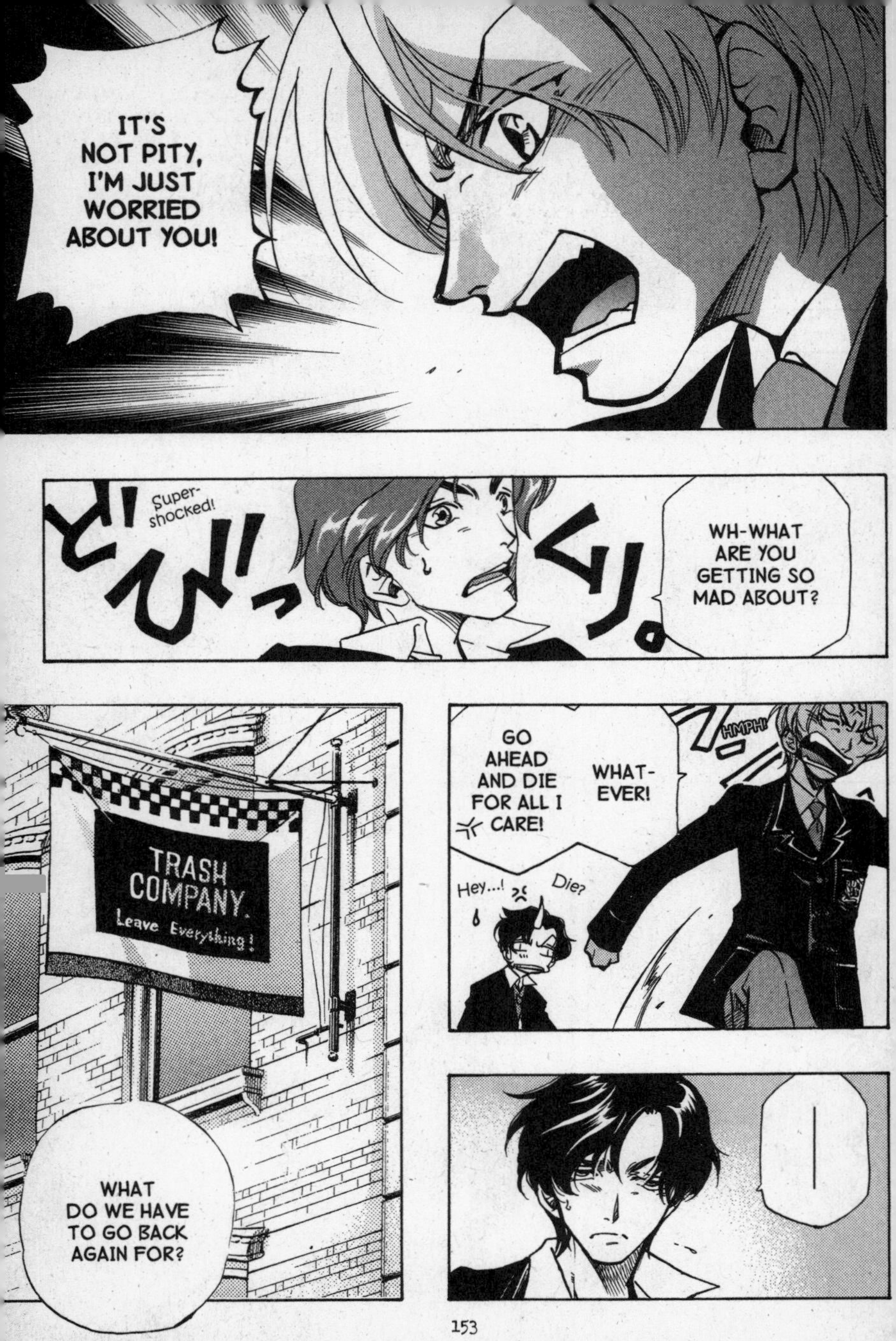
IT'S NOT PITY, I'M JUST WORRIED ABOUT YOU!
WH-WHAT ARE YOU GETTING SO MAD ABOUT?
どびっくり。
Super-shocked!
HMPH!
WHAT-EVER!
GO AHEAD AND DIE FOR ALL I CARE!
Die?
Hey...!
TRASH COMPANY. Leave Everything!
WHAT DO WE HAVE TO GO BACK AGAIN FOR?

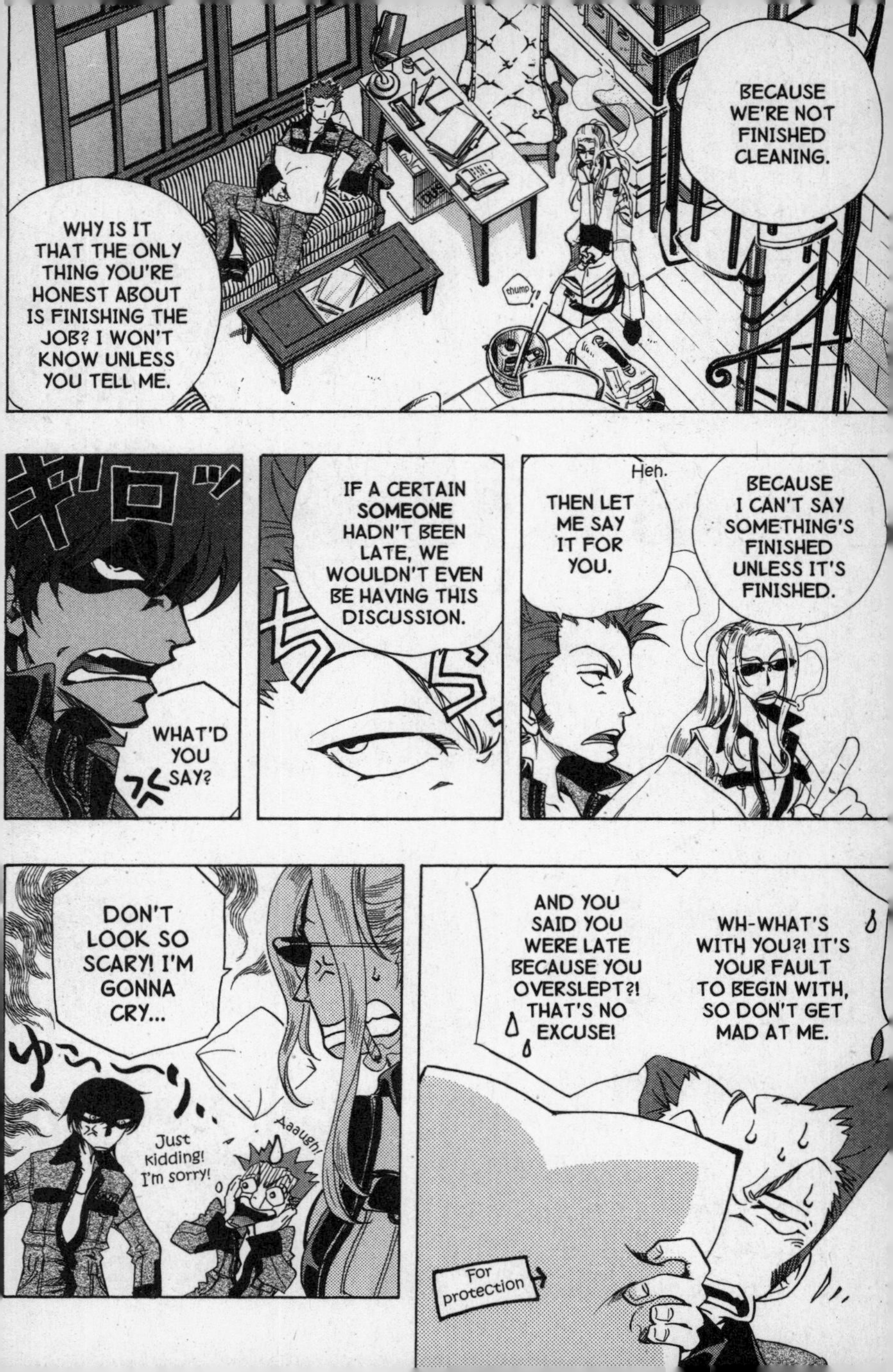
BECAUSE WE'RE NOT FINISHED CLEANING.
WHY IS IT THAT THE ONLY THING YOU'RE HONEST ABOUT IS FINISHING THE JOB? I WON'T KNOW UNLESS YOU TELL ME.
thump
BECAUSE I CAN'T SAY SOMETHING'S FINISHED UNLESS IT'S FINISHED.
Heh.
THEN LET ME SAY IT FOR YOU.
IF A CERTAIN SOMEONE HADN'T BEEN LATE, WE WOULDN'T EVEN BE HAVING THIS DISCUSSION.
ギロッ
WHAT'D YOU SAY?
WH-WHAT'S WITH YOU?! IT'S YOUR FAULT TO BEGIN WITH, SO DON'T GET MAD AT ME.
AND YOU SAID YOU WERE LATE BECAUSE YOU OVERSLEPT?! THAT'S NO EXCUSE!
For protection
DON'T LOOK SO SCARY! I'M GONNA CRY...
Aaaugh!
Just kidding! I'm sorry!

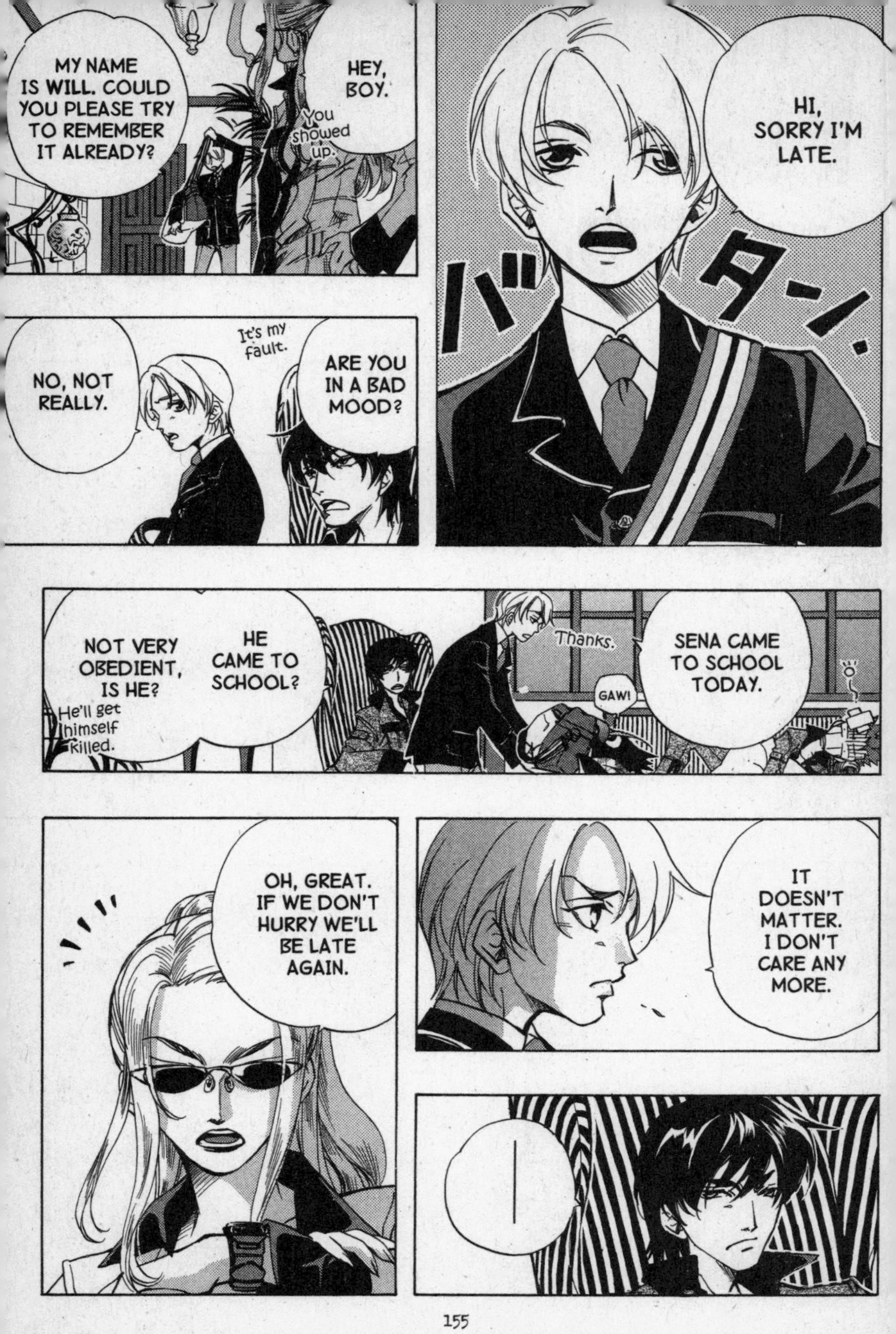

HI, SORRY I'M LATE.
バターン!
HEY, BOY.
You showed up.
MY NAME IS WILL. COULD YOU PLEASE TRY TO REMEMBER IT ALREADY?
ARE YOU IN A BAD MOOD?
It's my fault.
NO, NOT REALLY.
SENA CAME TO SCHOOL TODAY.
GAW!
Thanks.
HE CAME TO SCHOOL?
NOT VERY OBEDIENT, IS HE?
He'll get himself killed.
IT DOESN'T MATTER. I DON'T CARE ANY MORE.
OH, GREAT. IF WE DON'T HURRY WE'LL BE LATE AGAIN.

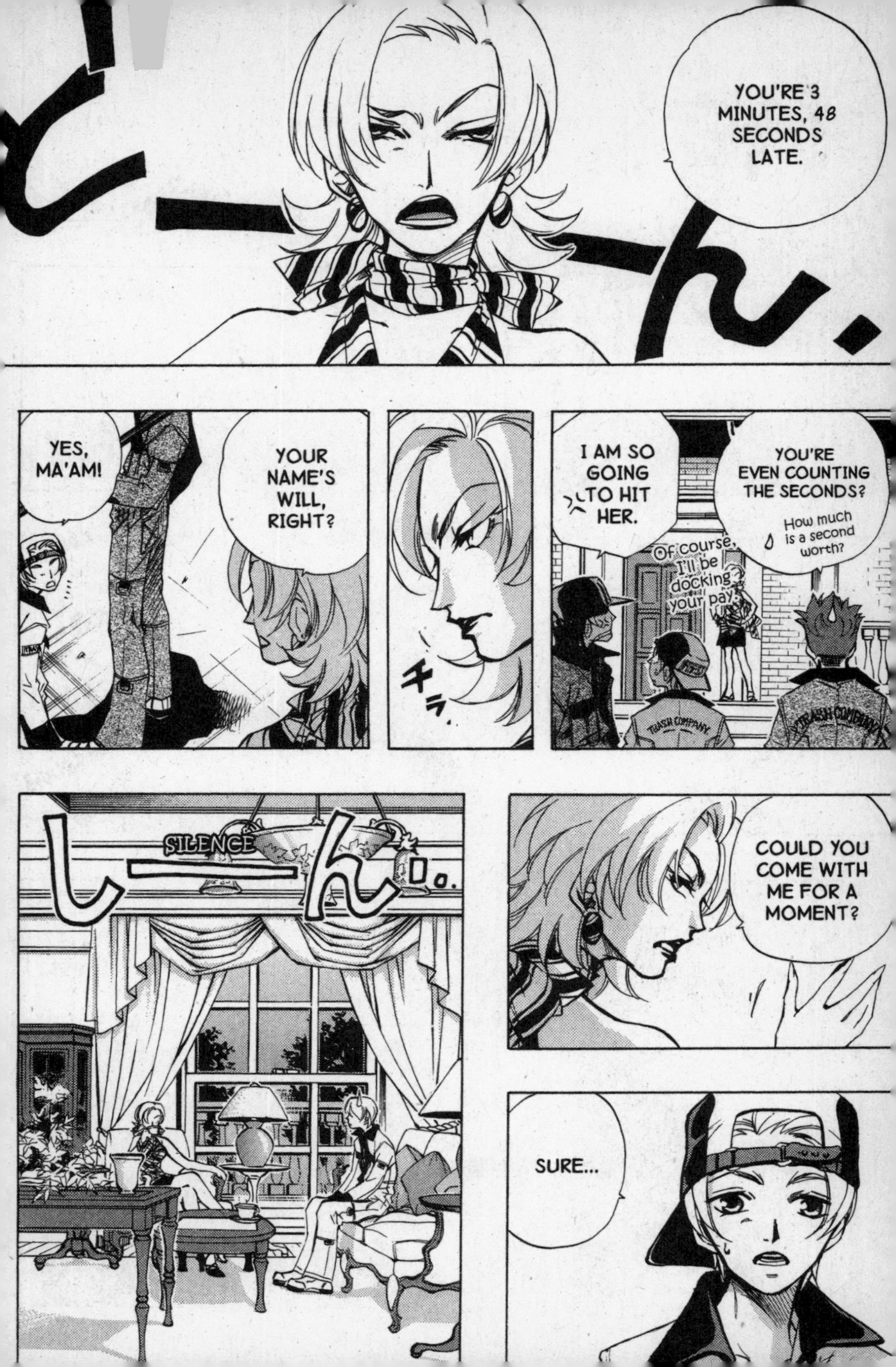
どーん。
YOU'RE 3 MINUTES, 48 SECONDS LATE.
YOU'RE EVEN COUNTING THE SECONDS?
How much is a second worth?
I AM SO GOING TO HIT HER.
Of course, I'll be docking your pay.
TRASH COMPANY
TRASH COMPANY
チラ
YOUR NAME'S WILL, RIGHT?
YES, MA'AM!
COULD YOU COME WITH ME FOR A MOMENT?
SURE...
しーん。
SILENCE

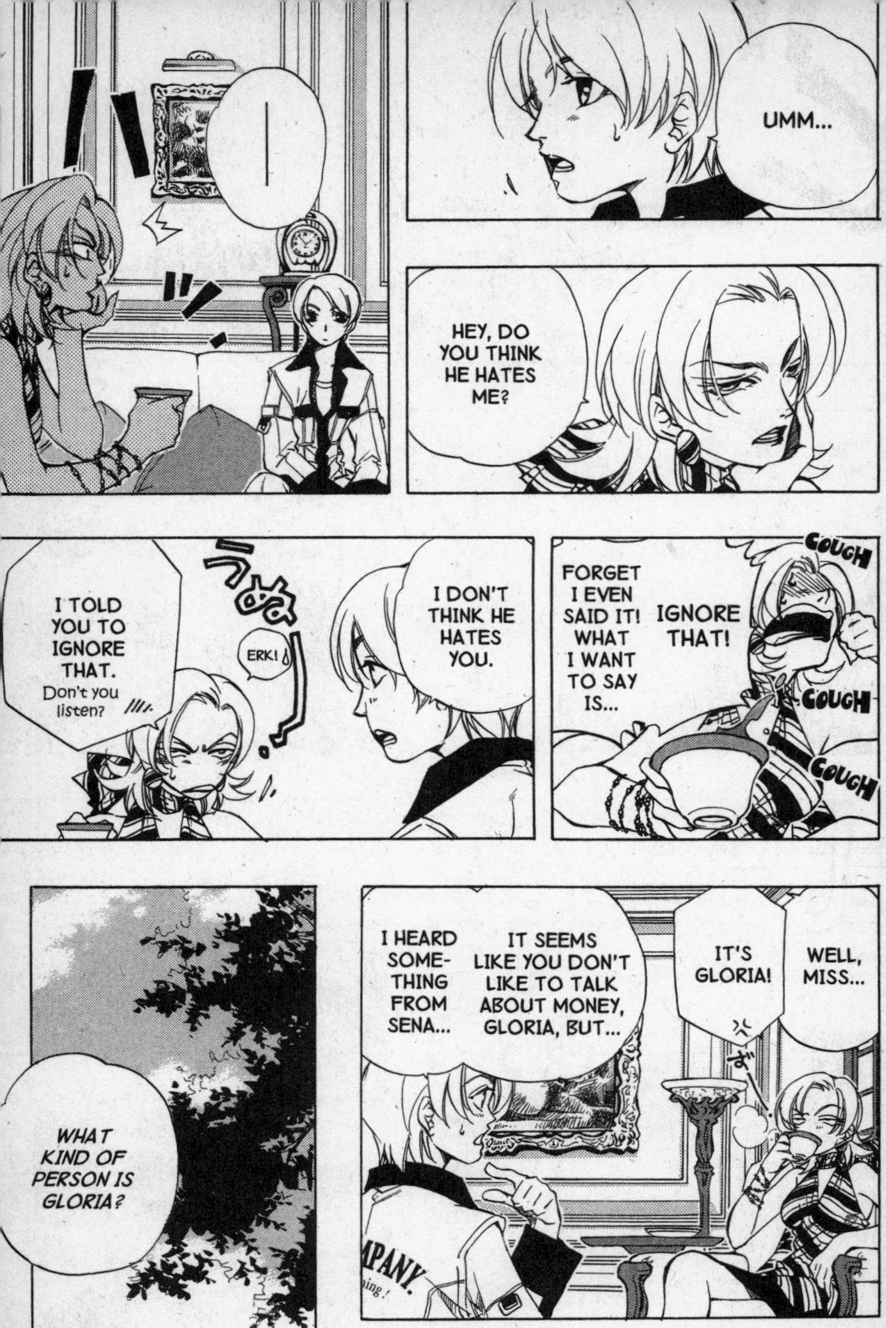
UMM...
HEY, DO YOU THINK HE HATES ME?
IGNORE THAT!
FORGET I EVEN SAID IT! WHAT I WANT TO SAY IS...
COUGH
COUGH
COUGH
I DON'T THINK HE HATES YOU.
ERK!
I TOLD YOU TO IGNORE THAT. Don't you listen?
WELL, MISS...
IT'S GLORIA!
IT SEEMS LIKE YOU DON'T LIKE TO TALK ABOUT MONEY, GLORIA, BUT...
I HEARD SOME-THING FROM SENA...
WHAT KIND OF PERSON IS GLORIA?

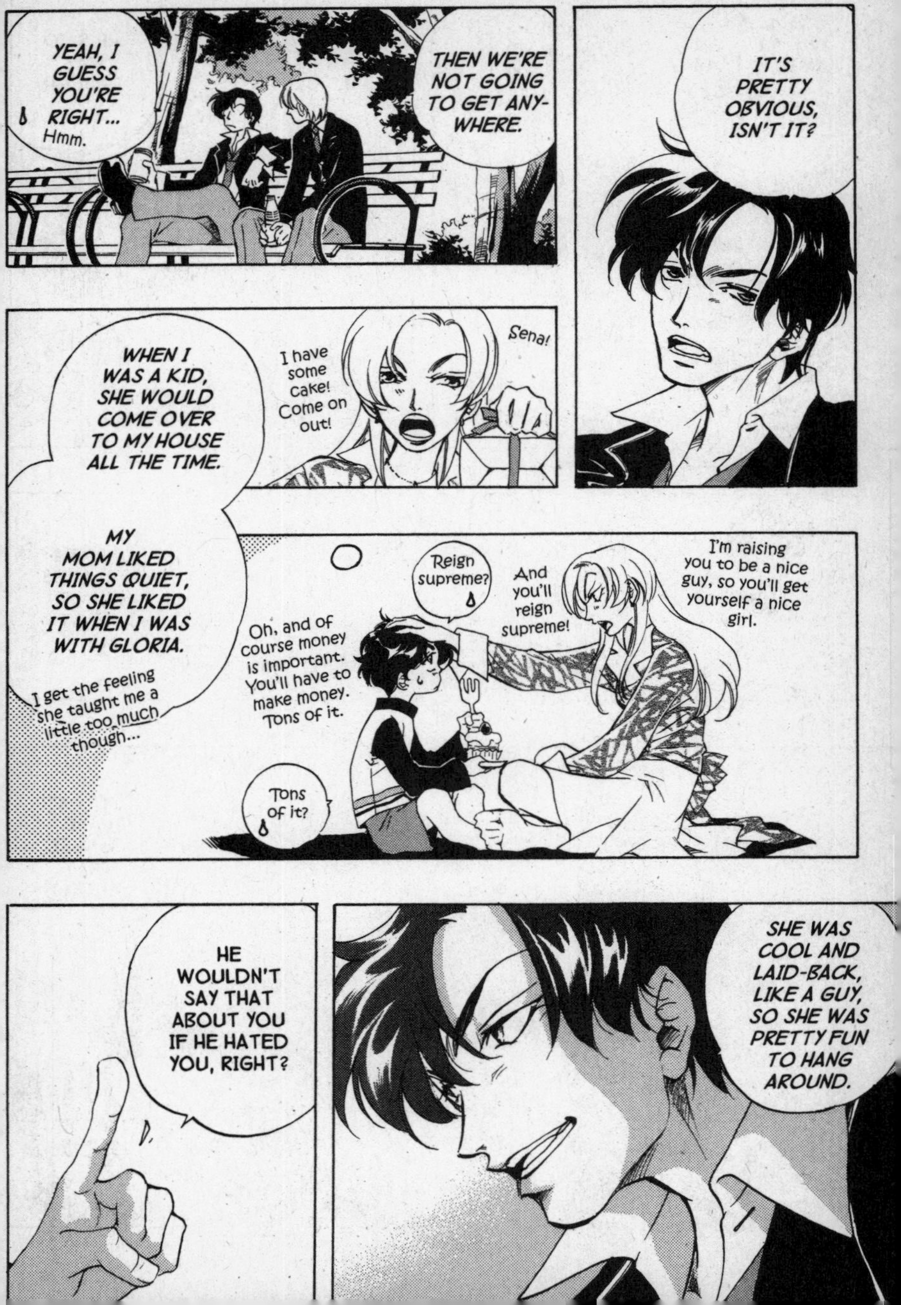
IT'S PRETTY OBVIOUS, ISN'T IT?
THEN WE'RE NOT GOING TO GET ANYWHERE.
YEAH, I GUESS YOU'RE RIGHT...
Hmm.
Sena!
I have some cake! Come on out!
WHEN I WAS A KID, SHE WOULD COME OVER TO MY HOUSE ALL THE TIME.
I'm raising you to be a nice guy, so you'll get yourself a nice girl.
And you'll reign supreme!
Reign supreme?
Oh, and of course money is important. You'll have to make money. Tons of it.
Tons of it?
MY MOM LIKED THINGS QUIET, SO SHE LIKED IT WHEN I WAS WITH GLORIA.
I get the feeling she taught me a little too much though...
SHE WAS COOL AND LAID-BACK, LIKE A GUY, SO SHE WAS PRETTY FUN TO HANG AROUND.
HE WOULDN'T SAY THAT ABOUT YOU IF HE HATED YOU, RIGHT?

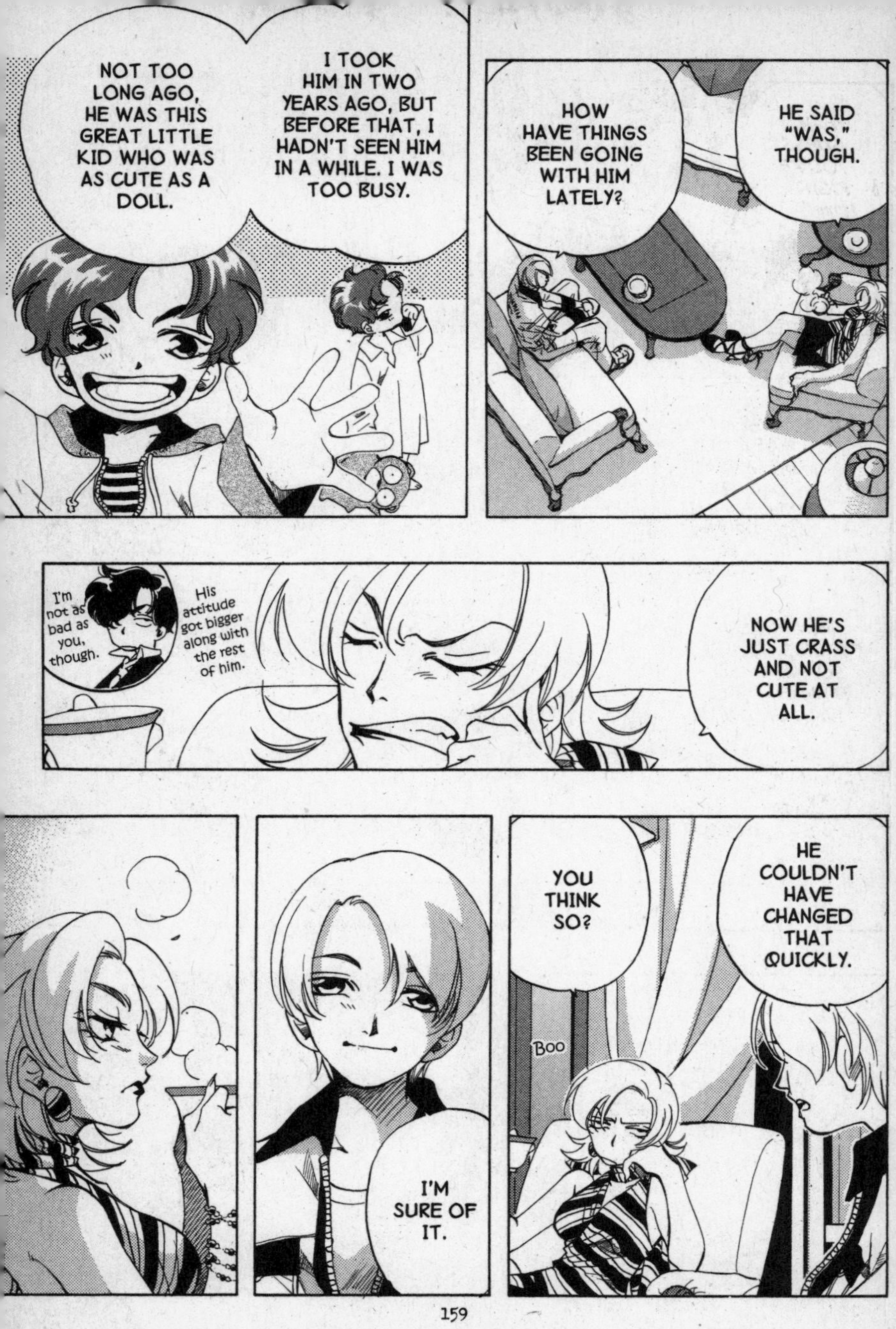
HE SAID "WAS," THOUGH.
HOW HAVE THINGS BEEN GOING WITH HIM LATELY?
I TOOK HIM IN TWO YEARS AGO, BUT BEFORE THAT, I HADN'T SEEN HIM IN A WHILE. I WAS TOO BUSY.
NOT TOO LONG AGO, HE WAS THIS GREAT LITTLE KID WHO WAS AS CUTE AS A DOLL.
NOW HE'S JUST CRASS AND NOT CUTE AT ALL.
His attitude got bigger along with the rest of him.
I'm not as bad as you, though.
HE COULDN'T HAVE CHANGED THAT QUICKLY.
YOU THINK SO?
BOO
I'M SURE OF IT.

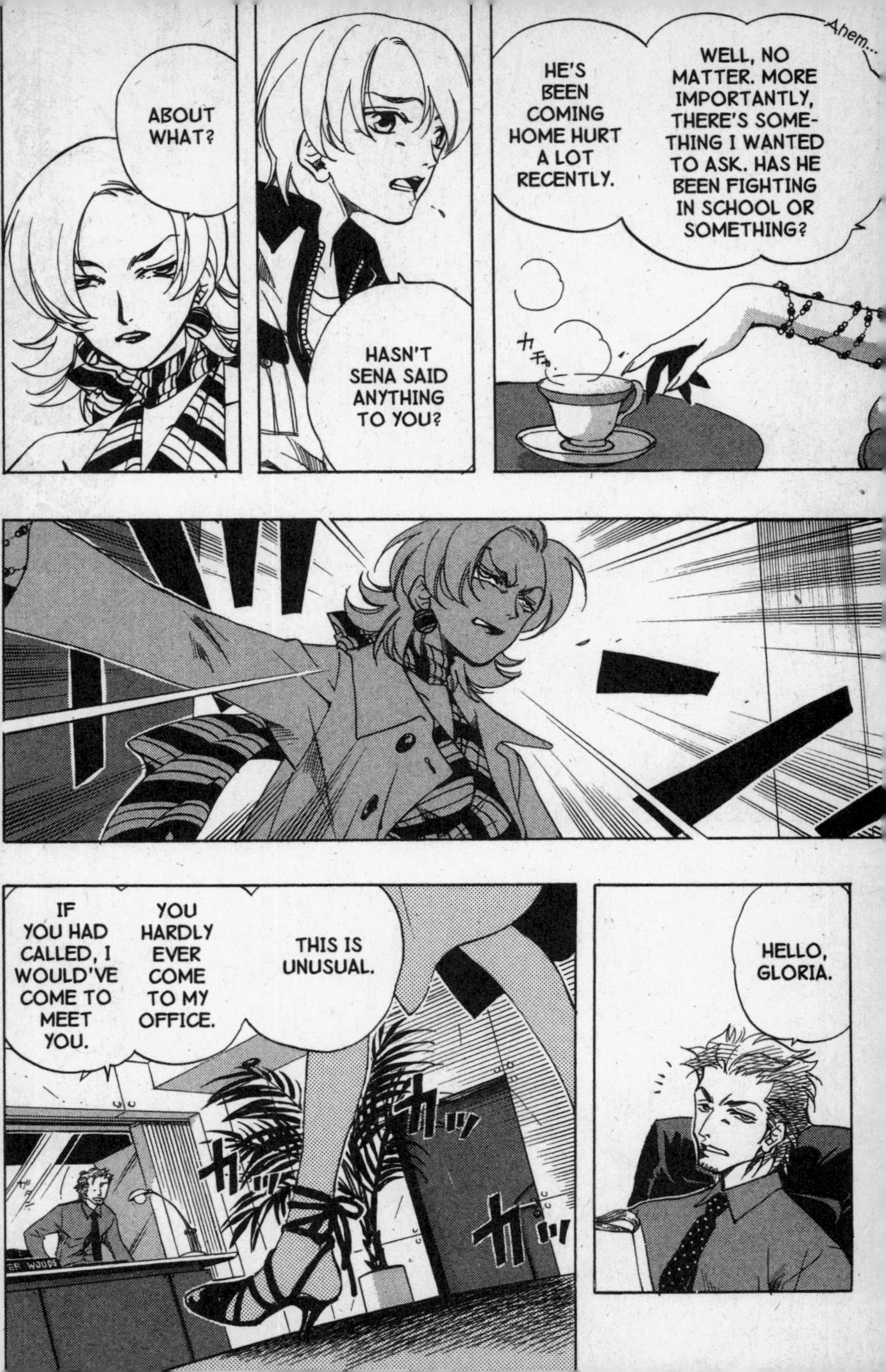
Ahem...
WELL, NO MATTER. MORE IMPORTANTLY, THERE'S SOME-THING I WANTED TO ASK. HAS HE BEEN FIGHTING IN SCHOOL OR SOMETHING?
HE'S BEEN COMING HOME HURT A LOT RECENTLY.
HASN'T SENA SAID ANYTHING TO YOU?
ABOUT WHAT?
HELLO, GLORIA.
THIS IS UNUSUAL.
YOU HARDLY EVER COME TO MY OFFICE.
IF YOU HAD CALLED, I WOULD'VE COME TO MEET YOU.

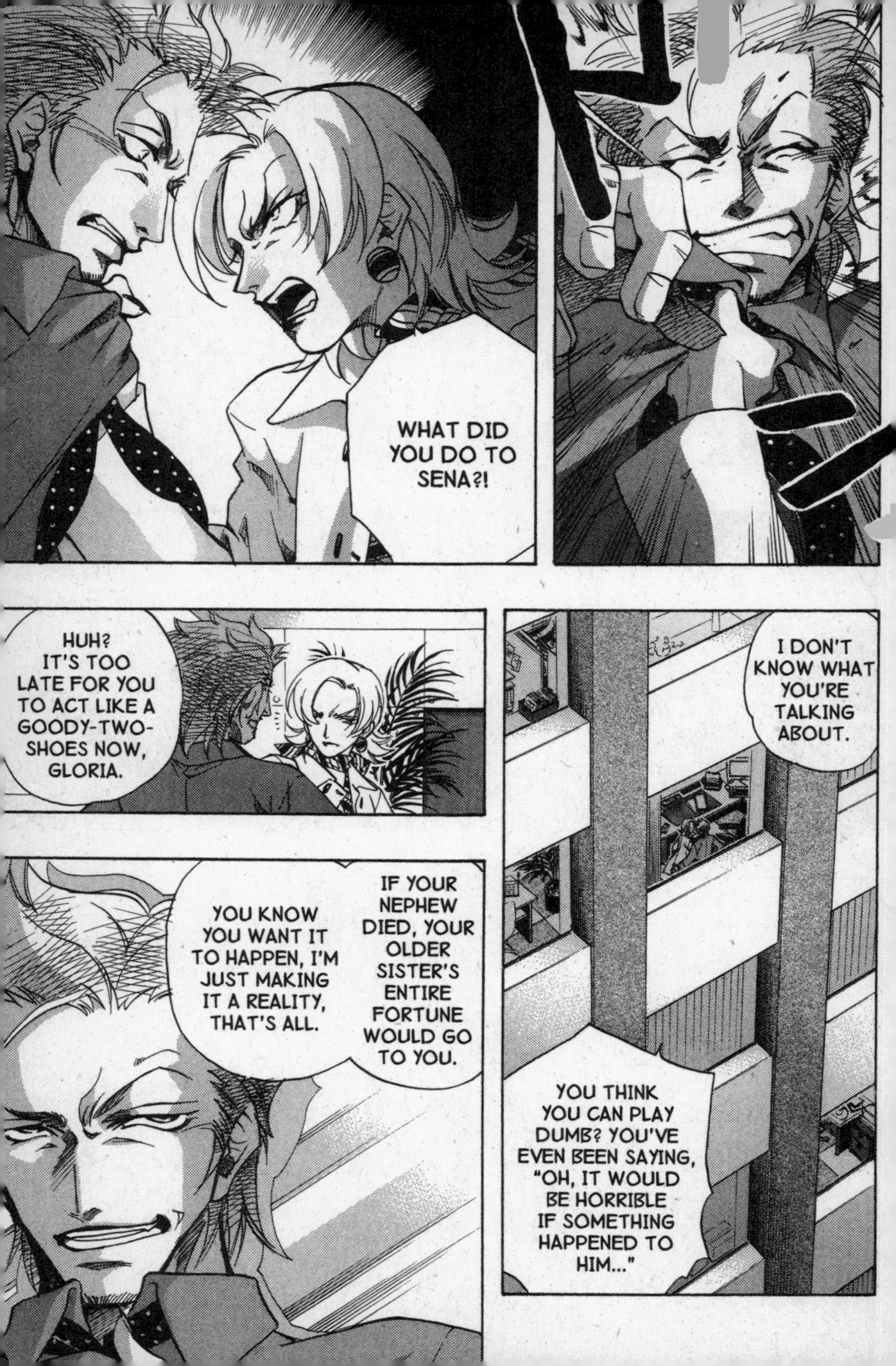
WHAT DID YOU DO TO SENA?!
I DON'T KNOW WHAT YOU'RE TALKING ABOUT.
YOU THINK YOU CAN PLAY DUMB? YOU'VE EVEN BEEN SAYING, "OH, IT WOULD BE HORRIBLE IF SOMETHING HAPPENED TO HIM..."
HUH? IT'S TOO LATE FOR YOU TO ACT LIKE A GOODY-TWO-SHOES NOW, GLORIA.
IF YOUR NEPHEW DIED, YOUR OLDER SISTER'S ENTIRE FORTUNE WOULD GO TO YOU.
YOU KNOW YOU WANT IT TO HAPPEN, I'M JUST MAKING IT A REALITY, THAT'S ALL.

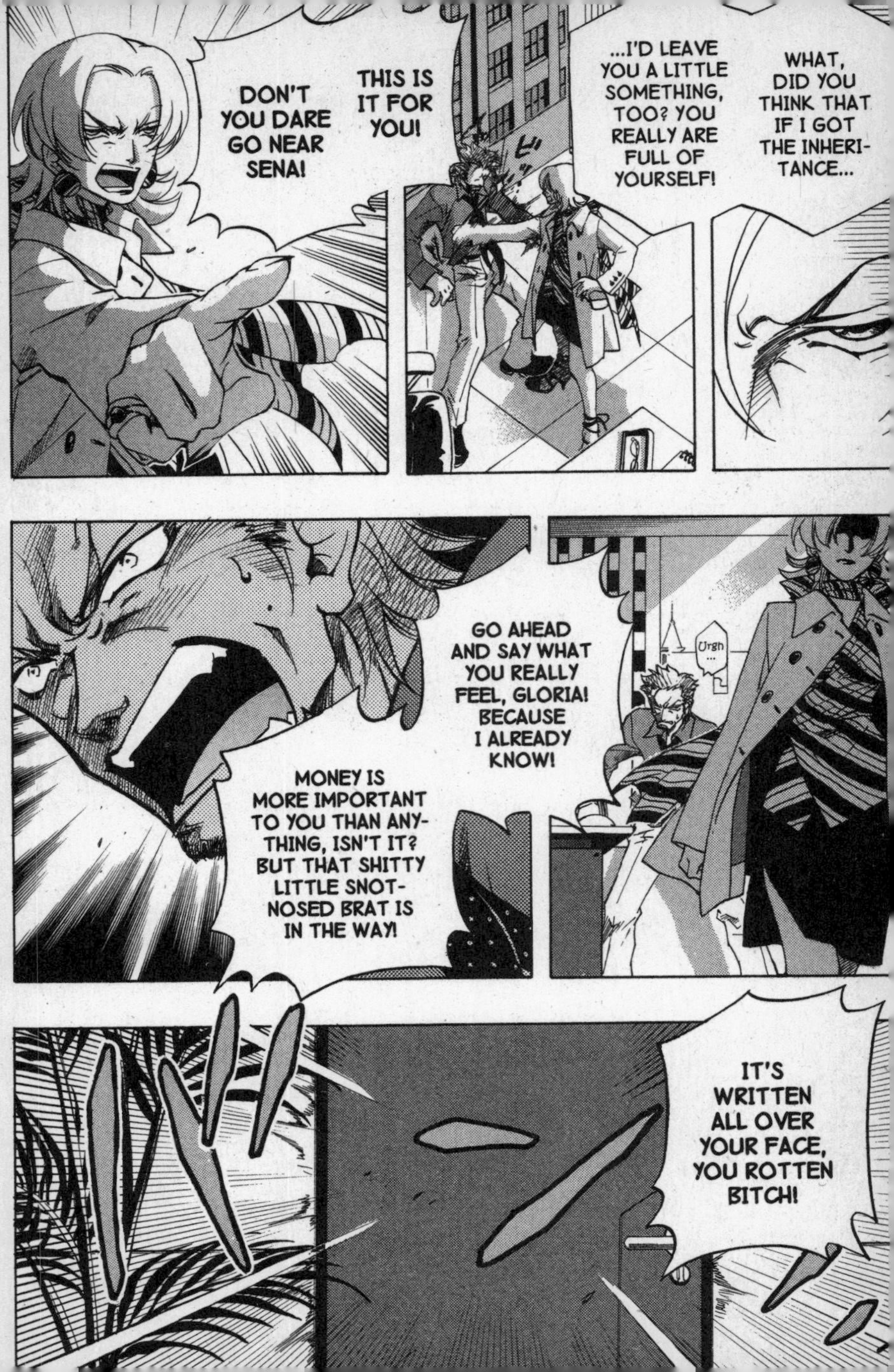
WHAT, DID YOU THINK THAT IF I GOT THE INHERITANCE...
...I'D LEAVE YOU A LITTLE SOMETHING, TOO? YOU REALLY ARE FULL OF YOURSELF!
THIS IS IT FOR YOU!
DON'T YOU DARE GO NEAR SENA!
Urgh ...
GO AHEAD AND SAY WHAT YOU REALLY FEEL, GLORIA! BECAUSE I ALREADY KNOW!
MONEY IS MORE IMPORTANT TO YOU THAN ANYTHING, ISN'T IT? BUT THAT SHITTY LITTLE SNOT-NOSED BRAT IS IN THE WAY!
IT'S WRITTEN ALL OVER YOUR FACE, YOU ROTTEN BITCH!

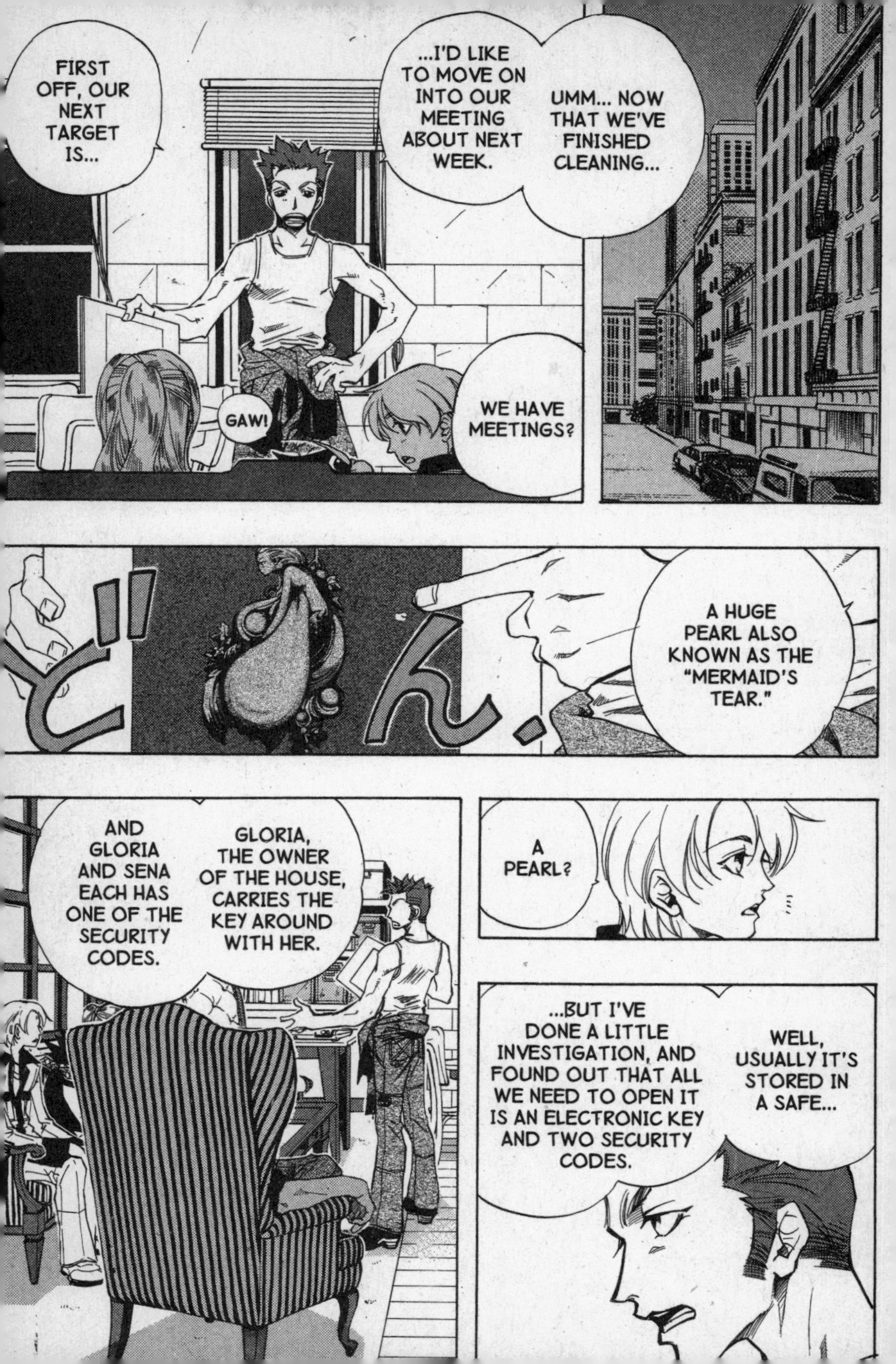
UMM... NOW THAT WE'VE FINISHED CLEANING...
...I'D LIKE TO MOVE ON INTO OUR MEETING ABOUT NEXT WEEK.
WE HAVE MEETINGS?
GAW!
FIRST OFF, OUR NEXT TARGET IS...
A HUGE PEARL ALSO KNOWN AS THE "MERMAID'S TEAR."
どん.
A PEARL?
WELL, USUALLY IT'S STORED IN A SAFE...
...BUT I'VE DONE A LITTLE INVESTIGATION, AND FOUND OUT THAT ALL WE NEED TO OPEN IT IS AN ELECTRONIC KEY AND TWO SECURITY CODES.
GLORIA, THE OWNER OF THE HOUSE, CARRIES THE KEY AROUND WITH HER.
AND GLORIA AND SENA EACH HAS ONE OF THE SECURITY CODES.

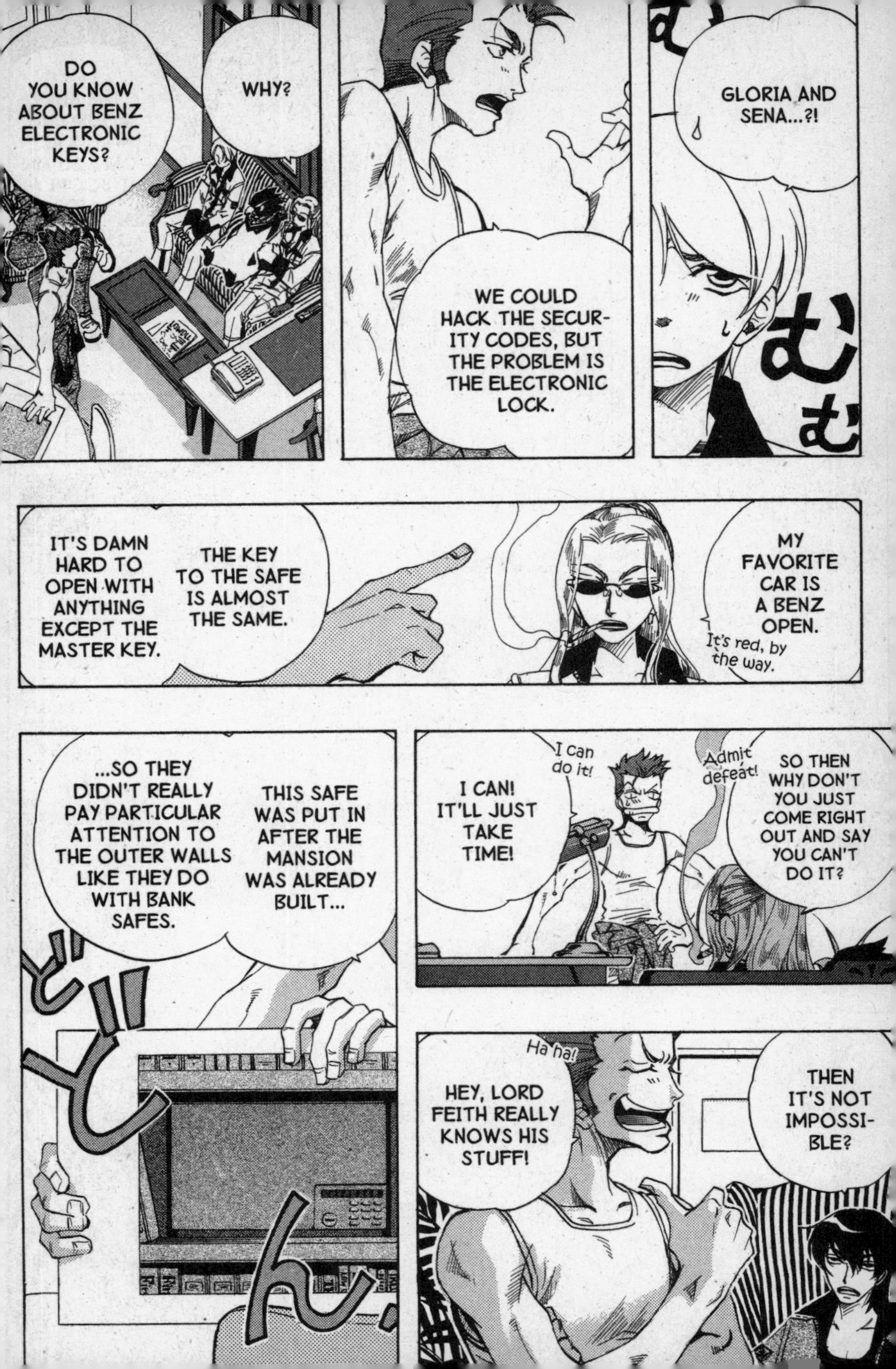
GLORIA AND SENA...?!
むむ
WE COULD HACK THE SECURITY CODES, BUT THE PROBLEM IS THE ELECTRONIC LOCK.
WHY?
DO YOU KNOW ABOUT BENZ ELECTRONIC KEYS?
MY FAVORITE CAR IS A BENZ OPEN.
It's red, by the way.
THE KEY TO THE SAFE IS ALMOST THE SAME.
IT'S DAMN HARD TO OPEN WITH ANYTHING EXCEPT THE MASTER KEY.
SO THEN WHY DON'T YOU JUST COME RIGHT OUT AND SAY YOU CAN'T DO IT?
Admit defeat!
I can do it!
I CAN! IT'LL JUST TAKE TIME!
THEN IT'S NOT IMPOSSIBLE?
Ha ha!
HEY, LORD FEITH REALLY KNOWS HIS STUFF!
THIS SAFE WAS PUT IN AFTER THE MANSION WAS ALREADY BUILT...
...SO THEY DIDN'T REALLY PAY PARTICULAR ATTENTION TO THE OUTER WALLS LIKE THEY DO WITH BANK SAFES.
どん

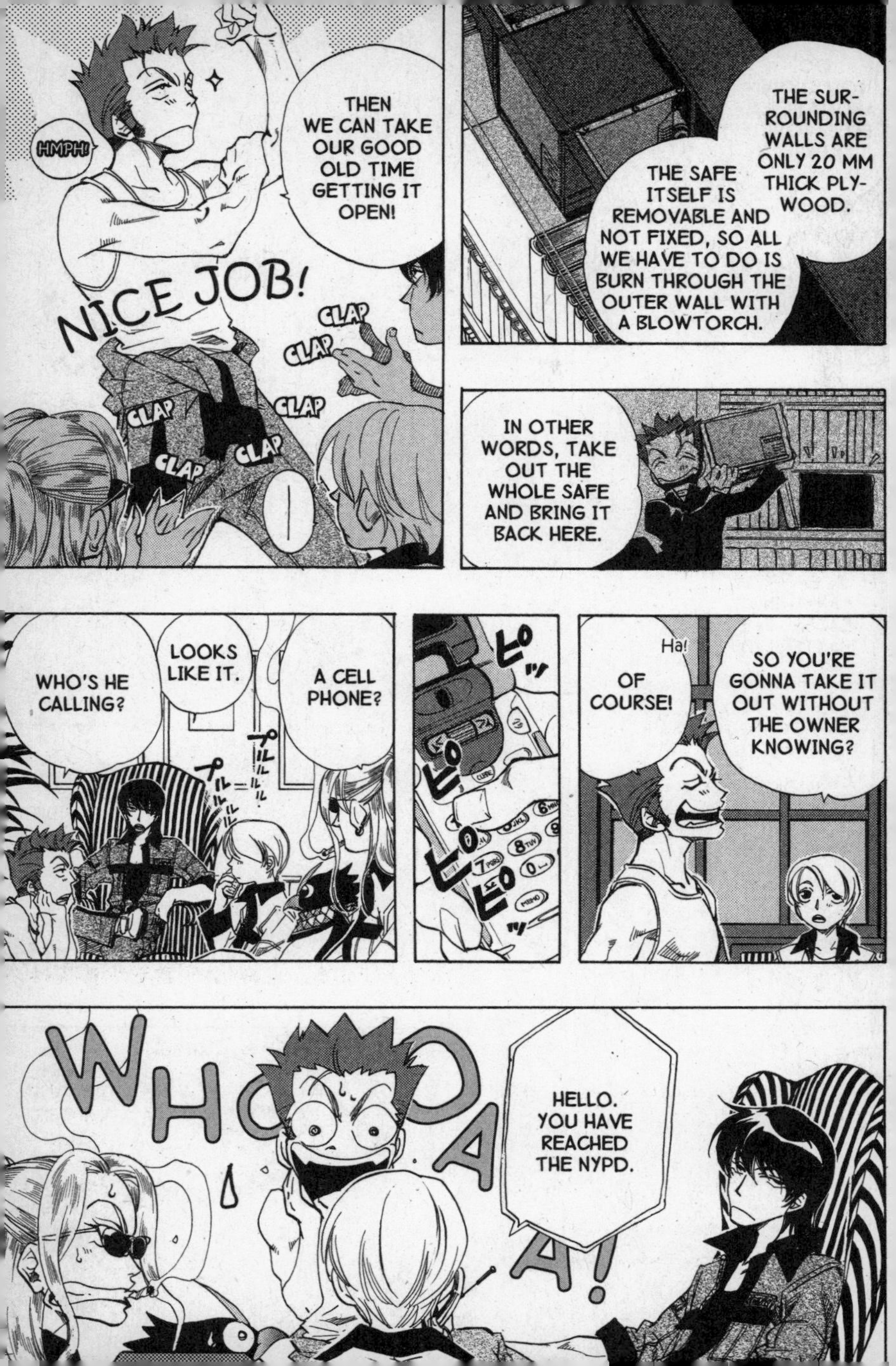
THE SURROUNDING WALLS ARE ONLY 20 MM THICK PLYWOOD.
THE SAFE ITSELF IS REMOVABLE AND NOT FIXED, SO ALL WE HAVE TO DO IS BURN THROUGH THE OUTER WALL WITH A BLOWTORCH.
IN OTHER WORDS, TAKE OUT THE WHOLE SAFE AND BRING IT BACK HERE.
THEN WE CAN TAKE OUR GOOD OLD TIME GETTING IT OPEN!
HMPH!
NICE JOB!
CLAP CLAP CLAP CLAP CLAP CLAP
!
SO YOU'RE GONNA TAKE IT OUT WITHOUT THE OWNER KNOWING?
Ha!
OF COURSE!
ピッ
ピッ
A CELL PHONE?
LOOKS LIKE IT.
WHO'S HE CALLING?
HELLO. YOU HAVE REACHED THE NYPD.
WHOA!

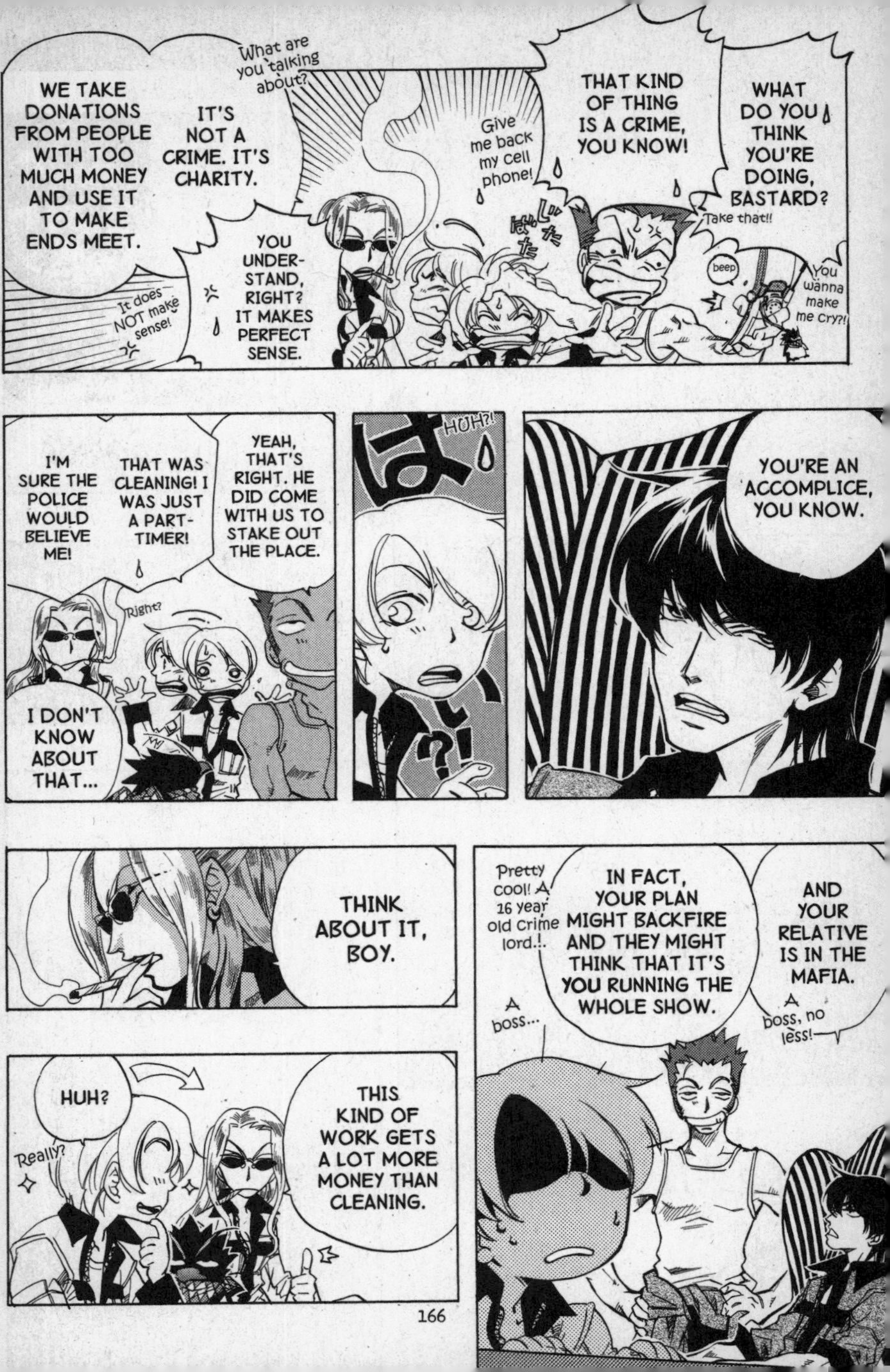

WHAT DO YOU THINK YOU'RE DOING, BASTARD?
Take that!!
beep
You wanna make me cry?!
THAT KIND OF THING IS A CRIME, YOU KNOW!
Give me back my cell phone!
What are you talking about?
IT'S NOT A CRIME. IT'S CHARITY.
WE TAKE DONATIONS FROM PEOPLE WITH TOO MUCH MONEY AND USE IT TO MAKE ENDS MEET.
YOU UNDERSTAND, RIGHT? IT MAKES PERFECT SENSE.
It does NOT make sense!
YOU'RE AN ACCOMPLICE, YOU KNOW.
HUH?!
YEAH, THAT'S RIGHT. HE DID COME WITH US TO STAKE OUT THE PLACE.
THAT WAS CLEANING! I WAS JUST A PART-TIMER!
I'M SURE THE POLICE WOULD BELIEVE ME!
Right?
I DON'T KNOW ABOUT THAT...
AND YOUR RELATIVE IS IN THE MAFIA.
IN FACT, YOUR PLAN MIGHT BACKFIRE AND THEY MIGHT THINK THAT IT'S YOU RUNNING THE WHOLE SHOW.
Pretty cool! A 16 year old crime lord..!
A boss, no less!
A boss...
THINK ABOUT IT, BOY.
THIS KIND OF WORK GETS A LOT MORE MONEY THAN CLEANING.
HUH?
Really?

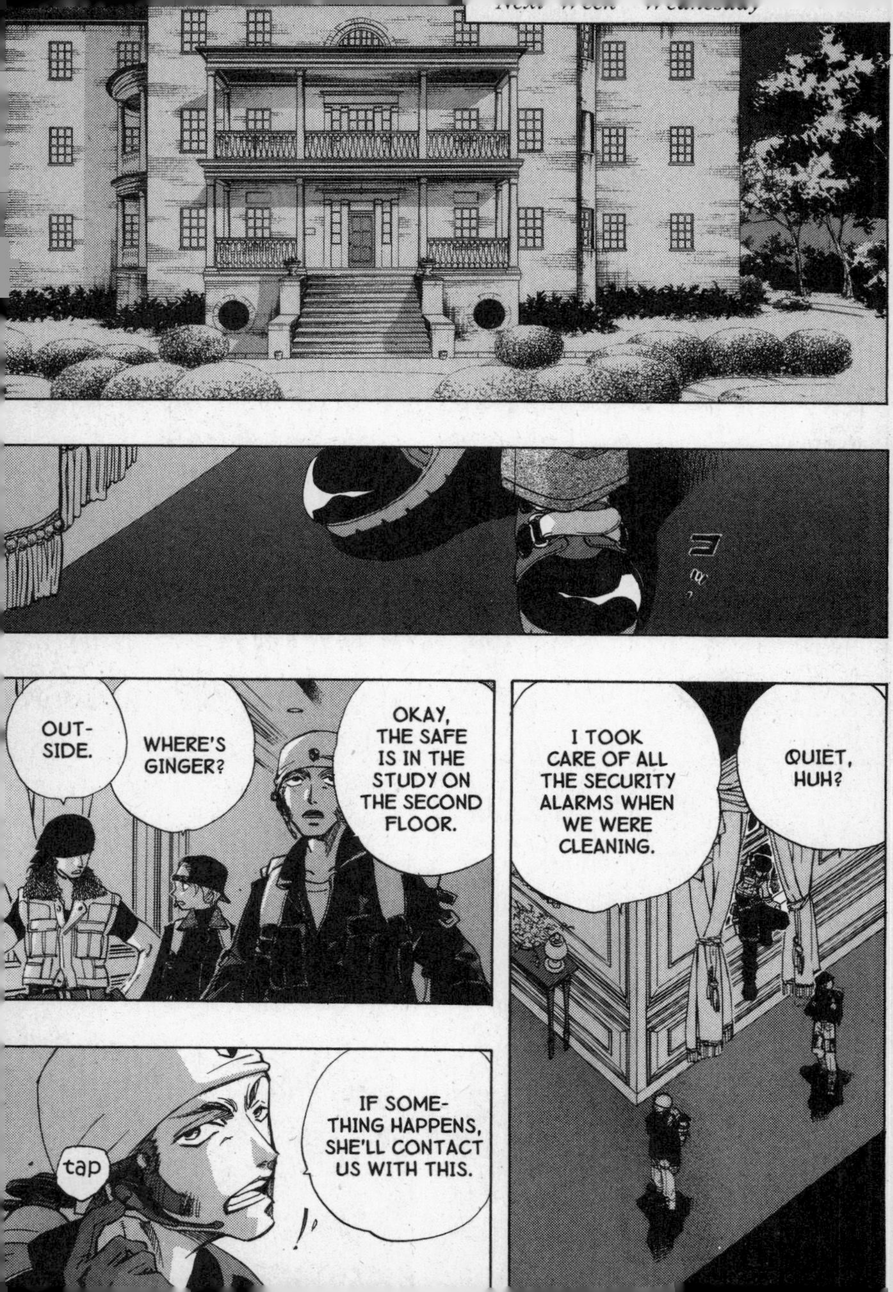
QUIET, HUH?
I TOOK CARE OF ALL THE SECURITY ALARMS WHEN WE WERE CLEANING.
OKAY, THE SAFE IS IN THE STUDY ON THE SECOND FLOOR.
WHERE'S GINGER?
OUT-SIDE.
IF SOME-THING HAPPENS, SHE'LL CONTACT US WITH THIS.
tap

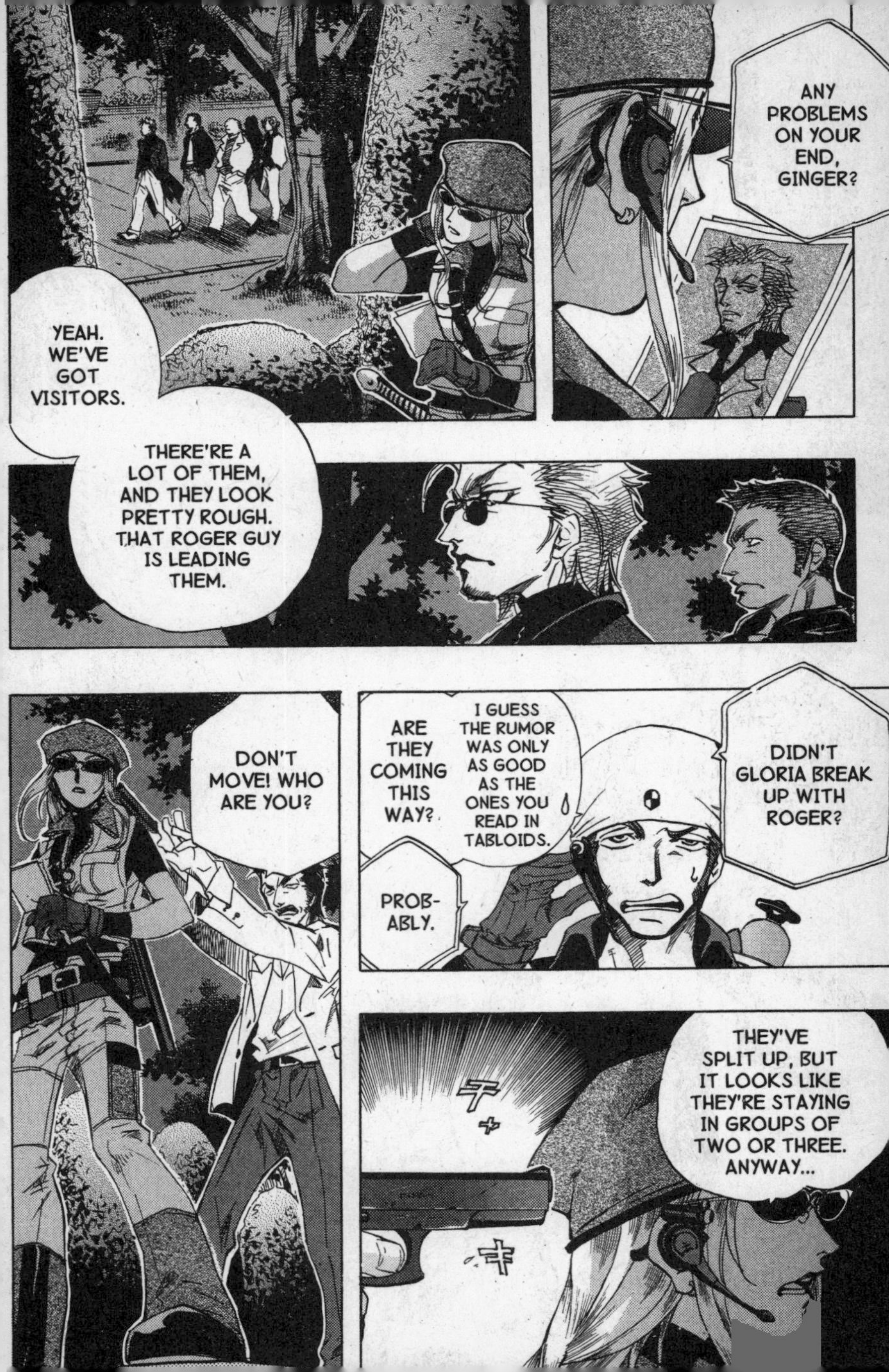
ANY PROBLEMS ON YOUR END, GINGER?
YEAH. WE'VE GOT VISITORS.
THERE'RE A LOT OF THEM, AND THEY LOOK PRETTY ROUGH. THAT ROGER GUY IS LEADING THEM.
DIDN'T GLORIA BREAK UP WITH ROGER?
I GUESS THE RUMOR WAS ONLY AS GOOD AS THE ONES YOU READ IN TABLOIDS.
ARE THEY COMING THIS WAY?
PROB-ABLY.
THEY'VE SPLIT UP, BUT IT LOOKS LIKE THEY'RE STAYING IN GROUPS OF TWO OR THREE. ANYWAY...
DON'T MOVE! WHO ARE YOU?

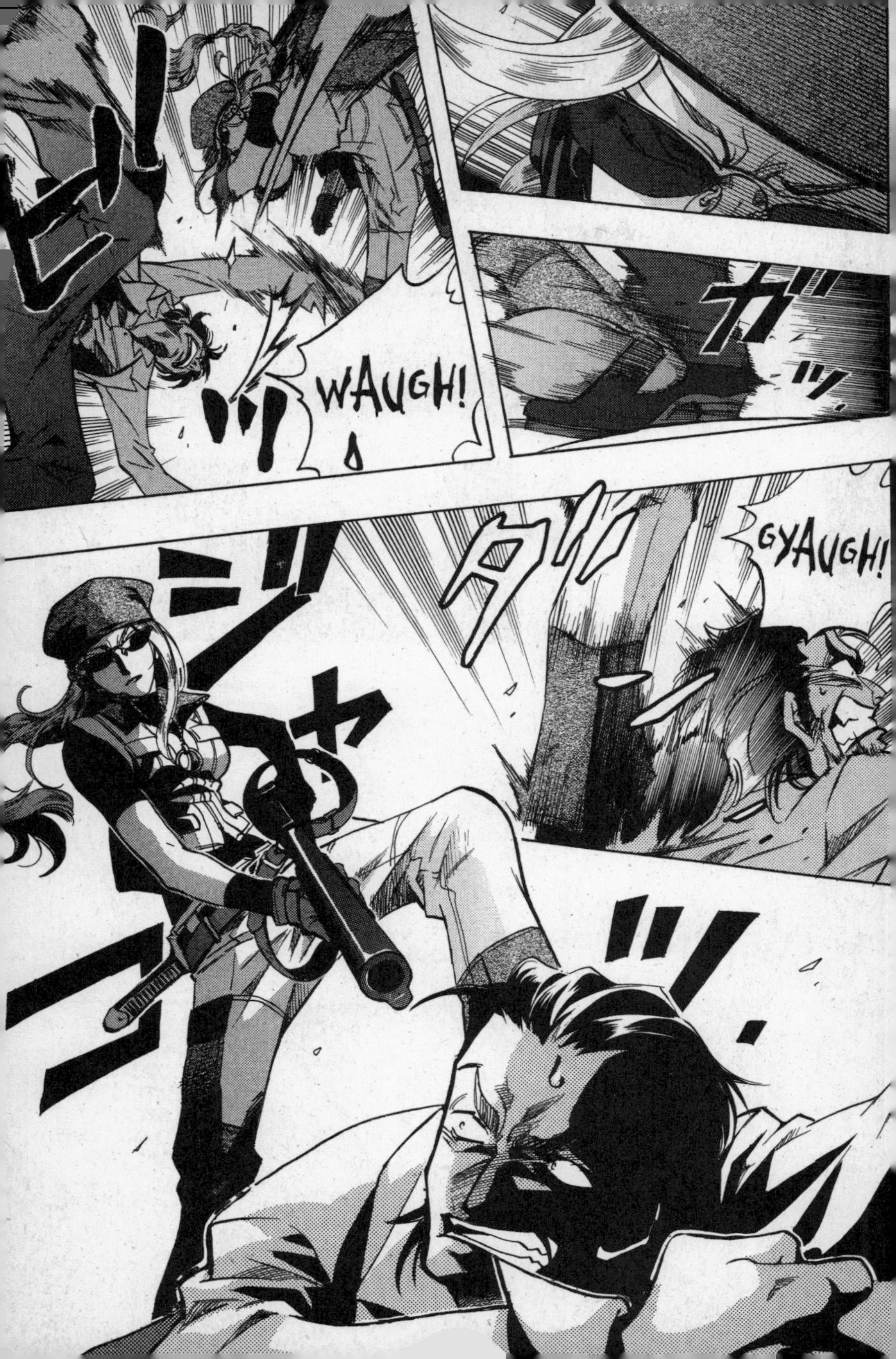
ガッ
WAUGH!
ダッ
GYAUGH!

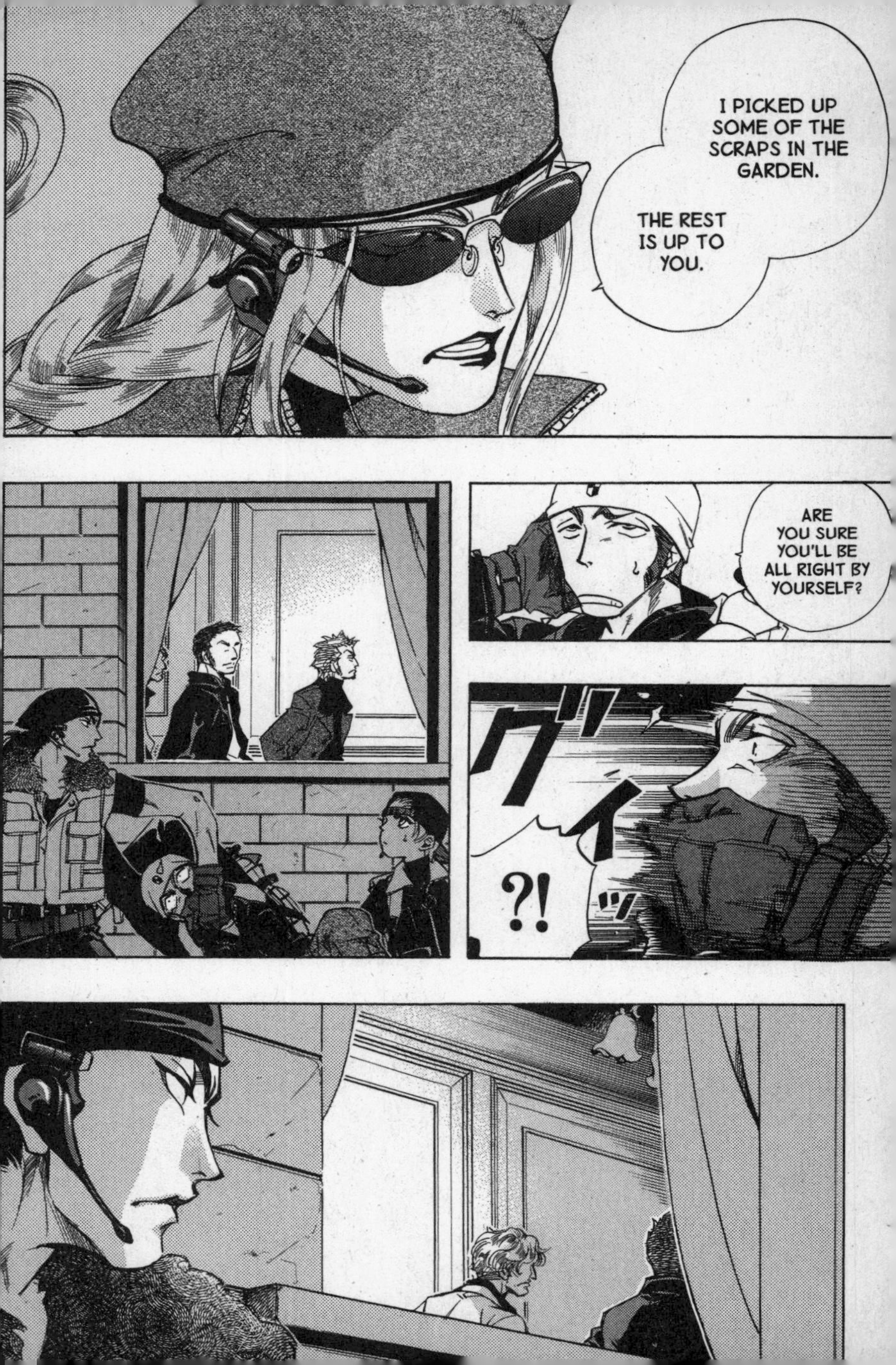
I PICKED UP SOME OF THE SCRAPS IN THE GARDEN.
THE REST IS UP TO YOU.
ARE YOU SURE YOU'LL BE ALL RIGHT BY YOURSELF?
グイッ
?!

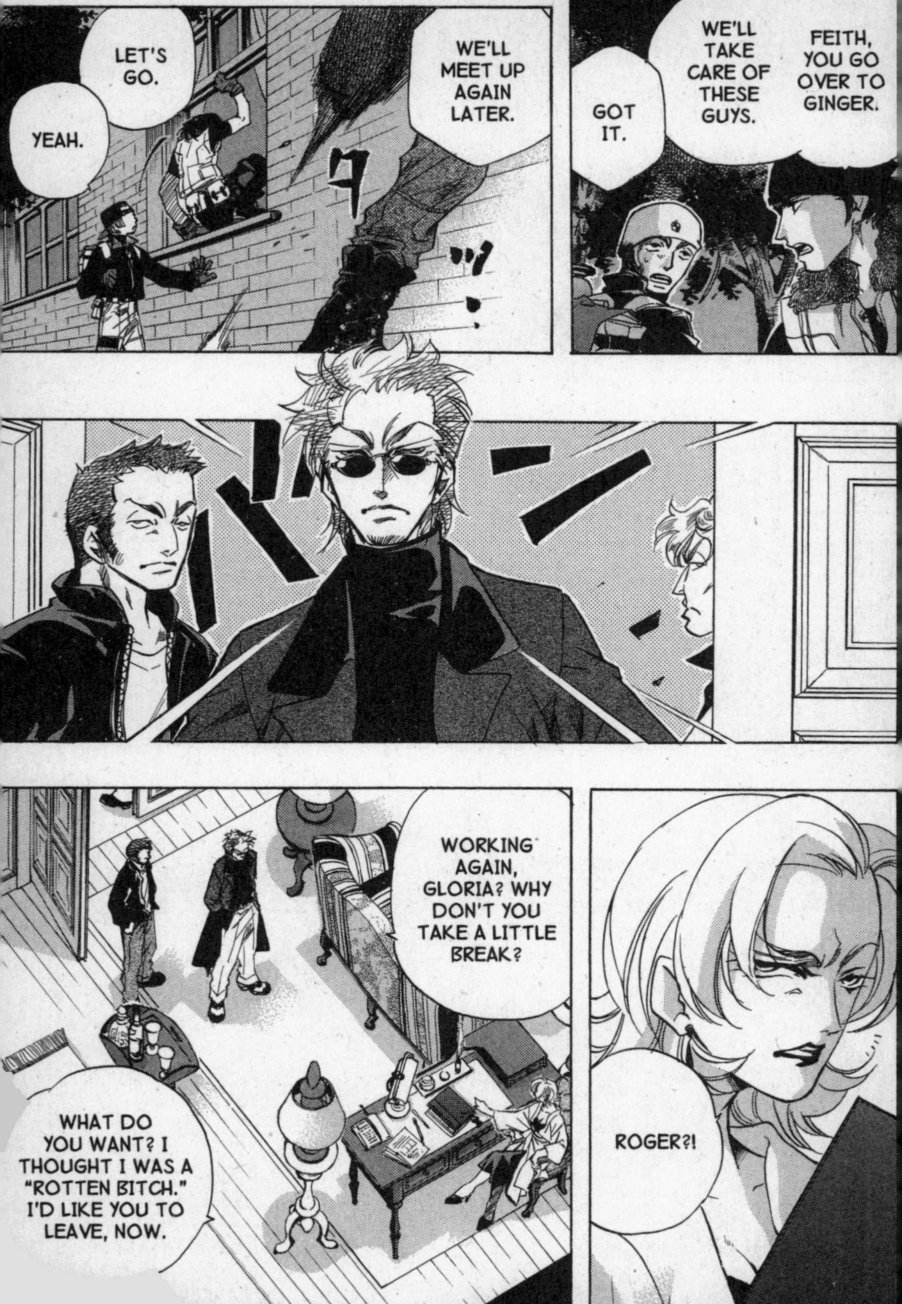
FEITH, YOU GO OVER TO GINGER.
WE'LL TAKE CARE OF THESE GUYS.
GOT IT.
WE'LL MEET UP AGAIN LATER.
LET'S GO.
YEAH.
ROGER?!
WORKING AGAIN, GLORIA? WHY DON'T YOU TAKE A LITTLE BREAK?
WHAT DO YOU WANT? I THOUGHT I WAS A "ROTTEN BITCH." I'D LIKE YOU TO LEAVE, NOW.

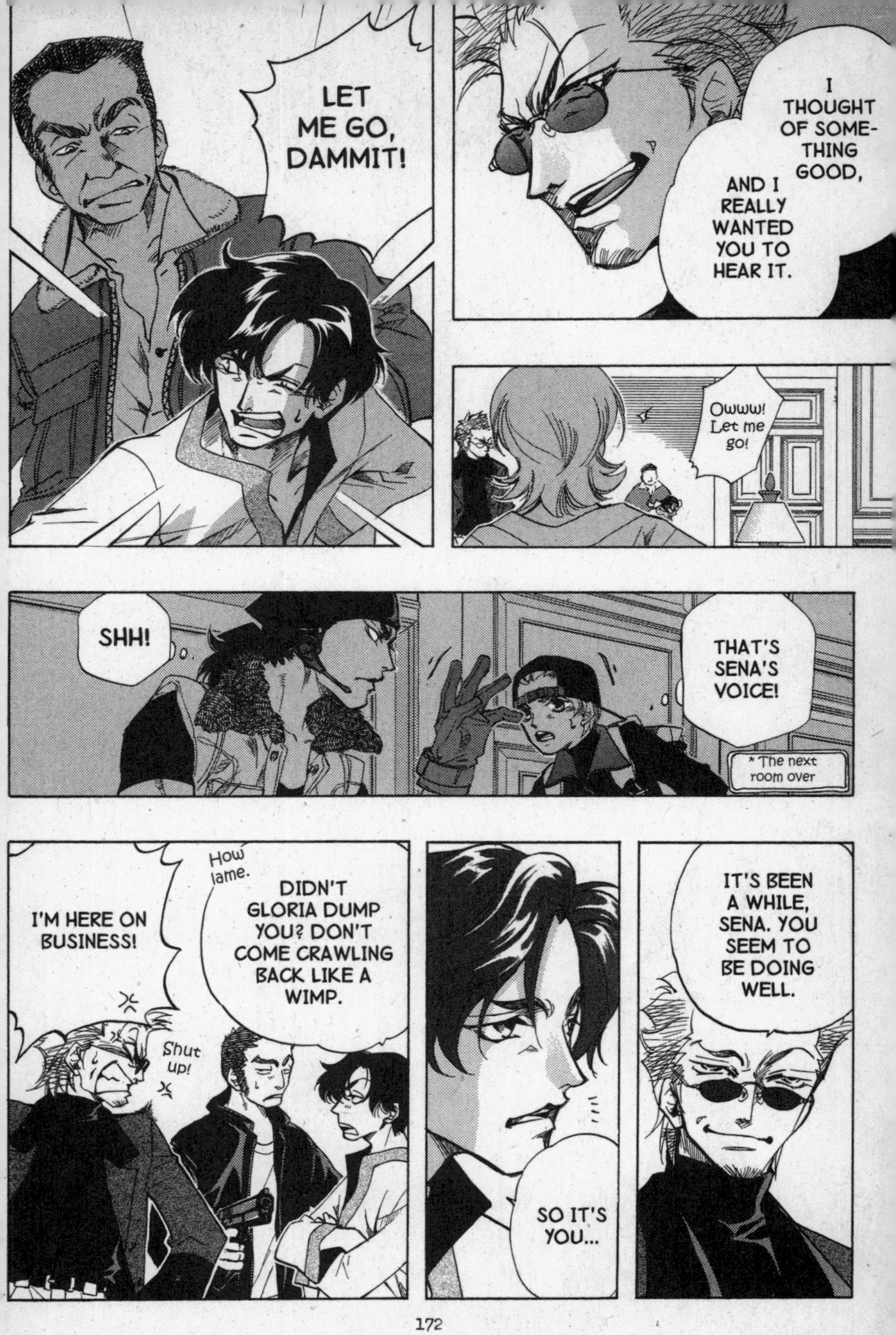
I THOUGHT OF SOME- THING GOOD,
AND I REALLY WANTED YOU TO HEAR IT.
Owww! Let me go!
LET ME GO, DAMMIT!
THAT'S SENA'S VOICE!
* The next room over
SHH!
IT'S BEEN A WHILE, SENA. YOU SEEM TO BE DOING WELL.
SO IT'S YOU...
How lame.
DIDN'T GLORIA DUMP YOU? DON'T COME CRAWLING BACK LIKE A WIMP.
I'M HERE ON BUSINESS!
Shut up!

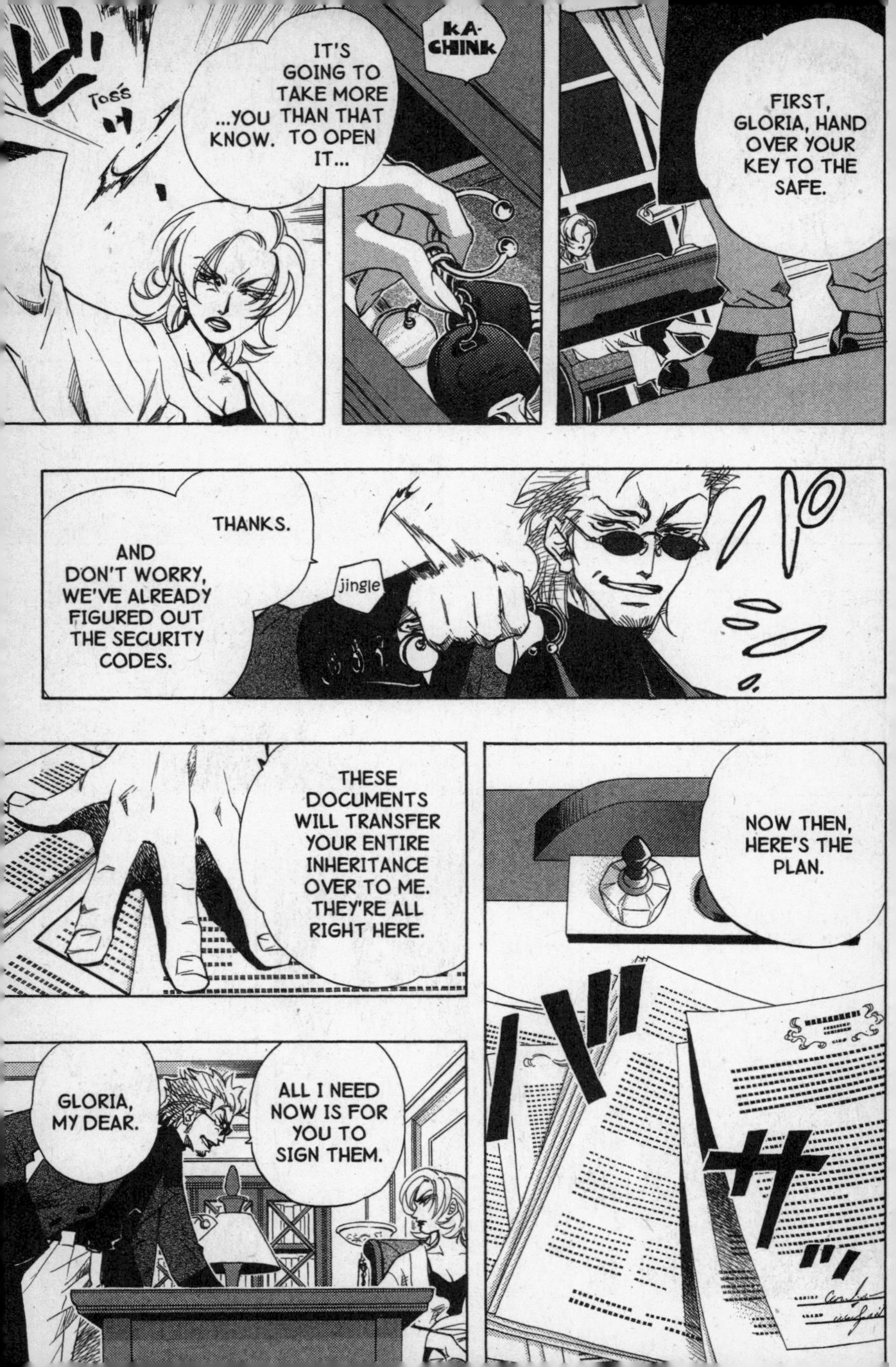
FIRST, GLORIA, HAND OVER YOUR KEY TO THE SAFE.
KA-CHINK
IT'S GOING TO TAKE MORE THAN THAT TO OPEN IT...
...YOU KNOW.
Toss
THANKS.
AND DON'T WORRY, WE'VE ALREADY FIGURED OUT THE SECURITY CODES.
jingle
NOW THEN, HERE'S THE PLAN.
THESE DOCUMENTS WILL TRANSFER YOUR ENTIRE INHERITANCE OVER TO ME. THEY'RE ALL RIGHT HERE.
ALL I NEED NOW IS FOR YOU TO SIGN THEM.
GLORIA, MY DEAR.

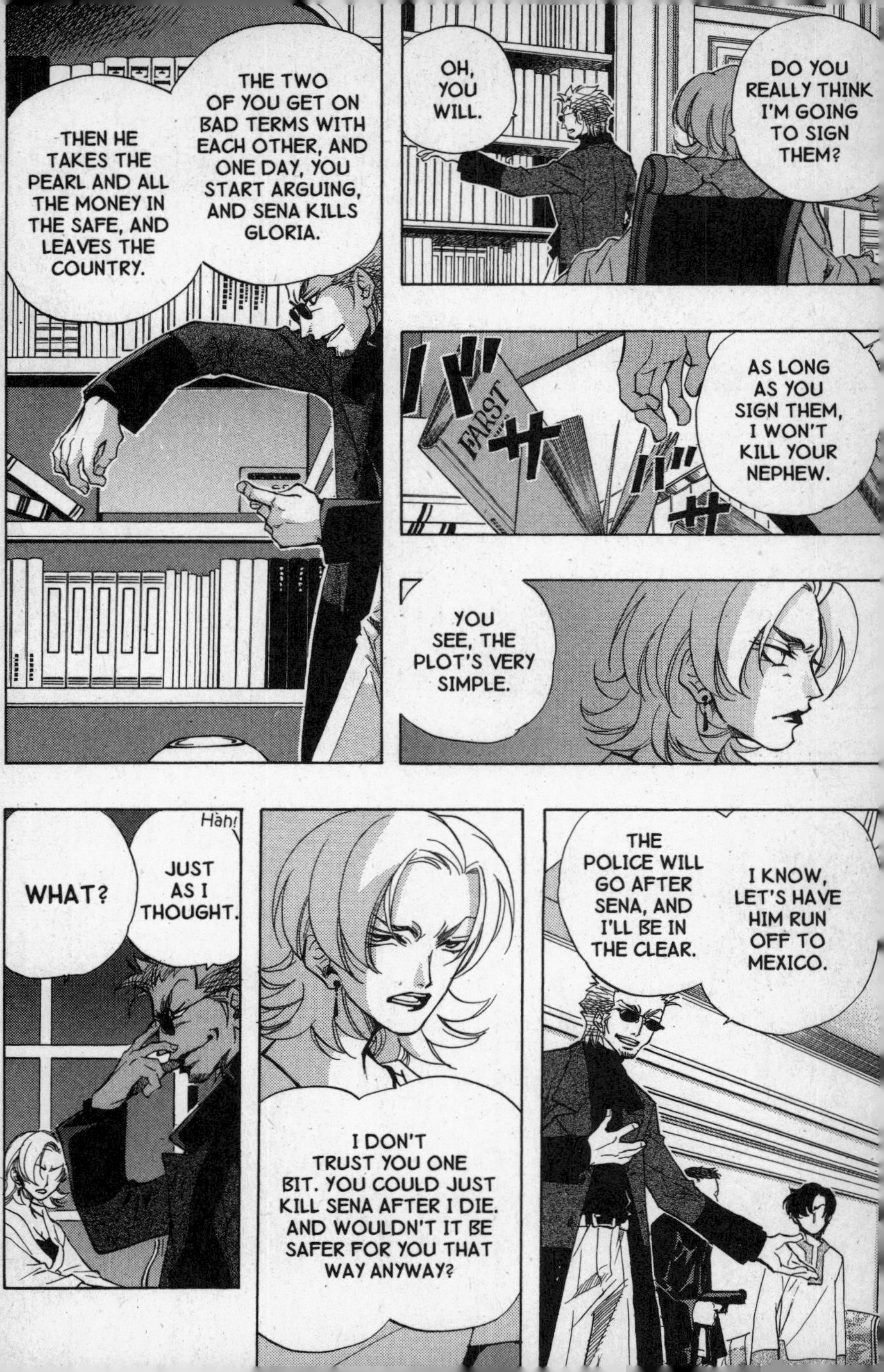
DO YOU REALLY THINK I'M GOING TO SIGN THEM?
OH, YOU WILL.
AS LONG AS YOU SIGN THEM, I WON'T KILL YOUR NEPHEW.
バサ
バサ
YOU SEE, THE PLOT'S VERY SIMPLE.
THE TWO OF YOU GET ON BAD TERMS WITH EACH OTHER, AND ONE DAY, YOU START ARGUING, AND SENA KILLS GLORIA.
THEN HE TAKES THE PEARL AND ALL THE MONEY IN THE SAFE, AND LEAVES THE COUNTRY.
I KNOW, LET'S HAVE HIM RUN OFF TO MEXICO.
THE POLICE WILL GO AFTER SENA, AND I'LL BE IN THE CLEAR.
I DON'T TRUST YOU ONE BIT. YOU COULD JUST KILL SENA AFTER I DIE. AND WOULDN'T IT BE SAFER FOR YOU THAT WAY ANYWAY?
Hah!
JUST AS I THOUGHT.
WHAT?

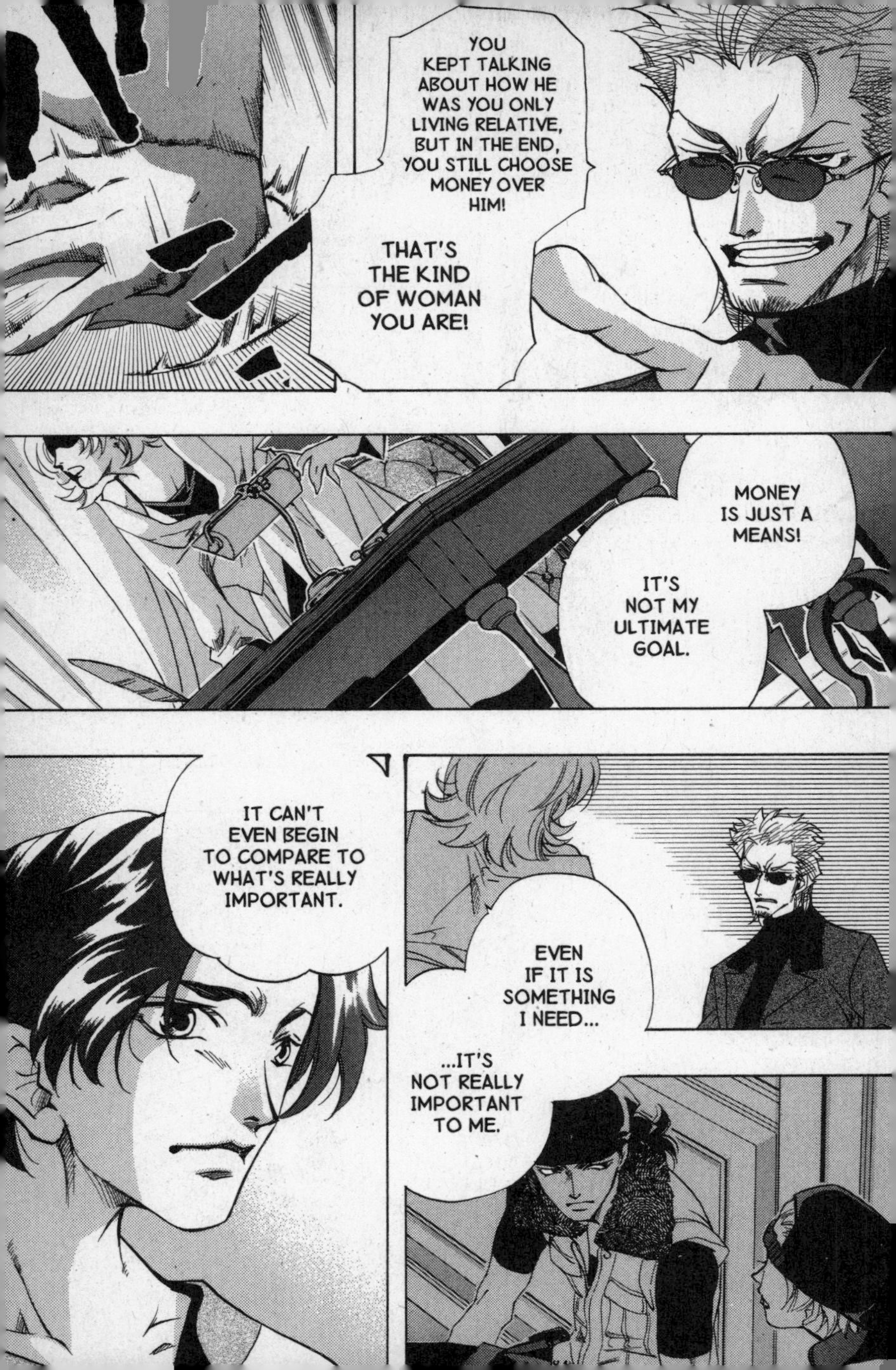
YOU KEPT TALKING ABOUT HOW HE WAS YOU ONLY LIVING RELATIVE, BUT IN THE END, YOU STILL CHOOSE MONEY OVER HIM!
THAT'S THE KIND OF WOMAN YOU ARE!
MONEY IS JUST A MEANS!
IT'S NOT MY ULTIMATE GOAL.
EVEN IF IT IS SOMETHING I NEED...
...IT'S NOT REALLY IMPORTANT TO ME.
IT CAN'T EVEN BEGIN TO COMPARE TO WHAT'S REALLY IMPORTANT.

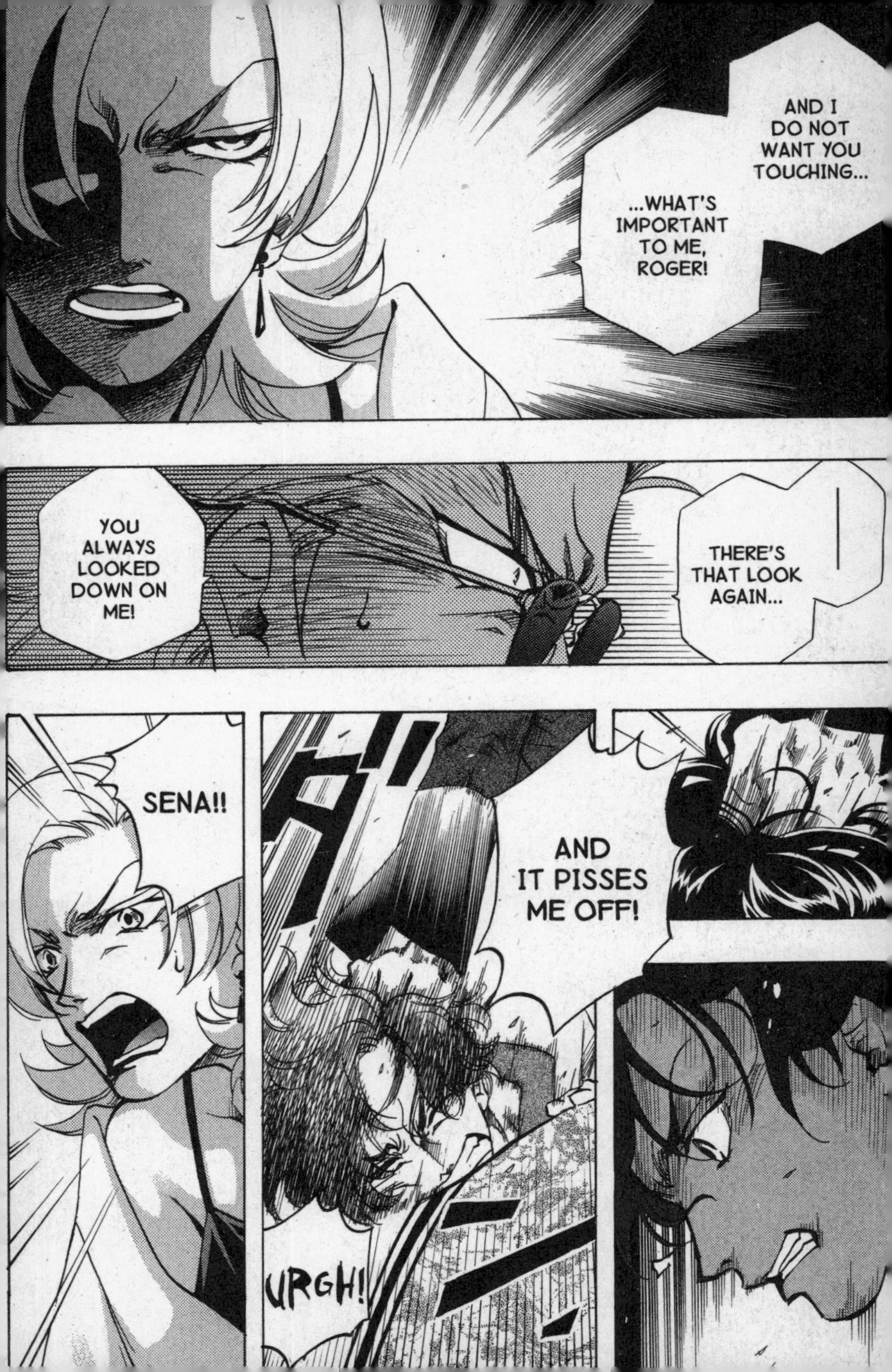
AND I DO NOT WANT YOU TOUCHING...
...WHAT'S IMPORTANT TO ME, ROGER!
THERE'S THAT LOOK AGAIN...
YOU ALWAYS LOOKED DOWN ON ME!
AND IT PISSES ME OFF!
URGH!
SENA!!

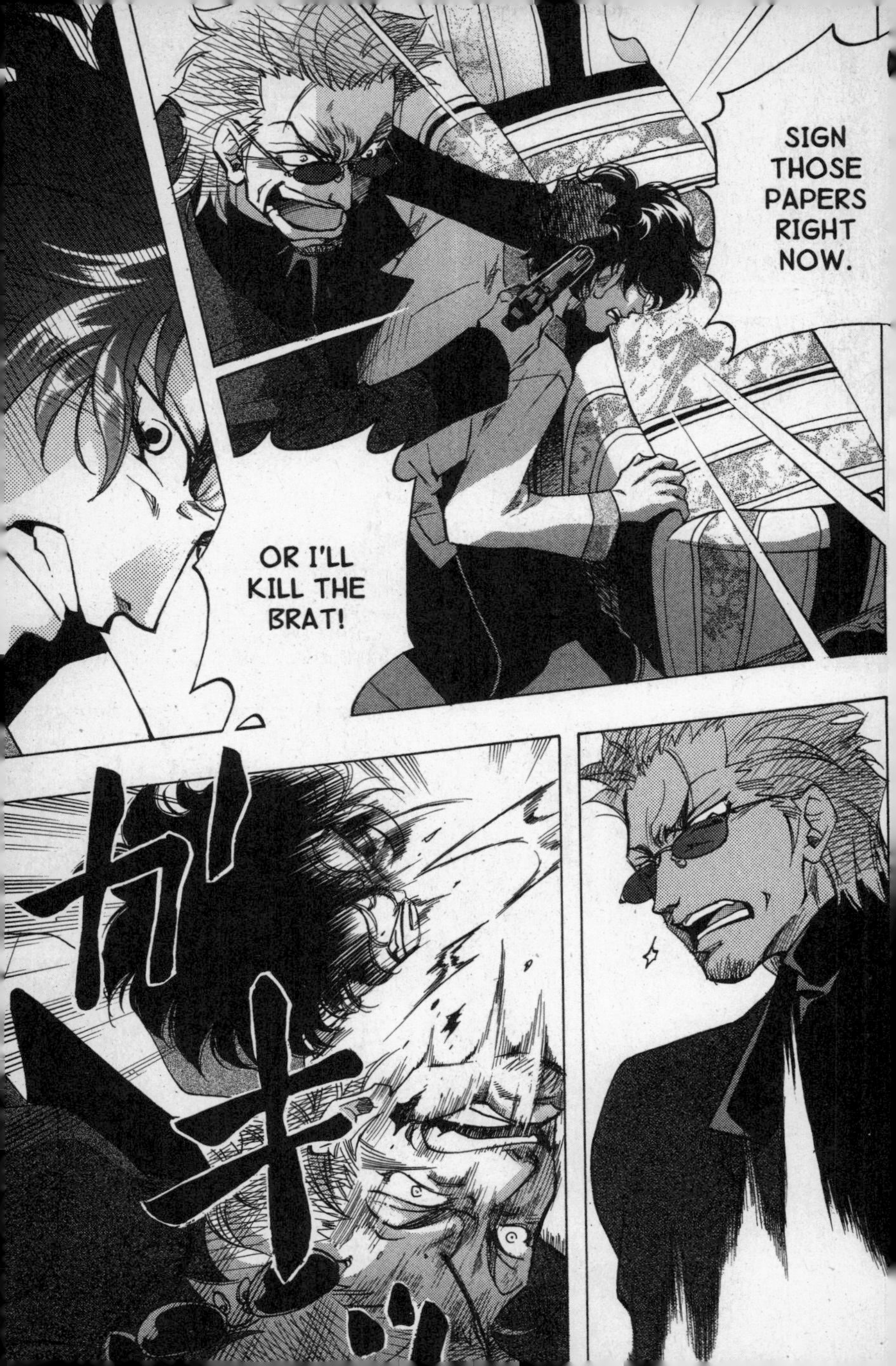
SIGN THOSE PAPERS RIGHT NOW.
OR I'LL KILL THE BRAT!
ガキッ

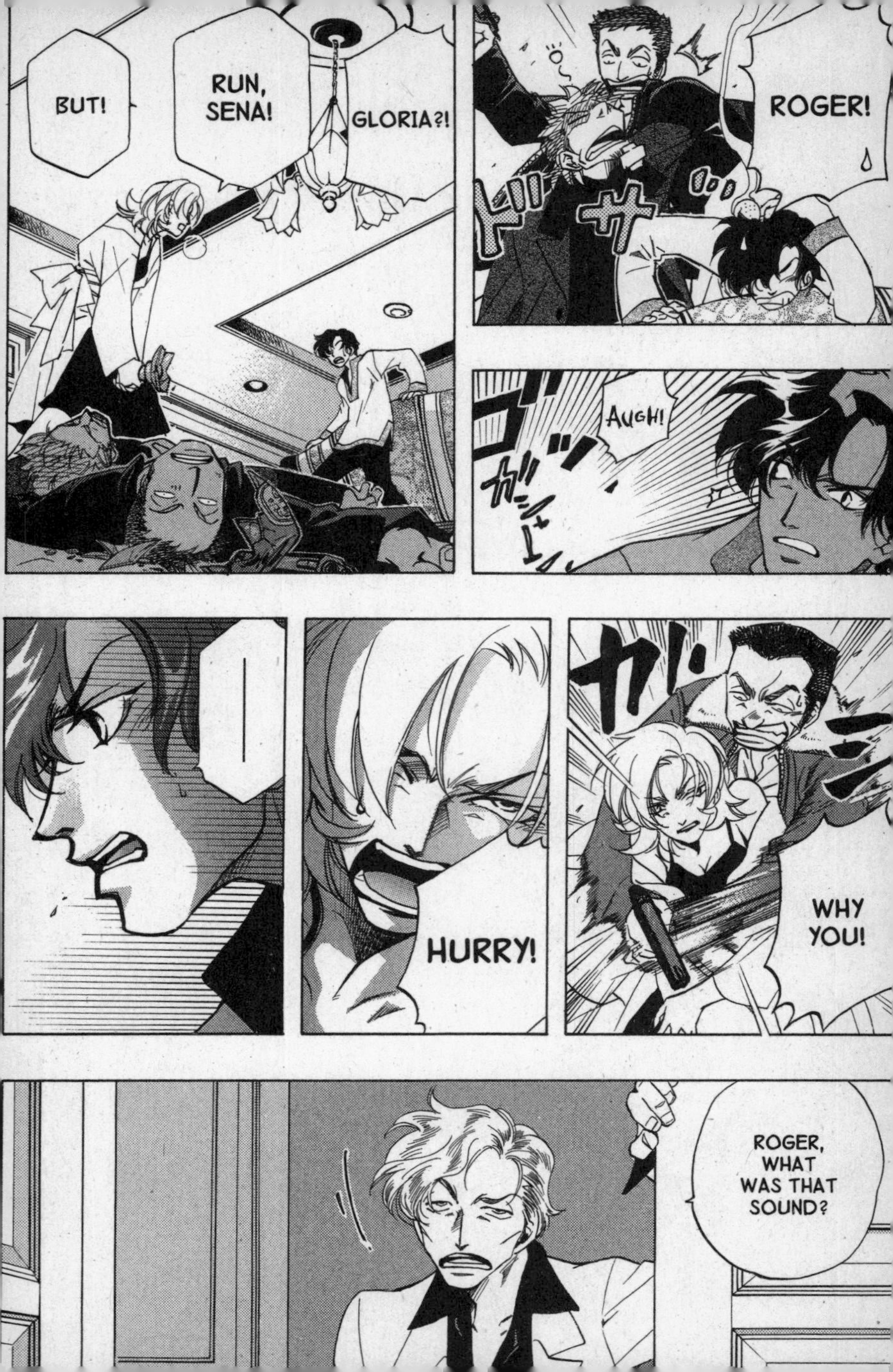
ROGER!
AUGH!
GLORIA?!
RUN, SENA!
BUT!
WHY YOU!
HURRY!
ROGER, WHAT WAS THAT SOUND?

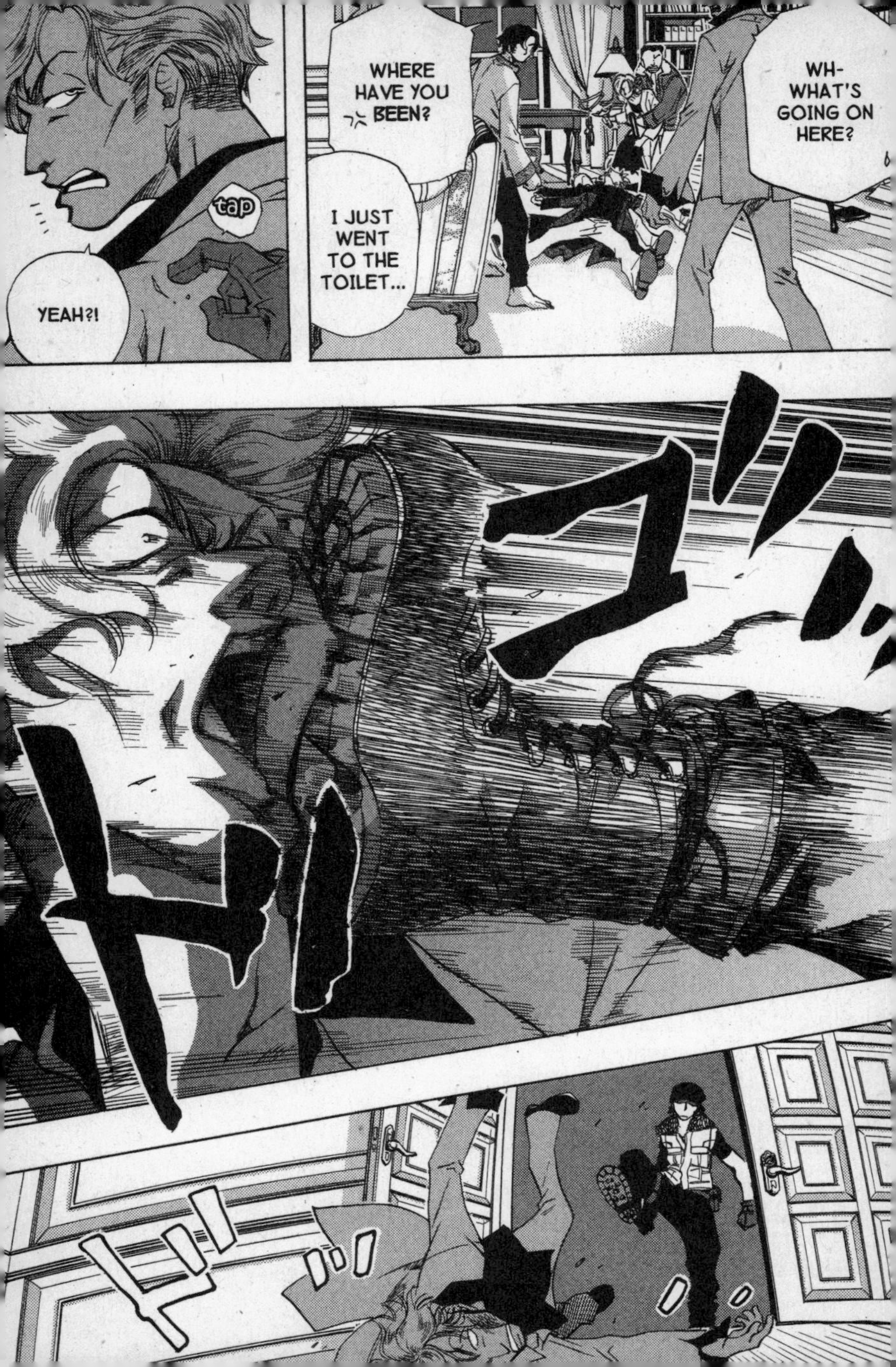
WH- WHAT'S GOING ON HERE?
WHERE HAVE YOU BEEN?
I JUST WENT TO THE TOILET...
tap
YEAH?!

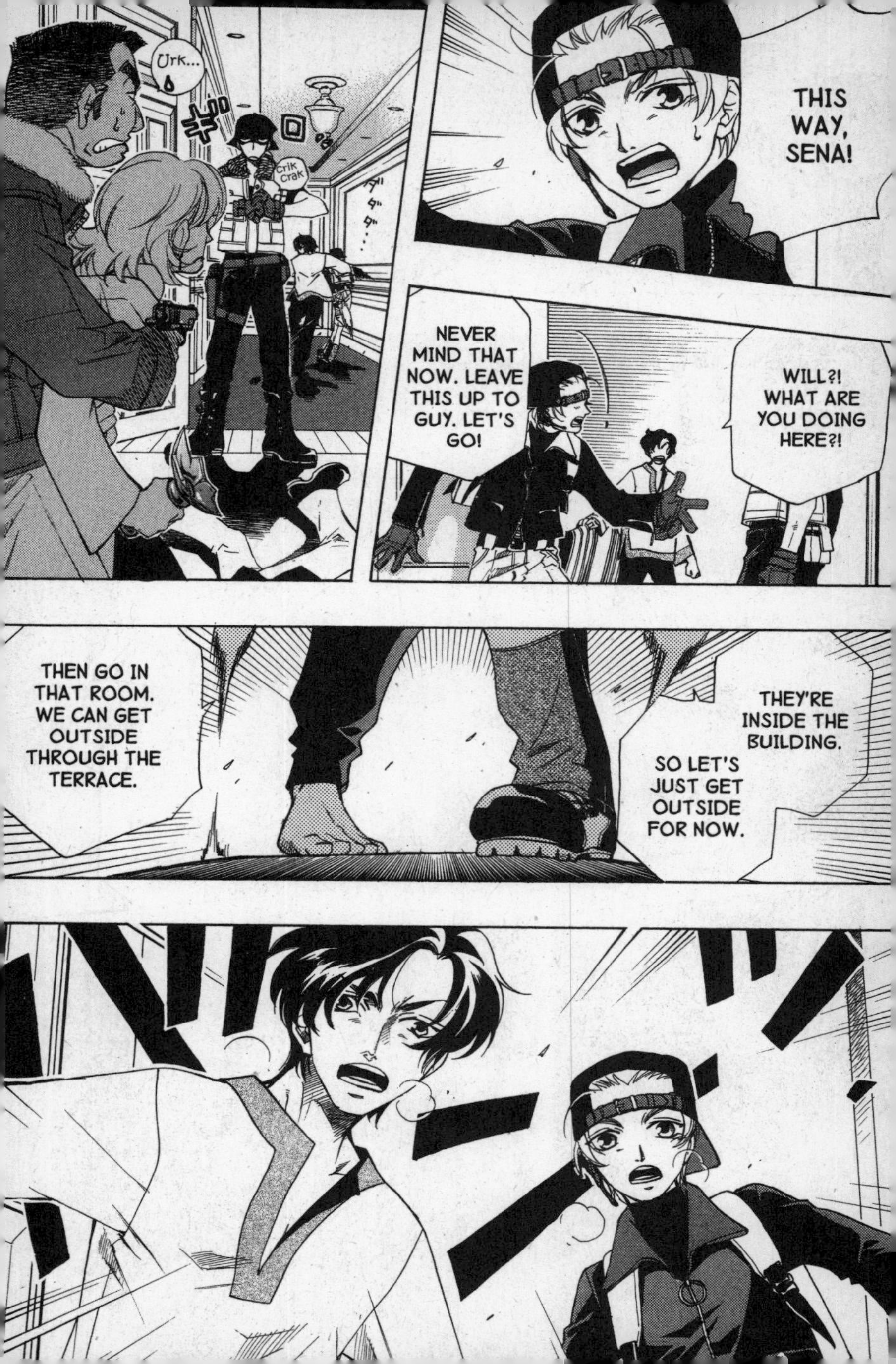
THIS WAY, SENA!
WILL?! WHAT ARE YOU DOING HERE?!
NEVER MIND THAT NOW. LEAVE THIS UP TO GUY. LET'S GO!
Urk...
Crik Crak
ダダダ…
THEY'RE INSIDE THE BUILDING.
SO LET'S JUST GET OUTSIDE FOR NOW.
THEN GO IN THAT ROOM. WE CAN GET OUTSIDE THROUGH THE TERRACE.

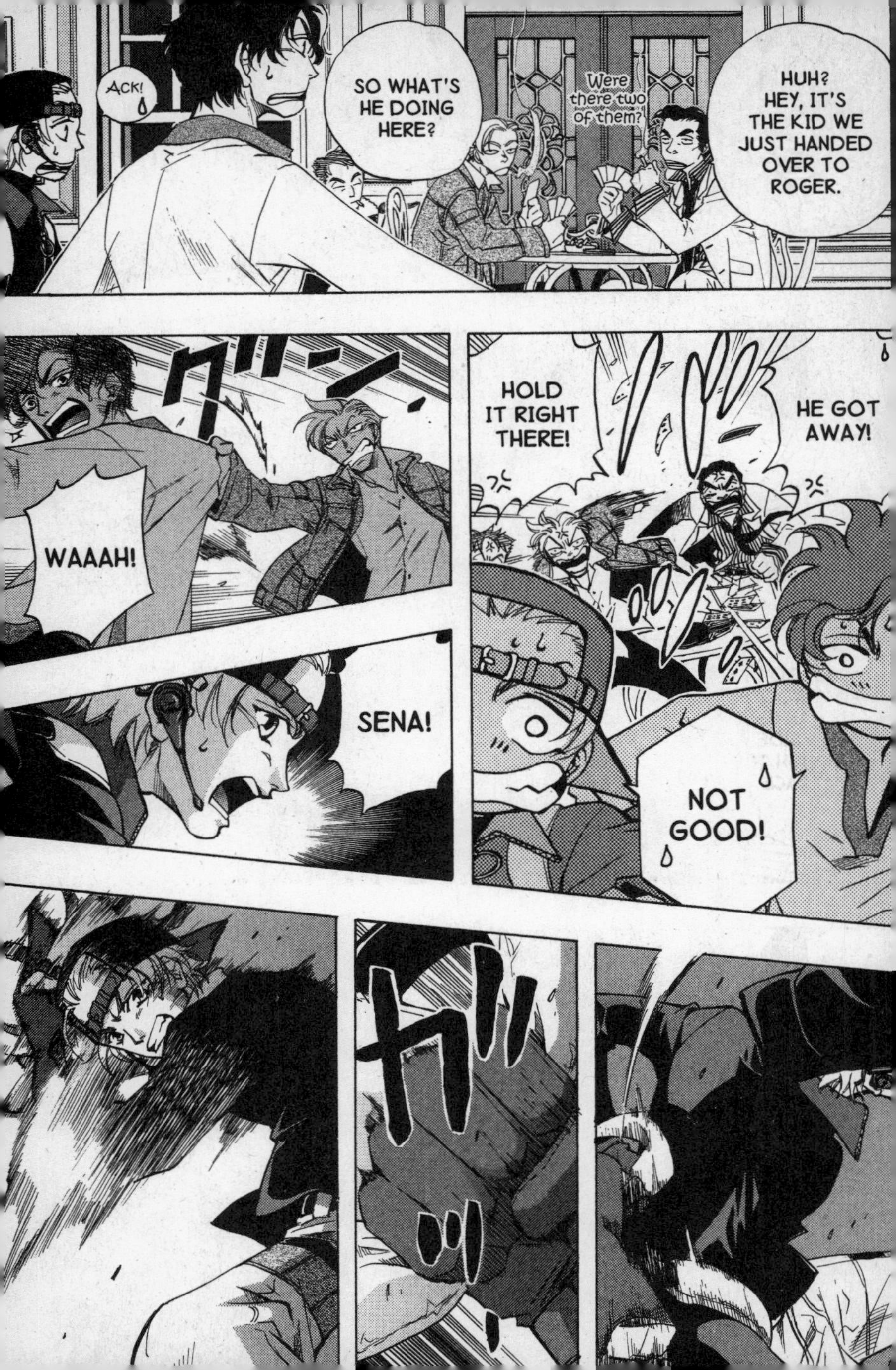
HUH? HEY, IT'S THE KID WE JUST HANDED OVER TO ROGER.
Were there two of them?
SO WHAT'S HE DOING HERE?
ACK!
HE GOT AWAY!
HOLD IT RIGHT THERE!
NOT GOOD!
WAAAH!
SENA!

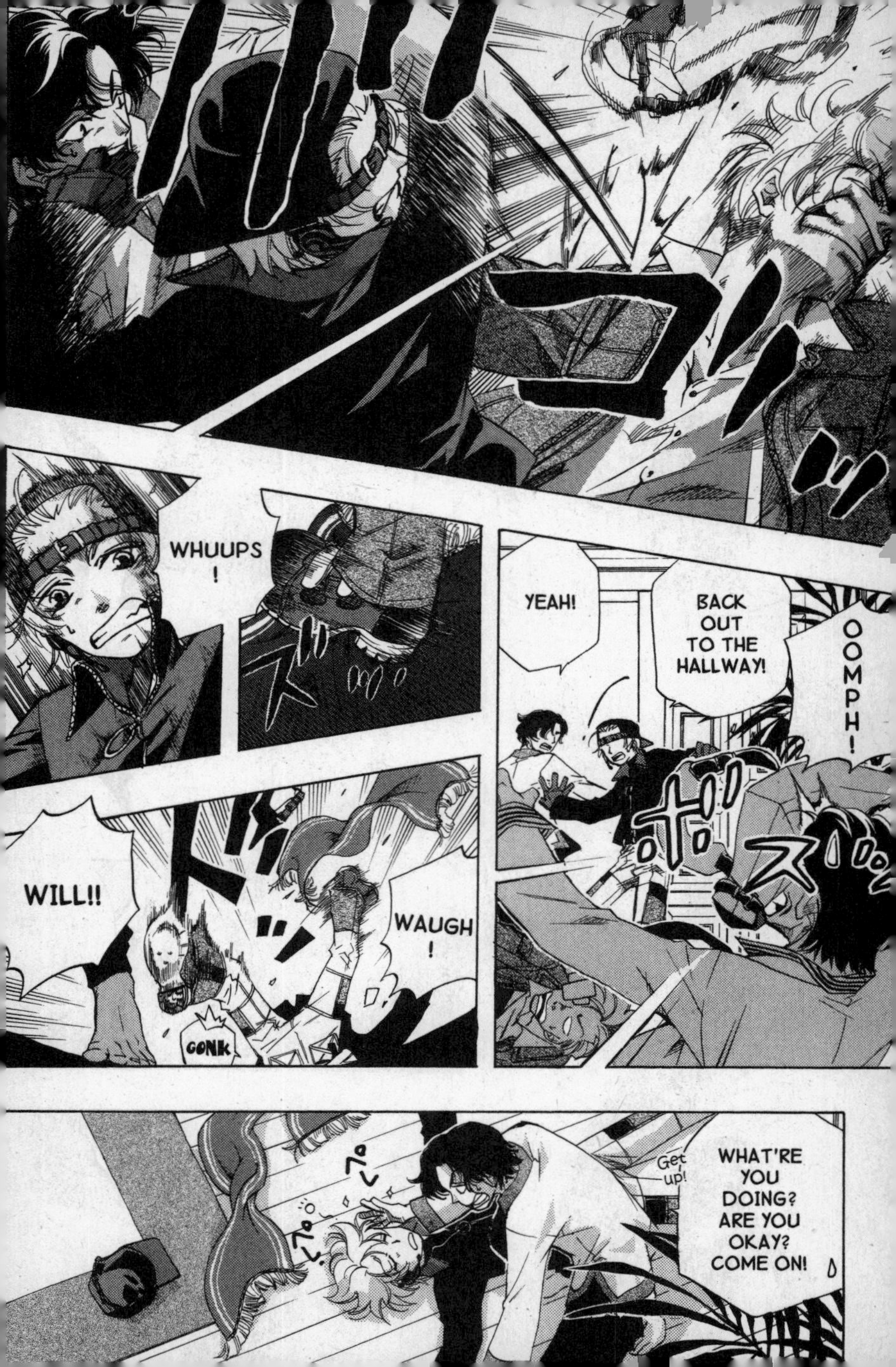
OOMPH!
BACK OUT TO THE HALLWAY!
YEAH!
WHUUPS!
WAUGH!
WILL!!
GONK
WHAT'RE YOU DOING? ARE YOU OKAY? COME ON!
Get up!

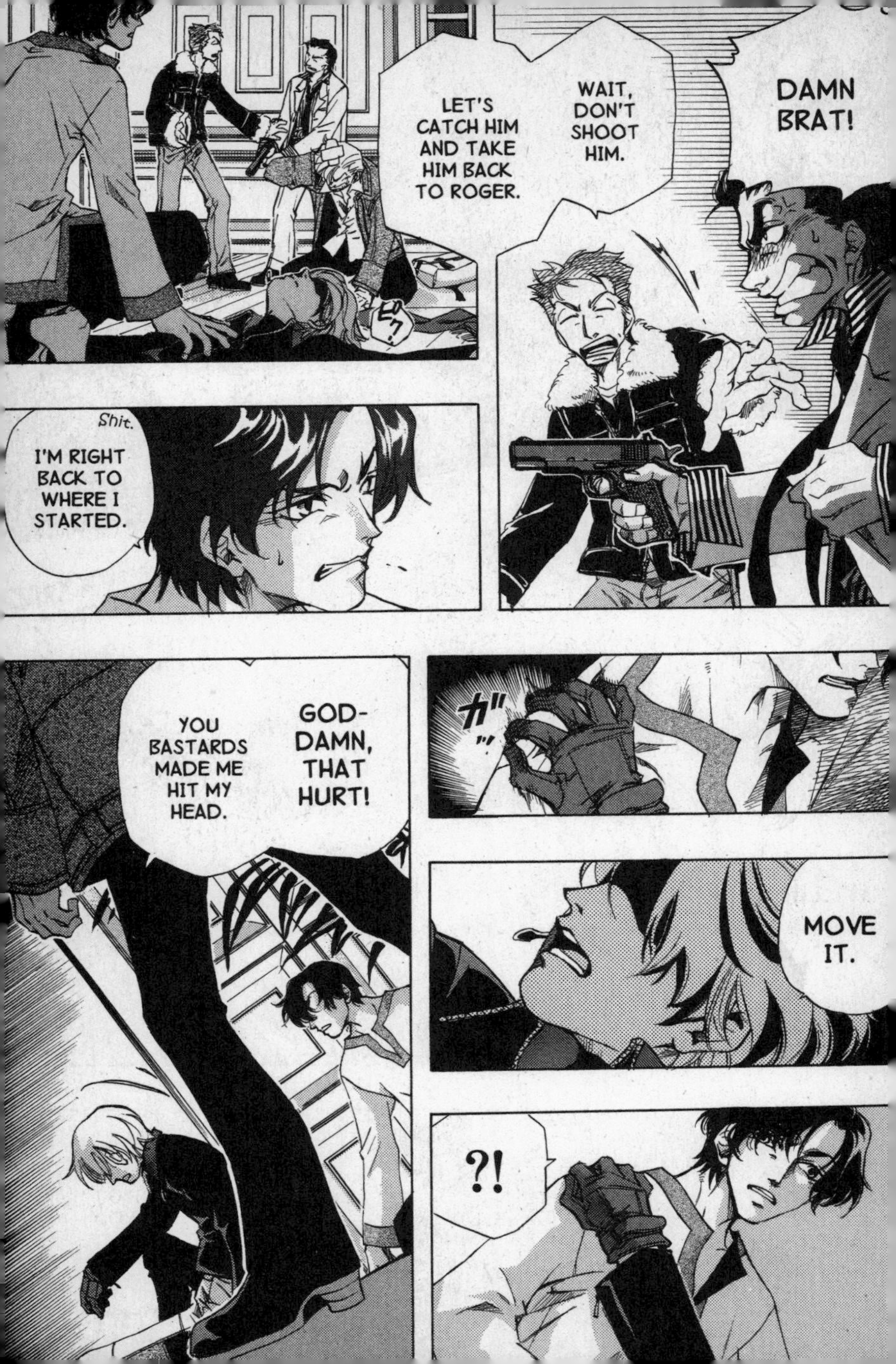
DAMN BRAT!
WAIT, DON'T SHOOT HIM.
LET'S CATCH HIM AND TAKE HIM BACK TO ROGER.
ピク!
Shit.
I'M RIGHT BACK TO WHERE I STARTED.
ガッ
MOVE IT.
?!
GOD-DAMN, THAT HURT!
YOU BASTARDS MADE ME HIT MY HEAD.

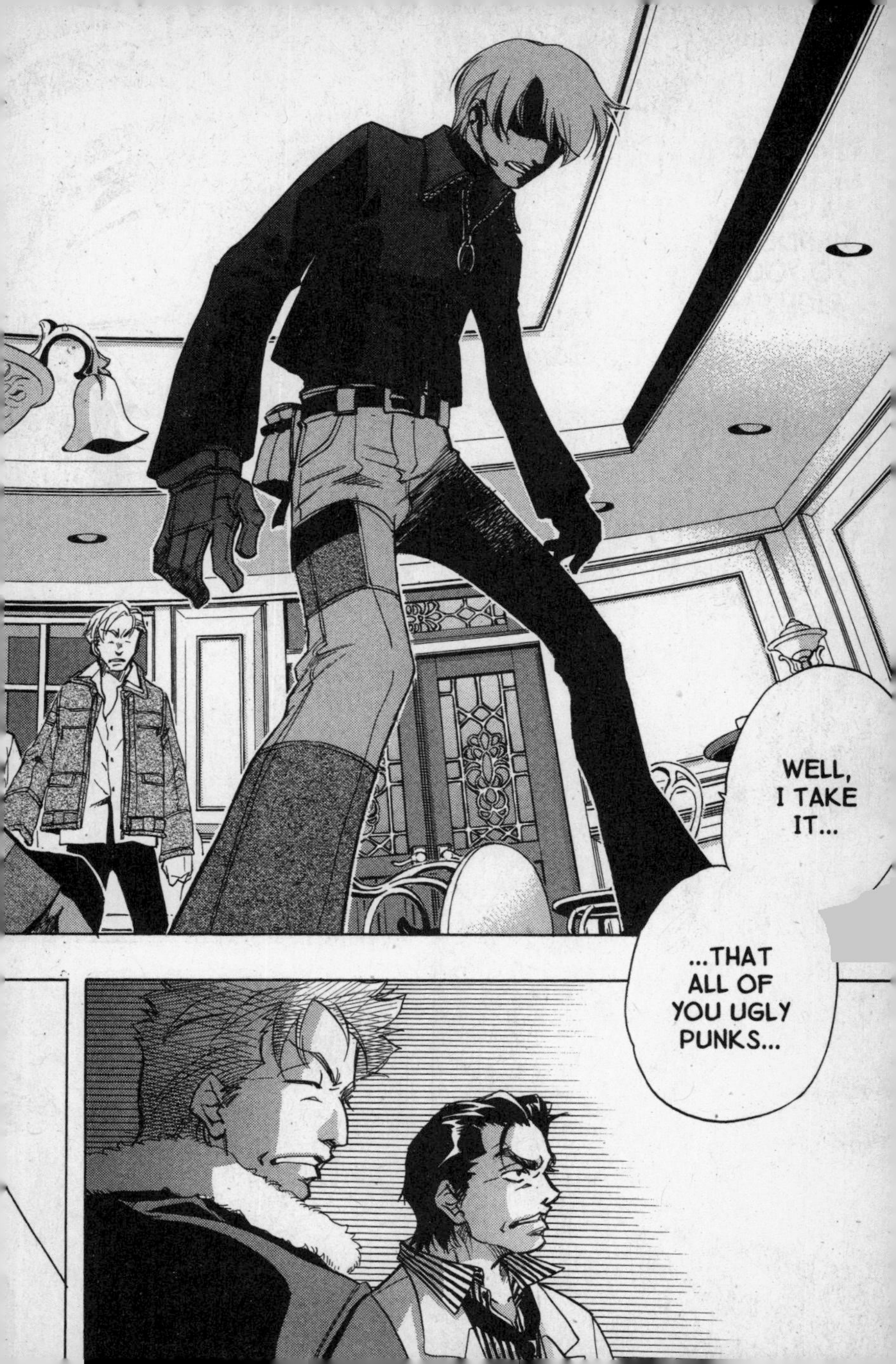
WELL, I TAKE IT...
...THAT ALL OF YOU UGLY PUNKS...

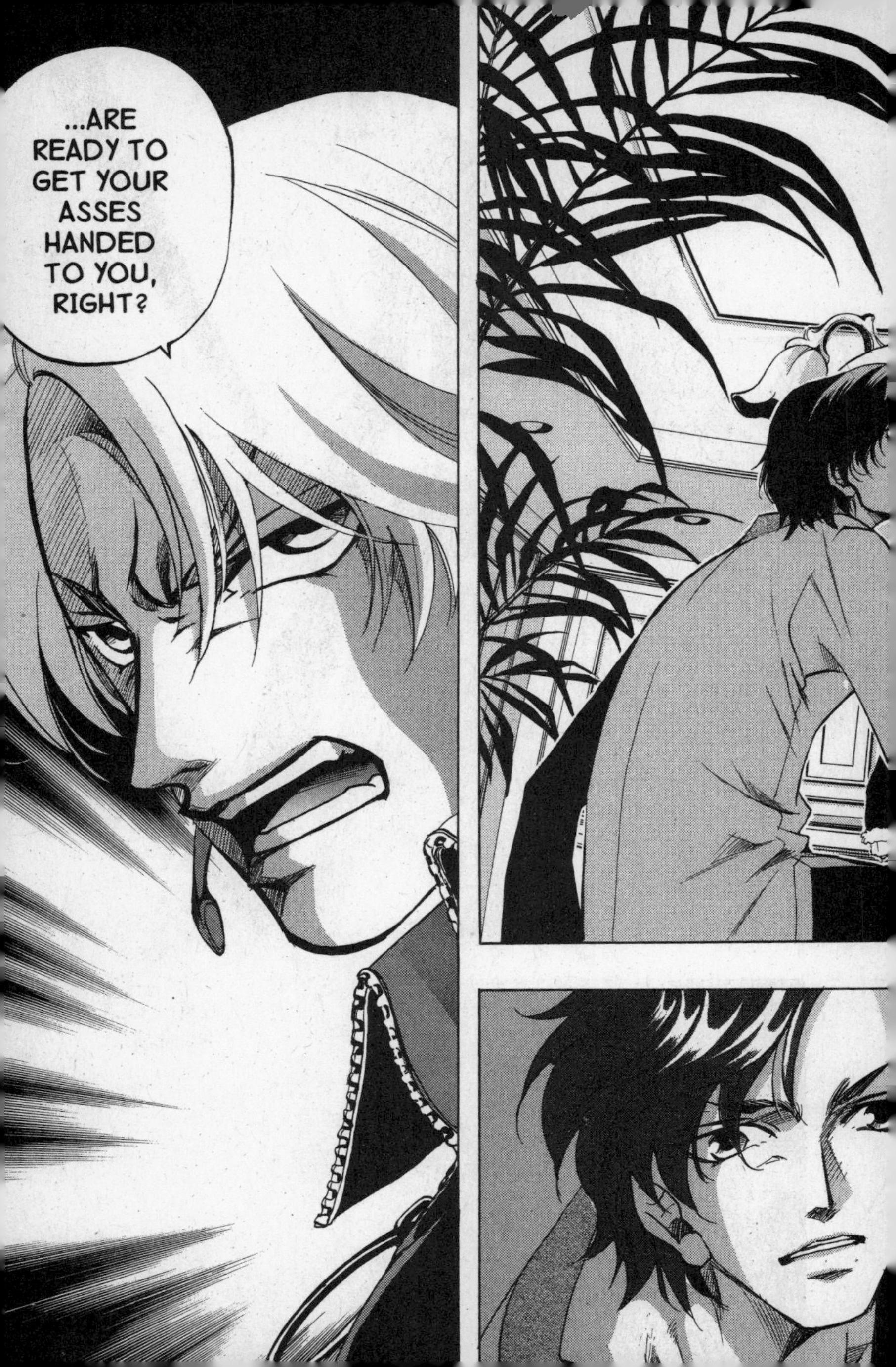
...ARE READY TO GET YOUR ASSES HANDED TO YOU, RIGHT?

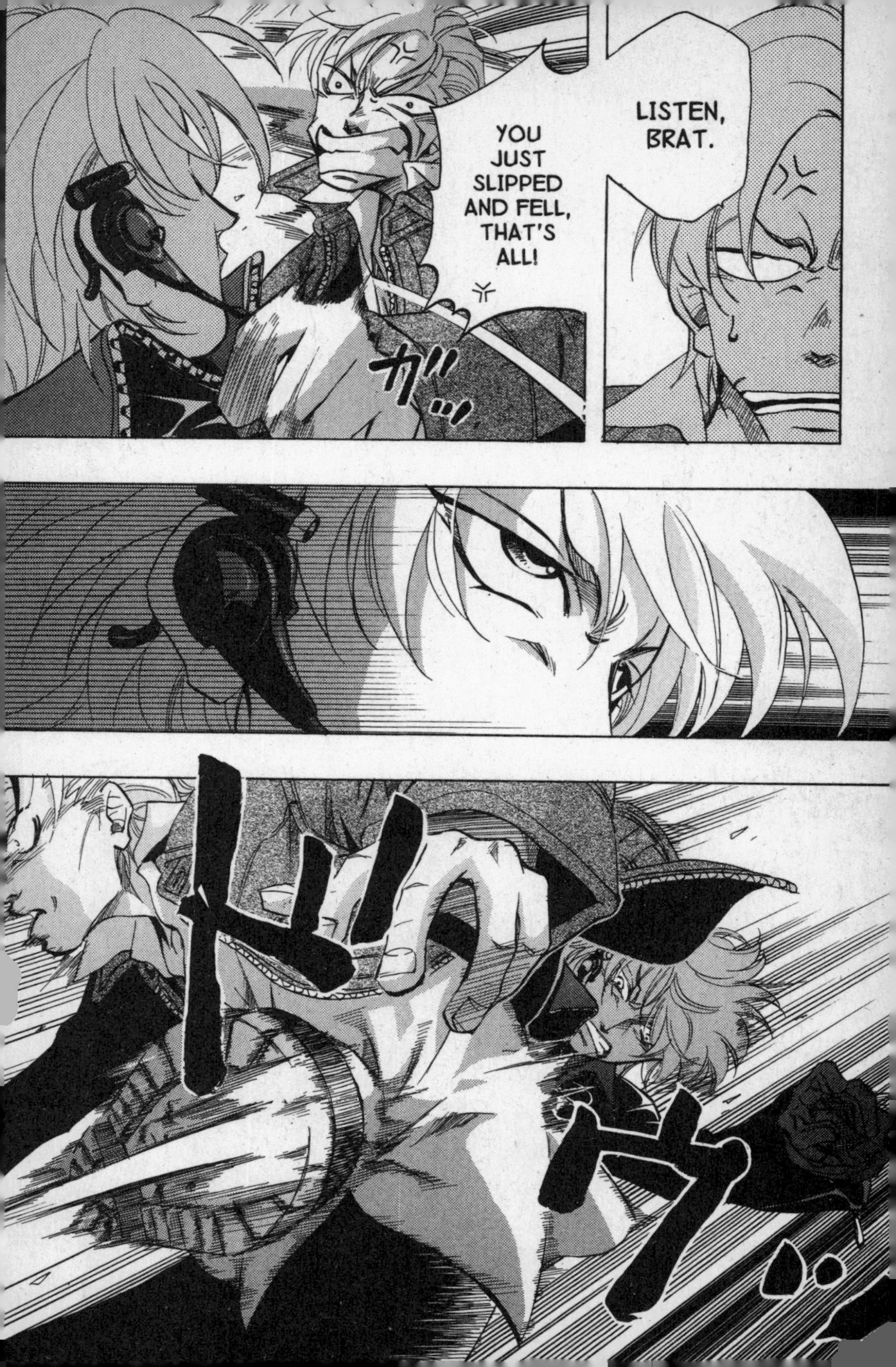
LISTEN, BRAT.
YOU JUST SLIPPED AND FELL, THAT'S ALL!
ガッ

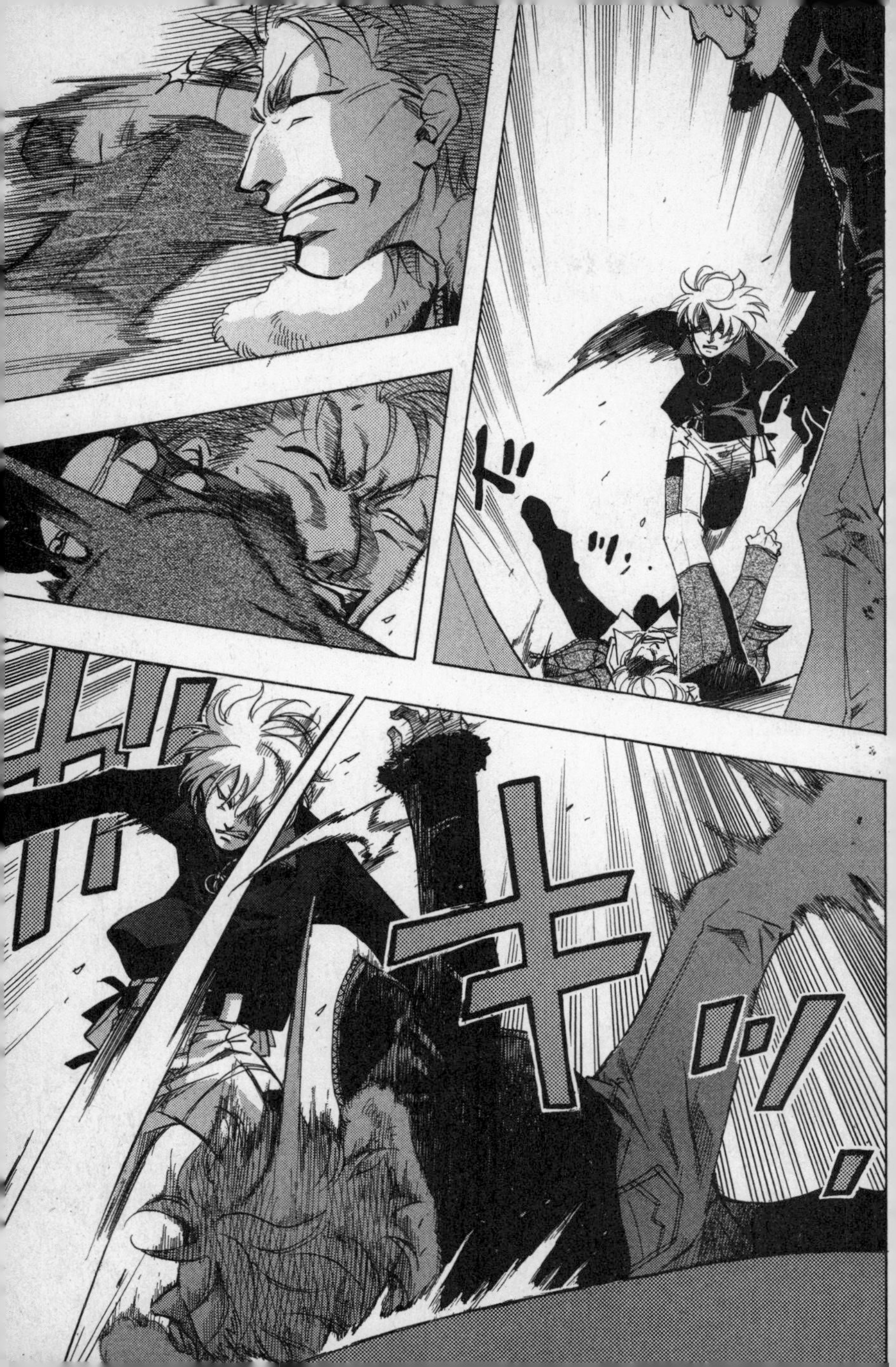
ドッ
ギン

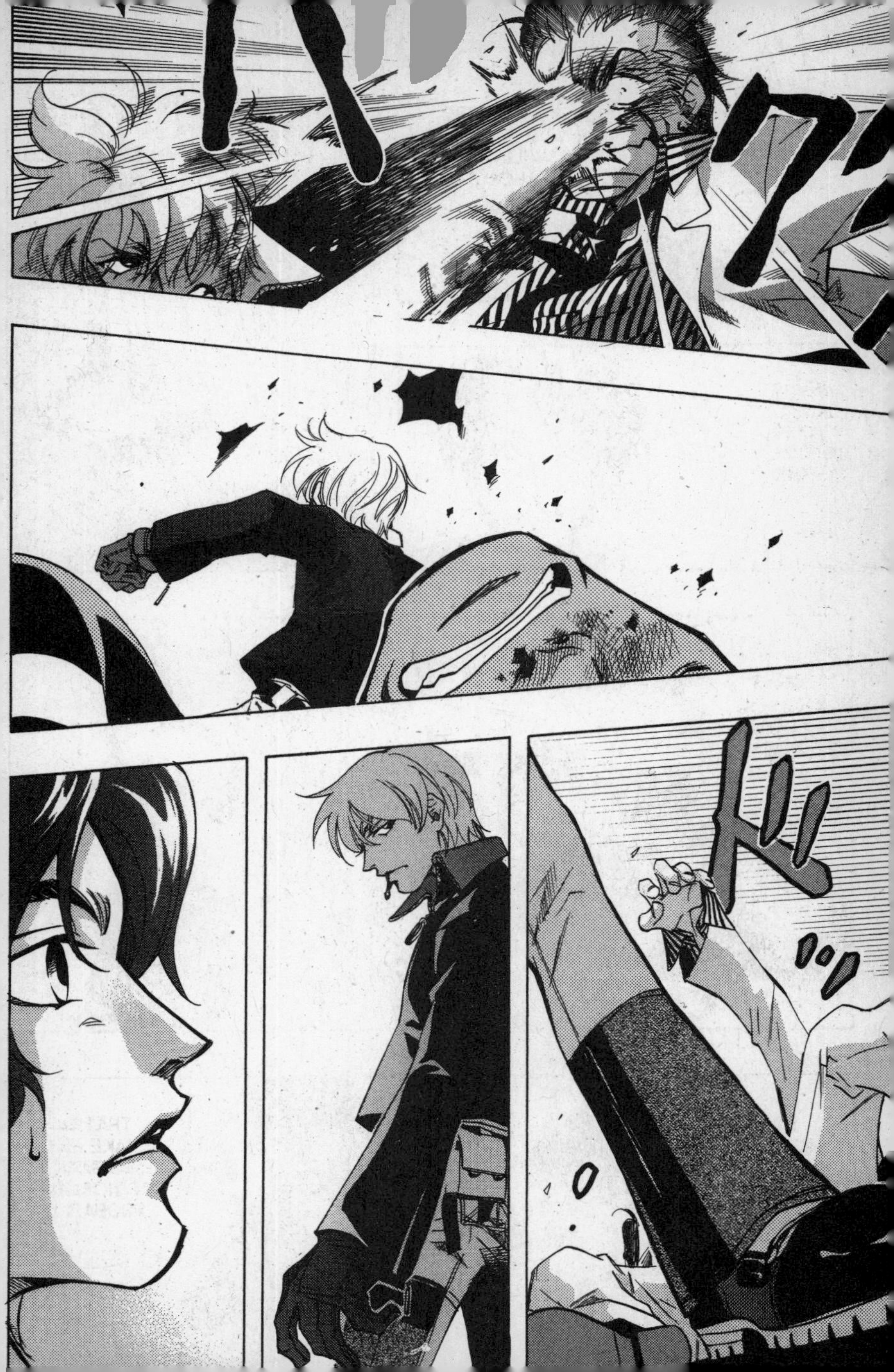

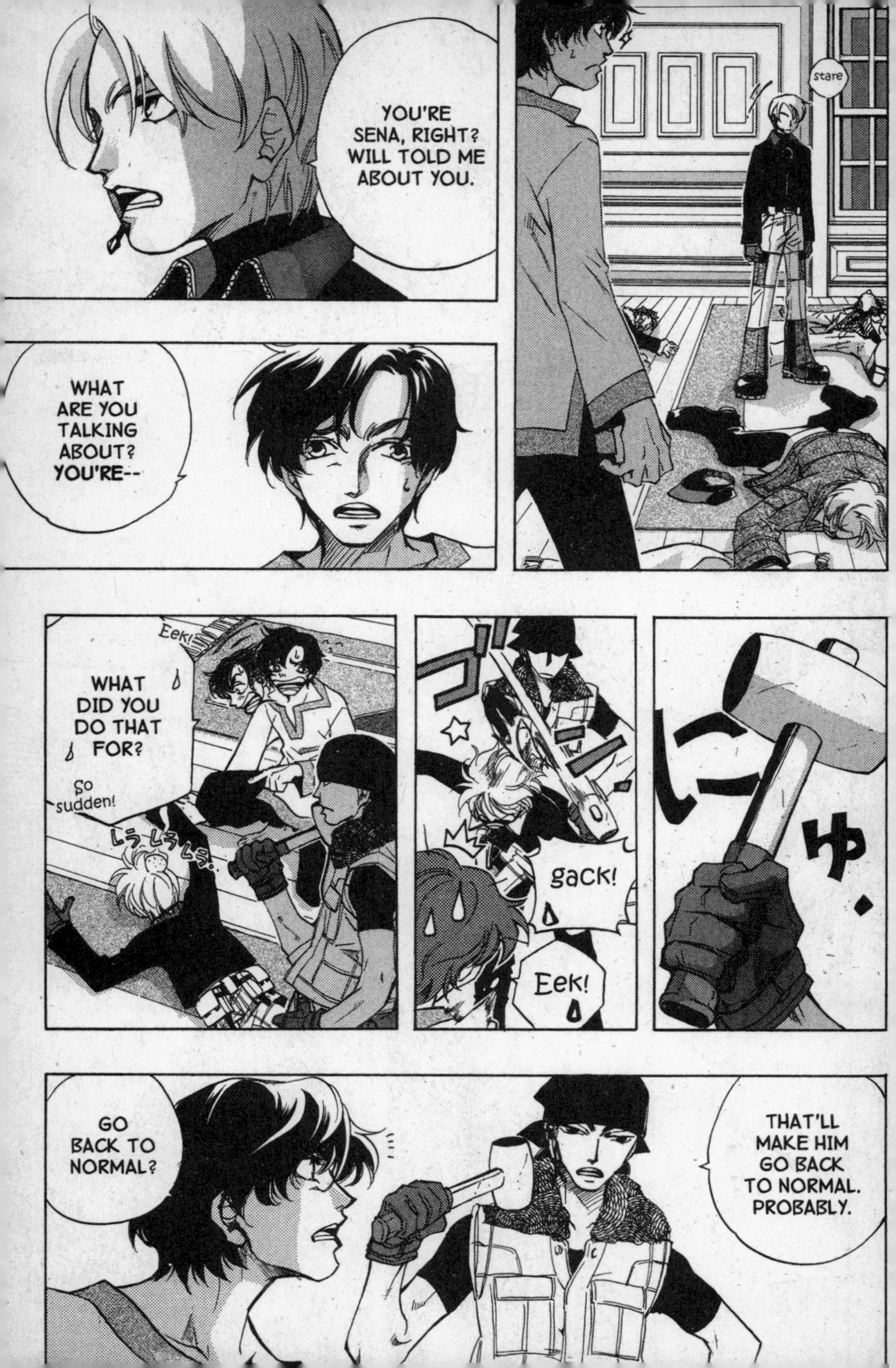
stare
YOU'RE SENA, RIGHT? WILL TOLD ME ABOUT YOU.
WHAT ARE YOU TALKING ABOUT? YOU'RE--
にゅ.
gack!
Eek!
Eek!
WHAT DID YOU DO THAT FOR?
So sudden!
THAT'LL MAKE HIM GO BACK TO NORMAL. PROBABLY.
GO BACK TO NORMAL?

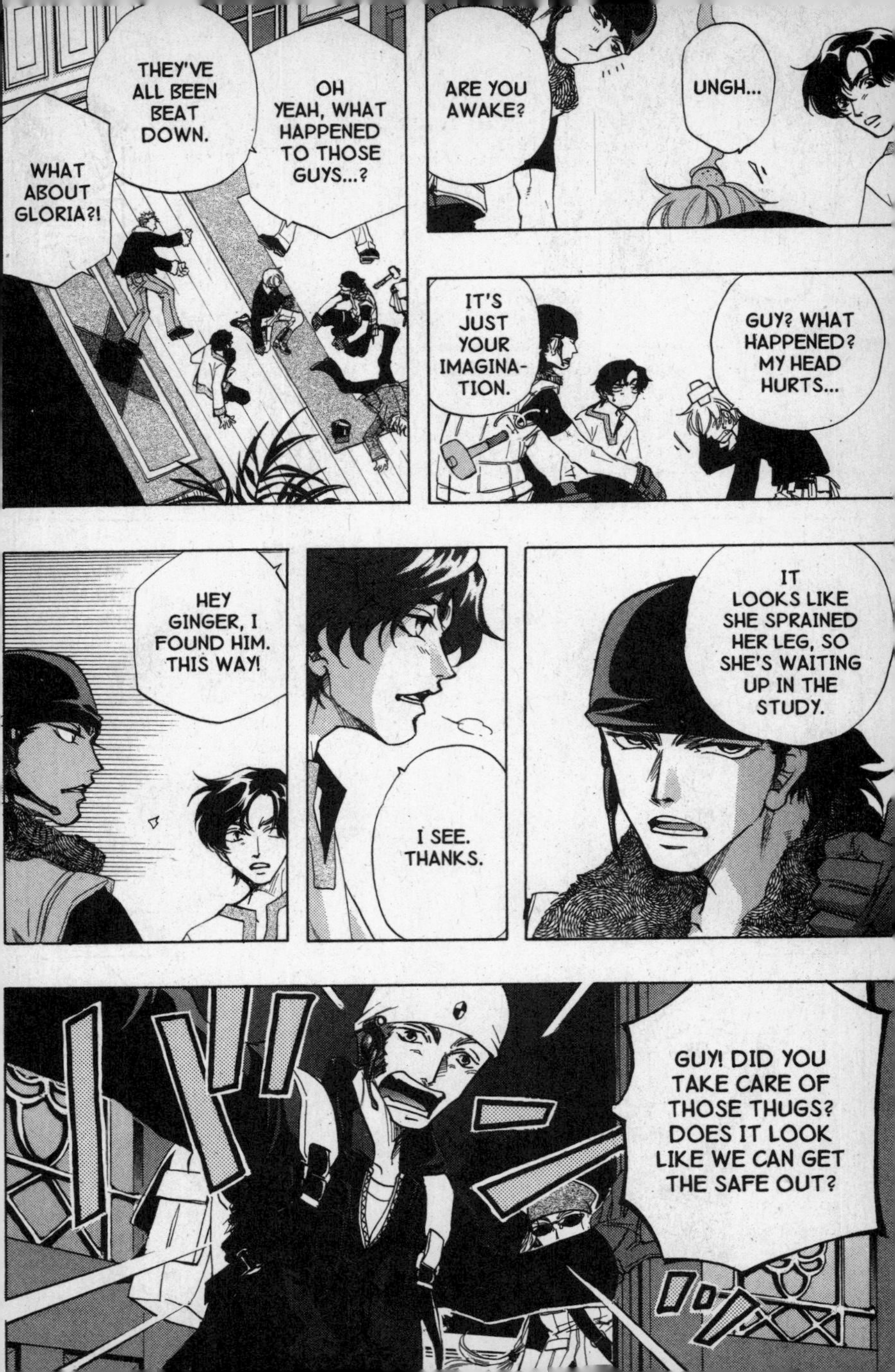
UNGH...
ARE YOU AWAKE?
GUY? WHAT HAPPENED? MY HEAD HURTS...
IT'S JUST YOUR IMAGINATION.
OH YEAH, WHAT HAPPENED TO THOSE GUYS...?
THEY'VE ALL BEEN BEAT DOWN.
WHAT ABOUT GLORIA?!
IT LOOKS LIKE SHE SPRAINED HER LEG, SO SHE'S WAITING UP IN THE STUDY.
I SEE. THANKS.
HEY GINGER, I FOUND HIM. THIS WAY!
GUY! DID YOU TAKE CARE OF THOSE THUGS? DOES IT LOOK LIKE WE CAN GET THE SAFE OUT?
DO-

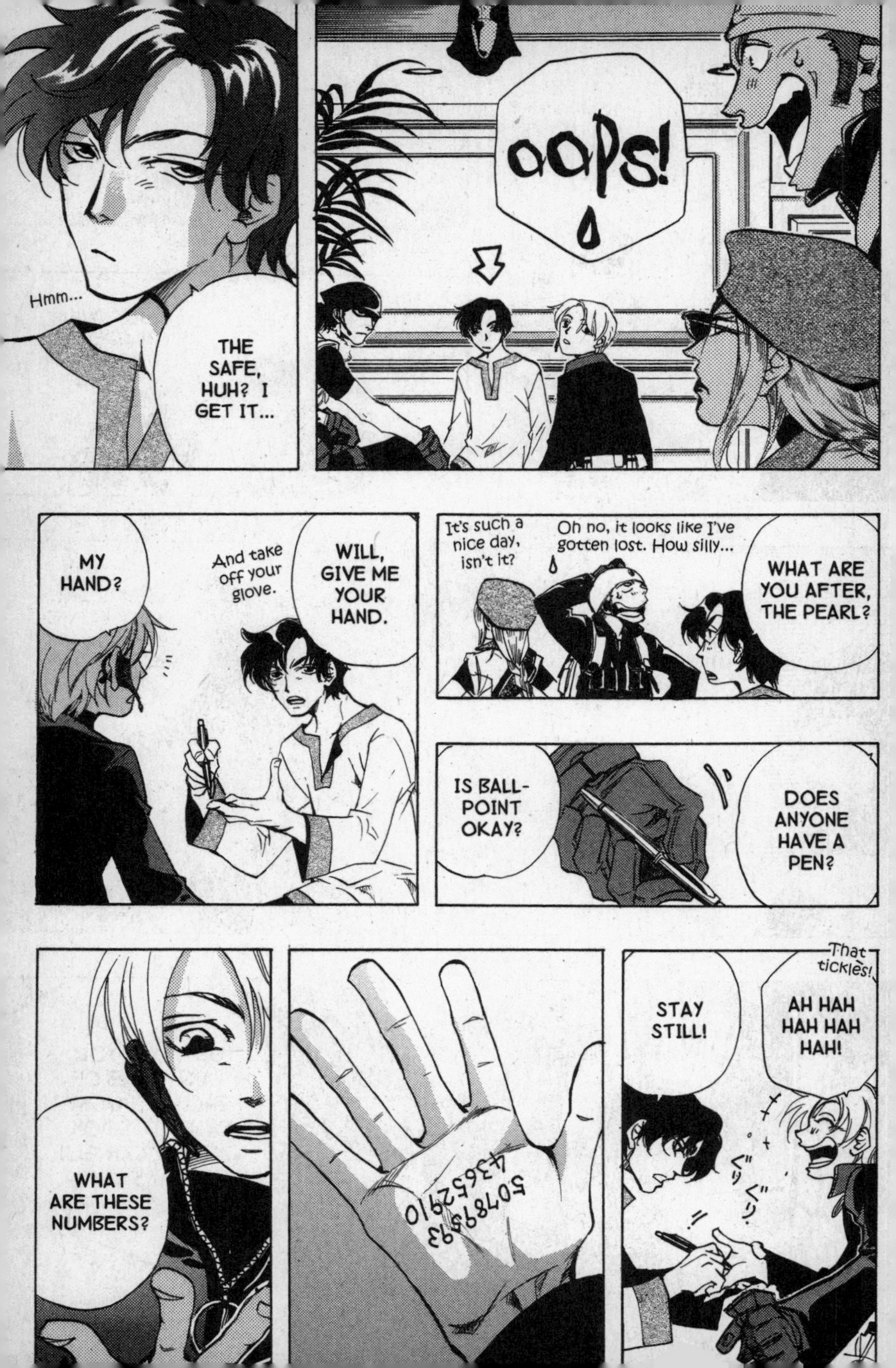
OOPS!
Hmm...
THE SAFE, HUH? I GET IT...
WHAT ARE YOU AFTER, THE PEARL?
Oh no, it looks like I've gotten lost. How silly...
It's such a nice day, isn't it?
DOES ANYONE HAVE A PEN?
IS BALLPOINT OKAY?
WILL, GIVE ME YOUR HAND.
And take off your glove.
MY HAND?
That tickles!
AH HAH HAH HAH HAH!
STAY STILL!
43652910
50789593
WHAT ARE THESE NUMBERS?

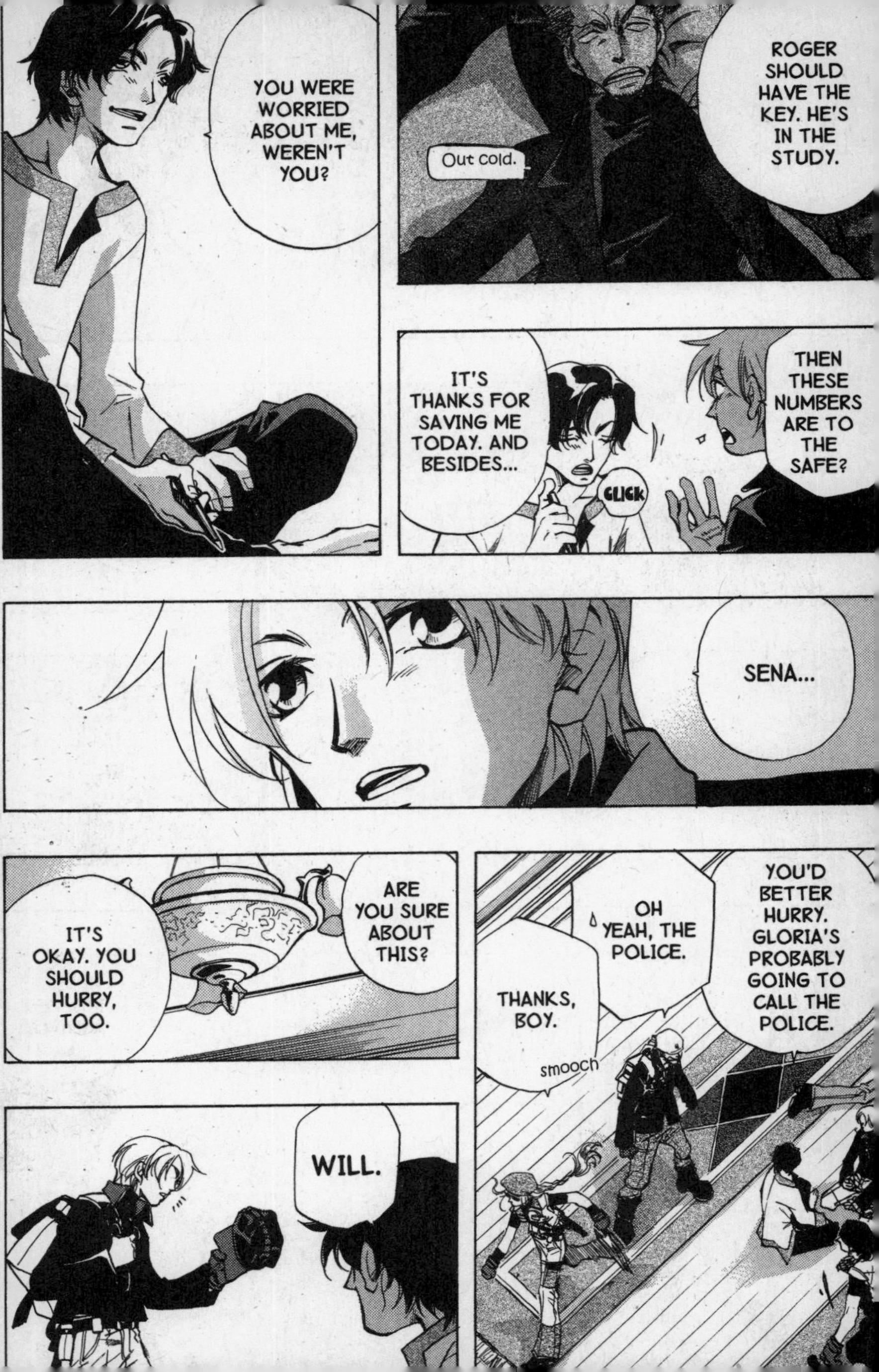
ROGER SHOULD HAVE THE KEY. HE'S IN THE STUDY.
Out cold.
THEN THESE NUMBERS ARE TO THE SAFE?
IT'S THANKS FOR SAVING ME TODAY. AND BESIDES...
CLICK
YOU WERE WORRIED ABOUT ME, WEREN'T YOU?
SENA...
YOU'D BETTER HURRY. GLORIA'S PROBABLY GOING TO CALL THE POLICE.
OH YEAH, THE POLICE.
THANKS, BOY.
smooch
ARE YOU SURE ABOUT THIS?
IT'S OKAY. YOU SHOULD HURRY, TOO.
WILL.

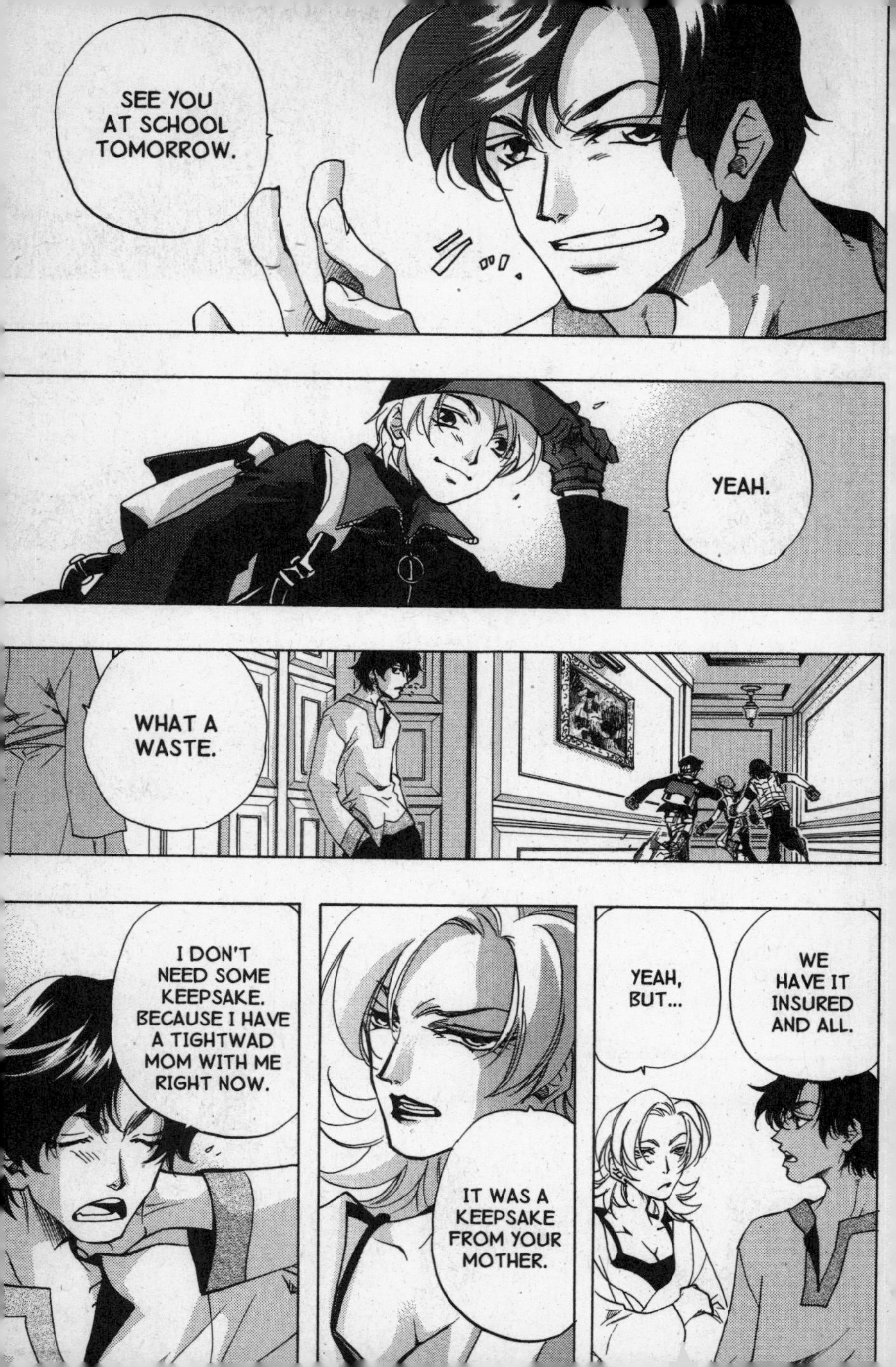
SEE YOU AT SCHOOL TOMORROW.
YEAH.
WHAT A WASTE.
WE HAVE IT INSURED AND ALL.
YEAH, BUT...
IT WAS A KEEPSAKE FROM YOUR MOTHER.
I DON'T NEED SOME KEEPSAKE. BECAUSE I HAVE A TIGHTWAD MOM WITH ME RIGHT NOW.

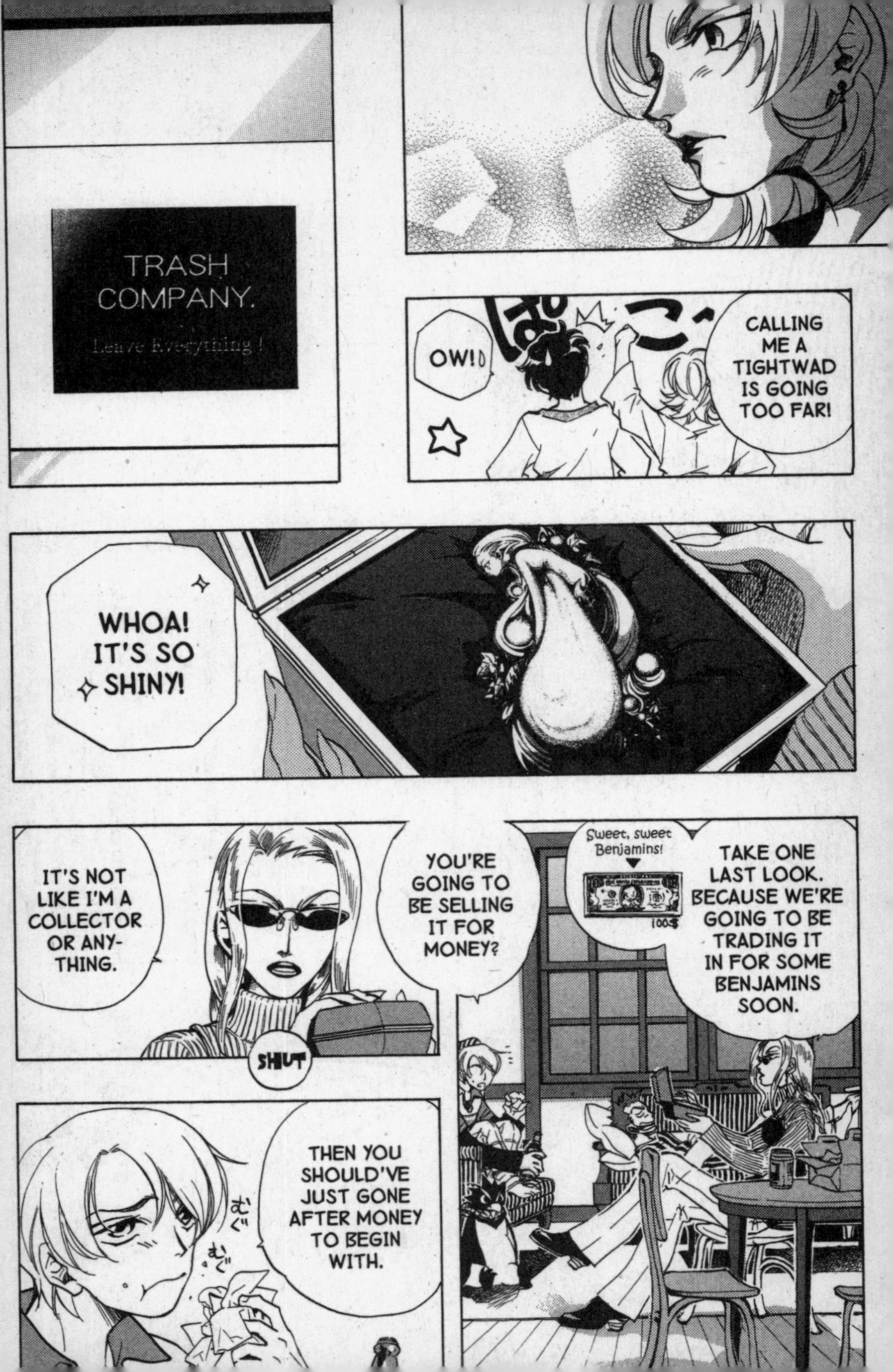
ぽこ
OW!
CALLING ME A TIGHTWAD IS GOING TOO FAR!
TRASH COMPANY.
Leave Everything !
WHOA! IT'S SO SHINY!
TAKE ONE LAST LOOK. BECAUSE WE'RE GOING TO BE TRADING IT IN FOR SOME BENJAMINS SOON.
Sweet, sweet Benjamins!
100$
YOU'RE GOING TO BE SELLING IT FOR MONEY?
IT'S NOT LIKE I'M A COLLECTOR OR ANY-THING.
SHUT
THEN YOU SHOULD'VE JUST GONE AFTER MONEY TO BEGIN WITH.
むぐ むぐ

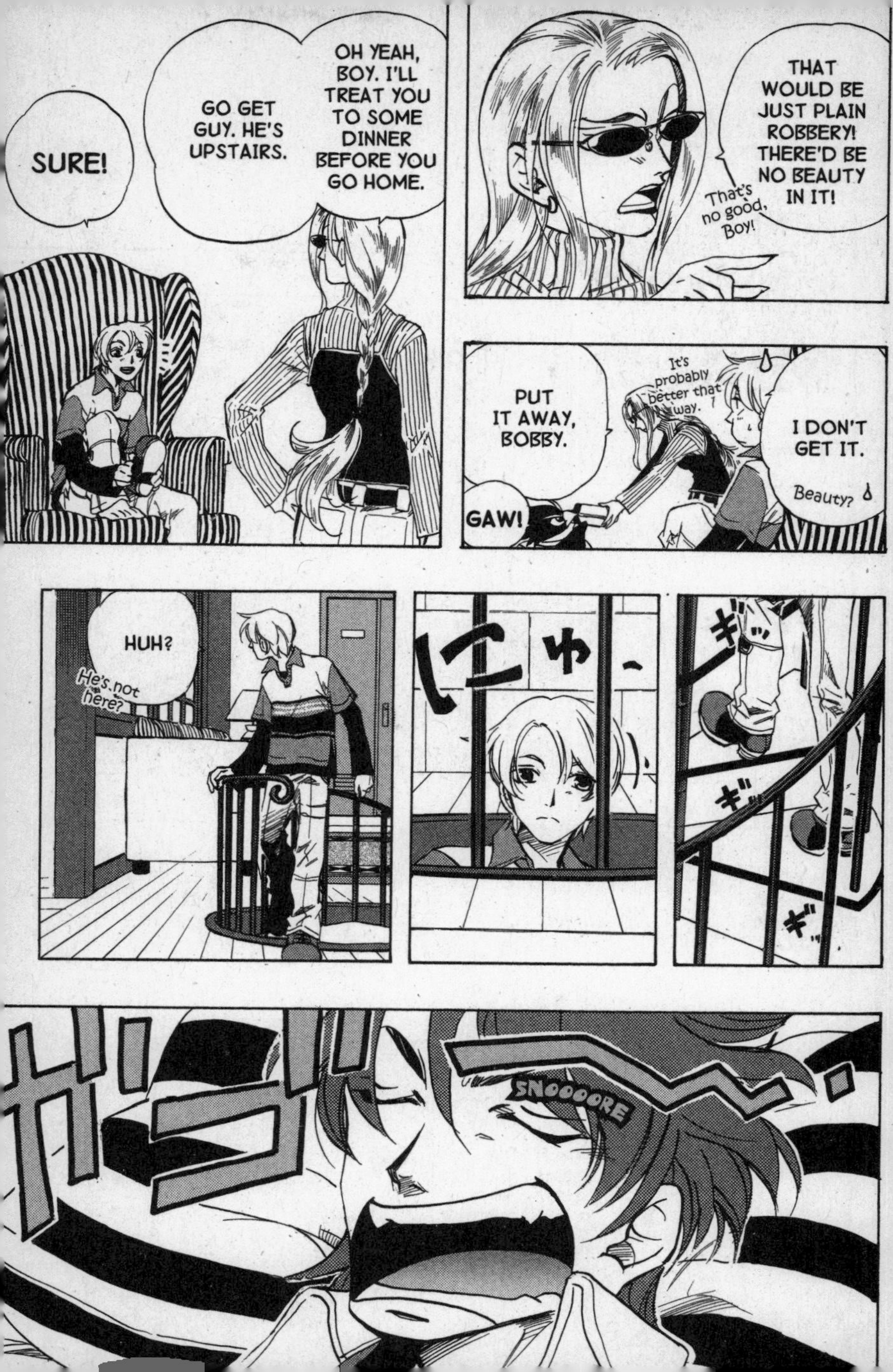
THAT WOULD BE JUST PLAIN ROBBERY! THERE'D BE NO BEAUTY IN IT!
That's no good, Boy!
I DON'T GET IT.
Beauty?
It's probably better that way.
PUT IT AWAY, BOBBY.
GAW!
OH YEAH, BOY. I'LL TREAT YOU TO SOME DINNER BEFORE YOU GO HOME.
GO GET GUY. HE'S UPSTAIRS.
SURE!
ギッ
ギッ
ギッ
にゅ
HUH?
He's not here?
SNOOOORE

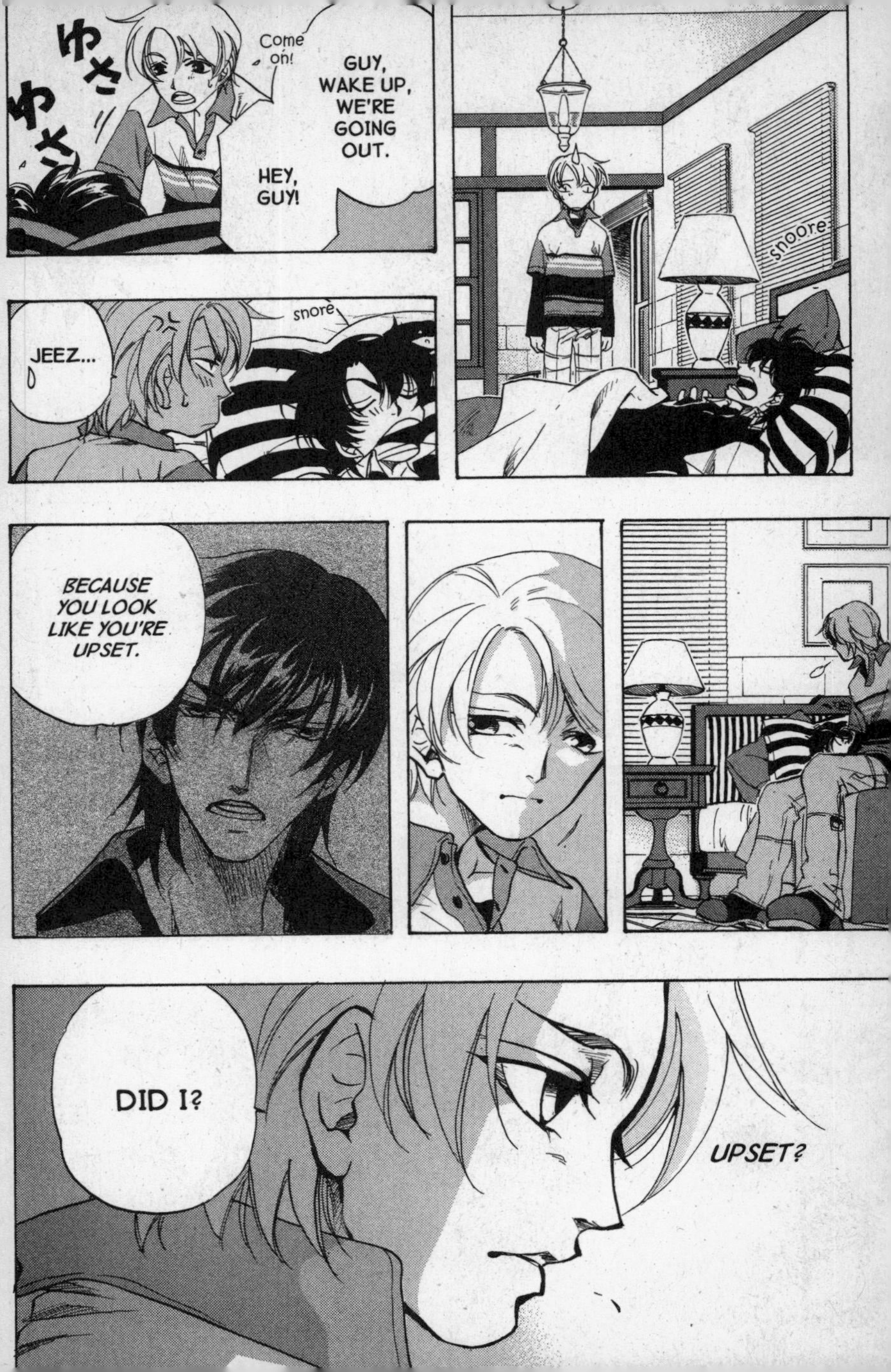
snoore
GUY, WAKE UP, WE'RE GOING OUT.
Come on!
HEY, GUY!
ゆさゆさ
snore
JEEZ...
BECAUSE YOU LOOK LIKE YOU'RE UPSET.
UPSET?
DID I?

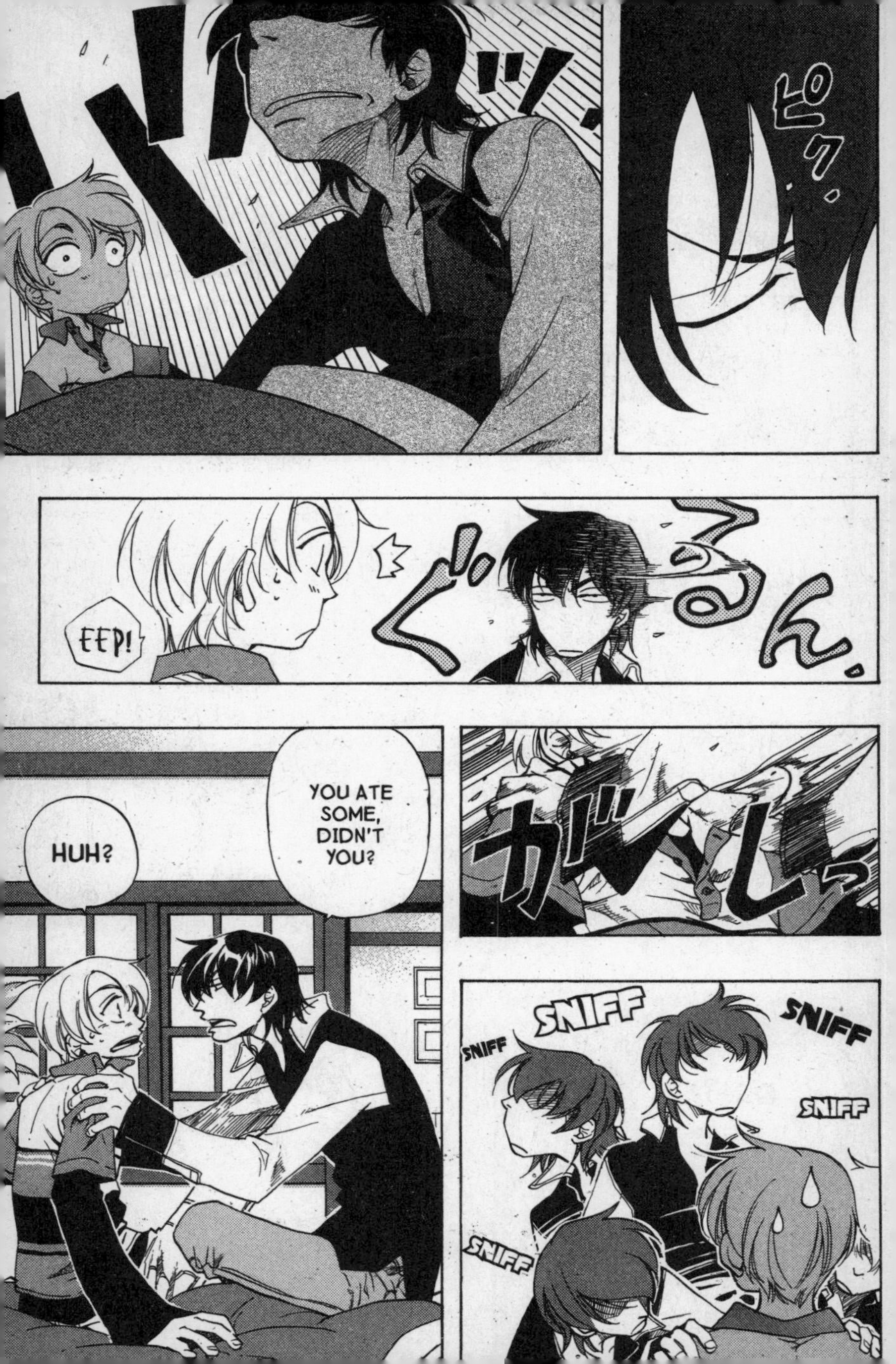
ピク。
ぐるん。
EEP!
がしっ
SNIFF
SNIFF
SNIFF
SNIFF
SNIFF
YOU ATE SOME, DIDN'T YOU?
HUH?

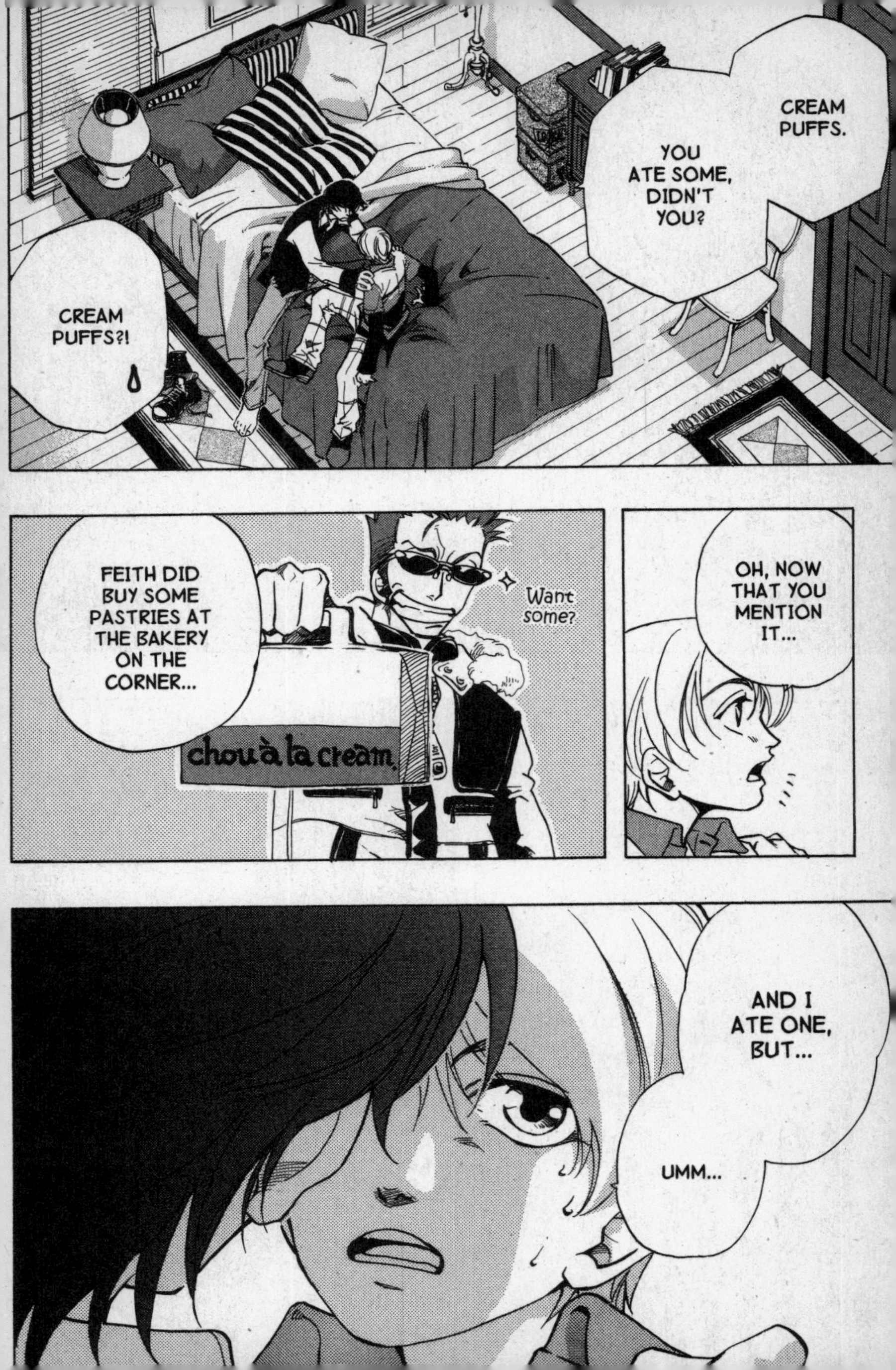
CREAM PUFFS.
YOU ATE SOME, DIDN'T YOU?
CREAM PUFFS?!
OH, NOW THAT YOU MENTION IT...
FEITH DID BUY SOME PASTRIES AT THE BAKERY ON THE CORNER...
Want some?
chou à la cream
AND I ATE ONE, BUT...
UMM...

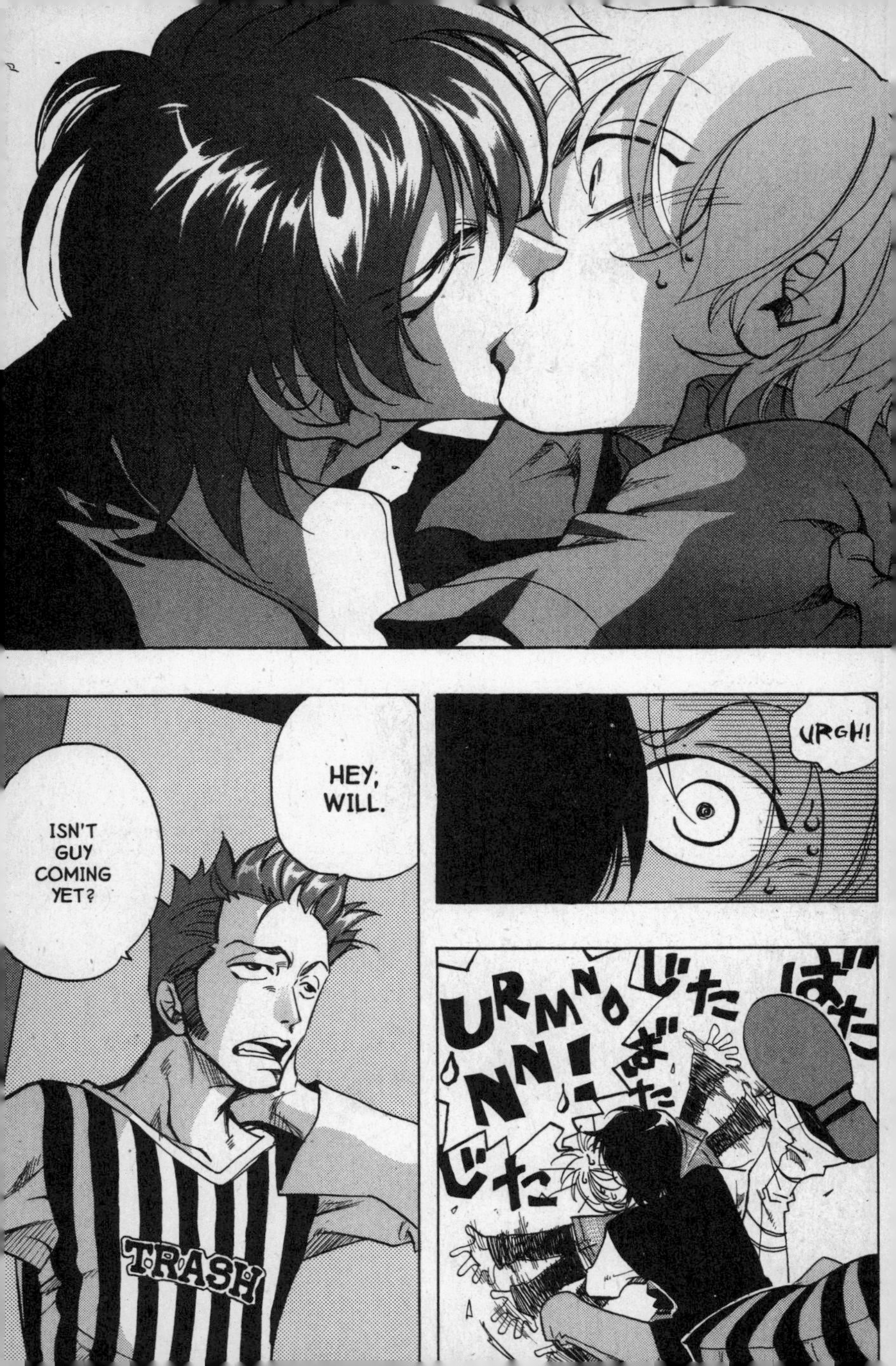
URGH!
URMNO NN!
じたばた
じたばた
HEY, WILL.
ISN'T GUY COMING YET?

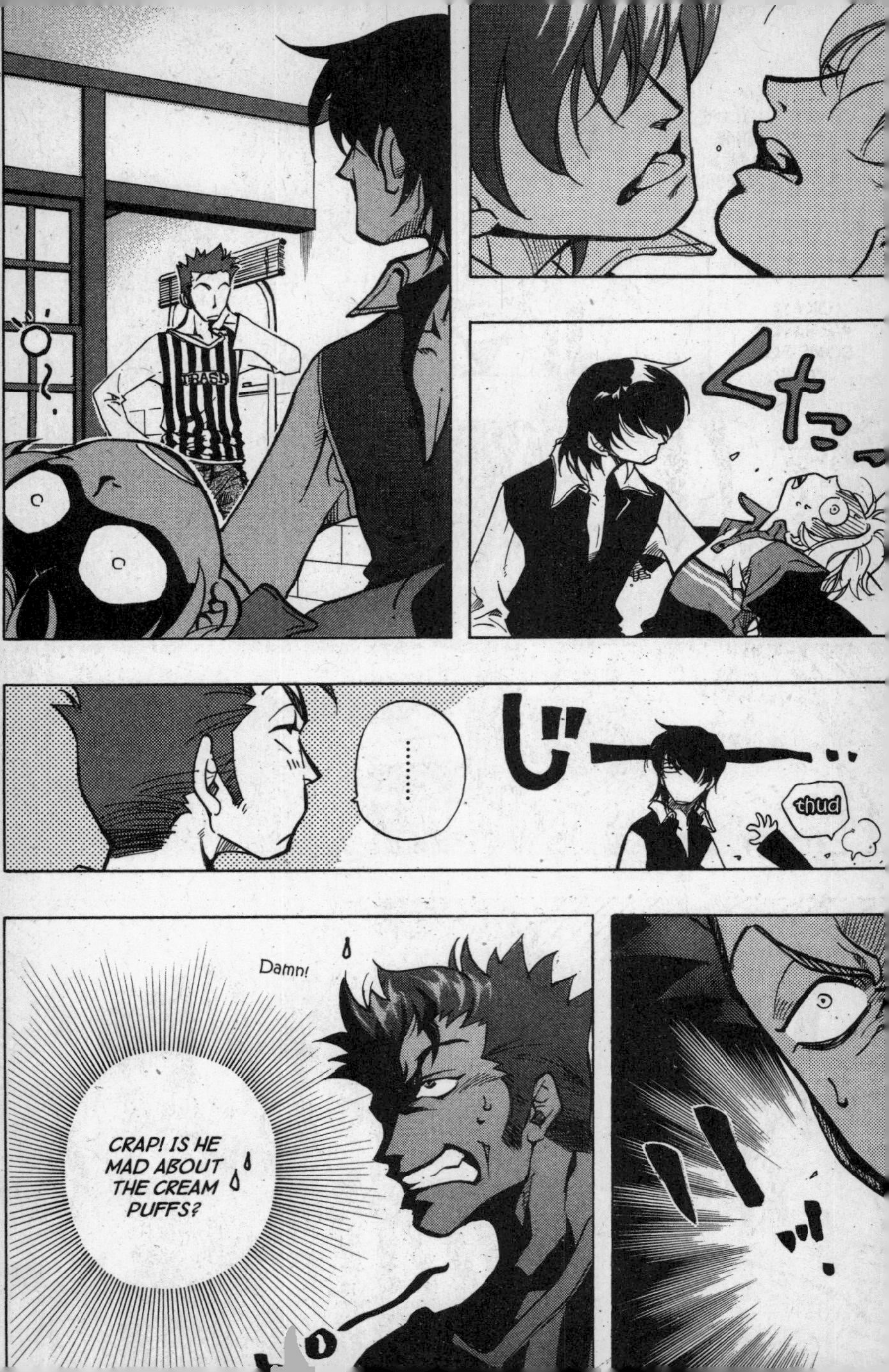

くたー
じーー
thud
......
Damn!
CRAP! IS HE MAD ABOUT THE CREAM PUFFS?

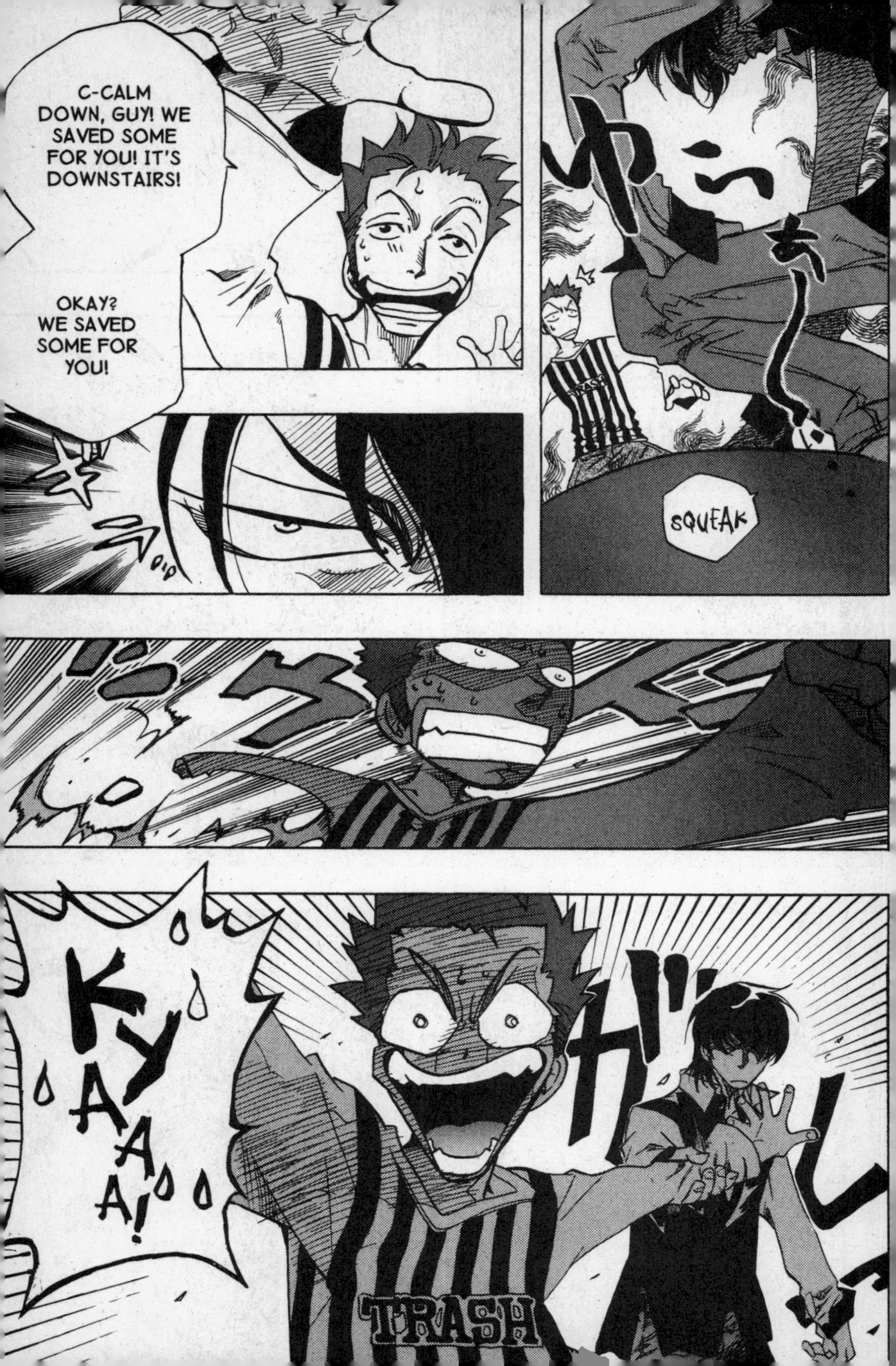
SQUEAK
C-CALM DOWN, GUY! WE SAVED SOME FOR YOU! IT'S DOWNSTAIRS!
OKAY? WE SAVED SOME FOR YOU!
KYAAAA!
TRASH

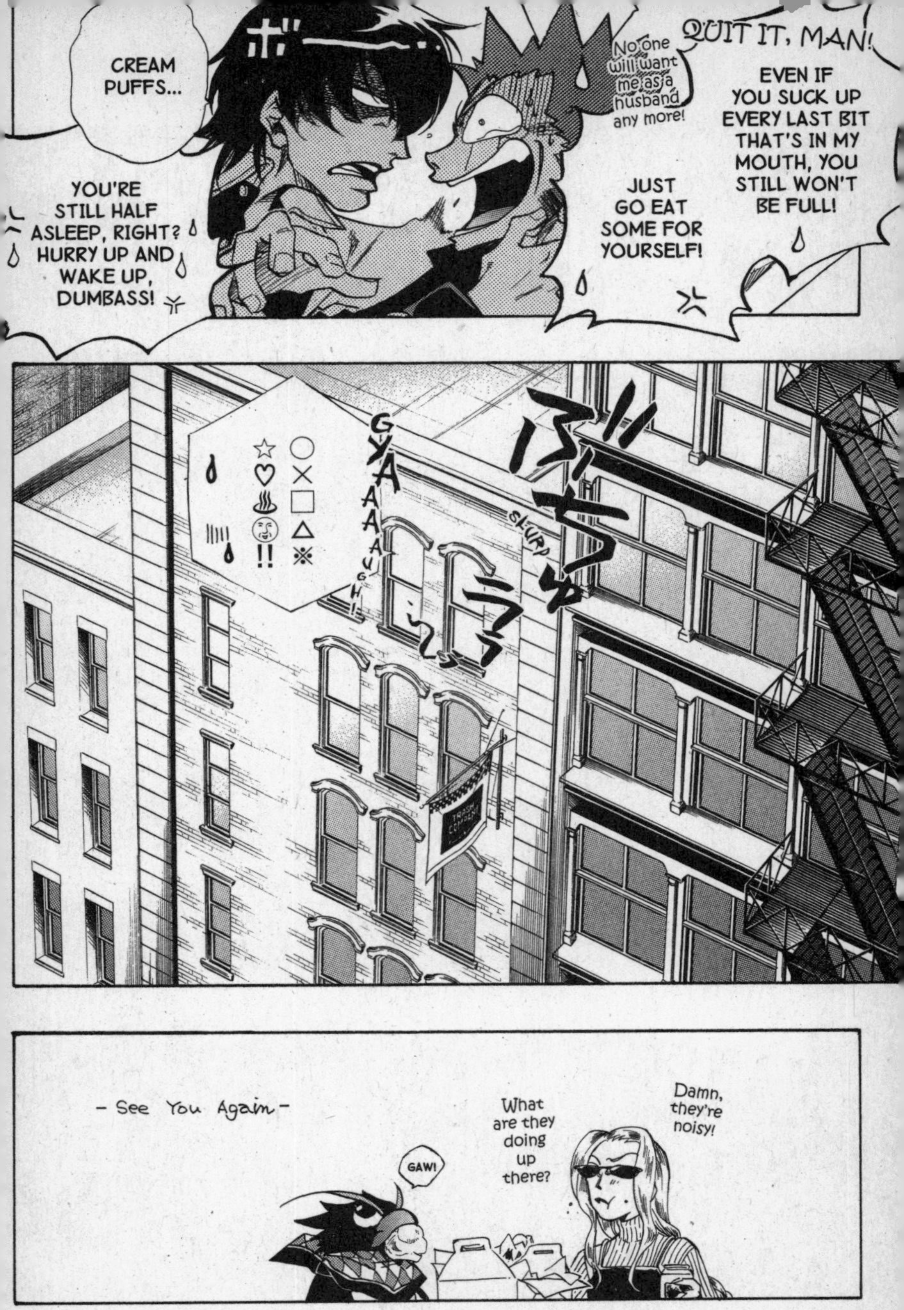
QUIT IT, MAN!
EVEN IF YOU SUCK UP EVERY LAST BIT THAT'S IN MY MOUTH, YOU STILL WON'T BE FULL!
No one will want me as a husband any more!
JUST GO EAT SOME FOR YOURSELF!
CREAM PUFFS...
YOU'RE STILL HALF ASLEEP, RIGHT? HURRY UP AND WAKE UP, DUMBASS!
ぶちゅ
SLURP
GYAAAAUGH!
Damn, they're noisy!
What are they doing up there?
GAW!
- See You Again -

number02 First Contact 02/END

GRENADIER クレネーダー ™

CREATED BY: SOUSUKE KAISE

TWO BIG GUNS CAN BRING PEACE TO THE WORLD...

Rushuna is a golden-haired Senshi—a gunslinger who travels the land with one purpose: to make the world a peaceful place with her high-caliber revolver and enchanting smile. However, her journey of nonviolence won't be easy and she may have to display her amazing gun skills and talent for reloading on the bounce.

THE MANGA THAT SPARKED THE POPULAR ANIME!

ACTION

OT OLDER TEEN AGE 16+

STOP!

This is the back of the book.
You wouldn't want to spoil a great ending!

This book is printed "manga-style," in the authentic Japanese right-to-left format. Since none of the artwork has been flipped or altered, readers get to experience the story just as the creator intended. You've been asking for it, so TOKYOPOP® delivered: authentic, hot-off-the-press, and far more fun!

DIRECTIONS

If this is your first time reading manga-style, here's a quick guide to help you understand how it works.

It's easy... just start in the top right panel and follow the numbers. Have fun, and look for more 100% authentic manga from TOKYOPOP®!